LAOS FILE

Dale Dye

"Dale Dye has a flair for telling stories and evoking images. His details about Marine life are accurate...Dye has the ability to draw the reader far enough into the story that the reader sees with the author's eyes and feels with his emotions...Dye's ability to tell a story the way it really happens is rare, and one sincerely hopes this book will not be his last...."

--Orlando Sentinel

"Capt. Dale Dye has done more than any other man alive to influence the way that America (and the rest of the world) views the US military."

-- Lt. Col. Dave Grossman, USA (Ret.)
Best-selling author, "On Killing," "On Combat"

"Dale Dye provides "firsthand knowledge...an inside view."

--Kirkus

LAOS FILE

DALE DYE

For Dr. Keith Collins
Many Thanks!
Dale Dye

WARRIORS PUBLISHING GROUP
NORTH HILLS, CALIFORNIA

LAOS FILE

A Warriors Publishing Group Book/published by arrangement with the author

This book is a work of fiction. Names, characters, places and incidents are products of the author's imagination or are used fictitiously. Any resemblance to actual events or locales or persons, living or dead, is entirely coincidental.

PRINTING HISTORY
Warriors Publishing Group edition/October 2008

ISBN: 978-0-9821670-0-7

The name "Warriors Publishing Group" and the logo
are trademarks belonging to Warriors Publishing Group

PRINTED IN THE UNITED STATES OF AMERICA

10 9 8 7 6 5 4 3 2 1

For Julia who understands war
and taught me about love.

And for Mike who pushed, pulled
and never let me down.

ONE
THE WORLD

1. Ozarks Mountains - February 1996

Death came creeping. Crawling, clawing, anxious to consume; the way it was, the way it always is. Death slithered under the ratty quilt, over the old soldier's distended belly, the final assault on a heart under siege. He stood helpless beside the knotty-pine bunk, feeling impotent, asinine. Knees hit the hardwood floor. A solid, icy jolt from the chunk of shrapnel still lodged behind a kneecap, up through the thigh into the base of his brain. Deal with it. Drive on. Face this death as he'd faced too many others. The End. Now drive on.

But a prayerful posture betrayed him. Words bubbling up from an artesian well dug years ago in a Lutheran Sunday School. *Yea, though I walk through the valley of the shadow of death, I will fear no evil...*

And the old soldier would finish it...as he always had when times were tight. *Because I am the meanest motherfucker in the valley.*

An eye popped open and rolled toward him. Red, white and blue in a single socket. *The flag still waves at twilight's last gleaming.*

"Checkin' out..." The old soldier groaned. "Almost there..."

"What can I do, Gus?" Death in the wire now, bayonet fixed, ready to rush. "Is there anything..."

"Charlie Mike..." Flag furled. Last transmission. *You may be suffering under a shitstorm but you will Continue Mission.*

Dropping his head on the old soldier's chest he heard a final volley of defiance. Hollow thumps from the last howitzer still firing. And death overran the old soldier's position. Gustav (No Middle Initial) Quick - crown prince and once heir apparent to the Sergeant Major of the United States Marine Corps - was now just another fucking stiff, a routine medevac.

*   *   *

Mid-winter dawn devastated the eastern sky as Shake Davis carried the corpse toward a pre-selected grave site. He'd dug the hole through frozen turf as ordered three days ago, in a shallow basin atop a pine-crusted knob behind the cabin. Sergeant Major Quick had fought off war demons from this mountaintop. Here he wanted to remain; planted high, a sniper commanding a broad field of fire. Here he'd perch, a gargoyle lurking in ambush, waiting for the Japs, the Koreans, the Chinese, the Vietnamese or the ghost of any gook he'd fought all his long life.

His shroud was a camouflaged poncho liner. Appropriate as the issue entrenching tool Shake used to spew rich mountain loam over all that was left of the man who taught, nurtured, kicked, cajoled, saved and salved him over a lifetime in uniform. When the hole was full, he folded the entrenching tool into a pick and dug the blade into the earth. There it stays; no nonsense, a grunt's gravestone.

Routine disposition of remains in accordance with the wishes of the deceased. Everything beyond the carcass - the detritus of a soldier's life: medals, citations, rifles, records and writings - packed and waiting inside the cabin. A few condolence calls - the list was mercifully short - and then haul it all back to the museum at Quantico. Just that and then handle his own baggage. There might be life after death but the larger mystery was life after the Corps.

Maybe I'll be back, Gus. He meandered down off the high ground, watching the pastel morning sky over spiky Ozark pines swirl like citrus in a blender. Maybe this is a good graveyard for dinosaurs.

* * *

Shake ran east on Highway 70, vaulted the Mississippi at St. Louis and bolted into Illinois. An overhead sign announced Effingham and by the time he slewed onto the bypass, wheels began falling off his resolve to escape. Run, but you can't hide. Death is light as a feather; duty heavy as a mountain. Or words to the effect that he was a procrastinator, coward, shirker; a shit-bird without much sense of the honor and ethics he preached to young Marines.

On the far side of town where the bypass bit back into an eight-lane exfiltration route, he spotted what was needed. Top Hat Motel had a vacancy and phones in every room according to the neon. More importantly, a package liquor joint was just across the parking lot.

Halfway through a double-knuckle of Old Busthead, he found the phone book. Scrawled stars in the margin indicated those with a need-to-know. Two, three...four old Corps cronies. Couple of very salty, very senior NCOs, Medal of Honor colonel, former lieutenant general living in Hawaii. Familiar names from the Marine Corps family album, all retired, all scattered.

He punched his glass into an ice bucket near the phone, poured painkiller, then cut it with cool water from the bathroom tap. Long night ahead, and he'd traverse many time zones to keep from blasting people out of bed with bad news. On the list were a few civilians from the Sergeant Major's other family but the gene pool was shallow this side of the grave. One and only wife dead of a stroke in 1970; she dwindled and then died after son - Marine First Lieutenant Kendall W. Quick - disappeared with helicopter and crew somewhere along the Annamite Cordillera.

There was a sister in Missouri who peddled antiques from a shop in Sedalia. Daughter-in-law Mindy, Ken's wife, somewhere in St. Louis; no number listed. And a grandson...Greenpeace, Puget Sound...not a big Sergeant Major fan. When Gus raised the subject of his grandson it was usually from the bottom of a glass.

"Kid needs a reality check..." They sat by the fieldstone fireplace cauterizing pain with whiskey and wood smoke, carving up what amounted to the Sergeant Major's estate. "Shoulda chased his ass down to Parris Island right after high school..."

"He might have been inclined to enlist if you hadn't retired when you did."

"Doubtful. His mom wasn't no big fan after Ken went missing."

"He'd have been the most popular boot on the Island, that's for damn sure. Daddy a war hero and grandad Sergeant Major of the Marine Corps?"

"Half right...but I wasn't gonna be no Sergeant Major of the Marine Corps."

"Bullshit, Gus. You were a shoo-in...everybody knew that. If you hadn't quit..."

"I never quit nothin' in my life, sonny-buck!"

"Then why'd you retire...before they announced the new Sergeant Major. It woulda been you and you know that."

"There's shit you don't know about...shit that ain't come to light yet..."

"Like what?"

"Like stuff I ain't got time to exploit or explain before I die. But you'll understand...one of these days...if you're half the Marine I think you are."

There were only a few more lucid moments before the honed steel glint finally faded from the Sergeant Major's eyes.

None of them - and none of the circumstances surrounding Gustav Quick's final hours - shed any light on nagging questions his old friend wanted answered before he had to bury the source in black Ozark soil.

*   *   *

Reactions from the Corps were mostly what he expected.

"Ah, shit. Good old Gus...he coulda been Sergeant Major of the Marine Corps, you know? Ah, shit..."

"Where'd you bury him? Uh-huh. He'll be happy there."

"Gus never shoulda retired. He'd still be with us today if he hadn't hung it up when he did."

"The Corps lost a legend. Him and Chesty Puller. There's a pair. Gus shoulda been Sergeant Major and Chesty shoulda been Commandant..."

"Rest in heaven...he done his time in hell."

"God bless him and thank you for calling." The three-star parked on his lanai overlooking Kaneohe Bay didn't sound ready to ring off and mourn. "By the way, have you notified DIA?"

"Defense Intelligence Agency? Nossir. Why would I do that?"

"You were very close to the Sergeant Major..."

"Yessir, I'm the one he called to...uh, handle it for the last few days."

"I presumed you knew..."

"What's that, General?"

"He worked for DIA...`72 to `76."

"I don't think so, sir. He was stationed at Eighth and Eye during that time...the Marine Barracks."

"Eighth and Eye had his records...DIA had his services. There may be materials they'll want to screen. Papers, files, that sort of thing. Anyway, once in; never out. You'd better let someone know."

Horizontal on a creaky double bed, Shake let his mind wander back over the past ten years. Had Gus been a spook? If so, did that have something to do with his unexpected retirement prior to being named for the Corps' prestigious top enlisted post? Gus would never talk about what made him leave the Corps he loved. Friends presumed it had to do with Ken being moved from limbo on the MIA list to KIA, the bureaucratic equivalent of a body bag; a hope-killing heartbreak the old man just couldn't bear. Enemies said it had to do with the lunatic fringe of the POW/MIA movement, a diehard gaggle of conspiracy-addicts and political gadflies using Gus Quick's high profile to keep ancient issues on the skyline. Lacking answers from Gus, he'd always sided with the former and disregarded the latter. But the spook connection - assuming there was one - cast a different light on the question.

He and Gus had both played the Special Operations game at various times in their career, but Recon Marine to Fed-level spook was a serious stretch. In all the years, at all the intimate opportunities, Gus never mentioned the biggest spook circus in the nation; an outfit that made the techno-geeks at Langley look like the slack-sack limp dicks they were generally considered to be by military shooters and door-kickers. What had he missed?

Seventy-two through seventy-six? Ass end of the war; peace talks. Kissinger and Le Duc Tho snarling over the shape of a table in Paris. Most of that time deployed one place or another, a bush-orphan except for the regular glut of angry letters from Shake's wife Jan, pregnant; feeling ugly, abandoned and betrayed. Doing domestic damage control at Pendleton in `75 when the call came from FMFPac WesPac: Vets fluent in gook required for Operation Frequent Wind, last call for loyalists and strap-hangers in Vietnam.

Red Cross rep at that refugee camp on Guam handed over a telegram and congratulations on the birth of his daughter. CO was sorry but no leave. Ass-deep in panicky zips; translators in short supply. Mail caught up a few weeks later. First photo of Tracey looking like a little prune...and a letter from the Sergeant Major.

Nothing special. Congratulations; chatty bat-shit about this guy and that. A few profane paragraphs indicating Nixon might be able to see the truth if he'd just stick that light at the end of the tunnel far enough up his ass. All scrawled on PX stationery and not a hint that Gus was doing anything other than staging dog-and-pony shows at the Marine Barracks in Washington. Was he under cover, for Christ's sake; doing some weird shit?

Who gives a damn now he's gone? What difference does it make? So he was a spook...so what? Wasn't a tour at Spook Central put the man's career in the toilet. So what did make Gus retire...

Instinct and experience told him the spook connection had something to do with it. An itch for answers broke over him like a rapidly-spreading rash. Maybe Gus could provide answers. He snatched at a jacket, felt for the room key and headed for the door.

Under the tarp over his truck-bed he found the career chronicles, a neat row of puke-green government-issue notebooks. Schooled in a system that could - and frequently did - bite you in the ass over details, the Sergeant Major was an obsessive record-keeper. It was all there - notes, thoughts, anecdotes - from 1944 when he enlisted to 1979 when he retired...except for the period in question. If the logbooks were gospel, Gus ceased to exist in '72 and magically resurfaced in '77.

He opened the log covering the short side of the gap. Familiar stuff. Most of that time they were still snake-eaters, members of a small Marine Recon detachment assigned to MACV/SOG, operating out of Danang. Log entries described how they and a few other Marines - mostly advisors to Vietnamese Marine battalions - helped trump the NVA grand-slam Easter Offensive.

Other entries were unfamiliar, revealing, irritating. It was Gus Quick that got him transferred - kicking and screaming - out of Vietnam back in '71 after a routine team extraction in the A Shau Valley turned into a shit sandwich. Shake's had enough...can't afford to lose him...requesting immediate orders to CONUS. So, Gus lied...said he had nothing to do with that.

And the business of career sabotage; just letting Gus rot in Vietnam? Bullshit. Sept. 71...Begged off orders again...offered me SgtMaj of 1st MarDiv at Camp Pendleton...primo slot but I can't go...belong here...with Ken...still a good chance to find him.

In the end, according to the log, it was a direct threat that finally shoe-horned Gus out of the combat zone. Last entry for summer of '72...orders to ceremonial duty at Marine Barracks, 8th and I Sts., Washington, DC. Three years of chickenshit a la carte. Goes against my grain. Called assignment monitor at HQMC. No more slack. Told me to take the orders or take a hike.

There was an asterisk. The reference was scribbled inside the logbook's back cover. * R. A. Beal - Washington. And a phone number in the 202 area code. Maybe R. A. Beal was DIA. And maybe Mr. Beal offered Gus a chance to side-step the dreaded tour at 8th & I. Maybe the spooks wanted somebody who had been on the ground, walked the walk and talked the talk. That profile fit lots of guys. Why single out Gus? Ken, of course. Vested interest in the subject matter. Reasonable.

Logbook on the long side of the gap was a pitiful piece of work. Angry rantings and accusations; long lists of cowards and criminals Gus wanted hung by the balls because they wouldn't believe there were Americans still captive in Asia. Entries for his last year of active duty at Camp Lejeune read like the diary of a madman; a steady descent into dementia. Ken Quick terminated with extreme bureaucracy; shifted from limbo on the MIA list to long gone on the growing roster of Americans Killed In Action/Body Not Recovered.

A slew of entries were viciously slashed, x'ed out, scribbled over...in one case, smeared with something that looked suspiciously like blood. The Whacko Brigade with promises to bring 'em back alive. They were all logged. Cheats, charlatans, shitheads, jungle-junkies who couldn't live without the war. And the lying, pitiful no-life, low-life military shoe-clerks who claimed to have been POWs and knew right on the money where we could find some more. Gus was on and off that bandwagon so many times he finally got run over by it. When the powerful people in the post-war POW/MIA picture ran out of polite responses, the Marine Corps told the Sergeant Major to shift his fire. When he refused, they told him not to let the door hit him in the ass on the way out.

So why keep me in the dark about it, Gus? What am I, the fucking enemy? He walked back to the phone, resolved to call that number in Washington when he was closer to the flagpole. Meanwhile, there was a bomb he had to drop on some folks in Sedalia.

*　　*　　*

"Mrs. Willis, Amanda Willis?"

"Yes? Can I he'p you?" The voice on the phone was Midwestern clipped, countrified. He could hear Jeopardy playing in the background.

"I'm Chief Warrant Officer Shake Davis, a friend of your brother..."

"Yes, Gustav has mentioned you...on the rare occasions when he calls or writes."

"Mrs. Willis...I'm sorry to have to tell you this..."

There was a mewling sound out of Sedalia but her voice was under control when she finished the thought.

"The Lord has called him home. I knew it wouldn't be long."

"Yes ma'am. The Sergeant Major died this morning at around seven. He was comfortable right up to the end. It wasn't too bad on him."

"I don't suppose there'll be a funeral. He said he didn't want one."

"No ma'am. I buried him near the cabin...where he wanted me to. The rest of his things he wanted sent to the Marine Corps Museum up in Virginia. He, uh...he left the cabin to me but there was some GI insurance in effect. It's equally divided between you and his grandson out on the west coast."

"I presume you'll be calling Bill to let him know?"

"Yes, ma'am. I have a number for him...but I don't know...there's no number listed for Bill's mother...Ken's wife? The Sergeant Major didn't give me any information."

"Well, no wonder, Mr. Davis. That's a painful topic in what's left of our family..."

He listened, remembering the pretty brunette Ken had met and married at Southern Illinois University. At Camp Pendleton where Ken was staging for Vietnam she made an impression. Unlike most of the maudlin war brides who haunted the post hoping their husband's orders to Vietnam would be magically cancelled, she seemed to understand a combat tour was not only mandatory, it was an esteemed rite of passage.

"After Ken was shot down over there, Mindy moved back in with her family in St. Louis. She grieved so hard they had to put her on pills. Years went by, you know. No information about Ken...nothing, except she got to taking more and more of them pills. One night a few years ago, she just took too many. She's buried there in St. Louis."

"I'm sorry, Mrs. Willis. The Sergeant Major never...I didn't know."

"Gustav took it kinda hard. Made him even more bitter about Ken seemed like. I don't wonder he didn't talk about it."

"Yes, ma'am. I should make some more calls. You have my deepest sympathy..."

"Thank you, Mr. Davis. And it appears I also have something for you. Gustav sent me a package, papers of some kind looks like. He wanted it mailed to you when he passed on. Shall I send it along?"

He gave his duty address at Quantico and hung up the phone. Then he went back to the bourbon, sipping and sensing ghosts rising from that fresh grave in the Ozarks.

*   *   *

"And the dynasty draws to a close..."

The voice was respectful, resigned, just a shade short of sad. Familiar gurgle and clink from Puget Sound. Bill Quick was having himself a stiff drink. "Suppose I ought to get busy and produce a son...ship him off to Parris Island so the Quick legacy won't fade...

"This may sound cornball, Bill...but I don't think you have to worry about that. As long as there are Marines, your granddad will be fondly remembered."

"And my dad..."

"Him too. For the short time we knew your father everyone thought he was a fine Marine, destined for great things."

"And shot down in his prime, as they say. Then my mom who just couldn't understand...and no one would explain it to her."

"I met your mom a couple of times. I think she understood."

"Uh-huh. Well, certainly at the end she understood it's better to be dead than not."

"Bill...I didn't call to hurt you or open old wounds."

"I know that, Mr. uh...Shake is it?"

"Nickname. Your grandfather came up with it. Used to say every time he turned around I was getting promoted. No muss, no fuss...just shake and bake. It stuck and I didn't argue. Sounds better than Sheldon..."

"Look, Shake...I don't mean to sound like a jerk here. I'm sorry about my grandfather. I really am...but I'm numb, you understand? There's been so much death..."

"I've been a Marine for thirty years, Bill. I know about death."

"Of course you do. It's what the Marine Corps is all about. It's probably why I'm the only Quick who got involved in preserving life rather than destroying it..."

"Bill, you've been drinking. So have I. Let's call a truce...in honor of your granddad, OK? There's some insurance money coming your way. Somebody from the Marine Corps will be contacting you shortly."

"Yeah, OK. I'll get this other stuff in the mail tomorrow morning."

"What other stuff?"

"This envelope my grandfather sent me. There are instructions to mail it to you if and when I find out he's gone."

2. Quantico

Three days left on his leave as he gunned the truck through the back gate at Quantico Marine Corps Base. Three days to dump the Sergeant Major's life on the museum's doorstep, deliver a few final lectures at the Warfighting Center, check on his retirement orders, see his daughter off to a new school, make yet another attempt to get his ex off the sauce, find a job, start a new life...fuck, all the time in the world.

Artie DeCampo, the retired Master Gunnery Sergeant who ran the Marine Corps Museum, helped him unload the truck. Like most former supply sergeants, Artie was an anal-retentive pack-rat, delighted with any treasure added to his trove.

"This stuff'll make a damn fine display, Gunner."

"Ought to, Artie. He was a damn fine Marine."

"Seems shitty, don't it, Mr. Davis? Guy makes it through Tarawa, Iwo, Inchon, Chosen, Khe Sanh, Hue, all that snoop-and-poop shit, four Purple Hearts...and then he gets eat up by that fuckin' cancer."

"I expect he'd have preferred an AK round between the running lamps, but he never bitched about it."

"Nope, he wouldn't. I seen him at the Staff Club in Danang after they told him his boy was missing...somewhere in Laos...where we wasn't even supposed to be. Never flinched that you'd notice."

"He was a True Believer, Artie. Capital T, capital B. He had the faith."

"Uh-huh. We was all like that at one time or another."

*   *   *

Stale air washed over him as he pushed into his spartan cell in the mainside Bachelor Officers' Quarters. He dropped the carbon-smudged inventory sheet on his desk and tugged open a window. Crisp, clean pine scent drifted on a winter wind. Maybe the cabin was the answer. Up there he could get by on a little chunk of his retirement check, hunt, fish, breathe...speculate on what the hell beyond being a Marine might make him happy.

Before the call came from the Ozarks, he'd spent much of his off-duty time packing, anticipating final orders, sorting through his interests and options as he stuffed souvenirs from a thirty-year king-hell, kick-ass world cruise into cardboard boxes. Not one goddamn germ of an idea came of it. Push come to shove, he was a pro; a high-speed, low-drag, gut-level grunt.

Hog-wallow happy when he was miserable down there in the mud and the blood and the beer. Beyond that he just didn't much give a shit.

In search of distraction he zapped his Sony portable to life and caught the CNN news at noon. Top story was a stunner; just what he needed to hear at this turbulent time of life. Apparently Slick Willie Clinton the artful draft-dodger was whomping up the old time revival spirit to heal yet another of the nation's ills. Cut to sound-bite.

Elmer Gantry up from Arkansas, croaking into a bank of microphones, surrounded by acolytes. Flanking him in wide shots, wheel-horses from big government and big business. All of them - unlike their leader - claimed honorable service in the late, great Southeast Asian wargames. Willie thumped the tub a time or two; allowed as how what he was gonna do was good for what ails us, and commenced to wrassle with the devil.

Cast out them demons of the past! Yes, Lord! Let me just lay on the hands here and fling out all that anguish and grief that tore the fucking country apart. Sure is a shame about that war, the whole generation of young Americans who never lived long enough to contribute anything useful, the unprecedented political and social upheaval that eroded a national sense of decency and integrity, not to mention the boys who might still be locked away in some Southeast Asian Alcatraz.

And it's OK that hundreds of thousands of innocent people were tortured or killed by a gang of stiff-necked Stalinist bastards who will not even admit to it, much less apologize for it. And a big ol' heartfelt *xin loi* to the veterans, the cripples, the crazies, the families who invested and lost, the moms and dads and wives and kids who are still waiting for closure. We have it from no less an authority than General William Tecumseh Sherman that war is cruelty and you cannot refine it. Naw, hell's bells my fellow Americans, we gotta get over it. We been through a righteous war since Vietnam. Yes, Lord...and then there was Desert Storm. A little short, a little shallow, piece of cake, really...but we won that sucker. We all got to understand...Vietnam was then; this is now. We gotta get on with Third World influence-peddling and make us a few bucks in this new global economy.

Therefore...king's X, ally, ally oxen-free, no harm, no foul...we are in bidness with the Socialist Republic of Vietnam. In fact, we are so deep in bidness with these opportunist assholes who are just now coming to grips with the promise of capitalism, that we're gonna send twenty of our most bright and shining representatives over there first thing next week. Amen...and we got the good ones packing right now. We got industry-types, bankers, brokers, farmers, engineers...and we even tossed in a few soldiers in case our new pals need a hand establishing their rightful hegemony over the entire eastern Indochina peninsula. Let's just get on over there and help these poor people out from under their own ideological shit-pile. Let's not be sore losers. And in conclusion, my fellow Americans, let me just say...in true humility...I told you so.

Zap to black and thank Christ the Sergeant Major didn't live to hear that. Finally far enough down the line to just sweep it under a lumpy rug. One big group hug and we're all warm and fuzzy. But that wouldn't deal with demons and war devils that still haunted his sleep. It wouldn't erase the faces of the dead, couldn't touch the gore-numbed places in his heart, wouldn't warm the war cold that froze his emotions.

And vets were irresistibly drawn back there? As if they were mindless metal shavings and Vietnam was a powerful, pulsing electromagnet. Eisenhower saw it coming. Soldier's perspective. Indochina - Burma, Thailand, Laos, Cambodia, Vietnam, all of it - was one big fucking quagmire full of quicksand. Good call, Ike. But the place worked on Westerners like an industrial-strength vacuum cleaner. It Hoovered us up and sucked us all into the bag. In the end - long after any conceivable reason for being there had disappeared - Vietnam seemed irresistible.

Except for me, he thought and reached for the phone. In my case, I go back to Vietnam when I am reincarnated as a rock ape, or a python, or a pissant...and not before. He tapped out the number he suspected might put him in touch with DIA or some cover set-up in Rosslyn on the Virginia side of the Key Bridge.

What he heard when the phone stopped ringing was the number he'd just punched repeated back to him. The voice was platonic, non-committal, sterile. He pictured a pair of wing-tips propped up on a GSA-catalog credenza.

"Uh, I was given this number for a Mr. Beal...R. A. Beal?"

"Mr. Beal gave you this number?"

"No. I, uh...I got it from a friend who is...or was, uh, connected with Mr. Beal. Is he there?"

"Your name, sir?"

"Listen, I'm Chief Warrant Officer Davis, a Marine down at Quantico. A good friend of mine just died. He had this Mr.

Beal's number in his files. Somebody who knew him pretty well told me he worked for DIA at one point in his career...and that I should notify them that he was dead. Like I said, there was this note in his files about Mr. Beal...so I thought I'd call..."

"And you presume you're speaking to someone from the Defense Intelligence Agency right now?"

"Well, Jesus...yeah. Ain't I?"

"I can take whatever information you want to provide."

"I'd rather talk to Mr. Beal."

"Sorry, Mr. Davis..."

"What? He isn't there...or I can't talk to him?"

"Both and neither..."

"Hello? Are we on the same planet here?"

"Mr. Davis, this is not a secure line. You'd be familiar with that concept?"

"Oh, yeah...but how do I know I'm talking to the right people on this unsecure line?"

"You are. Take my word for it."

"I'd like to...but I don't even know who you are."

"You can call me Mr. Bayer...or Bob...or whatever suits you."

"Well, listen, Bob...have you noticed how this conversation is beginning to sound like dialogue from a bad B movie?"

Low chuckle at last. "Yes...I suppose it all seems rather... arcane." Spook Bob had a sense of humor. Good sign. He could stop sparring.

"My friend was a retired Marine Corps Sergeant Major. Gustav Quick...no middle initial...died day before yesterday... Lake of the Ozarks. Like I said, there's some indication he worked for you guys back in `72-`76."

"And his personal effects? Papers, files, that sort of thing?"

"I hauled 'em all down here to the Marine Corps Museum. That's what he said he wanted done..."

"OK, Mr. Davis. Is there a number where we can reach you?"

He gave his private number in the BOQ and a number for the Staff Duty Officer at the Marine Corps Development and Education Command. He'd be one place or the other until his retirement orders negotiated the paper trail between the Navy Annex and Quantico.

"Listen...is there any way you can check for me? I mean, I'm not even sure my friend really worked for you guys. He never mentioned it or anything..."

Computer keys rattled on the other end of the phone. When he came back on the line, Bob sounded like a game-show host hedging bets.

"Let's just say you've called the right number."

"So you're saying he did work for DIA?"

"What I'm saying is goodbye, Mr. Davis. Thanks for calling...and have a nice day."

*   *   *

It was almost 1830 by the time he'd finished a cobweb-clearing run along the banks of Beaver Dam Creek, showered and negotiated outbound traffic to cross the base. Quantico's U.S. Navy Medical Clinic was closed. Hospital Corpsman First Class Judy Cavendish, who had drawn enough blood from him over the years to feed a family of vampires, had the duty. She was used to seeing Shake after normal clinic hours either checking on one of his Marines or visiting Navy pals.

"Commander Kybat's in the back, Gunner...finishing up some paperwork."

"Thanks, Doc. I told the Duty Officer I'd be here in case he calls."

"Aye, aye, sir. Scuttlebutt says you're gonna be needin' a retirement physical soon, Gunner. Laid in a fresh supply of needles for the occasion."

"Keep up the good work, Doc. I got a buddy in SEALs says they're looking for a few good women..."

In a tiny cubicle behind the administration desk, Doctor Art Kybat, Commander, U.S. Navy Medical Corps, sat reviewing patient files and sipping from a Diet Dr. Pepper can that smelled suspiciously of scotch whiskey.

"Hey, Shake. C'mon in and grab a seat."

"Greetings, Bat. How'ya doin', you old chancre mechanic?" Grabbing a plastic chair from a stack in the corner, he sprawled next to the desk and sniffed at the soda can.

"Want one?"

"Do I have to drink it out of a can?"

"Shit, man. This is the new Navy. No smokes, no dope. Sensitivity training every Tuesday. Tits may be referred to only in clinical terms. Day care center on every corner. Yes, it's after hours; yes, I'm done seeing patients, and yes, you have to drink it out of a can."

"Got it. Gimme one...light on the Doctor Pecker."

"Heard about the Sergeant Major..."

"Yeah. Shame, ain't it?"

"Uh-huh. I gave him his retirement physical. No indication of cancer. Except for looking like a goddamn piece of Swiss cheese from all the bullet and shrapnel wounds, he was in great shape."

"Doctor down in Missouri said it came on quick."

"Must have. Anyway, here's to him..."

They touched soda cans and drank. Memories of an old friend flashing in front of glazed eyes.

"So...when am I gonna do your retirement physical, Shake?"

"Pretty quick. Just waiting for the paperwork to drift down from on high."

"That why you came by?"

"No. I was thinking about Jan. My daughter says she's back on the sauce...vodka bottles hid everywhere."

"Cure didn't take." Doctor Kybat drained his drink and rattled a hook-shot into the corner shitcan. "Frankly, I didn't think it would. You gotta want to stop drinking...or you won't."

"She blames me, you know? Says our marriage was a sham. I married the Marine Corps and she was just excess baggage. Never there for her. Always running to the sound of the guns..."

"Listen, Jan says what all drunks say. It's everybody's fault but their own. She's sick, Shake...and she ain't gonna get better unless she makes a conscious, serious decision to stop drinking."

"Yeah, well, it's come to a head this time. Before the divorce, I could sort of keep a lid on her...and Tracey was a good influence. She didn't want to look like a fucking rummy in front of her daughter. But Tracey's transferring down to University of Miami this week..."

"And you're not going back?"

"Long past that, Bat. We'd just eat each other alive. She needs a new shot at life. So do I."

"Well, then she's a goner. She'll kill herself sooner or later. Solo car wreck if she's lucky. Cirrhosis if she isn't."

"She gave me twenty good years, Bat. I owe her."

"Think she'll give rehab another shot?"

"I think she will. Tracey's been working on her pretty hard. But I can't put her in some pissant wino tank. She gets embarrassed, you know?"

"How about the Betty Ford?"

"High-dollar deal, ain't it? Hard to get in unless you're an influential drunk?"

"High-dollar it is. But I know some people. I could get her a bed."

"How long's it take?"

"Three months, six months, a year. Depends on what kind of patient she is. And there's a mandatory follow-up program. You'd have to foot the bill for that."

"Probably take every cent I've got...just when I need it most."

"Probably. You want me to make a call?"

"Yeah, Bat. Go ahead. All those wars and worries, she rates a break."

*   *   *

Pausing in the passageway bisecting The Basic School's main classroom building he heard the twitter of forty hatchling second lieutenants. On the other side of the door they waited, anxious to check another block off the training schedule; hear what this old fart had to say, get it over with and get gone...out to the fighting Fleet Marine Force.

He taught what was known among the butter-bars in Quantico's preparatory pipeline as a skate-drill, a rare block of instruction during which you did not have to bust your ass at PT, wander through the boondocks worshipping a compass, or fire up a squad full of exhausted classmates to try your text-book solution to yet another tactical problem. In fact, all that was necessary to survive the prescribed meeting engagement with The Law of Land Warfare at TBS was an ability to fend off the dreaded Rack Monster and remain awake until Gunner Davis was through running his mouth.

Why his particular under-educated, frequently-profane mouth was chosen to run around the general topics of morality, ethics and honor on the battlefield was a mystery at first. He ran into Sherman Semple, his old platoon leader from Vietnam, who was now a Colonel commanding The Basic School. When he took the opportunity to ask Col. Semple why he wasn't teaching tactics, land navigation, weapons or any of the other standard subjects he knew better than a Baptist knows the Bible, the answer became a lesson plan.

"Shake, I'm not gonna have these kids drowning in psycho-babble bullshit. It's hard enough to get the job done while taking care of their Marines. But one of these days down the road, a few of them are gonna be confronted by tough decisions and no guidance. When it all goes to hell in a handbasket...like it always does...we've got to rely on them to do the right thing, the moral thing...take the high road instead of playing it safe. It isn't brain-surgery and it can't be taught like that. It isn't about knowing the right answers...most times there aren't any. It's about asking yourself the right questions, then having the courage of your convictions. You been there; you know exactly what I mean."

And so super-grunt became pseudo-philosopher, an irony not lost on colleagues who believed Shake Davis didn't know Nietsche from his own asshole. Still, he was the only Warrant Officer among the hot-runners who taught at The Basic School and he was the only one who taught Ethics and the Law of Land Warfare. He had a good fifteen years more time in service than most of the other instructors and twenty more than some.

They called him The Troglodyte when he arrived at Quantico but it didn't last. The joke was wasted on a man who had no idea what a troglodyte was and couldn't spell well enough to find it in the dictionary. And he didn't much give a rat's ass when he heard himself referred to subsequently as The Dinosaur. That he could spell and understand. Pre-historic fit a guy who became a combat veteran before you became an embryo.

As usual prior to entering a classroom full of fledglings that had been nit-picked to distraction over "wear and care of U.S. Marine Corps uniforms," he checked himself in one of the full-length mirrors spotted along the passageway. Slim, trim, just over six feet of old oak and chiseled granite. He'd pass muster even if his tailored uniform was on backwards or the shock of white hair remaining on his melon after a weekly high-and-tight suddenly turned purple.

All the young eyeballs would lock on seven rows of ribbons, capped by a Silver Star, Bronze Star, Purple Hearts and been-there badges that proclaimed he'd seen the elephant and heard the owl in Vietnam, Beirut, El Salvador, Panama, Saudi Arabia, Kuwait and Iraq. The gaudy stack pinned to his tropical shirt pushed the gold jump wings and silver SCUBA bubble right up to the shoulder seam. Normally he wore only the recon-rack and a few personal decorations, but this was his last class and somehow it seemed OK to brandish bona fides.

He was, after-all, a rare bird; recently promoted to Chief Warrant Officer-5, the new grade at the top of the warrant structure which had previously topped out at CWO-4. And he was a Marine Gunner - one of a relatively few infantry warrant officers as opposed to technical specialists - authorized to wear the bursting bomb device on his left collar opposite his rank insignia. Like all Marine warrant officers, he was commonly called Gunner, but in his mind the term always translated Warrior. If this final burst of sartorial splendor amounted to vanity or conceit, by God, he'd take the hit for it. After years of low-end drudgery and high-end danger, he was entitled.

Satisfied with himself, girded with martial credibility, he spun from the past, blew into the classroom and faced the future.

*   *   *

"So...was our boy Second Lieutenant Rusty Calley of the Americal Division a villain...or a victim?"

Hands waved at him from all over the classroom. Since there were no right or wrong answers in Gunner Davis's class, nearly everyone was anxious to respond. The hand on his right, flapping like a beached bass, belonged to a fervent, upwardly-mobile kid he'd taken to calling Spring-Butt Spencer, for a tendency to bounce up and down in a desperate effort to be recognized.

"Lieutenant Spencer...do you have to go potty? Or do you have an opinion?"

"Opinion, sir!" Spencer was just able to make himself heard over the laughter.

"OK. Lay it on us. Victim or villain?"

"Villain, sir...no question. Mitigating circumstances aside, he broke the generally-accepted law of warfare. In effect, he became a vigilante. Killed women and kids out of frustration with an inability to pacify his assigned AO."

"He says his guys got out of hand; they were fed up with the war and pissed off about the buddies they'd seen chopped up by VC operating out of that ville..."

"No excuse for what happened, sir. He was their leader and he failed to exercise control over his people."

"But he said at his court-martial...and a lot of veterans agreed...that what he did was nothing more than what the NVA and VC did to innocent people all the time to teach them a lesson about cooperating with Americans. What about that? Siddown, Spring-butt...give somebody else a chance to be the expert."

Second Lieutenant Margarita Chavez was a short, sturdy ROTC graduate of Pan-American University whose curvy frame was a challenge to Quantico's uniform tailors. "It can't be tit-for-tat, sir. You can't go around killing noncombatants just because the enemy does. You can't adopt their morality...or lack of it...and live with yourself."

"Live with yourself, Lieutenant Chavez? What about if you're gonna die otherwise? What if you can't tell who's a noncombatant and who isn't? What if you decide to leave a noncombatant alive today...and tomorrow he kills a couple of your Marines?"

"I don't know, sir. You'd feel pretty stupid, I guess, but I think you have to err on the side of humanity...and what's commonly accepted as ethical behavior..."

He nodded approval and finished her thought. "...in an unethical situation. That's about all the guidance you're gonna get. And in most cases, it's all you need. Look, nobody's saying you're expected to be The White Knight in combat. It's ugly out there in a fighting hole...bad ugly...and emotional to the point where reason goes right into the grenade sump. The key is mental discipline...in you and in your Marines. Hang onto your humanity no matter what that other inhuman bastard does. Don't let yourself fall to his level. Listen to your brain and your heart; not your gut. Do that. Don't let yourself get pushed off the moral high ground - in combat or out - and you'll be all right."

He paced the podium, checking his watch, snapping off the overhead projector on which he'd diagrammed Calley's sweep through the My Lai hamlet in southern I Corps. Almost end of the period; end of an era for him.

"Calley was a victim too, sir." Lieutenant Chavez was still standing at her seat, chin high, dark eyes blazing. Obviously, she had a point to make and was ignoring the whispers from classmates anxious for an early release.

"How so, Lieutenant Chavez? Fill me in on how Lieutenant Calley qualifies as a victim. You're not gonna tell me he was a scapegoat, are you?"

"Nossir. He got what he deserved, in my opinion. They even slapped a few wrists up higher in his chain of command...but they didn't go far enough...in my opinion."

He saw it coming and smiled. Highest marks for Second Lieutenant Margarita Chavez. She'd make a damn fine leader if they ever let her become one.

"How far up the chain of command should they have gone, Lieutenant?"

"All the way, sir...up to the people who bent the rules and allowed an unqualified, unsuitable individual to become a combat leader. He's a victim of a flawed system. He never should have been in uniform, much less wearing lieutenant's bars. The Army was in such a rush to find warm bodies for the Vietnam War that they let unqualified, unstable people become officers. What happened at My Lai was bound to happen...probably happened a lot more than we know about."

"Well done, Lieutenant Chavez. It did happen more than we know about. Believe me, I saw some of it. I've told you about the mass graves at Hue during Tet `68. They were chock-full of civilians - two thousand or more - executed by NVA or VC troops. Most of the killings were political or a result of feuds. Tet gave the guys with the guns a chance to settle old scores. It was sickening...and a lot of my buddies in 5th Marines wanted to do a little score-settling of their own. But we didn't. That's morality, ethics, honor. In the hard times, it's all you've got to keep you from becoming an animal."

His old alarm clock clanged to mark the end of the final hour. A class leader barked forty bodies to attention and he waited for the scrape and clatter to subside.

"I'll be retiring soon, Lieutenants. You're my last class at TBS. Thanks for your attention...and I wish I could have offered you more than opinions which, as you know, are like assholes...everybody's got one. Remember, vengeance is mine sayeth the Lord...and not yours, Lieutenant! Dismissed."

                    *   *   *

He turned from collecting map overlays to find Second Lieutenant Chavez staring at his sternum, locked into a rigid brace.

"Relax, Lieutenant. You did very well in this class. In fact, I think you'll do very well throughout your career if you don't let the bastards grind you down."

"I was wondering if I could ask you a question, sir. You're the only officer I've met here who was in Vietnam."

"If you're wondering why we lost, Lieutenant, I can recommend some good books. Or would you prefer the quick-and-dirty political betrayal version?"

"Nossir. It's about my older brother. He was a navigator on B-52s out of Guam. They got shot down in 1972 and then...nothing. He's listed as Missing In Action..."

"I'm very sorry to hear that...Margarita, is it?"

"Maggie, sir. And thanks. My Mom still mourns but I gave up on my brother a long time ago. What I was wondering about, what I can't understand, is why the Vietnamese don't just let us know what happened to him. They were gonna give everyone a full accounting...but on the news today, it said the Vietnamese are just kind of shrugging their shoulders..."

"Maggie, I'm sure as hell not gonna make apologies for the Vietnamese but maybe they really don't know what happened to our guys. And if they're just as clueless as we are about MIAs, they're not gonna bust their butts finding answers. These people fought a nonstop war for sixty years. If you count the bodies - north and south - they lost something like a million killed...and about 300,000 more missing in action. There's something like 100,000 families in Vietnam that list at least one relative as MIA. They accept that as the price you pay. They don't make a big stink about their MIAs and they don't understand why we insist on a strict accounting for all of ours. To them, missing after all these years is the same as dead."

"So we just abandon that moral position? We just write them all off as dead?"

"No, ma'am, we don't. At least not as far as I'm concerned. Anyway, you heard about lifting the trade embargo? There's a bunch of high-rollers and heavy-hitters headed over there next week. Cash talks; bullshit walks. Maybe we'll toss enough money in the pot to buy the answers. For your sake, I hope so."

He watched her trundle out of the classroom, headed onward and upward toward a glass ceiling with a distinctive Marine green tint. And then he followed her out into the brisk winter air, squaring his pisscutter over bushy grey eyebrows, wishing he could believe half the shit he shoveled.

*   *   *

Artie DeCampo seemed slightly pissed when he answered the return call. The message was only fifteen minutes old so he wasn't delaying the progress of Western civilization.

"What's the matter, Artie? They announce another budget cut?"

"Nah. Aggravation, you know? That's all it is. Can't get nothin' done for people dickin' around in the files."

"You're a museum, Artie. People do research in museums."

"Yeah. Guess so..." Unrest in the lair of the pack-rat. Sounded as if someone had actually walked into Artie's warehouse with a valid requisition...of all things...and an item was actually going to be issued from stocks. This did not please supply sergeants who believed equipment should remain in stock where it could be counted and fondled...as opposed to being issued to units where it could be used.

"So? You called, what's up?"

"There's this guy here, Gunner. Got ID from Defense Intelligence Agency and he wants access to all the stuff you brought in from Sergeant Major Quick."

"Yeah, it's OK. I called 'em..."

"The fuckin' spooks?"

"Turns out the Sergeant Major worked for DIA...few years...72 to 76. They probably want to make sure he didn't squirrel away some secret material or something..."

"What the fuck was a recon dog like him doing working for the spooks?"

"Beats me, Artie. He never talked to me about it."

"Bet it had something to do with his boy, you know? MIA investigations? Them DIA guys are heavy into that shit. I got some stuff down here makes reference to it...but most of it's blacked out."

"Uh huh. Well, Slick Willie says he's gonna get to the bottom of it. Heard it on TV yesterday..."

"Yeah...and monkeys are gonna fly outa my ass."

"Give the spook what he wants, Artie. Just make damn sure you get a hand-receipt."

"He gets nowhere near the door until I got signatures in triplicate...and a Xerox of his fuckin' ID."

He punched off, selected another line and tapped out the number of his ex-wife's house in Alexandria.

"Tracey? How you doin', honey?"

"Daddy! I was just going to call you. The stuff from the Betty Ford Clinic arrived FedEx just now."

"Think you can get your mom to go along with it?"

"No problem. It's an exclusive club. She likes that kind of thing. We`re talking spa here, right? Vacation, get yourself back in shape, new start, that sort of deal. Keep her from being lonely while I'm down there..."

"Don't remind me...while you're down there at the University of Miami getting educated and I'm somewhere trying to earn enough money to pay for it."

"Any job prospects?"

"I'll find something, honey. There's work out there, even for guys so old they fart dust."

"This is all bad timing isn't it, Dad? I could wait; work a year...or two."

"Negative! We been through all this before, right? I've got some savings. Been putting some away since you were born..."

"Yeah, but out-of-state tuition...and the Betty Ford thing..."

"Tracey, I got it covered. You packed yet?"

"Almost...but you don't have to drive me down there, Daddy."

"Taught my last class today. What else am I gonna do?"

"OK. We still having dinner tonight?"

"Roger that. Eight...down here at the Globe and Laurel."

"How did I know that? You took me there when I graduated from high school."

"It's tradition. You got orders...moving on? You pay homage at the crossroads of the Corps."

"Mom's up...gotta run.

"Go, Hurricanes."

"Right. See you tonight."

                    *   *   *

Flicking a set of sculptured nails at his proffered plastic, the cashier at the Officers' Club buffet indicated his lunch was covered in cash. She aimed an index spike at a dark corner and he saw a civilian waving him to a seat.

"Something tells me you'd be Mr. Bayer..." He slid his tray onto the table and shook a strong hand. The guy stood, nodded, smiled. He was mid-40's; sporting a neat salt-and-pepper beard. Blue blazer, maroon turtleneck and a rigid crease in faded Levi's. Not a rep tie or wing-tip to be found on his slim frame.

"Just a few minutes of your time if I might, Mr. Davis."

"You might...but only after you show me some ID."

He bit into his sandwich, munched and stared at the leather case in front of his plate.

"What can I do for you, Mr. Bayer?"

"Well, I've been down at the museum going through the Quick material...and I'm a little curious."

"So am I. Tell you what. You fill me in on a couple of things I've been wondering about and then I'll answer any questions I can. OK?"

"Within reason, Mr. Davis...and bearing in mind the need-to-know. Ask away."

"Did Sergeant Major Quick really work for you guys?"

"He did. Four years...between 1972 and 1976."

"I was his closest friend. How come he never mentioned it?"

"He was more operationally effective with no direct link to DIA. He worked undercover and under a mandated secrecy agreement."

"No shit? What did he do?"

"He was...an investigator."

"Investigating what?"

Spook Bayer sipped iced tea and pondered a ceiling fan for a long moment. "Mr. Davis, from time to time we employ people from the uniformed services with special backgrounds or expertise in a particular area. These people have got to be tenacious, motivated..."

"That fits the Sergeant Major's profile."

"Yes, particularly in the area of American POWs and MIAs in Southeast Asia. As you know, his son was on the MIA list until `76."

"And that's what he was doing for the DIA? Investigating POW and MIA stuff?"

"Correct. He was particularly useful at exposing scams. His insights from ground reconnaissance missions while he was attached to CCN were quite helpful to our analysts."

"Not helpful enough..."

Bayer propped his elbows on the table and ran a finger alongside his nose. "Mr. Davis, are you one of those hidebound people who think the Vietnamese are still holding Americans for ransom over there?"

"No, I don't think that, Mr. Bayer. But I think maybe the Sergeant Major did."

"Yes. He was adamant...and not willing to entertain evidence to the contrary. That's why his assignment with us was terminated."

"Well, that would explain a few of the radical things he said and did in the last few years he was on active duty."

"All quite understandable, I think. A presumptive finding of death is always hard to accept...particularly if it's your own son. Curiosity satisfied?"

"Yeah. Guess so. Your turn."

"Sergeant Major Quick's records and logs are extensive and complete...except for one period."

"Yeah, I noticed. The period he worked for you guys."

A notebook and pencil seemed to slither from the blazer into Bayer's hands. His voice shifted to the cadence of a lawyer conducting direct examination. "Do you have any knowledge of where the missing logbook might be at this time?"

He didn't.

"Are you aware of any other materials - written, photographic, reproduced or transcribed - relating to Sergeant Major Quick's employment with the DIA?"

Nope, nothing like that...other than the reference to R. A. Beal and the note in the existing log.

"Are you aware that under the provisions of the National Security Act of 1947, you are bound to reveal any knowledge you may have in this matter...under penalty of prosecution?"

Oh, yeah. Been to that concert. Got the t-shirt.

Spook Bayer stared for a long time before he blinked. Then he tore a page from the notebook and forked it across the table.

"This is my direct dial number and the number of my pager, Mr. Davis. If you run across anything later, please give me a call." End of official interview.

"Listen, I'm on your team, all right? We both get a government paycheck. What should I be looking for and why the hell are you so interested in it?"

Spook Bayer chewed his lip for a moment then slid back into his chair and plucked a french fry from the plate opposite him. "OK, cards on the table. Your friend worked on some very sensitive material concerning live sightings of POWs in Laos. He was focused on this issue because he'd run a lot of operations across the western border...along the Ho Chi Minh Trail..."

"And because his son Ken went down in that area..."

"Check. Motivation to the max. Regular bulldog about the Laos MIA deal. He was a real asset...until the evidence failed to support his beliefs. Then he went ape-shit...lost his objectivity...so we cut him loose. We've had enough disinformation and false hopes on this issue...just muddies the water and makes it hard to ascertain facts. Facts, Davis...not forlorn hopes or speculations or materials that can be taken out of context."

"You think the Sergeant Major may have some of this stuff in the missing logbook...assuming there is one?"

"He was a meticulous record-keeper, right? Why stop keeping records just because he was working for us? It doesn't happen that way in the intel game. We've all got stuff stashed away...occupational hazard. Bottom line is this: Some of the material he had access to might damage ongoing efforts to finally get a full accounting from the Vietnamese. We wouldn't want that and I don't think he would either."

"Well, thanks for the chow."

"My pleasure...by the way, would you be willing to let us look around that cabin in the Ozarks?"

Shake thought it over. Why not? Nothing left there now. He handed over a key and went back to his lunch. "Don't tear anything up, lock it when you leave and mail the key back to me." He stared out the O Club window, watching the GSA sedan turn right out of the driveway, heading in the direction of Quantico's main gate.

And so Spook Bayer explains the secret of Spook Quick. No major mystery, for Christ's sake. Sergeant Major was a little whacked out after '76. He was always saying the people in charge of investigating the MIAs had...what'd he call it? A mind-set to debunk...didn't want to hear anything that might indicate guys were left alive over there after Operation Homecoming. Makes sense a guy whose own son was in that category would stockpile any evidence...oh, shit!

He punched up the date on his G-Shock and headed for the door running hard, on the way to the unit mailroom.

*   *   *

Just one bulging envelope stuffed in his slot. Understandable. Mail from Sedalia would arrive before something from the west coast. It was thick, flexible; probably just what Bayer was after...or maybe he was infected with intrigue; falling into the spook syndrome. Maybe it was just the deed and documents related to the Ozark cabin and hilltop he now owned.

Negative. The Sergeant Major had been specific and meticulous about final affairs. Those documents were signed, notarized and on file at the county courthouse back in Missouri. So? Maybe these were copies...or a draft of the Great American War Novel Gus was always threatening to write.

Halfway across the parking lot, headed for his truck, he tore open the manila envelope. Inside was an inch-thick bundle of perforated computer paper, individual sheets attached to each other with the printer guide-track edges still in place. A yellow post-it note pasted on the first page: Close hold. Eyes Only. CWO Shake Davis USMC.

No legalese. No literature. Obviously intelligence related given the boldface slug that announced he was holding material classified Top Secret/Pinnacle/NOFORN. Could mean nothing or it could mean this stuff was hot enough to sizzle through flesh. No sweat...not with his current TS Clearance and a valid U.S. passport.

He flipped a few pages. No title, no cover-sheet; just an alphabetical list of names: last name first, first name last, middle initial. Underneath each name, a serial number, branch of service and a date. Didn't take a Mensa member to recognize a list of POWs or MIAs from the war in Vietnam.

So, did he have a need to know? Gus thought so...but Gus was a man obsessed; not necessarily a clear and lucid thinker on this particular issue. And that had to be the only reason for risking a felony offense; stealing classified material from the government he was sworn to support and defend.

Unlocking his pick-up, he fished out Spook Bayer's number and damn near dialed it on the car phone. The fever forced him to snap the receiver back into its cradle. Gus wanted him to see this...and Gus had never steered him wrong. Over thirty years he'd handled information classified all the way up through Holy Shit/Gee Whiz/Burn Before Reading. Except for the technical stuff, most security classifications were bullshit anyway.

*   *   *

By 1800 he had a throbbing headache and a very funny feeling about the material he'd been reading steadily for the past four hours. Sliding the half-moon specs down off his nose to rest on his chin, he closed his eyes and ordered bits of information to pass in review.

Computer-generated material; no question. There was a file number, document ID tag and some kind of flakey network address full of machine-speak symbols, punctuation marks and half-words. And there was no question the first part of the document was a list - 213 names - of American soldiers, sailors, Marines and airmen missing in action from late 1967 through early 1972. Common denominator: all went missing in Laos. Ken Quick was on the list along with all the known data about his shoot-down.

Part two of the material was less-organized, hard to mate with part one. Just slugs of information in random paragraphs from a different address somewhere in cyberspace. Highlighted references to locations all along the 500 or so miles of Ho Chi Minh Trail that ran through Laos. And background info on all sorts of odd bits.

Truong Son, Vietnamese for Long Mountains. Stony Beach, Bangkok. General Political Directorate, PAVN. NVA Group 559, the Truong Son Corps. Operations Homecoming and Linebacker II. VVA, not American vets...North Vietnamese Army survivors. The Cuban Program, Cu Loc, Fidel and Chico. Houses of Tradition, Lam Son 719, Vietnamese cross-border combat operation in 1971. *Doi moi*, "renovation" and *coi moi*, "openness."

Random computer dumps. Like excerpts from an encyclopedia, but in no discernible order. Some had to do with Laos, some didn't. Some related to POWs or MIAs, some apparently didn't. Geography lessons, geopolitics, some familiar, some meaningless. There was even material in transliterated Vietnamese which sorely taxed his memory of a language never used anymore unless he got a wild hair up his ass and drove to DC for dinner in a Vietnamese restaurant.

Fortunately, he found a full bottle of Tylenol in the drawer with the BOQ room list. He popped two pills, found his glasses and then a room number for Chief Warrant Officer Daven Morey, old panyo and OCS classmate. Daven was a data processing officer; a confirmed futurist, author of regular, esoteric articles in the Marine Corps Gazette claiming there was more power in megabytes than megatons. He lived topside on the second deck with a little furniture and a lot of gadgets. Time to pay a visit.

*   *   *

Daven had a date. His rooms reeked of PX perfume, ozone and overloaded electrical circuits. Sandra Settlemeyer, a civilian tech-rep charged with exterminating bugs in the base data processing system, looked up from somewhere deep in a Dungeons & Dragons program and waved. Two years before she'd done her level best to bring Shake and an Apple into the same grid square. It was never even close.

"Well, this can't be about computers. If you guys are gonna do grunt-speak, I'll take a break. Anybody need a Coke?" She saved her game, borrowed some quarters and headed for the soda machine in the BOQ lobby.

Shake pulled the print-outs from an envelope and walked over to where Daven sat surrounded by a suite of gadgets that looked like set dressing from Star Trek.

"I need to know what these two computer addresses are." He circled the blocks of type and plopped the papers down on a humming main-frame. "Can you figure it out?"

"I can run a few search programs...surf the net some. Where'd you get this stuff, Shake? It's fucking classified to the max!"

"Don't get your bowels in an uproar. It's some stuff Sergeant Major Quick left for me. I need to know where he got it...then maybe I'll know what the hell to do with it. OK? Can you help? And keep your mouth shut about it?"

"Question. Am I doing something utterly stupid for an old buddy...something that's gonna result in my lungs getting ripped right out of my chest?"

"Negative. If anybody did anything stupid, it was probably the Sergeant Major. All I want to know is where to return this stuff."

"Uh-huh. When do you need it?"

"Sooner the better. When can you have it?"

"Hard telling. Depends on what I run into. Before you retire anyway..."

"How about tonight?"

"No way. I'll be busy...putting my dragon in a certain dungeon."

"It's for the Sergeant Major, OK? I don't want shit smeared all over his reputation."

"Give it a shot...all I can do."

"I'm headed out. Machine's on down in my room. Leave a message if you find out anything. If I don't hear from you, I'll check back in the morning."

*   *   *

She was staring at framed photos along the back wall of the bar. All Marines, all legends, all ghosts haunting tiny Quantico town's one and only semi-famous landmark. Generations of professional Marines - filtered through Quantico as they were bound to be at one time or another - ducked through the back gate and wound up here to slake a thirst, cut boondock dust, resurrect flagging motivation or re-fight the last fracas.

Initiates - like the two butter-bar beef-babies flanking his daughter - came to the Globe and Laurel just to feel the Marineness of the place. Or to see if they could get laid. He nodded at a few regulars on barstool watch and rolled into a spoiling attack. Technically, both young officers out-ranked him, but they'd been in the Corps long enough to understand a veteran Chief Warrant Officer was a force outside the normal pecking order; a force to be respectfully reckoned with by all Marines...particularly second lieutenants.

"Sorry to pee on your parade, gents, but this lady is taken for the evening." Tracey kissed his cheek and pointed to her suitors.

"You probably know these guys, Daddy. They just got out of basic school." He caught the flash in her eyes as she brought a wine glass up to cover a broad grin. Thus cued, he glowered ominously and squinted at the plastic nametags on their uniforms. Right flank nearly choked on a mouthful of margarita; left flank opened defensive fire.

"Evening, sir...we were just...uh, celebrating a little. Orders came in today."

"And where has Mother Corps seen fit to send you, lieutenant?"

"Third MarDiv, sir...Okinawa."

"Well, then...our days of worrying about the Western Pacific are over. I'll make a few calls...just to let the Commanding General know you're coming."

She kept the lid on until they reached a table, but by the time the menus arrived Tracey was cackling, a rich rumble of mirth...her mom's kind of laughter...before the self-pity stifled it. "Classic, Daddy...beautiful. He won't sleep for a week. Like that time in Norfolk? You told that ensign there were claymore mines planted around the house."

"Never came back, did he?"

"Nope...and I got the message about dating young officers."

"You had enough action from the high school football team without some pencil-neck Navy staff puke sniffing around."

She shoved a lock of light brown hair - sun-streaked even in the winter - behind her ear and busied herself with a dinner selection. He sat stunned, realizing in that moment - out of all the time he'd spent watching his daughter develop - that he was in the presence of a beautiful woman. She demanded attention; drew glances from around the room, doing nothing more provocative than reading a menu. And he was about to cut her loose among the buffed and bronzed male population of the University of Miami.

"Tracey...listen, are you gonna be OK down there?"

"Far as I know, I am. They had an opening in the Ocean Science Program, I had the GPA, they approved a mid-term transfer, your check cleared..."

"That's not what I mean."

She laid her fork at the top of her plate and stared across the table; into eyes exactly the color of her own. "I don't sleep around, Dad. Not here and not down there. Does that make you feel better?"

"Yeah...truthfully, it does."

"I'll be twenty-one this summer..."

"I don't want to hear it."

"No, listen, Dad...let's take stock here. I'm gonna be OK, no sleaze, no disease, no unwanted babies, no asshole boyfriends. I've got a handle on it, OK? So stop worrying like I was sixteen or something. Mom's gonna be OK too. She was sober...at least when I left the house...and kind of excited about the Betty Ford thing. She wants to give it a shot and that's the first step, right? That leaves you..."

"I'm fine."

"No, you're not. Your best friend just died. You're about to become homeless after 30 years in the Marine Corps. Your pay is gonna be cut in half and you've got no job lined up. You're laying out big bucks for Mom and now you're faced with a three-year drain for me and college..."

"There's no sense in denying..."

"Precisely, Dad. There's no sense in denying you deserve a life...after all you've been through." She pulled a glossy pamphlet from her purse and laid it beside his plate. "It's not just a job...it's an adventure."

Pulling on his specs, he discovered that the route to that adventure could begin with the Naval Reserve Officers Training Corps. A highlighted portion of the pamphlet further revealed that qualified and accepted students could get a full-float scholarship through NROTC leading to a degree and a commission in the United States Navy.

"Don't choke, Daddy. There's a Marine option."

"Tracey, you don't have to do this. In fact, I don't want you to do it."

"Too late. I submitted the paperwork...and the nice Lieutenant Commander I talked to said there should be no problem for an Ocean Science major with my grade point average."

"Don't do this, honey. I promised you I'd pay the bills and I will."

"You can't afford it, Dad. You know damn well you can't. This gives me a chance to pay my own freight. Why are you acting so schizo?"

"It's not a good life for a woman! Take my word for it. I've seen it; I know."

"Things are changing, Daddy. You know as well as I do what's happening. Just look what's happened in the last couple of years."

"I know...and I know there's more to come."

"So, sky's the limit, right? There are lots of things I'll be able to do. What are you afraid of?"

"It's not what they won't let you do. It's what they might make you do."

"Like what?"

"Like lead a rifle platoon in combat, for instance. Suppose the social engineers force-feed this thing to the point that all restrictions are lifted and nobody with any sense bitches loud enough to stop it. Suppose you get caught up in some back-water shitstorm and get blown away. I've seen enough KIAs in my life to know my daughter is not gonna be one of 'em."

"My mind's made up. I'm gonna do this."

"Listen, I'm not retired yet. I can still make a few phone calls..."

"If you do that, Dad, I'll never forgive you for it."

He reached for her hand, hoping to ease the tension. She kept her fist balled, jaw muscles bunched. As she had on other issues over the years, Tracey Davis was making a determined stand. And, as he had done on most of those occasions, her father capitulated.

"So, if I become a high-paid Beltway Bandit...or if I win the lottery..." She smiled, uncoiled her fist and cradled his hand.

"Or if you capture a Leprechaun and claim his pot of gold, I'll resign, repay the loans and remain a puke civilian. Deal?"

*   *   *

The red light on his answering machine was pulsing steadily. Multiple messages. He hit the overhead lights, rewound, reached for a pad and pressed play. Jan...drunk but coherent: when was Tracey coming home...oh, and thanks for the Betty Ford thing...although she really didn't need it. Adjutant's office at MCDEC...retirement orders finally arrived... drop by and get his check-out sheet anytime. And Daven Morey: "Good news and bad news on your project. It's 2130...I'll be up til midnight. If you get back before then, come on up." Shake did.

Daven handed him a beer and a sheet of printer paper covered with queries, symbols and responses. He sat down on

Daven's rack and gave it a shot, but it just looked like someone was touch-typing with their fingers off the home row. "Other than proving I'm a computer illiterate asshole, what does all this mean?"

"Just gives you an idea of what I had to go through to get the job done."

"But you did get the job done?"

"First part was easy. That list of names? It's MIAs all right...from the Senate Select Committee on POW/MIA Affairs...sub reference something called the `Laos File' but I couldn't find out whose file it happens to be or any background on it at all. Good news is the info on the list was declassified by Bush in July '92. Executive Order 12812. It's all there...if you know how to read it."

"Terrific. We're off the hook. What's the bad news?"

"Part two. I surfed around looking for background on that stuff you underlined? Kept hitting minefields; interlocks and cross-references all over the place. Anyway, I tried a few trapdoors and thought I had the sonofabitch hacked on The Cuban Program and Group 559..."

"Yeah? Then what?"

"Then the defecation hit the oscillation, pal. Program started demanding a trace on the query...wanted to know just who in the hell was asking questions. I bailed and shut it down."

"Daven...please..."

"OK, look, there are certain files in certain data banks that are restricted...usually password restricted...but there are so many cross-references that if you know your way around the net, sometimes you can get in through a trapdoor...kinda like crawling in through a window when you forget your key. If the stuff is touchy enough, they sometimes put in an anti-hacker program that automatically tells them who's trying to gain access. Computer talks to computer and they got you. It's something like the cops doing a phone trace."

"So when you started asking about the Cuban Program and Group 559, they started a trace?"

"Roger that...but I shut down before they could get a handle on me."

"Who are they?"

"That address on part two? It's DIA."

*   *   *

If he was forced to fill out a score card, his next to last day in the Marine Corps would be rated somewhere between substandard and shitty. Disbursing was docking his separation pay for some long-forgotten dead horse he'd drawn in Naples. The friendly folks over at Marine Federal Credit Union kicked in the costly over-draft protection to keep his Betty Ford Clinic check from bouncing. A concerned corporal at Base Motor Transport highly recommended new brakes and shocks before he'd trust the pick-up to make Miami.

Now Master Sergeant Rafter Grimm, ranking guru of the command Adjutant's Office, was playing games with his orders. "Sorry, Gunner you can look but you can't touch."

"I need copies of my orders, Top. There are people all over the goddamn base waiting with bated breath..."

"Colonel Semple was on the horn when I walked through the hatch this morning, Gunner. Direct orders. Halt...one, two. You don't get doodley-squat until he talks to you...in his office...ASAP."

The staff sergeant stationed outside Colonel Semple's office knew better than to play gate-keeper with a salty senior warrant in the pissed-off mode. He pointed at the door with one hand and hit the intercom switch with the other. The colonel's visitor was inside the office to hear himself announced.

"Stand easy, Shake." Colonel Semple pointed to a couch and a coffee thermos. "Pour us a cup and have a seat."

"Colonel, we've known each other a long time. This meeting better not start with `have I got a deal for you'."

"You won't hear a sales pitch from me. Purely your decision...one way or the other. I told 'em that loud and clear."

"Told who?"

"Pentagon. Assistant Secretary of Defense for Plans and Policy. They got a job for you."

"Is this a joke, sir? Or does some dip-shit really believe I'd become an errand boy on the E Ring?"

"No joke, Shake. I got a call late last night. They want you to go to Vietnam with this delegation the President is sending."

His laugh was infectious. They sat chuckling, chortling, then whooping, dabbing at their eyes with paper napkins. "Christ, I told 'em when they called. I said putting Shake Davis with that bunch would be like putting a turd in the punchbowl."

"What in the hell prompted it, Colonel? Ain't nobody in the Pentagon knows me from Adam's off-ox."

"Computer dating, apparently. They had this other guy all set to go...small-arms background, spoke Vietnamese, buncha tours over there, advisor-type...then suddenly he gets reassigned somewhere; unavailable for one reason or another. So they plug in the requirements and ask the computer for a replacement. Your name comes up and my phone starts ringing."

"No way, colonel. No sale."

"Sure, Shake?"

"You know how I feel about that whole mess over there, sir. Closed book...and I have no interest in re-opening it."

"Well, I had to ask. Thought you might at least want to hear it. Scuttlebutt says the job search has been...uh, less than fruitful?"

"Yessir. Seems I'm a pretty tough sell on the civilian market. Defense contractors want an M-B-A not a C-W-O with a high-school equivalency. Even the cops are sending my letters back...too old to be a patrolman."

"Bucks gonna be a problem, Shake?"

"Yessir. Family expenses are pretty high just now...but I'll work it out."

"Why the hell don't you consider this deal in Vietnam? It's a steady paycheck for as long as the delegation is active."

"How much would they pay, sir?"

"What do you mean?"

"How much would the job pay...if I was to take it?"

"Shake, I don't think you understand. This is an active duty gig. The guy they want you to replace was an Army officer. You'd remain in the Corps...full pay and allowances...plus per diem for the whole time you're over there."

"No shit?" Another year...maybe more...full pay and then some...no living expenses. It would put him over the top. It also sounded just a little too ideal. "I'm at thirty this month, Colonel. By law, that's all she wrote."

"Waiver's on the way from Headquarters Marine Corps. You can stay for thirty-five if you don't go blind or get fat."

"How come a lowly warrant officer with all the high-priced help?"

"When have you ever met a lowly warrant officer? You'd have to ask the officer in charge of the military contact team about it, but I suspect they want a warrant because a warrant won't seem as threatening to the gooks as a bird colonel or a brigadier. Warrants get things done. Might get in with the NVA privates and sergeants and find out what's really happening."

"That's what they want me to do? Conduct some kind of technical inspection?"

"I'd bet that's it exactly, Shake. I'd bet the Pentagon Strategic Planning Staff would dearly love to have your take on the state of their military. I'd bet we're gonna start selling them bastards weapons before long."

"Jesus Christ on a rubber crutch!"

"Makes sense, Shake. We play the cards right and we give the American defense industry a much-needed shot in the arm, establish a buffer in the area and keep China off guard."

"Can I think about it?"

"Nope. Time is tight. They want you processed and standing tall out at El Toro on Monday."

"I promised I'd drive Tracey down to Miami tomorrow."

Colonel Semple walked to his desk and ran a finger down the calendar. "That's doable if you don't dick around about it. We can fax your orders through the recruiting station down there...and last time I checked there were regular flights from Miami to the Left Coast."

3. *Miami*

They blew past Cocoa Beach on Interstate 95 with Tracey at the wheel of his re-shocked and re-braked pick-up truck. He'd been pushing hard down the eastern seaboard, small-talking his way around the news he needed to break, when the Georgia radar-ranger bagged him south of Savannah. When he walked out of the Chatham County courthouse two hours later he was down seventy dollars and out of the driver's seat for the remainder of the trip. To keep from pouting he played with the radio.

"Leave it there, Daddy! Hootie and the Blowfish..."

"Hooters and the what?"

"Hootie...and the Blowfish...downeast rockers. I gotta get used to it."

"Christ, sounds like a gang of strippers from Olongapo in the Philippines."

"How would you know?"

"Been there, done that."

"Hope you got the t-shirt. Those days are over."

"Maybe not."

She glanced at him over the top of her shades and turned down the radio. "Is that it, Dad?"

"What?"

"What you've been wanting to tell me since we hit the highway. Are you moving out of the country?"

"Sort of..."

"Let me guess. Some sheik needs a gunslinger to guard his oil pipeline. No, wait...you bought into a bordello in Barcelona..."

"Tracey, I'm going to Vietnam."

"What?"

"Vietnam. I leave Monday."

"Correct me if I'm wrong, Dad. Aren't you the guy who told me you didn't leave anything over there you'd ever need to go back for?"

"That was before they made me a deal I couldn't refuse."

"Must be big bucks..."

"Big enough for what we need. They're letting me stay on active duty...full pay. I'm going with that Presidential delegation...the normalization team."

"Oh, my God! That's too much..." She laughed so hard he was tempted to grab the wheel. "My father...working for Slick

Willie Clinton. Next thing we know, you'll be a registered Democrat."

*   *   *

With Tracey busy at the Registrar's Office, he dropped her luggage at a dormitory, dug out a city map and headed for the Miami Marine Corps Recruiting Station where he'd been told to meet a Major Dave Martinez. Chasing the address he'd been given at Quantico led him to a high-rise Federal Building at city center. Rent-a-cop at the desk inside pointed to a bank of elevators and said the Marines were dug in on the top floor.

Major Martinez was in a post-PT cool down period, still wearing shorts and sweating from a racquetball game with one of his recruiters. "Sorry to greet you this way, Gunner. Independent duty, you know. Gotta grab your PT time when and where you can."

"No problem, Major. I won't keep you long."

"Relax, Gunner. Got the call from Colonel Semple yesterday. He says you're a hot property these days, extend every courtesy. No big deal for us. We do it all the time for Marines who come through Miami."

"I could use a cup of coffee...if it's not too much trouble." Major Martinez waved a hand and snatched at the phone on his desk. He was settling into a chair when a First Sergeant walked into the office carrying two steaming cups. There was something vaguely familiar about the man.

"This is my First Sergeant, Gunner." The Major grabbed the cups and handed one to his visitor. "First Sergeant Emmett Rea...Gunner Shake Davis."

"I've met the Gunner before, sir." The senior NCO extended his hand. "We served together with the BLT in Beirut. First battalion, 8th Marines, Gunner? I was a squad leader then...Bravo Company."

"I remember, Top. Good to see you again."

"You too, sir." The first sergeant headed for the door. "Let me know if there's anything I can do."

"So how's it going, Major?" He sipped coffee, not wanting to rush the meeting although he was anxious to get to a motel, shower and find a place for a nice farewell dinner with Tracey.

"Recruiting...here in Miami? Not too bad really. We get some good kids although the military isn't much of a draw anymore. Lots of Cubans interested in being Marines, though. Keeps us on top of the affirmative action quotas."

"Most of 'em make good Marines. Had a Cuban guy on the Drill Field with me...Parris Island back in 1977. Enlisted right off the boat from Havana. Outstanding Drill Instructor."

"Yeah...in fact, we'd be shipping a lot more of them but background checks are a problem sometimes. Lots of Cuban families down here are political. Sometimes I think that goddamn Castro is dug in down there ninety miles to the south just to piss me off."

"Well, things are changing in a hurry. Just look at where I'm headed."

"Never thought I'd see the day. Hope somebody's gonna pin their asses to the wall over the MIAs. You got any scoop on that?"

"Haven't heard a thing except what the President said on TV. Supposedly this whole junket has been laid on because they're making progress in resolving the issue. That's all I know."

"Well, give 'em hell, Gunner. We got the fax machine on stand-by. Your orders should arrive tonight. I'll give you a call."

"I better find myself a hotel." He set his coffee cup on the major's desk and stood.

"All laid on for you." The major extended his hand. "Sergeant Cruz in the Admin shop is a home-boy. He's got a room booked at the Belle Aire and an open ticket for you on Delta...Miami to John Wayne. You can leave anytime you want. When you're airborne we'll call El Toro and have somebody meet the plane."

Down in Admin, Sgt. Cruz marked Shake's map with directions to the hotel and told him the Marine Corps would handle the bill. The man had dark, brooding eyes, too much hair and an accent that smacked of Al Pacino as Tony Montana in Scarface.

"You truck, sir. Somebody gonna take care?"

"What's that, Sgt. Cruz?"

"You truck, sir. The vehicle you come down here in...parked outside?"

"My truck? No problem. I'm leaving it with my daughter."

"Yessir. Major want me to give you dis." Cruz dug in his desk drawer and produced a phone pager with a spring clip on the back. "You keep dis on you while you here in Miami. We need you...you hear de beep."

Seems like every officer in the Marine Corps carries one of the damn things these days but he'd always managed to slip the electronic leash. He signed for the pager, checked the controls and pressed the test button. Shriek sounded like a dump truck rolling in reverse.

"Damn! Doesn't this thing have one of those vibrator functions?"

"Government issue, sir..." Sgt. Cruz smiled and shrugged his shoulders. "Cheapest dey got."

"OK. Gracias, Sgt. Cruz."

"De nada, senor..." He was halfway to the door when Cruz caught him with a welcome suggestion. "You gonna try de comida Cubana while you here, sir?"

"You got someplace in mind, Sgt. Cruz? I'm supposed to take my daughter out on the town tonight."

"Bes' Cuban food anywhere, verdad? My cousin's place in Poquito Habana. I write it down for you. Make sure you try de pescada rosa con limon."

On the steps leading to the parking lot, First Sergeant Rea stood sucking on a cigarette. He heard footsteps, plucked the smoke from his mouth and snapped off a salute.

"Can't smoke inside government buildings anymore, Gunner. Gotta come out here every time I get the urge."

"Pain in the ass, ain't it, Top?"

"Roger that. You gonna be out and about tonight, sir?"

"Thought I might. My daughter's starting school over at University of Miami. I was gonna take her for dinner at a place Sgt. Cruz recommended."

"Little Havana? You be careful, Gunner. There's some mighty mean streets in this town."

*   *   *

It took two bottles of white wine and a pitcher of ice-water to get them through the spicy meal in Little Havana. The place was off the track, small, loud and breezy from an Atlantic rain squall that blew over the city while they were eating. They were the only two gringos in the joint except for a few who wandered in to pick up take-out orders.

"Nice place, Daddy."

"Came highly recommended. Local color..."

Tracey glanced at two Cubans slouched at a table nearby. "I think we're the local color in here."

He cut a quick look across the room. They were attentive, staring straight back, mucho machismo. Blousy silk shirts and high-speed white sneakers that likely cost just a little less than the layers of chunky gold jewelry they wore. Put that down to

Tracey and a clingy little mini-dress, part of her new Florida ensemble. Cold eyes above the pearly smiles. Pimps or pushers probably. He remembered the First Sergeant's caution and waved for the check.

It was two blocks from the restaurant to the spot where he parked the truck along one of Little Havana's main north-south streets. He walked with his arm around his daughter, anxious to get beyond the deserted sidewalks and dark alleys, into an area where their backs were covered by regular Metro PD patrols. Along Little Havana's main arteries, Miami cops kept the predators well away from the bodegas, pricey shops and honest street-people trying to turn a tourist buck.

"Get enough to eat, Daddy?"

"Yeah, plenty...more than I needed probably."

"You worried about your waistline?"

"Well, my plans to become a fat, sloppy civilian have changed."

She laughed and patted his belly. "That just reminded me..."

"What?"

"What you used to tell Gus Quick? When you guys had to baby-sit me and we'd all sneak off to the Staff NCO Club. You said you'd rather have a sister in a whorehouse than a brother who was a fat, sloppy civilian."

"Jesus, Tracey...you got some mouth on you."

"I come by it honestly."

"Guess you do at that. But you might want to talk a little more like a college student and a little less like a grunt on campus."

"Not much difference these days, Daddy."

They turned onto Biscayne Boulevard into a steady stream of tourists. Show time. Little Havana's nightly circus bathed in the orange glow of halogen street lights. Along the avenue in the direction of his parking spot a salsa quartet competed with a Jamaican steel drum band. Knots of swaying tourists milling around each group, chewing charbroiled meat off bamboo skewers. Every corner seemed to sport a carne cart or barbecue grill where strips of chicken or pork sizzled over smoky charcoal.

"Smells great. Want to get a meat-sicle before we head home?"

"You're hungry again?"

"Hey, listen, where I'm headed it might be nothing but fish heads and rice for the foreseeable future."

He bought two long bamboo slivers festooned with chicken chunks, green peppers and pearl onions. Tracey grabbed hers and maneuvered through the mob to watch the salsa band's conga drummer slam his way through a long solo riff. He was nibbling, trying to see past a tall Latino with acne scars on his neck, when his beeper began to wail.

While he fumbled to unclip the thing from his belt, a number of people in the crowd checked pocket or purse to see if their device might be responsible for the irritating screech. The tall guy in front of him turned, stared and reached inside his jacket. Pager in hand, he waved it at the man and smiled an apology.

"Sorry...it's me..." He punched the button to silence the beep and check for a phone number to call. The Latino was still facing him, still fumbling inside his jacket. He transferred the bamboo skewer to his left hand and held the device higher, more obvious. "Just somebody trying to screw up my evening..."

He glanced down at the LED display. Nothing but a series of 8's. What the hell? He was punching buttons, trying to determine if he'd made a control error when he spotted the white pistol grips against the black of the man's jacket. The gunman stepped back with his right foot and yanked harder at the pistol. As he swung it across his body the short, fat tube attached to the muzzle came into focus.

Can! Bastard's got a suppressor on the weapon. Adrenaline jolt...familiar, instant and electric. Drill the beeper directly at the shooter's face, lunge forward from the hips, slap the pistol aside. Focus hard and tight on counterattack...two muffled thumps over the shouts of people scrambling for cover.

Stay close...stay on the bastard! Shooter dancing backward. Trying for distance; get the weapon back in play. No fucking way, Jose.

He drove the bamboo skewer directly into the flesh underneath the man's chin. Meat, grease and blood splashed over his hand and ran down his wrist. Shooter spasmed and tripped over the abandoned conga drum. Reaching for the spike in his throat with one hand, shooter brought the pistol back on target with the other.

Drop it, you sonofabitch! Quit! Spin left, out of the line...stomp hard on shooter's elbow. Bone snapped and the semi-auto skittered across the concrete. He snatched at the little Colt Woodsman, dropped to a knee and centered the front sight on the shooter's nose.

"Freeze! Don't move!" He heard Tracey yelling something ...the whoop of sirens...weird Doppler echo off the store fronts along Biscayne Boulevard. He turned his head for just a second to see his daughter running toward him. "Tracey! Stay back...wave down those cops..."

In that instant the bloody shooter went to Plan B, jack-knifed a knee, reaching for the back-up piece in an ankle holster. No chance. Shooter caught two rounds from his own weapon: one through the hamstring and the other through the sternum.

* * *

They booked him at Metro Dade but the detective assigned to the case said it was just a formality. Clear case of self-defense with all the witnesses in the world willing to make statements. When the detective and his partner finished tape recording his preliminary description of events, Tracey was allowed into the interrogation room. She was visibly shaken but steadied up when she saw her father was fine and free of cuffs.

"Who was that asshole and why was he after you?"

"Beats me...both times." He hugged her, glanced at the cop and nodded. Detective Lieutenant Steve Berntson was a pragmatic veteran, a former Marine who admitted to being impressed by the way Shake Davis had handled himself in the crunch. He held a chair for Tracey and signaled for his partner to pour fresh coffee for all.

"Hitter for hire. Eddie Villachez...street name Mondo. Couple of outstanding wants and warrants. Used to be muscle for the dopers until INS busted him on a bogus green card. Last we heard they'd shipped him back to Cuba."

"Why did he try to shoot my Dad?"

Berntson shrugged and slugged at his coffee. "We got some people over at the hospital talking to him now. Subsonic twenty-twos didn't do that much damage, so he'll talk if we press the right buttons. If I had to guess, I'd say he either went nuts or he was on a job and got your father mixed up with another target. Hard to say with these dirtballs. Sometimes you never do find out what happened."

"Can we go home now?"

"You can. I need your Dad to hang around and do some paperwork. We can give you a ride."

"Take the truck, Tracey. I'll call you when I get back to the hotel."

She stood and took the keys, reluctant to leave. "You're not gonna put him in jail, are you? It was self-defense..."

"This is Florida, Miss Davis. Down here we figure a man's got a right to defend himself. Hell, your Dad shot the guy with his own gun. There's not a judge in the state's gonna do anything but laugh this one off."

When she was gone, he spent some time reading a transcript of his statement and scribbling signatures on a stack of forms. Detective Berntson left him alone, ducked out and found a phone to check on the shooter. He was back in ten minutes with a box of donuts and a pot of fresh coffee.

"Mondo is not a happy camper. That round you put into his thigh was a mite too close to the family jewels."

"Surprised I didn't put one up his asshole the way he had his leg hiked up..."

"Yeah, he was reaching for the snubbie Smith he had strapped to his ankle. Bastard was loaded for bear. Hornady hollow-points in the .22..."

"Subsonic ammo and a suppressor on a twenty-two. Hitter's gear."

"Yes, indeedy. He was out to whack somebody. In fact, according to my guys over at the hospital, he was out to whack you."

"Can't be. Had to be a mix-up. I'm just here to drop my daughter off at college. Gotta be on the west coast Monday. I don't know anybody in Miami...or in Florida for that matter."

"Let me ask you something...one old Marine to another. Are you political?"

"What?"

"Are you political? Have you got some kind of assignment in the Corps that might interest Uncle Fidel Castro down in Cuba?"

"No. Closest I've ever been to Cuba was on a ship that passed by headed for the Med."

"Uh-huh. You said you had to be out on the west coast Monday. What's that about...transfer or something?"

"Or something. I got orders to join the delegation that's going over to Vietnam next week. The deal about lifting the trade embargo...normalization of relations..."

"And as far as you know there's no connection between any of that and Castro or Cuba? No political linkage...Cuba and Vietnam...nothing like that?"

"If there's any linkage...I don't know about it. Why are you asking?"

Berntson selected a donut and tasted it. "Well, our boy Mondo says he's fresh off a boat. Only been back in Miami three days. He also says he was put onto you by a guy named Fidel."

"Castro?" Little alarm bells pinging somewhere behind his ears.

"Nah, no way. Mondo doesn't travel in those circles. However, if what he says is true, somebody down south of here wants you dead."

"Why?" Fishing in his memory for the names. Part two of the stuff Gus gave him? The Cuban Program? Don't even know what the hell it means. Can't be.

"That's a good question, Gunner Davis. And I can't think of an answer. Maybe Mondo's just feedin' us a load of shit, but I'm wondering about the way it went down. You say he turned and drew down on you after your beeper went off?"

"That's right. I looked at it but there was just a bunch of eights."

"So we don't have a convenient coincidence here. The beeper was a mark. Told him who his target was."

"Bullshit. The goddamn Marine recruiters gave me that beeper...so they could reach me. Nobody else would have the number..."

Berntson bit into his donut and shrugged.

"Are you saying somebody at the recruiting station set me up?"

"That's where I'm gonna be tomorrow morning to start asking questions."

"Better start with a Cuban sergeant named Cruz." Alarm bells clanging now. "He issued me the beeper and he sent me down to Little Havana for dinner."

"Check..." Berntson was scribbling in a notebook, licking sugar off his fingertips. "You know this guy? Ever have a run in with him...piss him off...send him to the brig or anything?"

"Never met him before this afternoon."

"Well, it's someplace to start..." The detective reached for another donut then changed his mind. He pointed at Shake's tattoo'ed forearm. "Force Recon, huh?"

"Yeah. Off and on for the last twenty years."

"Always wanted to give that a try but they had me stuck in MPs. Arrested a bunch of your guys one time for bustin' up a club at Pendleton."

"Well, you know how it goes..." He grinned and scratched at the tattoo, souvenir of a splendid liberty run...Kowloon, Hong Kong...jump wings over a Marine Corps emblem. "We tend to get the high-spirited types."

"And neither you nor any of your high-spirited types had anything to do with Cuba? No sneaky-pete operations out of Guantanamo?"

"No, never. I'd tell you if we did. Hell, it's no secret anymore."

"OK. We'll see what we can find out. Mondo's probably sniffin' glue. But...I'd be watching my back if I were you."

"I can go ahead and catch my plane tomorrow?"

"Far as I'm concerned you can. We got all the statements we need to keep Mondo off the streets. Bastard got what he deserved...even less...considering you didn't kill him."

*   *   *

"Major's down at Metro Dade, Gunner." First Sergeant Rea examined the pager parts on his desk, shook his head and scooped them into a desk drawer. "Lieutenant Berntson was on the phone at zero-dark-thirty this morning wanting us to lay hands on Sergeant Cruz and keep him desk-bound."

"And you did that?"

"Couldn't, Gunner..." The senior NCO pointed at a coffee pot and a chair. "Seems Sgt. Cruz picked today to go UA. The Major nearly shit himself trying to get down to the cops and get an investigation of his own started."

"Does Sgt. Cruz have a history of Unauthorized Absence?" The hot coffee was melting some of his jangled nerves. His orders were in hand and he had a reservation on the 1315 flight to Orange County where, presumably, he'd be clear of Cuban hitmen.

"Nothin' that shows up in his SRB. But I gotta tell you, I've had my eye on him for a while."

"How come?"

"Guy's too full of la familia bullshit, you know? Couple of times the State Bureau of Investigation let me know he'd been spotted at political rallies. He's just too...I don't know...too fucking Cuban for my taste."

"So you'd be willing to consider that he set me up?"

"You know what I think, sir? I think he did somebody a favor. I think somebody wanted to know where you'd be at such and such a time...without necessarily saying why...and Sgt. Cruz provided the information. When it turned out that somebody tried to kill you, Cruz realized he was in over his head and split for the hills."

"I still don't get it, Top. Why in the hell would Cubans be interested in me? Especially interested enough to sic a hitman on me?"

"Nothing springs to mind, Gunner. I was thinking you'd have the answer...if anybody did."

He slugged hot coffee, thinking hard about the material in the bag at his feet. Most of last night spent pouring over it. The Cuban Program...Fidel...Chico and Cu Loc. Somehow connected...to POWs or MIAs...to Gus Quick and his computer dumps...and now...God only knows why...connected to me.

"First Sergeant, you've been around a while...can you think of anything that would tie in Cubans with Vietnam or with POWs over there?"

"Huh? Jesus, you think this deal has something to do with Vietnam, Gunner?"

"I don't know, Top. Maybe...it's all I can think of right off the top of my head. Anything?"

First Sergeant Rea got up, put his hands on his hips and scanned the bookshelf behind his desk. "There's a book here...I seem to remember...here it is." He pulled a slim volume from the second shelf and tossed it onto the desk.

Bamboo Hell...Lieutenant Colonel Earl Gerheim...U. S. Air Force (Retired). Heart-breaking true story of a determined man who survived five years in one of Hanoi's most brutal hell-holes...

"This Colonel Gerheim was a guest lecturer when I went through SERE school up at Holmstead. He had something to say about Cubans. Christ, I can't remember exactly...I was suffering from a severe case of kick-ass..."

"Can I take this with me, Top? Read it on the plane?"

"Yessir, be my guest...but we might be able to go one better. Colonel Gerheim lives over in Coral Gables. I got his number. You could give him a call."

First Sergeant Rea got Lieutenant Colonel Gerheim on the phone, exchanged pleasantries, broached the subject and then introduced Shake Davis. Voice on the other end of the line gravelly; full of grit but fighter-jock cool.

"Welcome Home, Shake."

"Thanks, Colonel...same to you. Uh, the First Sergeant mentioned I'm headed back to Vietnam..."

"You can have that mission, pardner. One visit was plenty long enough for this old dog."

"Yessir...don't know how you managed it, to tell the truth. You have my utmost respect..."

"Tell you the truth, I'd feel a lot better if I had your respect for dodging the SAM those bastards slammed up my ass. First Sergeant Rea said you were interested in the Cubans over there?"

"Yessir. I'm a little ignorant on the subject, sir. Were there Cubans in Vietnam?"

"Just a few, Shake...but they were mean bastards. I came into contact with them at Cu Loc in Hanoi...1970..."

"Where was that, sir?"

"Cu Loc POW camp. We called it The Zoo. There was a couple of Cuban troopers there...intelligence types. We called 'em Fidel and Chico..."

He glanced at his watch but all he could see was gooseflesh rising on his forearm. "I never heard a thing about that, sir."

"Most people didn't. Anyway, Fidel and Chico were supposed to be there in Hanoi as English language instructors. That was clearly bullshit as we promptly discovered. They were on some kind of experimental team...supposed to torture the hell out of us and find out the most efficient ways to extract information or get us to sign propaganda statements. Let me tell you, Shake...those two cocksuckers were very good at it."

"What ever happened to these guys, Colonel?"

"Beats me. Probably living the good life in Havana. Decorated heroes for having tortured at least four Americans to death..."

"Colonel Gerheim...this is hard to believe, sir. I mean, they torture four men to death...Cubans soldiers in North Vietnam... our POWs...and we...regular Americans...we never hear any-thing about it?"

"Long time ago, Shake. After the war, with all the other sins and recriminations...they just faded into the mist, you know? I'm not even sure we know who they really were. Tell you one thing, though. One of these days, I'm gonna find out who they were...and I'm gonna personally lead the delegation down there that arrests their asses and brings them to trial. The sadistic bastards who ran the Cuban Program in Hanoi need to be strung up by their balls."

It was a long time after disconnect before he could speak. There it is...the Cuban Program. If Fidel and/or Chico...the Cu Loc Prison torture twins...are still alive, they'd be after anyone wanting to conjure up old ghosts. But how in the hell would they know about Sergeant Major Quick? OK...former POWs knew about them...wrote about them...talked about them in debriefs...so people in the American intel community investigating POW/MIA cases would know about Fidel and Chico...and vice versa. But how the fuck does that put me in the picture?

First Sergeant Rea refilled coffee cups and sat quietly until a decent interval passed. "Off hand, I'd say you got yourself a clue, Gunner. Anything I need to know?"

"Colonel Gerheim said all the right words, Top. Case of mistaken identity, I think." He stood, picked up his orders and drained his coffee cup. "Can you have one of your Marines drive me out to the airport?"

"I'll have a driver meet you down below at the main entrance, sir. Anything else?"

He scribbled on the First Sergeant's desk calendar. "That's my daughter's name and number here in town, Top. I'd appreciate your checking on her every once in a while. She's a Marine brat, so she'll be happy to hear from you."

"Don't worry about a thing, sir. Me and the wife will have her over for dinner...and I'll keep a sharp eye out."

He tossed his baggage in the back of the government motor pool van and settled into the passenger seat where a tanned and trim Lance Corporal was filling out the trip ticket. Just before they pulled out of the parking lot, the Marine driver retrieved a package from under his seat and handed it across the console. "First Shirt said to give you this, sir. It was forwarded from Quantico."

Inside the FedEx box was an envelope postmarked Puget Sound. Inside the envelope was Gus Quick's missing logbook and a letter from the grave.

*   *   *

Dear Shake,

By now I'm dust...or dug in wherever the hell Marines go when they die. Hope the burden of my last days was not too great because I'm going to call on you again to do me, our country, and the people who defend her, a great service.

This logbook and some other information you should have received from my sister in Sedalia outlines discoveries I made while working undercover with the DIA in 1972-76. I never mentioned this period to you for several reasons. I was ordered to maintain strict cover for credibility while I looked into the situation with American MIAs in Laos. It was easier to infiltrate the scam-artists if they thought I was just a distraught jarhead with a son on the MIA list, but that's not the main reason I kept you...of all people...in the dark. I did that to protect you. People involved with this discovery have been killed.

In fact, my primary source, a former NVA lieutenant who was living in San Pedro, was killed for giving me the initial lead and vital information concerning the fate of 213 American boys who were captured in Laos. When that happened, I decided to play this as close to the vest as possible. I'm mortally sorry but I didn't play it close enough. A letter I sent to an old panyo... a Cubano from the Bay of Pigs 2506 Brigade asking about the involvement of two Cuban military intelligence types in the Long Mountain March (see log for details) was intercepted and turned over to certain bad-asses in the Cuban State Security organization. The letter named you as the person to contact if anything unfortunate should happen to me. Watch your back!! The Cubans are in this somehow...and very touchy about it.

I continued to follow the leads, continued to investigate, until I was visited by a delegation of nasty gooks, former soldiers from their vets' organization, the Vietnamese Veterans Association (VVA), who wanted any and all information I had on American POWs in Laos. All this occurred in September 93 when Clinton lifted the restriction on American development projects in Vietnam. Big bucks hung in the balance. The gooks who came to see me knew I was on the Laos case and didn't want anything to disrupt the "inevitable normalization of relations" between us and them.

At first they tried to convince me that no one was likely to believe a senile old man whose only son was among the missing. When I told them about my source they got serious; made noises about having me killed. I called the sheriff and laughed the bastards off my property...but shortly after that, my source in San Pedro became the victim of a drive-by shooting. And so, I took the precaution of getting rid of the primary materials...the stuff you now have in hand. And I decided not to tell you anything about all this until after I was gone...to keep from placing you in danger...and to keep you from writing the whole thing off as the ravings of a sick old man. And yes, to obligate you to grant the last wish of a dead friend.

Shake, I was onto something...something big, incredible and very ugly. Unfortunately, what I discovered and duly reported up the chain of command couldn't be backed by solid evidence. I put together a pretty good circumstantial case, but the assholes in the DOD Office of POW/MIA Affairs didn't want to hear it. But that's not going to make it go away...especially if you look into it as I'm sure you will when you've read what I have to say in this letter and in the logbook.

Now, here's the shocker. I believe Ken is dead; have felt that way for some time. He was one of 213 American prisoners in Laos who disappeared while being herded up the Ho Chi Minh Trail for repatriation with Hanoi-based POWs during Operation Homecoming. What happened out there on the trail? It has something to do with B-52 strikes and NVA Group 559 which was in charge of carrying out Hanoi's orders to collect POWs from the Pathet Lao and bring them north. That much of the puzzle was given to me by my NVA source. What we need is the rest of the story and I'm counting on you to get it.

Were those boys killed by our own air strikes? If so, who's responsible? Did they die in some other horrible fashion? Or are they still prisoners somewhere? I don't know. What I do know is that the head-count was 213 live bodies on 20 December 1972 when all the POWs were corralled and counted before crossing the border into North Vietnam. My source was positive about that and he was an adjutant with Group 559 stationed at the Ban Karai Pass. None of them made it to Hanoi...not Ken...none of them. What happened? Why didn't any of these boys show up for Operation Homecoming? My last wish is to find out. We didn't lose in Vietnam, Shake, and we shouldn't suffer the indignities of a loser. I've given you theories which may lead you to the facts. Those facts can only come from one place: The People's Army of Vietnam. Before he was murdered, my original source told me there are records of the entire incident somewhere in the PAVN archives...supposedly in something called the "Laos File." He also told me there are "progressives" in the PAVN who might be willing to expose the incident provided sufficient motivation.

I know it's a lot to ask, Shake...and I know you feel it's time to let sleeping dogs lie...but please pursue this case. Don't let it all be in vain. Do what you can to locate sources, get at the Laos File, and find the answers. Honor, loyalty and good conscience

demand we do this. From wherever we go when it's over, I'm
relying on you. God be with you, son.
  Good hunting and Semper Fidelis.
                    *   *   *

Somewhere over central Texas. Knocked numb; nearly
breathless from a hard shot to the solar plexus. First pass at
letter and log...just a scan...but facts - if that's what they are - fly
off the page...drill into the brain like bullets. And the gist of it,
the nut of a very ugly fucking story, leaves you looking for an
air-sick bag.

Paris peace talks grinding along...1972...fourth agonizing
year of bullshit...both sides jackass stubborn...Kissinger tells
Nixon the Hanoi deal-makers have hit the brakes...hard. Clear
message scribbled on the ball bouncing around the American
court: Pay-up, Yankee Devils. War reparations, big-time. You
lost the case, now pony up the court costs. That much on the
record...such as it is.

Unrevealed background is the monumental ass-kicker.
Christmastime coming and White House war dogs still trying to
decide if there's an ace left to play. Meanwhile, back in
Hanoi...chess champs from the PAVN General Political
Directorate, responsible for wear and care of POWs, decide to
consolidate their gains. Prisoners from a number of North
Vietnamese camps...450 men, give or take, are assembled...
brought under one roof at the Hoa Lo or Hanoi Hilton complex.
Safe from vigilante-cowboy rescue attempts and all in a neat
little pile...ready for release on the red-letter day when the
Yankee Dogs finally capitulate.

Except for the guys in Laotian limbo...the poor bastards in
the hands of numb-nuts Pathet Lao prison warders looking for
a little post-war survival insurance. Takes a goddamn
delegation from the commie presidium to get those guys
headed north. Viet hard-liners...Cubans...even Russians...make
the trek to Vientienne and Pol Pot gets the word loud and clear.
Time to pop the geopolitical hole card...turn over all the Yankee
Air Pirates and other luckless lackies you've been holding in
those fucking caves. Time to head 'em up and move 'em
out...get these valuable assets up north where we can claim
they've been headed all along...international borders
notwithstanding.

Meanwhile in Washington, Pat pulls the switch to light the
National Xmas tree, circa 1972, as hubby Dick blusters over bad
news from the fucking Buddhaheads on the other side of the

world. Jingle bells, mortar shells, VC in the grass...take your Merry Christmas and shove it up your ass. Not enough honor in that peace for Tricky Dick who promptly flashes a go-code to the boys in the Big Ugly Fuckers on hot-pads in Thailand and on Guam. Down, set...hut, hut, hut...Operation Linebacker II is headed off-tackle.

Eighty-seven zillion tons of HE descend on the Ho Chi Minh Freeway from way the fuck up there where you can't even spot vapor trails. SOP, by God...we've done it before. Except that this time...unbeknown to our intrepid sky warriors...gaggles of American prisoners...broken down into manageable groups of ten, fifteen, twenty...are crawling up the trail like cockroaches under a throw-rug.

Each northward-bound group shepherded by a slug of NVA troopers from Transportation Group 559, the dedicated drones responsible for logistics and security along the Laos infiltration route since 1959...the same band of die-hard warrior-monks who reported themselves present and/or accounted for all along the Laotian traffic lanes until late 1974.

The Long Mountain March; your basic Old West cattle drive. And they damn near made it. Came together the week before Christmas '72 like a fucking Boy Scout Camporee, in Laos...on the home stretch, west of Khe Sanh and just south of the Ban Karai Pass, gateway to the People's Paradise. At that choke-point on the journey north something horrendous happened, something that made those POWs disappear. Logbook laced up, down and sideways with theories running from likely through maybe to no fucking way.

All hands pulverized into pink mist by an air strike? Not likely. If B-52 strikes were that good, there wouldn't be any ants left in the trail colony. Mass execution? Why? The Group 559 drovers were in charge of very valuable commodities and under orders to deliver them safely to Hanoi. Ambush by ground forces unknown? Have to be a humongous bastard to wipe out all trace of 213 Americans. Pathet Lao? Those assholes didn't take a deep breath without clearance from Hanoi...and they'd just turned the prisoners over; washed their hands of the whole deal. Pol Pot wouldn't sit still for something like that. What else? More Cuban shenanigans? So...213 Americans are somehow snatched out of Laos and delivered to downtown Havana? Russians? Chinese? No evidence. And why police up these 213 guys when they had 10 years to pick from the cream of the POW crop in Hanoi?

The answer, if the Sergeant Major's source was not completely full of shit, was in the Laos File...probably under heavily-armed guard in the most highly-classified section of the PAVN archives somewhere in Hanoi. Well shit, Gus...how about a side-trip to locate the Holy Grail and the Ark of the Covenant too?

Rumble and thump of landing gear reaching for Orange County earth. He slid the log and letter in his carry-on next to the computer dumps. At least they made sense now; an index to logbook references, a program providing background on players and puzzle pieces. Now what, Gus, you ruthless bastard? Solve the puzzle, obviously; find the Laos File...if it can be found. Search and ferret out a hungry gook progressive with the proper access, offer him a new Honda, carton of Salems, all-expense-paid stay at Disney World. Light the fuse and laugh like hell when the information rips the scabs off festering war wounds and sends Slick Willie's One World Express crashing off the tracks. Not bad.

4. Southern California

Marine Sergeant Julia Dewey was from Philadelphia by way of the El Toro motor pool. She was amiable, polite and professional which earned Sgt. Dewey respectable marks on Shake's list of things a good Marine NCO ought to be. Cruising south on the 405 Freeway she impressed him with her ability to negotiate California traffic in the wide wheelbase High Mobility Multi-Terrain Vehicle commonly called a Hummer or Humvee.

While he sat trying to control the ball-bearings rattling around in his head, Sgt. Dewey told him the airbase at El Toro was on the Congressional hit-list; due to be closed sometime next year. Most of the Marine fixed-wing squadrons - primarily Hornets and Harriers - due to become squatters on Navy turf at various air stations up and down the west coast.

As they blew through the main gate, he returned the sentry's salute and looked where she pointed. A long, low building on the right side of the main road was fronted by a *torii* and an ornate oriental brass bell, commemoratives of 3d Marine Aircraft Wing service in the Far East. Half of that headquarters building was the domain of the Marine Major General who commanded all Marine Corps Air Bases in the Western Area, according to Sgt. Dewey.

The other half had been "painted purple" or taken over by representatives from all the services on the Military Contact Team of the Hanoi Delegation. The theory, she explained as she deftly wheeled the Hummer into the parking lot, was that mixing all the colors of the various uniforms would result in something resembling purple.

"And that," said Sgt. Dewey, "is why they call a joint-service unit a purple-suit outfit."

"Thanks for the ride, Sergeant...and for all the good scoop."

"No problem, Gunner. Go through the main entrance and turn right. General Fowler's office is at the end of the passageway."

She wheeled out of the parking lot, on the way to deposit his baggage at the BOQ. He picked up the aviator's helmet bag that served him as a briefcase and passed under the *torii* hoping he could find a purple suit that fit.

* * *

Major General Gordon Fowler, United States Army, had the flinty gaze of a blooded combat leader. Hard contrast with the soft Texas twang in his voice. Little more hair and a Fender

Stratocaster, the guy wouldn't be out of place on a Lynyrd Skynyrd album cover. But he was airborne infantry, all the way; a Master Blaster from the star and wreath studded jump wings, and a multi-tour vet of the Asian unpleasantness from the clusters on his campaign ribbons. His right shoulder bore the yellow shield and horsehead of the 1st Cavalry Division. Air Cav in the Nam...not Marines but not bad.

"Glad to have you with us, Chief Davis...is that all right? We call our warrants Chief, but y'all have a different custom, I believe."

"How about Gunner, General...or just Shake? In our lash-up, a Chief is a senior enlisted sailor."

"Just give me a day or two to get it right..." Big grin. Honest, straight-forward, a sense of humor. Good vibes. "We cain't have our Marine Corps technical expert getting confused with a squid, can we? Anyway, sorry about the short fuse. We're all just getting to know each other. There's ten officers on the Military Contact Team and we leave for Hanoi in four days. You OK with that?"

"Piece of cake, sir...but I am a little shy on background briefings. What is it we're supposed to do over there?"

"Two primary missions, Shake. On the surface, we're gonna serve as liaisons between the PAVN and the civilian members of the normalization team. As you probably know, the Viet civilians may think they run the show, but the PAVN has been so important, so central for so long that they represent a big power bloc. If the civilians run into snags or stumble into a PAVN roadblock, we speak soldier-speak and get things underway again.

"Second part is to get an effective handle on PAVN capabilities, readiness, intentions, that sort of more standard military thing."

"And what exactly is it I'm supposed to do, General?"

"You're gonna be a primary player in mission two, Shake. You're gonna nose around every PAVN outfit you can find and make a professional assessment of their combat capabilities, equipment, morale, the whole shot. We've got people looking at air, arty and armor. Your mandate is infantry...especially small units, structure, leadership, weapons, equipment, logistics, training, integral supporting arms and the like. Can you handle that?"

"Yessir...but it would help to know why I'm doing it. Last time I looked we have their complete order of battle and a pot-full of tech intel..."

"Mostly guess-work, Shake. Assessments and analyses from techno-weenies who don't know which end of an SKS to point downrange. We're after humint...human intelligence... eyeballs on the target, so to speak. A guy with your background should be able to find the holes in their ground defense."

"Somebody up there thinking of going back to finish what we started, sir?"

"Negative!" Booming laugh almost drowned out by the roar of a Hornet hurtling down the El Toro active runway. "Somebody up there is thinking a lot farther down the line than that. We want to know where the holes are in the PAVN inventory so we can fill 'em up."

"Pardon me, general...but why in the hell would we want to do that?"

"China...the goddamn yellow horde." General Fowler shrugged out of his uniform jacket, stood and ambled over to a map of Asia tacked to a wall. His finger punched at Hanoi and ran north to the great glob of red representing the People's Republic of China. "Soviet Union may be in the toilet, Shake...but we cain't afford to relax. These boys up here...'bout a billion of 'em...are the new threat. And pardner...if they get froggy, they're gonna jump."

"Is that what they call strategic thinking, sir? Or do we just feel uncomfortable without somebody to hate?"

"It ain't idle paranoia, I'll tell you that...and I'll tell you why. Give it five or ten years and we better, by God, be ready to duke it out with the Chinese. They are a rising power, Shake. They've got a growing population and expanding nations always tend to push against countries around them. Nobody'd much give a shit if the Chinese were peace-loving little coolies, but that ain't the case. They fought a long war against the Japs, another against us in Korea; they fight regular border wars with Vietnam and India and they just won't let the Chinamen on Taiwan live in peace.

"You can see from just looking at the map that China is huge. What you cain't see is their attitude towards the rest of the world. Fact is, they're paranoid about anybody that ain't Chinese and they're a bunch of diehard racists. The average Chinese don't have a clue about the world outside China and he don't give a damn about democracy. What he's got on his mind is history, incidents like the Opium Wars where the Chinese got beat up bad by round-eyes, including Americans, who poisoned their country with drugs.

"The Chinese are building more and more economic muscle and a lot of that money is going into their military which is making them harder to deal with on a peaceful basis. They keep it up, shorten their supply lines and get somebody to sell 'em a decent fighter aircraft...we can kiss off the concept of influence in the area. Unless...we keep the Chinese occupied with other things, worried about somebody else...somebody closer to home."

"Like the Vietnamese..."

"Check. Like a southern neighbor strong enough to resist Chinese expansion and influence."

"Jesus, General...I gotta tell you...it's a mind-bender. We fought the bastards for 10 years, did everything we could to destroy their military program...now we're gonna shrug it off...rebuild a bigger and better version of the NVA?"

"Take the long view, Shake. It's a new day; a new administration duly elected by the American people, with new policies and programs. Like it or not, guys like you and me are honor-bound to support that."

General Fowler leaned on the front of his desk, folded his arms and stared hard into his visitor's eyes. "You look like you been kicked by your horse, Gunner Davis. You ready to ride with us? Think you can hack it?"

"Don't know, sir. What do you think?"

"I think you're a professional who gets the job done. You've got the background, the experience and the language ability...and you've got my complete trust and confidence. Does that help?"

"Yessir, it does." He rose and extended his hand. "I'll brush up on my Vietnamese and give it my best shot."

"I know you will, Shake. And, by the way, there's a mission two-alpha you should be aware of. All of us on the Military Contact Team are gonna assist in any way we can with resolving the MIA situation..."

"Don't we have some guys already over there handling that?"

"Uh-huh. The Joint Task Force/Full Accounting...but they seem to be stuck in some kind of rut. Buttin' heads with the PAVN right and left. We're supposed to find out what the problem is and do what we can to fix it. Major Dwyer is honcho on that project and you'll get a full briefing tomorrow. Now, get some dinner and some sleep. We start early around here. See Major Dwyer for in-briefing at 0730. Name's on a door down the hall."

5. *The Ozarks*

On a hilltop overlooking Lake of the Ozarks, the man who calls himself Bob Bayer shivered in the chilly breeze blowing up off the water, flicked a half-smoked cigarette into the dark and re-entered the musty cabin. The four men he'd left meticulously strip-searching the place were huddled near the fieldstone fireplace drinking hot cocoa from paper cups.

"We gonna get off this mountain before Christmas, guys?"

"It's clean here and everywhere within a fifty meter radius outside, Bob. Nothing like what you're looking for."

He nodded and crossed the room where a man in a checked wool lumberjack coat sat noodling on a sophisticated laptop.

"Nothing here..."

The countermeasures specialist from Defense Information Systems Agency nodded but kept his eyes on the symbols and digits dancing across his screen. "Didn't really expect to find anything, did you?"

Bayer maneuvered, trying to make eye contact. No use. Bathed in electric orange compu-glow, the guy sat staring, soul-less as a jack-o-lantern. A modem plugged into the cellular phone at his side chirped. The Voodoo King of the Pentagon's Information Vulnerability Analysis and Assistance Program gave it a soothing pat.

"So...it looks like Davis must have the material."

"You're the spook; not me..." Voodoo King shrugged and executed a neat keyboard paradiddle. "But if you're asking, my guess is he's got it. Doesn't take a genius, right? We get a hit from a computer in Quantico...Davis is in Quantico. The address the hacker queries is not public knowledge, but would appear on the material copied from the Task Force data-bank. Davis gave the address to some hacker and asked him to see what he could find. Q.E.D. Davis has got the material."

"And where is he now?"

"El Toro Marine Corps Air Station..." Voodoo King rapped, tapped and re-tapped. "Arrived at 1624 local from Miami on Delta 225. Picked up by a Marine driver and delivered to the base."

"Thanks. Don't disconnect until I get back." The man called Bayer walked outside, let his eyes adjust to the dark, and then strolled toward a cream-colored Dodge van spattered with mud, slush and road tar. Working man's wheels if you missed the small satellite comm dish on the roof. Bayer's boss sat in the back, surrounded by sophisticated transceivers, reading a stack of faxes. Bayer swiveled the passenger side captain's chair and reported.

"Turned it upside down, inside out...nothing. Consensus is that Davis has got the stuff with him out at El Toro."

"As I presumed. Well, very soon we'll have the premise, postulation and proof all in one geographical area. Things are looking up, Robert."

Bayer's boss was a spook of the *ancien regime*, a patient, calculating veteran of hot and cold wars, currently running a multi-mission DIA task force with the leverage and latitude to focus major assets where and when he - and he alone - thought they were needed with few, if any, questions asked. His organization was so complex and compartmentalized that it was virtually invisible. Like a giant squid it had tentacles that reached everywhere and the ability to disappear in a cloud of murky ink.

"He's got everything Quick had...and he's put it all together by now. Question is...does he believe it and will he act on it?"

"A man like Davis can't help but act on it. Look at his record, Robert. He has no aversion to jousting with windmills. He's done it before and he'll do it again. Davis is not the question here."

Bayer's boss rubbed at swollen, arthritic knees no longer capable of supporting his beefy frame. The left joint had gone first, shortly after a Mauser round tore through it just off the beach at the Bay of Pigs. The right knee fell victim to the brutal ministrations of a Cuban interrogator who made the most of a gringo plaything before repatriation efforts slammed the lid on his toy-box.

"The question is...does he have a fair shot at completing the puzzle?"

"Hard telling, boss...but I agree he's got a better shot at his level than anything else that's been tried. This isn't the kind of thing one government agency shares with another government agency, that's for damn sure. Way too many powerful bodies in the shrapnel fan..."

"So where do we stand here, Robert? What's your take on the elusive bottom line?"

"I'd say that depends, boss...on your perspective. As usual, there are a whole hell of a lot of perspectives involved in something like this...."

When his boss motioned for him to continue, the man called Bayer closed his eyes and tried to grasp the pattern being painted by seemingly disparate events. "One way of looking at it...something like this could bring down a sitting President. Vietnam would be very much back in the news and that would not play well with Slick Willy's draft-dodger image. Another view...we finally get some verifiable, supportable answers to the MIA questions. That's good. On the other hand, if something like what we suspect turns out to be true...it might blow the whole Vietnam-as China-buffer strategy right out of the water..."

"The China-buffer theory is bullshit...always was and always will be. It's what the administration is using to pump the economy, boost exports, create jobs...while they jam their liberal agenda up everyone's ass and suck the guts right out of this nation!"

"You won't hear any arguments from me."

"No. And we won't hear any arguments from anyone else when it's all said and done, Robert. This is a win-win situation. We just might give some brave men and their families' final peace...and while we're at it, we dash some very cold water on a bankrupt foreign policy."

The man called Bayer nodded and reached for the door handle. "I guess for now we let Shake Davis do his thing, and hope he turns up what we're looking for..."

"Precisely..." Bayer's boss rubbed his knees. The pain was almost constant now but he was afraid of the drugs they offered to relieve it. "Mr. Davis has the keys, clues and credibility. That's why we saw to it he was assigned to the IRDG. If his friend Quick was correct about the Laos situation, then Davis - a simple veteran with no apparent axe to grind - may well find the proof."

"And if he doesn't?"

"Back to square one, Robert...with a single notable exception."

"Fidel..."

"Precisely. If the Miami incident is an indicator, we've found the bastard's hot button."

The man who calls himself Bayer cracked the van door admitting a gust of cold Ozark air. "I know I've asked you this before, boss...but are you dead certain it's the same guy?"

"Oh, it's him, Robert. You can take that to the bank. I'm an Ochoa-Desidro groupie...have been since the day the bastard broke my leg with a pry-bar in Havana. I've followed him to Chile, Angola, Peru, Vietnam, Guatemala, Salvador, Grenada...you name it."

"And you really think this Laos File thing is gonna smoke him out of his hidey-hole...after all these years?"

"If what we believe is in that file is really there? Yes, I believe Fidel will rise to the bait. He's a haunted man, Robert...marking time, ducking and weaving, waiting for the hammer to fall."

"Hence the trade overtures to Havana..."

"A little goose to keep him hopping, that's all. If Fidel thinks he's about to be given up by State Security in exchange for some minor intelligence concessions, he's going to get nervous. One of the things he will be most nervous about is his role in Vietnam vis-à-vis the Americans who will have his balls firmly in hand."

"So he'll go after the Laos File and try to destroy it."

"Of course he will...now that we've let him know it exists."

"What if he succeeds?"

"We have assets in place..."

"Our man on the JTF..."

"Precisely." Rodney A. Beal lifted the receiver of the scrambler phone and waved the man called Bayer back to work.

6. El Toro

Sign on the wall outside the office simply said MilCon Personnel - MAJ J. C. Dwyer USA. That simple introduction did its subject no justice. Shake tried to muster his standard reporting-for-duty growl but whatever it was he finally said to announce himself sounded like someone stepped on a cat.

The field grade army officer seated behind the solitary desk in the office simply nodded, accepted his orders and began to read. He shuffled into a loose parade rest and considered certain facts now in evidence. Fact One: Major J. C. Dwyer is a female. Fact Two: She is an asian female...probably of Thai stock if his experience in Bangkok fleshpots was any yardstick. Fact Three: If Chan Dwyer knew she was a very beautiful woman, she did not let it affect her demeanor.

"Welcome aboard, Gunner Davis. Have a seat." No tinkling temple bells, no shy flutter of silky lashes. She nailed him with a direct glance and pointed at a chair. Her voice was a rich alto, somewhere mid-range between Ann Murray and Suzie Wong.

"Let's get to it. First names OK with you?"

"Fine..." He stuck a paw across the desk and wrapped it around her slender hand. "Call me Shake. It's a nickname..."

"I'm Chan...except when the general's around. I guess he gave you the mission picture last night? OK, we've got ten officers on the Military Contact Team which is just one part of what's called the International Relations and Development Group or IRDG. The twenty-six civilian members are from all different disciplines. We are at their service if and when they need to work with the PAVN. Meantime, the 10 of us - four Army, three Air Force, two Navy and you - each has a distinct area of expertise..."

"Yeah, the general kind of sketched that in last night. We're gonna conduct a kind of low-key technical inspection...see what they've got...what they need."

"Rog...and all that information will be compiled and collated through me...wearing my Military Intelligence hat."

He squinted at her lapels. "But you're wearing..."

"A-G brass...right. The general thought M-I sounded a little too much like spy. So, for this trip, I'm Adjutant General Corps all the way...a no-threat, no-sweat paper-pusher."

"And I'll be reporting to you?" The new purple suit was beginning to feel a little more comfortable. Regular, close contact with Chan Dwyer might be stimulating.

"You'll be on a fairly loose leash, Shake. It's gonna take a while for us military-types to build relationships within the PAVN. We can't expect too much too soon. The good news is they've adopted a policy based on what they call *doi moi* and *coi moi*. You know those words?"

He felt a slight chill run through the pleasant buzz chatting with Chan Dwyer provided. "Yeah, I'm still a little rusty...but loosely translated, *doi moi* means renovation and *coi moi* means something like openness." And both terms are contained in the Sergeant Major's notes.

"Check. Those are the official SRV buzz-words. Supposedly, they want this normalization thing so badly, that they're gonna throw open the doors, full cooperation, no hard feelings..."

"You buyin' that?"

"Nope. My semi-certified Asian opinion is that they're gonna show us what they want us to see...and nothing else until we make the right contacts."

"And we've got some kind of clue about who they are?"

"Won't know for sure until we get over there...but I can tell you who they won't be. They won't be any of the die-hard commies or the stiff-necked old sweats from the Nghe Tinh Group."

"Whoa, Chan...I'm lost now..."

"Nghe Tinh is a province in central North Vietnam, the ancestral home of Ho Chi Minh and the heartland of hard-core communist revolutionaries. The Nghe Tinh Group is a sort of an old-boy alumni association...the guys who want to kick butt rather than kiss it. Think of it as a kind of Vietnamese John Birch Society.

"Fortunately, they're considered a lunatic fringe with no real power. What we need are the young turks, the educated PAVN apparatchiks that started ascending to power after the Sixth Party Congress in 1986."

"Check. No truck with the commies; look for the starry-eyed progressives. Anything else?"

"Yeah...we've all got a collateral duty. Without making major waves, we stay on the look-out for any information concerning MIAs, remains, dispositions, that kind of thing."

"General Fowler mentioned that. What's the story?"

"Let's just say the JTF guys over there might benefit from some fresh perspective. Don't talk this around, but I think it's an attitude problem. Our guys can be just as stiff-necked and self-righteous as the Vietnamese sometimes. That doesn't play well with the PAVN...so as we form relationships...we provide a second venue for collecting information and saving face."

"Let me ask you a personal question...your opinion only. What do you think happened to the guys on the MIA list?"

"Personally? I think they're long dead. Maybe a few wound up in the old Soviet Union someplace. Might even be some who were turned...or just gave it up as a lost cause and are living somewhere over there on a rice farm. I don't think any of them are in secret prisons if that's what you mean. But that's not the issue, is it? The issue is to find out what happened to them...and to give the people at home a final accounting."

"Close the book on Vietnam...once and for all."

"Uh-huh. We're gonna have to do it. Sooner rather than later or we'll be stuck in a time-warp...just like the Vietnamese."

*   *   *

Over the next hour in Chan Dwyer's office, more specific mission information flowed. He caught what he could, made a few notes...but mostly he sat quietly and admired his new boss. She was wise, witty, intelligent, professional; able to slip smoothly between female charm and soldierly demeanor. The transition was always fluid and natural, never abrupt or startling. No wonder she was a key player on the Military Contact Team. She'd melt the Vietnamese...military and civilian...right out of their Ho Chi Minh sandals.

"That's about it for now, Shake. Any questions?"

"Just one...right away, if I may?"

"Shoot."

"I'm headed off base tonight...have a little dinner...look around Little Saigon...sort of re-orient myself, so to speak. Would you like to go along?"

She pondered the invitation for so long Shake was sure he'd stepped over some personal foul-line in Major Chan Dwyer's court. He was pondering an apology when she finally nodded and smiled, waving a dismissive hand at the paper covering her desk.

"I guess this stuff can wait...maybe some of it will disappear. OK...you're on. What time?"

"Maybe 1900...or thereabouts. I've gotta see about a car."

"No problem. I've got a rental. Meet you here at 1900?"

He walked out of her office headed for his own just down the passageway. Million things to do before departure. He had to read stacks of intelligence, meet the rest of the Military

Contact Team, check on Jan, call Tracey, stock up on personal items at the PX. And put his thoughts on a higher professional plane where they concerned a certain superior officer.

*   *   *

Her Budget rental was a Geo sub-compact convertible that fit her frame comfortably but left him contorted like a B-17 belly-gunner. He slid the seat back as far as it would go then levered himself around until he could squeeze his knees under the dash. Waving off her apologies, he navigated and admired her profile. The broad, flat oriental masque got lost in the Chan Dwyer genetic battle. From his perspective she looked delicately angular.

Wind noise made conversation difficult. He answered her casual questions by leaning across the front seat which brought him a pleasant waft of citrus. Soap not perfume, he suspected. Chan Dwyer didn't seem like the sort of woman who would use perfume bottle to hose herself down. By the time they reached the 4th Street off-ramp, she had his unofficial bio from Southeast Missouri cotton-patch to penultimate duty station at Quantico. Her interest seemed genuine so he rattled it all out, including a failed marriage chapter and a full addendum on daughter Tracey.

"You must be very proud of your daughter..." She swept into a public parking high-rise and snagged a ticket from the machine at the gate.

"Yeah, I am. Tracey is the one thing in my life I can honestly say went right." He helped her raise the convertible top and secure it. "Although how in the hell she turned out so great with an old man like me, I don't know."

"False modesty, Shake. I read your service record. Stumble-bums don't last as long as you have in an outfit like the Marine Corps. In fact, I've heard it said that the reason you don't find losers in the Marines is because there are just so many opportunities for losers to get killed."

"Luck plays a big part in it...or fate or karma or whatever the hell. Anyway, I seem to have survived with all the right parts in all the right places."

They turned a corner onto Little Saigon's restaurant row and he unconsciously slowed. Heady, pungent, fecund aromas...always did it...always lifted the safety cover and mashed that mental button. There was that moment when just inhaling swept away the years, diminished the miles and dumped him - alert, vibrating, alive - back in Vietnam.

"Should I be on the alert for flashbacks?" Chan Dwyer stood ahead of him on a street corner; glowing with a neon aura, back-lit by gaudy restaurant signs. He was unaware that he'd stopped walking and not a little embarrassed by it.

"Sorry..." He joined her and glanced around at the redolent noodle shops, fancy oriental eateries, import stores, herbal medicine emporiums and acupuncture clinics. "It's the smells...just something about them. Nothing else smells the same. Take a deep breath..."

She complied and closed her eyes, savoring, tasting. "Very Chinese...Szechuan...spicy."

"Close...most of their cooking is Chinese based anyway. But smell that kind of medicinal thing? That smell that sort of hits you up here in the sinuses? That's camphor wood. Most of the villagers used it for cooking fires, still do I'd guess. We used to smell it on the wind and you knew you were either close to a ville or the gooks were...oh, shit...I'm really sorry."

"About what? Gook? It's Korean, actually. Comes from *mi-guk* meaning foreigner. Our guys brought it home from the war."

"I'm gonna have to be a little more sensitive to these things. Really, I apologize."

"Forget about it, Shake. I'd rather not hear it but it's no big deal."

"Out of my vocabulary...as of now. I promise."

"Yeah? What's that they say about old dogs and new tricks?"

"Merely involves the proper motivation. I'm very motivated not to offend you...for any reason."

This time she stopped in mid-stride. He backed up a few paces, stared down at her and shrugged. "I mean it, Major."

She stared back, considering the possible implications. "Is that a superior officer thing...or a boy-girl thing?"

"I don't know for sure..."

"Way too soon for the latter, so I'll presume it's the former." She turned abruptly to survey the neon. "You're the veteran. Where do we eat?"

"Well, we don't want bogus chow since we came all the way down here. I'd say we avoid the flocked wallpaper joints, forego the ivory chopsticks and follow the smell of camphor wood." They walked on, sniffing, shopping for something that seemed ethnic on one hand and sanitary on the other.

Chan Dwyer picked up the conversational threads but he detected a certain distance, a veneer of frost that was absent before he let his battleship mouth over-ride his rowboat brain. He half listened, absorbed with smacking himself around for acting like an ancient adolescent.

Keep it up, asshole. She'll nail you to the bulkhead and you'll deserve every bit of it. Hello? Earth to Shake, come in...you just met this woman, for Christ's sake and you work for her. She's a superior officer...your superior officer with a mission in life that does not include playing hide the salami with a guy fifteen years older...is that right?

"You mind me asking how old you are?" He steered her into a noodle shop that came to his attention mostly because of clean tablecloths. "You seem pretty young for field grade."

"Thirty-two last April...but Asians don't show it so badly...thank God."

"But you're not completely Asian...I mean you're...shit, I better just shut-up and order."

"No, it's OK. I'm used to it. I'm a half-breed actually. My Dad was an Air Force lifer...ordnance tech at Nakom Phenom Royal Thai Air Base. My Mom was an English teacher on base; half Thai, half Chinese. Michael Dwyer married Kuladee Chan and they begat me...Jade Chan Dwyer. I am living proof that Dad humped something besides bombs in Southeast Asia."

He chuckled at what was obviously a familiar story easily told. "Well...no offense...it's a lovely pooling of genes. So how did you wind up in uniform?"

"I don't know...soldiering appealed to me...some kind of mystical legacy from the Mongols maybe. Anyway, I enrolled in ROTC at Washington State. I'm conversant in Chinese so Military Intelligence got interested in me after I graduated and made it through OCS. Can we eat now?"

"You can point and pray or I'll translate." He handed her a mimeographed menu in Vietnamese.

"I'm lost. You order. Spicy is OK for me. My mom judges the quality of a meal by how much you sweat."

He ordered in Vietnamese from a beaming waiter who immediately ignored the meal request and started talking about his time in the ARVN. Shake listened politely, caught nearly everything; and then complained of thirst. That sent the ex-ARVN lieutenant scurrying for a freezer and two bottles of chilled *Ba Muoi Ba* beer.

"What was all that about?" She poured from the bottle and took a healthy belt. "Sounded like you ordered everything on the menu...or is it like Chinese? Sometimes takes a lot of sound and fury to make a little point."

"Nature of the beast in this particular Little Saigon and every place else where Vietnamese refugees wound up, I suspect. The minute I spoke Vietnamese, he presumed I was a vet out to re-capture my lost youth or something. They get a lot of those guys, I guess. Naturally, he had to tell me all about his combat time with the Hac Bao...Vietnamese Rangers...and how he single-handedly saved Saigon..."

"There's a note of sarcasm in there..." She grinned and carefully rubbed the rough edges off her wooden chopsticks as the waiter returned with their meal.

He ladled pungent *nguoc mam* sauce over her plate of pork and noodles and cut a glance at the waiter mopping tables across the room. No predatory wariness in those dark eyes, no nimble tension in his movements. Guy had a lot more experience with outgoing than incoming.

"Ten to one he was an ARVN shoe-clerk. Most of the really bad-ass combat guys wound up dead or in re-education camps. It's the same in the Vietnamese restaurant I go to every once in a while up in DC. Every waiter, busboy and cook was an airborne blood and guts snake-eater of one variety or another. Can't find a truck driver or clerk to save your ass when you ask about their ARVN service."

"It's the same with American vets, isn't it?" She sampled the spicy fish sauce, made a face and asked for another beer. "I mean, you get a bunch of guys together who served in Vietnam and there won't be a rear-echelon type in the room. Every one of them will claim to be a LRRP or a SEAL or an SF guy or some variation of Freddy Krueger in camouflage."

"It's amazing...." He felt strangely comfortable with her; willing to share thoughts he normally kept private. She's a hell of an intel officer, he decided, and that has very little to do with foreign language aptitude.

"Truth is the tooth-to-tail ratio was something like twenty-five or thirty-to-one, you know? Thirty guys in the rear for every poor bastard outside the wire. I used to wonder how we got any food or fuel or convoys or supplies or administration done. Who did all the dreary, routine stuff if every vet you meet was out beating the bush with a bayonet between his teeth?"

"Does that kind of thing piss you off?"

"Used to...not any more. I am what I am and I did what I did. These other guys want to play Walter Mitty...let 'em."

"Bullshit. I think they ought to be called on it."

"Why...this late in the game?"

"Because it's dishonest, not to mention dishonorable." She slugged at her beer but it was something besides alcohol painting the flush across her cheekbones. Somewhere in this idle conversation Chan Dwyer's switch got flipped.

"It's an insult to the guys who did it for real...guys like you, for instance. And other people get hurt by the lies..."

"I'm hearing something more than righteous indignation here, right?"

"Yes."

"Well?"

"I'm trying to decide whether or not I want to tell you something."

"Why not? I'm harmless."

"I don't think so. In a lot of ways I think you're a typical Marine. See the objective, lock and load, hey-diddle-diddle...right up the middle. Given certain circumstances, that makes you damn dangerous."

"Guilty as charged, I guess." He pondered his beer, avoiding the challenge, feeling very much like a seventeen-year-old horse's ass. "But I'd like to put it in perspective for you."

"Do that...please." She seemed genuinely interested rather than simply professionally curious.

"I am a typical Marine in a lot of ways. Never been much of a planner or plodder. Mother Corps says go, I go. She says fight, I fight. Fair enough...it's the life I chose, right? But...nothing's ever subtle with me. Everything's always a goddamn head-on collision...act fast, follow your instincts. I always feel like...I don't know...like I'm just one little step away from a bodybag. Too much time out on the razor's edge maybe...but I push it, grab for the gusto, no compromise. Live like that...well, you find yourself apologizing a lot."

Chan Dwyer reached across the table and squeezed his hand. "I don't think you've got all that much to apologize for...and I've always kind of liked Marines anyway. They're fun to watch."

"Thanks for that, Chan..."

"No problem. Puts me in mind of a Tac Officer I had in OCS...world-class jerk. Somebody called him on it and he says, OK...so I'm an asshole. Does that make me a bad person?"

They roared and whooped at the image; repeating the line in a number of variations and accents. "Ah, Jesus..." Shake mopped at his eyes with a paper napkin. "It's such a comforting thought. You can be an asshole and still be a nice person..."

"Not always you can't..." Chan shook her head and poured beer into her glass. "There are exceptions."

"Uh oh...the story you were going to tell me?"

"A little slice of life having to do with bogus vets..."

"Let's hear it."

"There was this guy...I met him just after I got out of OCS...while I was waiting for orders." She piddled with the remnants on her plate, pushing noodles into odd shapes with a chopstick.

"Anyway, I was full of Army fervor, chockablock with glorious heritage...feeling like a part of something big and important. So, I met this guy at a party, he said he was a vet and we started going out. He was very handsome...very mysterious...seemed reluctant to talk about his time in Vietnam. Naturally, I just had to hear all about it...so I pried.

"He told me some horrendous stories...all about being a LRRP...missions deep in VC country...missions in Laos. Even claimed to have been captured once...and tortured before he made a heroic escape. He had me thrilled to the gills, I'll tell you. It was like sitting at Daddy's knee. I adored him...for all the wrong reasons. So, by the time I go off to the MI basic course at Ft. Bragg, we're playing Ken and Barbie and talking about getting married..."

"When did you find out he was bullshitting?"

"Wait. I'm coming to that. Now Mom and Dad are not real keen on this concept. Dad thinks it will interfere with my career...we should wait. So this guy comes over and cries the poor-ass about war trauma and my Dad withdraws his objection. Least he can do for a fellow vet, right? Mom has been reading tea leaves or something and she warns me to steer clear. Naturally, being a big girl and knowing my own mind, I don't listen. We get married as soon as I finish at Bragg and head off for my first posting at Ft. Monroe."

"What's he doing all this time?"

"Driving a truck...cross-country hauling. Can you believe that? And he claims to have a degree from Stanford. Says he's not sufficiently recovered from the war to begin looking for a better job. We move into an apartment near the fort. He quits the truck-driving game and starts hanging around the Officers Club all day. That's when he hit the tripwire..."

"Started telling tall tales to the wrong people, huh?"

"Yeah...and the real vets let me know he was full of shit right away. I couldn't believe it. Not my husband. So I use my MI training and run a background check on him."

"There it is..."

"Yeah. Turns out he was a not-so-distinguished Spec 4 with some terminal transport outfit at Cam Rahn Bay, way in the rear with all the gear. Never got any further from the flagpole than Long Binh and Vung Tau. In short, a complete and utter fraud. Did ten months in country... including an Article 15 for running a busload of people off the road...and then got sent home... where he received a general discharge under honorable conditions."

"Holy shit..."

"And that degree from Stanford turned out to be a high school GED certificate from some adult education center in Bakersfield."

"Guy missed his calling. He should have been an actor."

"He was good all right...very well read and a memory like a sponge. When I finally confronted him with it, he even tried to convince me what he did in Vietnam was so secret that the official record was just a cover story. I was in a lawyer's office the next morning."

"Did he contest the divorce?"

"He whined for a little bit...until my Dad showed up with a sixteen-pound sledgehammer. Anyway, he is no longer in my life."

"And you've been single ever since?"

"Once bitten, twice shy. But I have a social life and it's satisfactory. I'm not a monk...and my career...my work so far has been rewarding. I like who I am and I'm happy with things the way they are right now."

"That's quite a story, Chan..."

"Yeah, well it's like they say...shit happens."

He called for the check and reached for his wallet but Major Chan Dwyer insisted on paying.

*   *   *

On the streets outside, Little Saigon's late shift was just coming on duty. Corner cowboys...oriental scatterlings...

straddled their Hondas and honked at each other in pidgin Vietnamese. Sanyo boom boxes with more power than tactical nukes throbbed and pulsed with the pissed-off growl of gangsta rap. From an apartment window across the street, the nasal wail of a Saigon siren on a black-market tape competed between cuts.

As they turned toward the parking garage, he caught two of the punks staring. They sat side-by-side on a 250cc Kawasaki rigged for dirt. The tallest of the pair wore his coarse black hair in a bowl-cut that might have been fashioned in fifteen seconds by a pissed off barber in one of the local *hut toc* shops. His shorter partner sported a scraggly mustache and long, manicured nails.

He maneuvered between them and Chan, nodded, and mumbled a greeting in Vietnamese. Both cowboys stared through hooded eyes then swung around, kicking the bike to life. He caught some of what they said over the snarl of the engine, putting a hand on Chan's elbow, steering her out of the shadows.

"Not the Vietnamese equivalent of have a nice day, huh?"

"What I said was. What they said wasn't."

"Loosely translated?"

"Well, there was a certain racist flavor to the comments, Chan. They seem to think this goofy-looking roundeye bastard should leave their women alone. Their women - meaning you - would be a lot happier with what they've got to offer. Something like that..."

"Not on their best day..."

"Don't sweat it. Just street creeps; another legacy of the war. These guys are the U.S. import version of what we used to call Saigon Cowboys...greaser punks...mostly ARVN draft-dodgers or deserters who hung out on street corners; roared around town on their Hondas causing trouble."

Chan paid the man at the parking garage then braked to power the convertible top down. "Little cool night air to clear our heads..." He nodded but kept his eyes on the passenger-side wing mirror. A single headlight glared from half a block to the rear. Over the strains of a forlorn tune...lost love lamenting...he distinctly heard the snarl of someone goosing a two-stroke engine.

*   *   *

They were in light, late-night traffic about a block from the freeway on-ramp. He was leaning across to turn off the radio when he heard a concussive pop over his right shoulder. The safety glass windshield bowed outward and shattered into a series of jagged spider-webs. He stayed low, listening to the two-stroke roar up from behind on his side.

"Turn hard, Chan! Anywhere..."

Peeking over his seat-back, he saw the two unpleasant cowboys skirting a line of parked cars. Same bike, same two assholes; one on front bent low over the handlebars while his buddy in back struggled to change magazines in a MAC-11, boxy little nine-mil rattle-gun. Closer...pushing hard...another gob of flame from the muzzle...hard, hollow smack of rounds blowing through the Geo quarter-panel.

Chan kept them moving; avoiding the tendency to hit the brakes. Smart...use the car as a weapon...blow through the ambush. Third burst clipped off the rearview mirror and turned the rest of the windshield opaque.

"I can't see!" Chan was craning her head to steer, dark hair blown straight back by the wind stream. He popped upright and bashed at the glass with a forearm, knocking clear a reasonable slit, showering both of them with shards. She swung hard right onto a side street and mashed the gas.

He heard the bike downshift over the clang of incoming rounds. Better weapon and a stable firing platform; they'd catch a tire or the gas tank.

"In my purse...behind the seat!"

"What?"

"There's a weapon in my purse!"

He snagged her bag, tore through the zipper and felt the bulk of a revolver. The cowboys were nearly on them when he swung around and cut loose...all six rounds; piss on aiming. The bike dropped rapidly to the rear. Unlikely he hit the bastards but they clearly didn't relish the idea of a sitting duck biting back. She slowed the Geo and he watched the bobble of light as the cowboys jumped a curb and punched the Kawasaki into an alley.

"Good Christ! What was that all about?" She was trembling but in control of her voice. More angry than upset; soldier instincts.

"You got ammo?" She blinked at him for a long moment, and then reached for her purse where he'd tossed it on the floorboards and dug. Silently she handed over a speed-loader full of .357 hollowpoints. He stabbed the rounds into the cylinder, twisted the release, snapped the weapon closed and handed the empty clip back to her. Holding the weapon inconspicuously down at his side, he opened the door and inspected the damage. She stayed behind the wheel, letting the combat veteran assess the situation and direct a course of action.

Streets dark and deserted; no gawkers, no sirens, no visible reaction to what likely happens all the time in this part of town. "I don't think they'll be back. Probably scared the shit out of 'em when I returned fire."

"Well, you certainly scared the shit out of me. What were they after?"

"Same two punks who shot their mouth off when we left the restaurant." Sorry, sport...no simple answer. Slipping into quicksand way over my head. Strike two...and another pitcher wants to blow me out of the box...keep me from swinging for the truth about an obscure incident 23 years ago and half a world away from here and now. "Either they figured to rip us off or they were serious about that racist remark."

"Bullshit. Didn't look like a rip-off to me. You do that on foot...out of a dark alley. Those guys were trying to kill us. Get in and we'll find the cops."

"Tell you what, Chan..." His gut was tight, a painful knot just under the sternum, pumping sour bile up into his throat. "Let's not do that directly. Let's get back to the base...I know the area; we can stay off the freeway. Let's report this to the military authorities. Let the MPs sort it out...nobody got hurt."

"You're thinking it might interfere with the mission?"

"Yeah, I am. We don't want to get caught up here in a police investigation. Let's just report it through the chain of command, make our statements and drive on."

She nodded, punched out a little more vision area and cranked on the engine. "I'm thinking the general will not be happy, but he'll be less upset than he would be if he had to replace two key officers in two days."

Determining they were beat-up but road-worthy at low speeds, he eased back in the Geo and sat examining the hefty Smith & Wesson Model 19. A Tyler grip bolted on the front-strap...in .357 magnum with a two-and-a-half inch barrel...hard glow of tritium inserts...would have helped if he'd had time to use the sights. "Nice weapon, Chan. Why was it in your purse?"

"Well, you ungrateful bastard..." She jerked the Geo into gear and steered where he pointed.

"Just wondering is all..."

"It's always in my purse...or somewhere I can reach it."

"You've got a concealed carry permit?"

"Let's just say I've got credentials to cover it."

"I get the picture...Military Intelligence."

"You get the picture..."

They were silent for a long time, letting the crisp Southern California air soothe jangled nerves; erode the hard edge of an adrenaline rush. "You gonna take that weapon to Vietnam?"

"What? No, I'm gonna leave it in the armory at the base. Why?"

"I don't know...maybe you should take it. They've probably still got Honda cowboys in Ho Chi Minh City. They'll have AK-47s and a lot more experience."

*   *   *

Naturally, they were stopped cold by the MPs at the Trabuco Road gate. By the time Chan finished flashing her credentials and talking to the Provost Marshal Duty Officer, they were surrounded by curious MPs and a photographer was strobing all over the area snapping evidence shots. The riddled rental was impounded but the duty officer offered them a ride back to the BOQ.

She stood smiling under the soft glow of a standing security light. He just shook his head and plopped down on the BOQ steps. Sleep was going to be an elusive commodity and he had at least one phone call to make.

"I feel like that guy in the Peanuts cartoons, you know? The little kid with the black cloud that follows him everywhere. Believe it or not, a similar thing happened to me in Miami just before I came out here. I was dropping my daughter off at college."

"Really?" She sat and idly patted his back. "Someone took a shot at you in Miami?"

"No shit. Cuban guy tried to nail me..."

"Listen, Shake, my intelligence instincts are starting to vibrate. Come by the office tomorrow, I want to ask you some questions...official capacity, OK?"

"Yes, ma'am. I'll be there." He stood and stretched, checking his watch. She stared up at him, grinned and shook her head.

"Leave it to the Marines. It's certainly been stimulating."

"It has at that." He stuck out his hand to help her up. "We still pals?"

Major Chan Dwyer held onto him, stretched and pecked him lightly on the cheek...sisterly but stimulating...before she headed for the BOQ door. He followed her but stopped short of his room where a bank of pay phones nestled just off the main passageway. He dug out the Metro Dade PD card from Lt. Steve Berntson and punched in the numbers.

*　　*　　*

Commander Jeff Ault, former deck-ape on a Dixie Station destroyer and current junior officer on the contact team's Navy contingent, swung by the PMO to pick him up just before noon. Most of the morning had been spent in conference with Santa Ana PD investigators and an Orange County Sheriff's detective who happened to be a police academy classmate of Lieutenant Steve Berntson in Miami.

"What's the scoop, Shake? I saw the car in the impound lot. Looks like you guys got hit with a broadside from a five-inch thirty-eight."

"Felt like it, I'll say that. The Santa Ana cops seem to think it was some kind of Vietnamese gang deal. Apparently there's an oriental mafia down there or something. They figure the guys got a nose-full of coke and took exception to a round-eye squiring an oriental around their turf. Happened before, they say..."

"General Fowler pissed?"

"Not too bad. Me and Chan saw him this morning right after he got in. He'd already seen the initial report and talked to the cops. He seems willing to write it off as your basic gang-related drive-by."

"Lots of other things on his mind. We leave at 0930 tomorrow."

"Roger that. Once he found out we weren't gonna be held up by the cops, it sorta became a non-issue. Chan told him the car was covered by insurance and we were on to other things."

"Life goes on, Shake. Let the cops deal with it."

"Yeah. I told 'em everything I know."

Not quite. After the uniformed cops delivered their opinion, he spent a private hour with the OCSD detective trying to link the Miami incident with what happened in Santa Ana. No doubt by now the danger was connected with the information he had on MIAs and the players in that game more than twenty years ago. And that, as far as he was concerned, made the problem nebulous. He didn't really have any information...at least nothing that could nail Cubans - or

Vietnamese for that matter - with anything binding or precarious. What he had was speculation; a puzzle with critical pieces missing. Only one thing was certain, Berntson and his Orange County colleague agreed: solving that puzzle posed a serious danger to Cuban and Vietnamese parties unknown...and by extension, to Shake Davis.

He was prone to call Spook Bayer, dump the whole thing in his lap and retrograde his ass right out of the line of fire. Tempting...but his gut objected. Sure as hell, that would burn the book before it got read. Bottom line becomes obvious. If faceless bastards are trying to blow me away for what little I've got, then I've very likely got a whole hell of a lot more than I think I do.

*   *   *

He reported to Chan Dwyer's office right after chow. She nodded curtly and waved him to a chair, her MI hat clearly and squarely on her head for purposes of this encounter.

"Tell me about Miami."

"OK...but it's not gonna make much sense unless I give you some background." Question remained as he began to talk...just how much background to provide? A certified MI officer would have spook connections in one closet or another. Was Chan Dwyer as well-connected as she was well-armed? If he gave her the whole picture, would she paint him into a corner; bring the DIA into play?

In the end he kept it simple and superficial. Just a bunch of theory and speculation. Maybe there was an answer to a big part of the MIA question somewhere in it. Maybe not. Maybe 213 Americans died or disappeared along the northern sector of the Ho Chi Minh Trail back in 1972. Or maybe they didn't. Maybe the Cubans had something to do with whatever happened. The only thing he felt instinctively confident about was that someone in the Peoples Army of Vietnam could clear those muddy waters.

She listened intently, dark eyes flashing from him to the legal pad where she jotted notes on key points. He rambled for about 20 minutes, folded his arms and shut up.

"Wild story..."

"Yeah, I was prone to just let it simmer, you know? At first I figured the Sergeant Major was off on some kind of spook tangent. Then the letter where he cites a source, and the source gets dead...I don't know..."

"I could see these people...whoever they are...going after him, but why you?"

"Yeah, that question came up in my own mind after the Miami deal. It appears he mentioned me as the heir apparent in a letter to a Cuban buddy. He was looking for information on a couple of Cubans that were apparently involved in POW interrogations. What, if anything, they have to do with the situation and MIAs on the trail, I don't know."

"Well, one thing you should know. There's an apparent connection between the interested Cuban parties and the interested Vietnamese parties. I'd say coincidence is out of the question here."

"Uh-huh, that occurred to me. Anything else?"

"Well...I think you must be onto something. You've got some people running scared at the thought of your pursuing this matter."

"Maybe I should just turn it all over to the spooks; let the JTF guys or the Pentagon POW people get into it."

"What would that get you?"

"It would get me out of the line of fire..."

"Is that where you want to be?"

"Look, Chan...Gus Quick was my best buddy; he did a lot for me and I owe him. Hell, I'm a veteran and just as pissed as the next guy about the MIA thing. I'd like to know what really happened. I'd like for the families to be able to put it behind them...come by a little overdue peace of mind. And if those bastards pulled some kind of shitty deal, I think we ought to know about it, but how am I gonna do something that all the government agencies and heavy political hitters haven't been able to do for the past twenty years?"

"Well, we know they loathe and distrust our government in any and all of its permutations. Maybe they see you as the dragon-slaycr, the guerilla warrior who wins where huge field armies can't. It would be very much in their tradition. I mean, given where we are now in the normalization process, it's fairly clear that the USG is ready to accept whatever explanations are given about MIAs and POWs, right? Then along comes Crusader Rabbit with a different agenda..."

"Shit, Chan...it just seems so far-fetched."

She touched fingertips to the corners of her eyes and exaggerated their slant. "Let me give you a little oriental perspective here. There is always the matter of honor, or reputation...or saving face...to be considered when an Asian is trying to get beyond a blemish or a bad incident. Shame can be worse than death...witness the ritual suicide thing. So when you've done something bad, you go to great lengths to cover it up or shift the blame or pretend it doesn't exist. You resist, way beyond reason or logic, any attempt to get at the truth...especially from official parties and agencies who would use the truth to punish you or shame you."

"I'll buy that. Fits my experience."

"OK, Shake...now extend to this case. Let's say something horrible really did happen to those POWs...something that would amount to a war crime. Let's say exposure of that incident would create such a storm that the normalization process would break down. You'd be branded a criminal by the rest of the world and your own government would string you up by the heels for dumping them back into the economic dark ages. What are you gonna do?"

"Everything I can to keep the incident from being exposed..."

"Check. The real question is what to do now?"

"Suggestions?"

"Go to Vietnam. See what develops."

"Yeah? If they're trying to blow me away in my country, what's gonna happen when I get to theirs?"

"Listen, Shake, I don't think this is a concerted SRV government operation. If it was, the Sergeant Major would have died of something besides cancer...failing that, you'd be in a morgue somewhere. I'd bet good money the enemy is a person or persons outside their government... somebody with something serious to hide. You're probably safer in Vietnam than in America right now."

                    *   *   *

Over an azure expanse of Pacific, the Air Force C-141 Starlifter climbed, engines sucking and blowing, clawing for altitude; nosing toward a course that would lead to land at Hanoi's Noi Bai Airport. He knew from experience there was nothing to see, nothing to do that would make the long leap over the Pacific Rim any faster or less tedious. Below them, for the next nineteen hours, nothing but an undulating carpet of blue until it gave way to the green expanse of northern Vietnam's Red River delta.

He found a flat spot on a cargo pallet aft of the luggage stacks, wrapped himself in a poncho liner and lay down to sleep. Whatever future waited in Vietnam, it could not be as bad as what he'd encountered there in the past.

7. Hue - 1968

Sometime in mid-February...after Tet anyway, the brand new year of the...what? Monkey...or some kind of horrible oriental fucking monster. Year of the Gook? Yeah. Fits. Nguyen of the North and his ball-busting sidekick Victor Charlie leaping Hue City's tall buildings in a single bound. How's that go? Hard to focus in a shit-storm; brain concussed, sparking on and off line in this miserable, lousy, constant, consuming, mother-fucking rain. Supergook of the fighting 6th NVA Infantry Regiment...more powerful than a locomotive...faster than a speeding bullet, able to bend the badboys of Delta Company, 1st Battalion, 5th Marines with bare hands. There it is...and who, disguised as an evil communist cocksucker, fights a never-ending battle...

That's all...the sonofabitch just won't quit. Dug in all along these goddamn ancient walls, taking advantage of the Biblical proportions. Moat 40 feet across, mossy stone walls 40 feet high and 40 feet thick...and Luke the Gook dug in hard and deep...like deer-ticks all along that 40 foot width... burrowing...sucking the life out of the Marines who keep bashing helmeted heads against the rock; ducking the king-hell hailstorm of bullets that cascades down on us.

Wounded twice...three times? Who the fuck knows? All hands bleeding into the same goddamn boat. Just fifteen or twenty bushrats left of the 200 that set sail on this sinking ship. Been at it for two weeks now. Shitshot Yankee in King Nguyen's Court and you will climb those walls and you will tear down that disgusting commie Kotex of a flag flying over them and you will keep at it until we are forced by circumstances to roll your dumb dead ass into a poncho.

On your feet, douche-bag. It don't hurt 'til the bone shows. You're a medevac when you can no longer get your boots under your butt and squeeze a trigger. Meanwhile, advance...find a way to get your ass up onto that wall. Chamber another round in that Matty Mattel plastic M-16 and drive on...advance to contact, climb the walls and kill the gooks. Code of the Grunt: Assault the fucking high ground. Take no prisoners and do not become one.

Air, arty and naval guns blew you an access, didn't they? Day late and a dollar short...but who's counting? Politics are part of the modern war process. We had a little trouble getting clearance from the friendly gooks to use the heavy stuff on the unfriendly gooks. Dig it: Monte Cassino syndrome. See, you got to weasel and waffle if you want to die while gently capturing a national monument. It's the Citadel...and it's the ancient imperial capitol of the Annamite Kings...so get the fuck up there and do what Marines do. We ain't got all day...and a lot of them reporters back there on the other side of the Perfume River got deadlines to meet.

And somehow, miraculously at dusk the next day, there we stand, the conquering heroes of Delta One-Five. On the wall; mangled gooks at our muddy feet, bearded, bloody, drooling with exhaustion, high on death...ours or theirs...doesn't matter. Philly Dog, the Southerner, Doc Toothpick, Sully, Smitty, Steve the Storyteller, Reno, Zeke, Al the Kike, all bloody, battered lumps: non-breathing, non-effective, non-hackers, somewhere between down there and up here.

And I'm senior so I give the orders. Dig in; get a line...squeeze the bastards trying to get out of Hue City between us and the ARVN who finally decided to lend a hand in taking their sacred place back from the sacrilegious. Just hold tonight, people. All over by morning. Here comes Marvin the ARVN at dawn, locked and loaded; ready to kick ass and take names. Should have known. Fucking sergeants get paid to know. There ain't no skate.

Air waves over Hue crackling with radio traffic. General Giap...this is Nguyen of the North in Hue...how copy, over? Have you lima-charlie, Nguyen...send your traffic. General Giap, we have suffered a monumental ass-kicking here. Them fucking Marines just seem to want to die. They are now on the Citadel walls and we are surrounded, trapped. Situation desperate. Interrogative, General Giap...may we have permission to withdraw from Hue? Nguyen of the North, this is Giap of Dien Bien Phu...be advised you will fight in place and you will die in place. There ain't no skate. How copy, over?

Some salute and stay. Others, the ones who hit our wire-thin lines up there on the wall at zero-dark-thirty, are desperate to live. Macabre images, brain-burned by flickering illumination rounds, choreographed to the owl-hoot of falling flare canisters. Enter the gook who lives forever in my soul.

Fifty percent alert. Fourteen swinging dicks on line and holding the southwest sector of the wall. Oriented west-east. Charlie Company somewhere to the left. Alpha 1/5 and the ARVN below us on the right. Dead ahead, according to the only officer we've seen in the past week, an ARVN Ranger battalion poised for a dawn assault on the Imperial Palace...over there in the dark to our northwest.

And somewhere out there in the gloom, between us and the ARVN, a shit-pot full of hard-wired gook survivors with an option: blunder east into a fresh battalion of ARVN Rangers full of news media macho...or slip out of the noose to the west, through a thin, bloody line of U.S. Marines suffering from a case of terminal kick-ass. No choice, no challenge.

Grenades come first; a sparking shower of ChiComs, tincans fixed to wooden handles, packed with shrapnel and high explosive. Full alert from the first burst. Then the Great Grenade Exchange. Kids fighting with snowballs from an ice fort, swapping ChiComs for M-26s and back again. Short fuses; rim-shots and air-bursts. Scrambling in the holes like spastic shortstops. Hot grounders; pick 'em up and peg 'em back.

No idea how many live bodies left in the line; trying to find out when he blows into my hole...stinking of sweat and fear...sobbing with each gasping breath. Smell him; feel him before he snatches at my neck and tries to drive a knife into my heart. Blade deflected by a battle dressing on suspender straps. Bent forward...desperate search for a weapon...somewhere on the bottom of the hole...but the Gook From Hell's got me locked up tight. Feel his knees kicking at my kidneys as he stabs again...wild and flailing in the dark. Rusty steel bites deep in the left chest but he misses the heart mark.

Grab the knife hand for leverage and spin. There, you sonofabitch...lit by mortar illum...scraggly, stinking, insane bastards face-to-face at last. U.S. Marine meet Supergook. This ain't shadows and this ain't a lump in the bush and this ain't some slant-eyed demon backlit by muzzle flash. This stinking, scary, wired, weirded-out sonofabitch is the enemy! And in the next blinding burst of flare-light over our killing hole, I see his soul. Down in there deep, beyond religion and politics and genetics, is ugliness and insanity. There is murder, hate, horror and things so cold, cruel and brutal they make me scream. And he screams too...seeing the same things in the same combat-fractured mirror.

He has to die...now, immediately...groping for a weapon as he wails and gouges my eyes. Blinded...but something on the rim of the hole...a helmet. Supergook drives a fist into my windpipe and scrambles to recover his blade. Swing hard and desperate...last gasp with a full pound of moulded steel helmet. Impact like a ripe melon...and again...and again. Hit him hard in the face with the helmet...feel blood from a broken nose...and hit again, desperate to kill. Opened his right cheek to the bone...skin flapping...blood gushing...bare bone and teeth...a ghoul in the next flare burst. And he's gone into the night; a one-trick pony of hard-edged, agonizing, near-death nightmares.

TWO
THE NAM

8. Hue - 1968

Prone, soaked, shaking. Back again; in that stinking shallow depression, stabbed by icy gusts of the wet wind that blows across ancient walls and howls off into the night. Death wind. Soldiers say it sucks the life out of them as it passes. Death wind through the city of death...and no way out except to die.

Or get through the Americans huddled in soggy holes...just ahead...just over there in the dark beyond Captain Phuong's bloated corpse. Or maybe somewhere a little left of that...near where Sergeant Xuan collided with the artillery round. Only a leg left to mark the intersection; a bloodless stump and swollen foot, cocked up into the death wind. Good job, Comrade Xuan...with your stumpy toes pointing toward the enemy. Good work for what's left of a senior soldier of the Trinh Sat reconnaissance platoon. We'll remember your leg in the 800th Battalion of the 6th Infantry Regiment...if any of us remain to remember.

Americans over there beyond the butcher's block; white, black and brown shapes, squinting pig-eyes into the dark. Seen them all before, bulky giants covered with clattering piles of useless equipment; huge, violent men who stumble and stagger through the jungle. And these Americans are Marines...ugly, brutal men who fight like rabid, raging animals when cornered. And how will we fight now...ten or twelve ghosts in the dark...remnants of the Trinh Sat platoon? Is there a way out of this corner?

Death wind shifts and...smell the Americans? There just ahead...ten meters...maybe a little more. Filthy musk; warm unwashed bodies in wet uniforms. And food...cheese? Yes...and greasy meat that bloats their bellies and brings the stink of bowel gas. Heavy scent of oil slathered on their black rifles and machineguns.

Sapper snake slithers nearby. Senior Sergeant Phuoc will lead the rush. Whispers in the dark, covered by the rippling drumbeat of rain. Some comrades will stay and fight. Others will slip away to the west, through the Americans, and regroup outside the city. Our platoon must find a hole in the net. Follow

Sergeant Phuoc, find a hole, probe and push...grenades first...then rush.

Just two grenades left in the shoulder pouch. Probably soaked, probably duds. Unscrew the base cap, probe for the arming string; wrap it around the little finger. Heave the grenade and the string pulls a striker, creating a spark; igniting the fuse. Or not...if the wax seal on the handle has cracked and the fuse is wet. Just five rounds remaining in the SKS. They'll be gone in the initial rush and no time to reload at this range. Hinged bayonet broke off when I used it to pry up a manhole cover on the south side of the city. Move the short, sharp utility knife from behind the canteen to the front of the belt. It will come to that...no doubt...in minutes now...just a few more moments.

Trembling as the death wind blows black gobs of cloud across the moon. Mating with a soggy, cordite-stinking patch of bloody dirt, domain of the maggot, kingdom of the flesh-eating worm. Black lumps squirming and scrunching in the dirt left and right. Soon now...live or die...and the words come. Code of the Liberation Army: I swear to fight firmly for the people. I will go forward in combat without fear; will never retreat...

And the target moves...out there in the dark...swish and squeak of a wet poncho, the shape of an American steel helmet. Edge of a hole; an American in there and he must die...now! Flash and crunch of grenades. Sting and shriek of hot shrapnel. Five rounds into the dark and into the hole; wrestling with a grunting devil. Grip with the knees while the slick, feral animal bucks and roars beneath me; grip as I did on the back of father's water buffalo long ago and far to the north of here. Knife in hand even as the panicked animal smashes backward crushing us into the mud and slop at the bottom of the hole. Slash and stab...again...behind the collarbone...reach for the heart... again...again and again.

Slick with mud, rain and sweat, the animal twists between battering knees. And in the guttering light of a dying flare, an image burns through my eyes, into my belly and up where it freezes my heart. Green eyes, red-rimmed and bulging; lips in *rictus* snarl stretched over teeth filmed with blood. Copper stench of fresh blood and sour stink of fear. And with every breath that blows from his heaving lungs, the animal spews a red mist into my face. Stab again...and blade bites flesh. Die, you pig-bastard...die now...please!

And pain...horrible, throbbing pain explodes in my face. Stars and swirls in the night sky over the animal's shoulder. Something hard and heavy...hurting, crushing my nose...blood streaming into my mouth. Choking, spitting the red mist back into his demon face. Below the temple...lance of pain...cheek crushed...flesh flapping under my right eye. I will die here...or I will escape...but I will not kill this animal. He will not die...but I will...if I don't get out of this hole. Slash wildly, kick clear of the killer and scramble from the soggy gravesite.

*   *   *

Concussed and pumping blood, Sergeant Than Duc Minh staggered into the darkness; ran blindly until the adrenaline was depleted. He passed out somewhere on the west side of the Citadel where he was found by a patrol of fleeing survivors from the K4B VC Infantry Battalion.

9. Hanoi - 1996

He wakes up, trembling and drenched in sweat, as usual at this stage of the dream that hounds him like a jungle predator. The dream stalks Than Duc Minh, hovering like one of the American helicopter gunships; always out there on the horizon of his consciousness ready to pounce. It is the face of the American devil who scarred him so brutally that wakes him early and denies further rest.

At times like this Minh hugs his knees, buries his head and hears petty men rising from the shambles of the Party, proclaiming the purity of "Our Great Spring Victory." Party hacks are never constrained by facts and they won't let you be confused by them. Ignore the zombie veterans in nine remote hospitals around the country. Unlike the penitent and tortured American war-criminals, there are no Peoples Army combat veterans suffering from war-related psychological problems. Minh and his few friends - old warhorses who keep the Nghe Tinh Group alive in memory of fallen comrades - know the depth of such nonsense.

The best lies are those you believe to be true. And lies come easy to young men in clean uniforms who never had the painful cramps or felt the warm ooze of shit on their thighs as they lay gasping in some dark jungle ambush. Easy words for peacetime pundits, who mark their status with pockets full of ballpoint pens and gaudy Seiko watches. A true lie from the mouths of babes who never felt the sting of hot shrapnel or the deep, penetrating pain of a bullet. They have not seen The Beast and so The Beast does not exist.

Senior Sergeant Than Duc Minh gazed out a window at the glow spreading like fine liquid gold over the capital of his country. A similar glow spread through his chest. With all its faults; despite its foolishness at times, it is my country; the ark of my ancestors...and I love it. Inside a bitter man dwells a staunch patriot. If only the two would stop fighting each other.

Still...such things are karma, like the dawn of this day he'd rather miss. Somewhere behind the rising sun, the enemy was droning toward his country once again, a much-discussed event that the bitter man viewed as an insult and the staunch patriot saw as national jeopardy. Regardless, The Beast would not let him sleep away the day and a PAVN pensioner was still subject to military discipline. Work was waiting and Minh worked in a place full of constant reminders that the great red shark of state often ate its young.

Minh rose, stretched some of the pain from arthritic joints and peeked through the woven bamboo curtain that separated him from the family of four also living in the cramped twenty-meter-square cubicle on the second floor of a stucco building near Hoan Kiem Lake at city center. The only other man in the apartment slept soundly with one thin arm draped over his wife's lumpy form. It would be another two hours before the man untangled himself and trotted off to his tiny desk in a dark corner of the moribund Ministry of Trade. Ten minutes after that, the woman would trundle her two daughters off to school and begin another day of constant complaining to anyone foolish enough to stop and listen.

Minh shuffled quietly across the apartment in bare feet to reach a small sink and a bucket of cold water. He scrubbed at his face and ran a finger roughly around his teeth and gums. The woman kept a small, ornately-framed mirror over the sink and each morning he tried diligently to avoid looking into it. No use. In pursuit of early morning stimulus, his eyes always found the mirror and froze. And this morning - as they had nearly every morning for the past 26 years - his eyes confirmed what he already knew. No magic in the night; nothing changed. He was still the ugly, disfigured old soldier who haunted the archives at the Central Military Museum.

He lingered on the image as he did on rare occasions when he was sure no one was watching him watching himself. And he remembered the days before Hue, days when mirrors revealed a warrior prince rather than a scar-faced frog. An angry, puckered keloid ridge slashed across the right side of his face from the top of his ear to the edge of his nose. The malaria-addled doctor in the A Shau Valley field hospital said it had been festering too long before treatment. There was nothing he could do to reduce the scarring. And there was certainly no way for him to re-construct the shattered cheekbone, so he removed most of it and sent Sergeant Minh to a rest camp across the border in Laos.

Eventually, Minh reached a better hospital at the major PAVN logistics base near Tchepone where he was an ugly but otherwise able-bodied soldier with a low status on the medical priority list. He stayed at Tchepone for three months, watching the right side of his face fall and develop a permanent concavity between eye and jaw that left his head looking unbalanced;

skewed and deflated like a ball kicked out of round. Eventually the scar tissue contracted and sucked the right side of his mouth into a permanent, sickly smirk. Offered an opportunity to stay in Laos...quite likely to die under American bombs...he volunteered to hide out with PAVN Group 559, the Truong Son Corps. And what horrible things happened so long ago seemed like the events of yesterday when he let himself look in a mirror.

Outside, the slate roofs of Hanoi's old colonial buildings began to soak up morning sun as Minh turned to retrieve his faded, patched green uniform and sandals. He dressed as he usually did on the veranda of the small apartment while water for his morning tea heated on a charcoal brazier. Below his perch, Trang Tien Street was coming to life with the hiss of rubber tires and the squeak of rusty bicycle chains. A Soviet GAZ-31 jeep bearing Ministry of Defense markings belched blue clouds as it turned left onto Dien Bien Phu Avenue headed for the Citadel...not the one from his dream, but PAVN headquarters, the warren of barracks, shops and buildings where he worked.

Minh squatted, sipped the tasteless tea and stared at the building across the street from his own, a mirror image of muddy beige stucco, stained by coal fumes, crumbling from low maintenance. No escape there. Every one of the twenty tiny apartments in that building would constrict and confine the same as the one at his back. They would reek of too many people in too little space and mildew from the constant, cloying Hanoi humidity. He wanted to move; find a refuge with some room. And he wanted to escape the clutches of Mrs. Thanh Thi Ngoc, the PAVN colonel and senior curator who ruled the Central Military Museum like the battalion commander she wanted to be rather than the petty bureaucrat she was.

Minh retrieved his old military pith helmet and squared it perfectly over his eyebrows, the same way he'd worn it every day of all those years in the jungle. The feel of an old, sun-bleached friend caressing his scalp and forehead was one of the small comforts he enjoyed each morning. It marked him as a veteran fighter, a defender of the nation...and it answered questions about his scars before they were asked. Still two hours before he had to report for work, but Minh left his apartment building and turned right, sighting on the tall grey spike of the Cot Co watchtower on the perimeter of the Citadel.

Near the intersection of Dien Bien Phu Avenue, he stopped and bought a bowl of *pho ga*, thick stew with chicken and plump noodles. The squinty-eyed woman who ladled his portion and a little extra was an old friend who allowed him to take the bowl and return it on his way home. Carrying his breakfast to the corner, Minh spotted another old friend squatting over a wheeled cart, breaking glass bottles with a small hammer, getting ready for another day of labor as one of Hanoi's freelance bicycle tire repairmen.

Old Tran always took to the streets early, staked out a prime spot and stayed late. The leg he lost to an American mine near Cua Viet made him less mobile than the competition. As Minh crossed the street to share his breakfast, Tran waved and scattered a handful of sharp glass shards into the street, an old trick that guaranteed him a brisk business repairing punctures.

"Good morning, Comrade Tran. A good day today..."

"It will be...when the bicycles hit my minefield." They shared out the stew and ate silently for a few moments, watching the shadows shorten along the street. "You look tired, Minh. The dream again?"

"The dream...and the dragon lady waiting up the road... and the shit-hole where I live."

"We've lived in worse places. Be happy you're not eating dirt in some tunnel with the Americans tossing grenades into your lap. That can really ruin your sleep."

"I could go south...live with my brother-in-law in Hue..."

"And I think you've had enough of Hue. Too many ghosts..."

"Well, I'd like to get out of Hanoi...at least until the Americans leave."

"Then you would be gone somewhere for a long time, Sergeant Minh. The Americans arrive today...sometime around noon if you believe the radio...and who knows when they will leave? Last time they stayed ten years."

"We don't need the Americans, Tran..."

"Look around you, my friend. Our money is worthless. You need a kilo of dong to buy a kilo of rice. No more Russians, no more rubles, no more reconstruction. We need something..."

"But not from the Americans, Tran! If we deal with them, we kiss the snake. It is an insult...to you and to me...and to all our brothers who died."

"Look at it from another angle, Minh. This is only justice. This is the Americans finally taking responsibility for what they did to our country during the war. This is the loser paying tribute to the winner."

Old Tran got busy with a blow-out and Minh wandered up the street toward the Citadel. An hour yet before the museum opened, but Mrs. Ngoc would already be at her post, preened and posing, prepared to gloat in case the Americans dropped by to visit. But that was unlikely according to the Nghe Tinh Group which always had an opinion about such things.

The Americans were coming to build and spend; not bluster and snoop. No dignity in having their pointy noses rubbed in the ashes of defeat...and everywhere you looked in the Central Military Museum, the Americans - even more than the French and Japanese - were portrayed as abject losers. Mrs. Ngoc would be disappointed. Minh felt much better as he neared the tall, ornamental iron gate of the museum.

The spongy old rump-sprung Russian Lada Mrs. Ngoc drove to work was parked between the Chinese 122mm howitzers flanking the entrance to the museum administration building. She'd be in her office drinking tea for the next hour so; probably drooling over the American mail-order catalogs she collected. As one of the museum's few long-term fixtures, Minh knew the truth about Colonel Ngoc and her assistant Major Hiep.

Museum curators were appointed as learned, dedicated caretakers of the country's huge, minutely-detailed collection of wartime documents and artifacts. But beyond the superficial aspect of giving visitors a good show, neither Ngoc nor Hiep knew or cared much about the material they guarded. Officers like Ngoc and Major Hiep saw no active combat in the war with the Americans and they took no pride in the nation's long military history. They were simply adept players in the PAVN General Political Directorate, a couple of nimble *aparatchiks* and consummate political tacticians. What power they enjoyed stemmed from their post as gatekeepers of Vietnam's most prestigious professional military research and intelligence facility. Minh saw them as prime examples of the rot pervading the ranks of his army; peacetime pragmatists perfectly willing to deal with the devil and disregard the consequences. Resentment of pseudo-soldiers like Ngoc and Hiep drove Minh into the ranks of the Nghe Tinh Group where the old virtues of service and sacrifice were kept alive against the suffocating cloud of greed spreading over Vietnam.

Rounding the left side of the bland grey administration building, Minh entered the museum's interior courtyard paved neatly with smooth slate tile. When he wasn't stuck up on the second floor endlessly arranging records or rearranging displays to suit Mrs. Ngoc's whim, he spent his time in this inspiring space. At the center of the square, mounted on a whitewashed concrete pedestal was a Russian MIG-21, the all-weather interceptor Europeans called Fishbed for some odd reason. This one was a true sky-shark, tail number 4324 with fourteen red stars on its nose to mark victories over American planes. Debris from many of those victories was cleverly stacked around the base of the pedestal, each piece marked with aircraft type and date of destruction.

He wandered toward a sleek SA-2 Anti-aircraft missile, remembering the early days with Group 559 when he helped emplace those lethal darts, aimed at the marauding American planes that flew recklessly over the great trail trying to cut his army's lifeline to the south. Despite his creeping ugliness and the heart-breaking, terminal message he sent to the girl waiting for him at home, those had been good days...except at the last...except for the Long Mountain March.

"There you are, Sgt. Minh! Come quickly..." He cringed, gave himself a moment to rearrange his facial muscles from snarl to smirk, and turned to meet Mrs. Ngoc's charge across the courtyard. A waspish creature in a severely tailored uniform, she had liver spots on her hands and wispy, grey-streaked hair that constantly escaped a tight little bun knotted and pinned at the base of her skull. She had a screechy parrot's voice and an irritating habit of singing certain syllables of certain words.

Mrs. Ngoc was a pragmatist, a proponent of *realpolitik*, full of progressive plans for the country...and she rarely shut up long enough to listen to anyone but a few superior officers in the General Political Directorate, the prestigious and powerful soul of the entire PAVN military structure. Mister Ngoc left her childless in 1975 and took his infantry battalion of the 341st Division to face the Saigon puppets at Xuan Loc. He died there and Minh deemed him a lucky man.

"Good morning, Mrs. Ngoc..." By military rights he should address her as colonel, but Mrs. Ngoc let everyone know she thought such titles were "trivial remnants of rampant militarism; politically incorrect for a progressive republic poised on the brink of sweeping international relations." Despite such sentiments Mrs. Ngoc could shout and strut like a training cadre corporal when she thought it facilitated matters at hand. Apparently this was one of those times.

"Where have you been, Minh?" She glanced at the dainty Casio on her wrist as though it might provide an answer. "I have been looking for you everywhere..."

He squinted at the sky, gauging time by the sun's proximity to the tall spire of the Cot Co Tower. "Still twenty minutes before opening, Mrs. Ngoc." He swept a hand casually toward the rows of captured armor and artillery that lined the edges of the courtyard. "I have been contemplating our great victories...in which I played some small part..."

"This is not the time to dwell on the past, Sgt. Minh. We are looking to the future. The Americans arrive today."

"Of course..." He relaxed his facial muscles as much as possible, emphasizing the involuntary smirk which he knew irritated Mrs. Ngoc. "...and will the Yankee Pirates be visiting our little command?"

"A visit is not on the official itinerary I received from headquarters...but there are soldiers with the group...some of them veterans of the fighting in the south...who may wish to visit. We must be prepared."

"I have faced them before. I am prepared."

"Our orders are to cooperate fully and treat the Americans with respect, Sgt. Minh. Perhaps I should send you away..."

"Not necessary, Mrs. Ngoc..." And no chance, dragon lady. Minh's position was secure as long as he remained privy by right of authorship to a certain file in a certain locked cabinet buried deep in the archives. "I have no desire to confront Americans...ever again. Should they visit the museum, I will be at my desk in the archives. Or would they be welcomed there also?"

"Of course not, Minh. Why must you be so irritating; so reactionary?"

Minh blinked but did not answer. Mrs. Ngoc knew his attitude, and over the years she learned that he held her and other progressive upstarts in the GPD in contempt as traitors to a cause that cost Vietnam millions of lives; prompted the willing and noble sacrifice of an entire generation. If they chose to ignore that for the expedient of ending a world trade embargo now that the Soviet supply line had disintegrated, so be it. His forgiveness bore a much higher price-tag.

"Some of the lights in the Truong Son display in the exhibition hall have burned out. Change them. We have a group of schoolchildren arriving in thirty minutes."

"We have no spare bulbs, Mrs. Ngoc."

"We have them now...specially flown in from Taiwan. You see? The Americans are already making things happen. We will soon be on the road to economic recovery...and that is the real victory, Sgt. Minh." She pressed the display button on her watch, smiled at the diminutive electronic beep and turned for her office in the administration building. "See Major Hiep for the new bulbs, change them quickly and then remain at your desk until lunchtime."

*   *   *

An entire wall of the concrete exhibition hall that connected the administration building with the amphitheater containing the Dien Bien Phu diorama was given over to a photo-mural of the Ho Chi Minh Trail. It was another of Minh's favorite displays since he knew most of the places depicted intimately from service with Transportation Group 559, responsible for defense, traffic flow and maintenance of the spider-web trail complex running more than 500 kilometers along the western edge of the Truong Son Mountains. Beneath the map, in full detail for military students who studied here, was a listing of major PAVN units which used the trail to infiltrate south from 1959 to 1975. His original unit was listed - the 800th Battalion of the 6th Infantry Regiment which turned east into the A Shau Valley in 1967 to face the American Marines.

Minh ran his eye over the trail, checking bulbs that marked SAM missile batteries, radar installations, vehicle parks, major choke-points, base areas 609 and 702, primary axes of infiltration, and sites of major battles with American Special Forces or Saigon puppet commandos who tried to cut the trail. Three spots were dark: Tchepone where he left the hospital and became a member of the Truong Son Corps, Ban Loboy Ford where he splashed across the Ben Hai River, full of spirit and ardor back in 1967 before he knew anything of war...and the Ban Karai Pass...a place best forgotten.

He changed the burned out bulbs and then turned out the overhead lights to gauge the effect. It looked like an arc of stars, a spray of twinkling light in the night sky. One of the bulbs...up in the northern sector...blinked intermittently. He knew what it was...the Ban Karai Pass. Faulty wiring...or a wink to remind him of a shared secret.

Minh walked toward the rear of the main exhibition hall and stepped up onto a concrete walkway which led past the reeking latrines. He didn't mind the smell so much as it served to remind him that most of the people who worked here were indeed full of shit, but it offended Mrs. Ngoc. He'd have to see the headquarters staff commander soon for a team of soldiers to muck the place out. Climbing the steps to the second floor, Minh reached the padlocked steel door leading to the museum archives. He selected a key from the ring on his belt and clicked open the lock. Beyond the heavy door was a dusty anteroom, the outer-sanctum guarding deep, neat ranks of metal file cabinets, the complete archives of the People's Army since it came into existence as the Viet Minh in 1945.

This was his real domain, containing the spindly wooden desk where he spent most of the time he wasn't out playing handyman around the museum. Minh checked to see that the electricity was working then switched on his small hotplate to heat water for tea. Dust danced in the sunbeams streaming through the shutters so he threw open a window to air his office.

With a warm teacup soothing some of the morning ache in his fingers, he eased into his chair and stared at a stack of damp documents to be filed. A damp breeze through the window reminded him to apply again for a dehumidifier. The archive files, crammed into hundreds of long, locked drawers would not tolerate much more river bottom humidity. Perhaps now that the Americans were tossing money up into that muggy air...

Minh lit one of the five daily cigarettes allowed by his tight budget, sucking hard to ignite the soggy Japanese tobacco, and returned to the window. In the museum courtyard below him, a gaggle of children wearing red neckerchiefs was being prodded into the Dien Bien Phu diorama. He could already hear the strident tones of martial music overlaid with tape hiss as the automatic playback responded to a teacher's cue. That modern building; even the one he was standing in, wasn't here when he first came to the museum back in 1973.

Back then he'd been policed up from an obscure outpost on the Chinese border where he'd been sent almost immediately after returning to Hanoi from the Long Mountain March. It was a remote assignment designed to keep his face hidden and his mouth shut while the Army general staff decided what to tell the General Political Directorate. He was half asleep, staring across the Red River into China when the helicopter arrived to whisk him back to Hanoi...for a historical debrief, they said.

At the hands of senior GPD officers, it turned out to be a hysterical interrogation. They wanted the truth about Ban Karai Pass. They sat him down in a room of that building over there...the one originally built in the 1890s as headquarters for the French Army Signal Corps in Indochina...and told him to write it all down, leave nothing out and be brutally honest about what happened out there on the trail. Minh did as he was instructed, fully expecting to be jailed, executed or at the very least sent back to the border where he would die of boredom, disease or a Chinese bullet.

None of that happened. He had General Giap to thank for it. The wily old field marshal, veteran campaigner, architect of Dien Bien Phu and all the subsequent great victories, turned out to be a compassionate man. He read Minh's report, looked at his ravaged face and offered him a job, small pension, a government apartment and the gratitude of the Peoples Army.

His first task had been to review, collect and collate all the information on events concerning The Long Mountain March of 1972. It was top secret work; an emotional roller-coaster for one of the few remaining survivors, but Minh was a diligent and dedicated soldier, penitent and grateful for his salvation. He amassed all the statements, reports, accounts, investigations, maps, orders, lists and documents and recorded the gist of each in a compact log that became known to a very select few as the Laos File. Most of the information was garnered from seven surviving eyewitnesses, all from Group 559...and all dead now except for Minh...and the Cubans. But those two bloody bastards likely died in some self-inflicted shitstorm...probably in Angola. Minh savored the image of swarthy carcasses bloating under the African sun, being torn apart by jackals.

Even now thinking of the Cubans made his palms sweat. He butted his smoke, wiped his hands and pulled the key ring from his belt. At the back of the record repository, in the top drawer of a plain green file cabinet secured by a beefy Soviet padlock, he found the red logbook, the Laos File. He turned the pages slowly, noting references for supporting documents in his own cramped handwriting. It was all there and there it would remain under lock and key as long as he lived.

Minh put the Laos File back in the nondescript cabinet and snapped the lock on one of the most brutal and sensitive incidents of the long war with the Americans. He was not allowed to destroy it as he'd often wanted to do - General Giap had been adamant about that - but as long as he lived the terrible truth of the Long Mountain March would never stain the proud record of brave soldiers who died for Vietnam.

*   *   *

Russell Rockwell Thurman, Chief of the International Relations and Development Group, led his coterie of 36 jet-lagged roundeyes through the interminable reception line in a spacious conference room of Hanoi's seedy Dan Chu Hotel. There was a distinct pecking order both among the Vietnamese, neatly lined up around the room at precise intervals, and among the Americans who milled themselves into some semblance of a semi-democratic conga line.

Thurman, the 50-year-old veteran diplomat who had parlayed his stick-time as a dust-off driver out of Pleiku into a world-wide air freight and shipping conglomerate, shook as many hands as necessary and then disappeared into conference with Vietnamese Premier Do Muoi followed by a host of secretaries and interpreters. General Fowler was in the front third of the line and quickly paired off with PAVN General Nguyen Phu Dinh, the current Army Chief of Staff. Others in the IRDG located counterparts from various government ministries or state committees, shanghai'ed interpreters from the pool of English-speaking Vietnamese waiting on the periphery, and began forging relationships over brimming bowls of iced shrimp and bottles of warm beer.

Shake Davis was dead last in line with only some relatively insignificant flesh left to press. The conversational tapes he plugged into on the airplane added fluid to his Vietnamese and unlocked a flood of forgotten vocabulary which garnered several polite compliments from the people he met. Still, he seemed to be an orphan when the pairing off was finished.

Chan Dwyer was sampling spicy pork patties, surrounded by three PAVN officers - two men and a woman - who were all talking at the same time. She was nodding and chewing, working her patented charm. He wandered in that direction and overheard Chan giving a polite version of her oriental heritage story. Apparently her counterparts all spoke English. She waved, but he held off joining the group and snagged a beer from the ranks of bottles on a long central table.

Warm as walrus piss. Chill the shrimp until it makes your fillings ache, but they can't come to grips with the concept of cold beer. *Nuoc da*...gotta find some ice. He searched the length of the table and found a glass, crunched it into the ice-bed beneath a layer of shrimp and poured beer. Ahhhhh, better.

Nothing dehydrates like a long TransPac flight stuck in a sardine can sucking thin air.

"You can always tell a veteran..." The man speaking Vietnamese at his shoulder was a short, stocky officer wearing the purple tabs of the SRV Navy.

"But you can't tell him much." Shake offered his hand and a smile. The officer laughed politely, bowed slightly...really only an exaggerated nod...and shook hands.

"I am Lieutenant Pham, Peoples Navy. My father fought in the war. He always drinks his beer with ice."

"Old habits die hard, Lieutenant Pham." He started to introduce himself, but Pham waved a hand and switched to English which he spoke passably, minus nuance and most adjectives.

"You are Senior Officer Davis. A Marine officer, I am told."

"I'm a Marine...but not very senior. Much of my time was spent as an enlisted man. We can switch to Vietnamese if you like. It might be better for me to practice..."

Pham seemed relieved and more relaxed when they returned to his native language. "I was told you speak our language...but perhaps not so well...and communication is very important."

"Of course it is. Tell you what, Pham. We'll stay with Vietnamese until I get lost and then switch to English. You do the same...and please call me Shake."

Pham pondered the name for a moment but politely let it pass without further comment. "We will be together much of the time while you are here. I have been assigned as your escort officer."

"Well, that's great. I was beginning to think I was to be left on my own..."

"Oh, no, Shake. We go where you want; see what you wish. All doors open. I am selected because of my specialty...infantry...from ships...landing..."

"Thui Quon Luc Chin..." That's what we called them in the south...Vietnamese Marines...probably same deal here.

Pham frowned and switched to English. "Does not translate well. These words...from the war...from before. We now say naval infantry."

Check. And so do the Russians. Okay, Pham...whatever, we're gonna have to march on common ground. "I will remember that. And when we visit some of your naval infantry units, we'll see if there are differences."

"You wish to visit small units?"

"Yes. Infantry units; nothing larger than a battalion, I think."

"I am directed to show you what you wish to see." Pham shrugged, trying hard to express what he was thinking in polite terms. "They do not say...exactly...the purpose of your visit to these units."

"I am not a spy, Pham. Spying would serve no purpose as there is no war between our countries. Your concern these days is China. That is also our concern. The American military people here have been directed to observe, to see where you might need help in strengthening your defenses."

"And your country would provide this help?"

"That's what I'm told."

Pham plucked a shrimp from the ice and chewed, pondering the imponderable. "This is all very difficult to understand..."

"Yes. But I believe it will get easier as we go along." He spotted Chan Dwyer circulating among the military people in the room. She waved and he nodded.

"I'm being called away, Pham. When will I meet you again?"

"We have been ordered to report each day to the offices of the State Committee for Cooperation and Investment. When you decide precisely what you wish to see, I will join you there or call for you here at the hotel."

He shook hands, polished off his beer and joined Chan Dwyer in the hall outside the meeting room. She was in tour-guide mode, checking names off a spreadsheet.

"Meet your counterpart?"

"Yeah. You?"

"Three of 'em. One each for transportation, billeting and miscellaneous. What's your guy like?"

"Blank slate so far. Too young to have fought down south, but his dad did. Seems anxious to please."

"I've got you and Jeff Ault as roomies. That OK?"

"Great. Just point me in the right direction."

"Your gear should already be in the room." She made a mark on the spreadsheet and handed over a large brass key. "General Fowler has called a meeting with everyone on the Military Contact Team. His suite at 1900. Be there..."

"Roger that. Uniform?"

"Anything but...civilian clothes from now on unless you're on official duty."

"Hope he likes Levi's. I don't have anything else."

* * *

"Welcome to the SRV, folks. He'p yourselves to beer, water or soda. It's on ice in the back of the room." General Fowler's suite in a lofty corner of the Dan Chu Hotel was a distinct cut above the muggy cave Shake shared with Commander Jeff Ault on a lower level. The place was packed with exotic fruit baskets wrapped in pastel cellophane. Shake counted three telephones on a desk near the general's laptop, modem and fax machine.

"My initial meeting with Premier Muoi and General Dinh went very well. We had some frank discussions and I'm fairly confident we can be of some help here. Mr. Thurman and his team are being set up for business and have met their counterparts, so the show is officially on the road.

"Let me just point out one thing to you. When Mr. Thurman met with the Premier, the PAVN Chief of Staff was right there at his elbow. That point was not lost on Rock Thurman, believe me. It serves to illustrate what a strong influence the military still has in this society. I was not surprised to see it and we discussed the implications right after the meeting broke up. Rock Thurman feels...and I agree...that we need to get our heads together right away and determine how we'll mix the soup.

"For instance, Mawk Arnold, the road construction and highway guru on the IRDG, has discovered his primary source of technical expertise and skilled labor pool is PAVN combat engineers. Civilians may lay out the roads, but soldiers are gonna do the building. That sort of thing...

"I'll be working on that and plugging you in where you seem to fit. Meanwhile, here's the mechanics. We'll all be living at the Dan Chu when we're in Hanoi. If you're on the road, draw money from Chan and you're on your own. No black market dealing. That's strictly taboo and I don't want our fiscal wizards pointing fingers in this direction while they try to help stabilize the local currency. Pay the going price for what you get and remember the basic exchange rate is about 3,000 dong to the dollar.

"Chan Dwyer is the hub of our wheel here. She's gonna have an office over on Dien Bien Phu Avenue near PAVN headquarters and when you're not somewhere else on business, be there. That's where we meet our counterparts every day and pick up individual assignments. There's phones and fax but I'm told the service is spotty. If you need to call or fax home, do it from there and we'll foot the bill.

"Uniform is civilian clothing when you're here in Hanoi. When you're on the road visiting commands, wear the appropriate duty uniform. In short, keep it simple and low key. Now, we've got a weekend ahead of us with not much to do. You're all dismissed until Monday morning 0700. Chan will be making maps from the hotel to her office and distributing them over the weekend. Questions? OK, get outta here and let me get some work done."

Shake was near the door and nearly gone when General Fowler bawled at him. "Hey, Shake! Remember what I said. Don't be out there selling those jeans on the street."

"No sweat, General. I sell these and I'll be reporting for duty buck-ass naked."

*   *   *

Commander Jeff Ault left the hotel at dawn for a tour of Hanoi's Thirty-Six Streets, the old French colonial part of the city. Jeff's guide was his Navy counterpart Commander Thien, described as "a little brown-water, gun-runnin' sonofabitch who claims to have been a torpedoman second on one of the boats that attacked the USS Maddox in the Tonkin Gulf."

Shake rattled around the room for an hour, putting some final thoughts into a note for Tracey and then went down to the lobby restaurant for tea and egg noodles. Dressed in jeans, jungle boots and a prized red polo-shirt with a Marine Corps emblem embroidered on the chest, he selected a three-wheeled cyclo from the ranks in front of the hotel and haggled with the driver over the price of a ride to the Committee for Cooperation and Investment. Naturally, the driver had no idea where those offices might be, so Shake told him to head for Dien Bien Phu Avenue.

Should be easy to spot. Somewhere near the PAVN headquarters. Walls and a tall watch tower. With Chan stirring the stick they'll have trucks and vans and cars lined up three deep. Gooner techies re-wiring everything for high-speed ops.

Look at 'em out there. Early Saturday morning and the joint's got more jump than the Tokyo Stock Exchange. Dylan ought to get his ass over here and add a few verses to The Times They Are a-Changin'. Wake up and smell the *nguoc mam*, Nguyen. Better start swimmin' or you'll sink like a stone...and these people have got the word lima charlie. Feel the beat all over the place. Like lemmings lined up on the edge of a cliff; waiting for the first furry little sonofabitch to leap over the edge...head-first into a raging torrent of capitalism.

Second thoughts...some shit never changes. Entrepreneurs and street hustlers here in Hanoi just like the slicky-boys in Saigon, Bien Hoa, Vung Tau, Quang Ngai, Danang, Hue, Dong Ha. Give 'em half an idea how to turn a dishonest dong and they'll run with it. Look at that shit. Right here in the heart of commie country there's a guy looks like a fucking flamingo in a neon pink track-suit hawking Taiwan treasures. Get 'em while they're hot and decadent, folks. We got batteries for your transistor radio. We got plastic bowls and kitchen crapola that out-lasts Tupperware. We got Shisedo cosmetics guaranteed to convert a lady from frump to fox. We got boot-leg tapes and players with gadgets that make 'em more fun to watch than to play. Eighty-six that *ao dai*, lady. Squeeze your butt into a pair of Guess jeans and top it off with a Grateful Dead t-shirt. Step right up...

As predicted, the offices of the Military Contact Team were easy to find. He paid the driver with a double handful of local currency and dodged through a mob of workmen to find Chan Dwyer holding down a central desk with a phone at each ear while her counterparts directed traffic. He waved his letter at her and mouthed the word "fax?"

"Ding Dong..." She dropped one of the phones to her shoulder and looked around for the female PAVN captain on her admin team. "Can you show Mr. Davis how to send a fax, please?"

As the diminutive officer in uniform and braided pig-tails dialed the overseas code and the Miami number, Shake jotted a note on the cover-sheet asking First Sergeant Emmett Rea to pass the fax along to Tracey as soon as possible. They stood waiting for the connection, watching the chaos slowly recede as people and equipment fell into place. The woman at his elbow seemed to be familiar with some master plan and had the muted, precise manner of most female officials in Vietnam.

"Ding Dong?"

She smiled and began to feed his fax into the machine. "Our major does not have your command of the language. My name is Captain Dinh Duong."

"You should teach Major Dwyer to speak Vietnamese."

"Not necessary. I have Chinese and English. So does she."
She checked the transmission report and proudly held it up for
him to confirm his message had arrived in Miami.

Chan was off the phone, assembling a gigantic copy
machine when he started for the door. "Looks like you're stuck
with the duty this weekend..."

"Looks like it. Gotta get this beast up and running so I can
make some maps. Can't have you grunts getting lost out there."

"Need a hand?"

"No, thanks. It's coming together slowly. Where you
heading?"

He held his snapshot camera up for her to see. "Goin' for
the gusto right off the bat. Ho Chi Minh Mausoleum. My
daughter will never believe it unless I've got pictures. Why don't
you toss a frag in the middle of all this and come along?"

"Love to but it's not gonna happen. The Old Man's already
sending over assignments from the hotel. And you're on the
road Monday, by the way."

"Where to?"

"Commander Ault's gonna inspect some ships or
something at Haiphong. Apparently there's grunts or Marines
involved. Anyway, he wants you to go along. I'll have all the
details sometime tomorrow."

Captain Dinh Duong led him back out into the street. "Bac
Ho lies just there," she said pointing up the road past the PAVN
Citadel. "They do not allow flash pictures inside."

Kham ong ngu lam. Thank you very much, Miss Ding
Dong...and not to fret. Wouldn't think of flashing Uncle Ho.

*   *   *

Lines at the huge limestone mausoleum marking the last
bivouac for Uncle Ho were long and silent. People stood
mutely; reverent sweat running down their faces like teardrops
in the muggy air hanging over the pristine square. Even kids
seemed to sense something eerie and kept a lid on natural
inclinations to turn the rare, uncluttered space into a
playground.

Easy to count at least three generations here...waiting for
the few moments allowed each citizen to pay respects to
everyone's treasured relative; the man who took on all colonial
comers, sucked 'em dry and sent 'em packing. Something
about that bony, bearded old bastard lying in there; refusing to
rot or be forgotten. Something capable of wiring about a million
ohms of kick-ass resistance into the circuitry of people who

didn't know politics from pigeon shit...and didn't care. Uncle Ho knew which buttons to push; knew how to turn passive peasants into snarling freedom fighters ready to die in droves. Get past the speeches and high-flown phrases...shuck it right down to the nut-cutting...and it was all about that old intangible...inspirational leadership. The kind of stuff JFK brought bubbling up in American hearts; the kind of effervescence LBJ and RMN extinguished like Alka-Seltzer.

He stood in line for a half-hour; looked like at least another before he'd be close enough to make the cut of ten visitors at a time allowed inside the mausoleum. He watched the clouds, switched to the scrubbed pavement and finally offered a smile for the few people who bothered to look in his direction. Then the ghoulish nature of it all got the better of him: This is like digging through the rubble in Berlin, frantic to glimpse the scorched lump of evil, twisted Nazi maniac who caused all the pain and suffering of an earlier war.

What the hell was he going to do in there, standing near the skinny sack of formaldehyde that used to be Ho Chi Minh? The answer struck as he left the waiting line and let himself down on the grass beneath a spindly shade tree. He was here to thumb his nose. Like the kid who got his ass kicked by the schoolyard bully, he was here to gloat...because the bully got the ultimate comeuppance.

*   *   *

"Gonna give it a pass?"

Jolted by American English, he squinted up to see a short red-haired man standing over him. Tone and posture read military which was confirmed by a faded tattoo on the back of the outstretched right hand: Birdie on a Ball, Marine. He shook hands as the man dropped to a seat at his side.

"Mike Stokey, Gunner. Light colonel of Marines...fish out of water...attached to the JTF here in town."

"Nice to meet you, sir. Seems you know who I am."

"Uh-huh. From the advance personnel roster they sent over...and from a previous life...back when I was a hard-charging Recon corporal and you were a salty-ass team leader running missions out of Dong Ha."

"No shit?"

"No shit. Got out of the Recon business after the tour in '69, went to Language School at Monterey and back for tour two right at the end...with an Interrogator-Translator Team. Break for college...OCS...The Basic School...you know the drill."

"Jesus...sorry. I don't remember..."

"Wouldn't expect you to. You were busy and so was I. Besides, in those days, doing what we did, it didn't pay to make too many friends."

"There it is..."

"So, you gonna pass on paying your undying respects to Uncle Ho?"

"Yessir. Think I will. Seems...I don't know...what? Futile?"

"Uh-huh. Just as well. I been in there...and it's not worth the wait. Anti-climax, you know? On top of everything else, he ups and dies of natural causes. Piss poor performance for a martyr."

"Think I'll just get a long-shot so my daughter will believe I was really here...then find something else to do."

"You drink beer, Gunner? Or is that a silly question?"

"Yes...and no, Colonel. You're on point."

*   *   *

A cyclo driver, complaining loudly about two heavy Americans stressing his legs and springs, deposited them at a small joint near the foot of Hai Ba Trung Street where an old French-built bridge spanned the Red River. They took a table with a view of the sultry sampan traffic; far enough from the street to avoid choking on fumes, and ordered beer. For a fistful of dong, the teenage waiter brought them glasses, ice and his unswerving promise not to let resupply falter.

"So how's it feel to be in the belly of the beast?"

"Pretty weird. Alternates, you know? Sometimes I feel like I'm back running Recon missions...watching, laying up somewhere too damn close to the enemy. Other times it's hard to imagine there was ever a war with these people."

"It was all a long time ago, Shake. Not many of the people milling around out there on the street remember anything about it. And those that do don't dwell on it. Most of the old soldiers you meet shrug it off. They won...just like they always knew they would...and life goes on. What's next, you know?"

"Must make your job kind of tough."

"Sometimes it's enough to piss off the Pope. Joint Task Force for Full Accounting. We call it JTF...Just Totally Frustrating. You wouldn't believe some of the shit we've run into..."

"How's it work?"

"Basically we work off the DOD MIA list and try to determine a status for the guys on it. We work with an SRV government outfit called the Vietnam Office for Seeking Missing Persons, beat the bush, dig around old crash-sites, interview people who might have knowledge of Americans back during the war, deal with con artists who try to sell us dog bones. It can be a mess."

"Making much progress?"

"Nah, shit...not so you'd notice. We've managed to find a few, move some more from missing to KIA Body Not Recovered, but the gooners are not overly cooperative. There's all kinds of problems. We're pretty sure the PAVN General Political Directorate, the outfit that was responsible for POWs during the war, has a stash of remains hidden somewhere.

"I mean, I've been on digs where we mysteriously turned up bones that had obviously been carefully preserved before they were planted where we could find them. And we know some guys were shot trying to escape right after capture or beat to death by pissed off villagers, but you can't get any of the old farts to talk about it. No matter what you tell 'em, they're all afraid to talk. Really frustrating, you know? Especially for the vets on the JTF. I mean, we all feel an obligation to find the answers. Least we can do..."

"I heard you've been at odds with the PAVN."

"Who told you that?"

"Briefers back in the States..."

"Huh. Well, at least they're not kidding themselves about progress on the issue. Listen, this is not for public consumption, but Marine to Marine, we've got a little problem at the leader level. General Varney is a great guy, really dedicated to the cause, but he's got this attitude that pisses the Viets off something awful. He tries to beat 'em up...pin 'em down...treats 'em like lance corporals.

"I mean...it's understandable. He's under a lot of pressure...self-inflicted and otherwise...to come up with the answers, but he rankles the Vietnamese and that filters down to us guys in the field. They won, you know...and they feel like things should proceed at their pace and in the manner they decree. Bottom line is they've got other things on their minds and frankly, they could give a shit less about our MIAs."

"How about Laos? You guys able to do much over there?"

"Laos is a whole other ballgame, Shake. We got ten back from the Pathet Lao during Operation Homecoming and that was that. There's something like...I don't know...just under 300 guys we're pretty sure were alive on the ground at one point or other. You ask the Laotians and they say they returned everybody they had. NVA in Laos had most of 'em anyway. But you ask the Viets and they just shrug. Never heard of any of the guys on the Laos MIA list. It's the one question we're probably never gonna find the answer to..."

"Colonel Stokey, let me ask you something. You ever hear of a thing called the Laos File?"

"You mean the stuff we've got at the JTF, information on the guys who went missing in Laos?"

"Nossir. This would be something the PAVN has."

"I'm sure they've got plenty of stuff in the military archives but...like I said...they claim no knowledge whatsoever on MIAs in Laos. They tell us to talk to the Laotians...who tell us to talk to the Vietnamese...big fucking circle-jerk."

"You ever meet Sergeant Major Gus Quick?"

"Never met him personally, but I know his son was on the Laos MIA list for some time. I'd have to check, but I think they came up with enough information to make a presumptive finding on him."

"Yessir. He's listed as KIA Body Not Recovered. Anyway, the Sergeant Major died a couple of weeks ago and he gave me some information he'd developed when he worked for DIA. What it boils down to is a theory. He believed the NVA herded a bunch of POWs taken in Laos up the trail in 1972, headed for repatriation...and then they just disappeared. He also believed the answer to what happened to those guys is in something called the Laos File...which he claimed is maintained by the PAVN."

"Did he say what he thought might have happened?"

"There are all kinds of possibilities. He just seemed convinced that if somebody could get to this Laos File, we'd have the answer to what happened to 213 guys who never came home. That number included his son Ken, so he was naturally pretty anxious to clear up the mystery."

"Listen, Shake...I'd love to buy into that, I really would...it would solve a lot of problems and give a lot of people back home some peace, but these goddamn theories are a dime a dozen, you know? We're still trying to check out the caves near Viengxay over in northeast Laos where there are supposed to be a bunch of guys still alive."

"Has anybody ever asked the PAVN about the Laos File?"

"Not that I know of..."

"What could it hurt?"

"Well, if it exists...and there's something dirty in it...it wouldn't help matters for them to know we know about it. Might put 'em back on their high horse and start 'em making new noises about war reparations."

"Seems to me that's already happening, Colonel. I mean, the IRDG is over here to rebuild the country, right?"

"You got a point there, Shake. Maybe we could quietly broach the subject and see what happens. I got a guy over at the Central Military Museum where all the archives are kept. Name of Major Hiep...he's GPD but he's also a real budding capitalist. Might be a place to start anyway..."

"Can I meet him?"

"Yeah, I guess so. You busy tomorrow? Sunday's usually a slow day at the museum. Hiep's junior man on the curator staff so he catches the duty."

                              *   *   *

Lieutenant Colonel Stokey left him in the central courtyard and went to set up the meet with Major Hiep. Cordial cooperation was insured by the carton of duty-free British cigarettes and the Frank Sinatra show tunes tape they brought along as ice-breakers. Having worked with Hiep on previous MIA projects, Stokey felt fairly certain he could judge from the curator's reactions if the Laos File was a lead or another dry hole.

He wandered around the courtyard, drawing curious glances from the few Vietnamese visitors, until he reached a T-54 tank on the right flank of the administration building. The placard confirmed what he suspected. It was the same heavily-photographed vehicle of the NVA 203rd Armored Brigade that smashed through the gates of Saigon's Presidential Palace on the last day of April, 1975...a day that lived deeply in his own personal infamy. He was contemplating what he could have done with a LAAW had he been at those gates on that dark day when Lieutenant Colonel Stokey returned and led off in the direction of Major Hiep's office.

Nguyen Manh Hiep sat sucking on one of his newly-acquired cigarettes as they entered. He was a polished figure with a perpetual smile, thinning hair and dark liquid eyes. He shook hands, poured tea and apologized for his limited command of English. Shake responded in Vietnamese which led to a long-winded description of his background and the military school at Monterey where he'd learned the language. They settled into polite conversation and Minh seemed genuinely delighted to be speaking in his own tongue with two roundeyes.

"Major...like many professional soldiers, I'm an amateur historian..."

"Yes, yes. I understand. I am a professional soldier and a professional historian. I understand completely. It is very good that Colonel Stokey has brought you here. It will give you a whole new view of the war in which you fought."

"Your museum is very impressive. We have nothing like it in America...but I am particularly interested in the aspects of your...uh, War of Independence...which involved operations in Laos."

Hiep grinned and winked at his visitors. His expression was just short of a gloat as he lit another of the gift cigarettes and offered them across the coffee table. "What is your expression? A cat in the bag...no, a cat out of the bag. We no longer deny these things. Our operations in Laos were very extensive. In fact, from a historical standpoint, they were the key to victory."

"Yes, Group 559, the Truong Son Corps..."

"You are very well informed, Mr. Davis."

"Thank you, Major. I'm interested in the question of captured Americans in Laos. I'm told you have all the records here in your archives."

"Yes, we have very complete records...but I'm afraid there is not much on your countrymen who were taken prisoner in Laos. As I recall, we received some ten men from the Laotian People's Liberation Forces and they were turned over at the end of the war as specified in the agreement between our countries..."

"But our records indicate as many as three hundred Americans were shot-down in Laos. Why do you suppose only ten were taken prisoner?"

"We must assume the rest were killed in crashes...or possibly killed by the Laotians if they survived being shot down. I'm sure your Task Force and our people from the Office for Seeking Missing Persons will eventually find the answers."

"And there would be no helpful information in your archives?"

"I think not. Communications with the Laotians were difficult and not always pleasant. Our archives will certainly bear that out, but I'm certain they contain no information...other than that on the ten men we turned over to you at the end of the war."

"And your archives are the central repository for such information?"

"Yes, we have everything here...very extensive, very complete. The record of every American captured during the War of Independence."

"Major...is there something in your archives called the Laos File?" Shake studied Hiep's oval face through a cloud of tobacco smoke. He seemed to be pondering, searching his memory, but there was no flicker of surprise, no twitch of guilt or embarrassment.

"Of course we have many documents dealing with Laos. The complete operational history of Group 559, for instance...but I know of no one document or compilation that we call the Laos File."

"This would be a record of some 213 Americans captured in Laos..."

"No. I can say for certain there is no such document in our archives...and I can say for certain that we did not capture any more than 10 of your countrymen in Laos. This much is certain. Perhaps you should ask the Laotians..."

Hiep directed a discreet glance at the clock on his wall. Was it nervousness...a desire to bring this line of questioning to a close?

"Major Hiep, I have...or had...a friend...he's dead now...whose son was shot-down in Laos. There has never been an answer regarding what happened to him. Would it be too much to ask for you to check your archives for information?"

"Our policy is openness and reconciliation, Mr. Davis..." Hiep stubbed out his cigarette, rose and walked to his desk. "If you'll give me the name, I'll have our archivist check immediately..."

Shake got his notebook and pen, wrote Ken Quick's full name, rank and service number on a page and handed it to Hiep. The curator picked up his phone, dialed and spoke Vietnamese to someone on the other end named Sergeant Minh. He smiled, held the receiver to his ear and smoked his way through another cigarette before he got a response.

"I'm sorry, gentlemen, but our archivist has checked the master index and listing for all American prisoners. This man does not appear in either place. That means he was never a prisoner. If we presume he died, there is no record of our having recovered his remains. Is there anything further I can do for you?"

Outside the wrought-iron gates of the Central Military Museum, they paused to search for a cyclo. Lieutenant Colonel Stokey glanced at Shake Davis who seemed lost in thought. "What do you think?"

"Hard tellin'. Didn't look like he was lying, did it?"

"Nope...but Hiep is a cool customer. I'd like to have seen the reaction on the other end of the phone..."

"Yeah. What was the guy's name? Sergeant Minh?"

"That's what I heard. He's probably the main man but I've never met him."

"Think we could arrange to meet him...and maybe read some of that stuff on Group 559?"

"Guess so...let me work on it."

Major Hiep watched his visitors hail a cyclo, lit a cigarette, then hurried across the courtyard and up the steps to the archive section. Senior Sergeant Minh was staring out the window, watching the departing Americans.

"Was the name in the file?"

"Yes. He was one of them." Minh stared at the cigarette in the Major's nicotine-stained fingers until he was offered one. "No need to check, Major. I know all the names."

"Where is the Laos File?"

"Where it always is..."

"Perhaps we should move it. I do not think the Americans will let it drop. If they believe the file exists, they will keep pressing to find it."

"There is nothing to worry about, Major. The Laos File is my responsibility under direct orders from General Giap. I will show it to no one; do nothing with it until and unless he orders it."

"General Giap is retired; a sick old man...out of the political picture."

"If that is so, Major, I will phone him and see if he wants me to turn the file over to you."

Major Hiep sucked a nervous puff deep into his lungs and waved his hand to dismiss the suggestion. He might be politically ostracized and retired, but General Vo Nguyen Giap remained a major influence on the people and the Peoples Army. An officer challenged that icon at extreme career peril.

"It is just that I am not comfortable with retaining such information here."

"The file is my responsibility, Major..."

"I do not understand why General Giap will not allow us to destroy it."

"What happened happened, Major Hiep. Destroying the Laos File will not alter that."

*   *   *

Turning to the window, watching Major Hiep storm across the courtyard, Minh felt a sudden chill. General Giap was old and infirm, really only a figurehead trotted out on State occasions. What might become of the Laos File if he should die? What would become of the file's custodian...and very likely the sole living survivor of the Long Mountain March? Small fish always fry first. A life in the ranks had taught him that if nothing else.

For the first time since his only known address was somewhere in the jungle, Minh felt the painful rumble low in his belly. He locked the archives and stumbled down the stairs to the reeking latrines.

10. Hue

Atop a small hillock claimed as a private sanctuary, he sat smoking; carefully not thinking too deeply, savoring the aroma of fine Cuban tobacco. Up here rich smoke rose to mingle with the delicate scent of papaya. Absent immediate goals and pressure to reach them, life was as good here as it was likely to be anyplace else. His cigars were a sensual luxury along a fairly barren road and this little hill - rising just thirty meters above the surrounding countryside - was about as close to heaven as he needed to get.

Fine, he thought, letting smoke trickle from his mouth into his nose. Entirely sufficient...and no need to search for greater insight. Away from the clamor and nonsense, the striving and strife, the poltical intrigue, a simple man arrives at a simple truth. Heaven is merely the absence of hell.

It occurred to him in a burst of frigid clarity less than a year after he came to live with the militant monks of the Hoa Hao sect...and at that moment his brief foray into the mysteries of Buddhism ended. Marx - his shaman for so many years - arrived at the right conclusion for the wrong reasons. Religion is indeed the opiate of the masses but the addiction is instinctive and apolitical. Churches - Catholic monoliths of his boyhood or rambling pagodas like the one below this hill - are simply opium dens where addicts go to escape hell. In the end, neither the shape of the pipe nor the flavor of the smoke matters.

Yes...no need for deprivation, self-sacrifice, secret mantras or navel-gazing inspired by temple gongs. The earthly veil of tears...purgatory...the concept of a middle ground...all non-sense. If you are not in hell...you are in heaven, *verdad*? Still, there was no use - and no practical point from where he sat - in trying to share this insight with the little Buddhaheads below. They needed the pursuit more than the goal...and former Master Sergeant Carlos Alejandro Reyes of the Intelligence Branch, Army of the Socialist Republic of Cuba, needed the monks of the Hoa Hao to preserve heaven.

A bicycle bell jangled somewhere below his hill. The cigar was nearly finished but he saved the butt in a notched bamboo container. He never knew when the next package of clandestine delights might arrive and his sole supplier walked a slippery slope back in Havana. *Habana linda*, where heaven is denied by decree and hell is always just a political misstep away.

"Brother! Brother, I have been searching for you!" Han, the local boy who ran errands for the Hoa Hao monks, slid off his bike and ran up the hill. Two years past when the boy's father resettled in Hue following assignment as manager of a small furniture factory, Reyes began to cultivate the family's friendship. Everyone knew his ties to the monastery were more practical than spiritual, so it was easy to bring small gifts, socialize, show an interest in business and the family...and eventually gain free access to one of the only private telephone lines in Hue capable of making and receiving overseas calls.

"There has been a call..." Han steepled his hands and bowed, a ritual greeting for monks observed by the Buddhist faithful which Reyes did not discourage. "At first they spoke the other tongue...but my mother was able to talk with them in English..."

Reyes offered the boy a slice of mango and a sip from his water gourd, waiting patiently. They had been through the drill before and there was no great mystery. Only one person knew how to reach him. In fact, only one person outside Vietnam knew where he was. So, Fidel had called. It only remained to see if there was a message or if he had been instructed to return the call.

"This is the number, brother..." Han revealed a slip of paper with a country code and number in his mother's spiky hand. He glanced at it briefly...Havana...but not the usual dead-drop phone machine. Some new house or office Fidel had chosen to avoid the hungry young lions looking to thin the herd at the top of Cuba's lethal mercenary apparat. "There was no message, but you are to call back at nine-thirty tonight. My mother says you are welcome to eat with us and then use the phone."

"Thank you very much, my friend...and please tell your mother I will be honored to eat with you this evening."

*   *   *

Han bowed again and scampered down the hill to retrieve his precious bicycle. Reyes followed, thinking the can of pickled Serrano peppers and red beans he would sacrifice in exchange for a paltry meal and access to the phone were a fair trade. It was nearly four months since Fidel last called. Tonight he could double the cigar order and feel confident his old Commandante from Cu Loc and the Long Mountain March would fill it gladly.

The Americans were here and the Americans always made Fidel nervous. Likely he wanted reassurances from a trusted agent-in-place. Since his flight from Vietnam in 1972, Fidel lived on a brittle edge in the murky world of Cuban paramilitary operations. His fortunes were precarious, tied by constantly unraveling political knots and governed by the whim of Tyche Fortuna, the ancient Greek goddess of gamblers and mercenaries. It was the sort of gut-grinding hell that Chico stayed in Vietnam to avoid.

*   *   *

Just inside the gates of the Hoa Hao compound on the fringes of Hue's south side residential sprawl, a group of senior monks sat plotting the future of their faith. As usual on such occasions, the leadership gathered in a grove of wind-stunted palms between the temple steps and the communal well. Chico Reyes, a blatantly failed acolyte who was tolerated by the order on the basis of a sacred plea for political refuge delivered at that very spot, paused at the well to refill his gourd.

He was near enough to hear the discussion but not so near that there was any chance of his being asked to participate. The topic was potential proselytizing on the part of the Americans. There was some fervent dread that the sticker price of war reparations might include hidden costs related to Christian missionaries. Many of the senior monks seemed convinced the IRDG came complete with a bible-thumping Christian chaplain.

As usual when such meetings took place, the air in the grove was filled with fear and loathing; threats and plots. The Hoa Hao were political and religious in equal measures; had been since the first time Reyes heard of them as an obscure bunch of Buddhist zealots who militantly hated Vietnamese Catholics, Vietnamese communists, Montagnard animists, foreign missionaries and moderate Buddhists, meaning any of the faithful who did not follow the teachings of the Hoa Hao. They were among the most powerful jokers in the deck each time Saigon - or Hanoi for that matter - tried to shuffle and meld religious differences during the war years. Political refuge was a traditional cornerstone of Hoa Hao dogma which is what led Chico Reyes to Hue when he decided to stay in Vietnam rather than return to Cuba.

There had been a similar council meeting then during which his fate was decided. He'd made no effort to falsify his background as a soldier, the Hoa Hao were well-connected and could easily check. He stood before the senior monks and told the truth in Spanish-accented Vietnamese. There was no future for him now that the war with the Americans was ended. He was a lowly enlisted man with a facility for languages who would be sent somewhere else to die if he returned to service in Cuba. The communist cadre in the north was purging non-Russian foreigners. And he was tired of war...tired of being on the point of a political bayonet...he wanted to search for inner-peace...to study the teachings of Buddha.

The religion business was subterfuge, of course, but it was entirely sufficient for the Hoa Hao monks. They accepted him, sheltered him and tried to show him the true path. Eventually they tired of the game and simply tolerated him as they would a favored pet that pissed on the potted plants.

Chico Reyes sauntered across the temple courtyard, watching the plumes of dust raised by the slap of plastic sandals on his feet. He was safe here; an accepted, almost invisible anomaly in the community. Life could be tedious, but there was a regular stipend from Fidel - which he multiplied through business contacts - and Hue provided sufficient distractions to keep his grapes from withering.

There were times over the years when Chico got bored and contemplated getting back to the action, but reports from Fidel always disabused him of the notion. Cuban mercenary forces - sometimes with official backing; sometimes without - were on a world tour, covering more miles than a rock band...and dying, dirty and desperate, in turbulent shit-holes from the Caribbean and Eastern Europe to Africa and the Middle East.

He knew how lethal it was out there on the razor's edge, snorting and snarling with the madness upon you and your finger tightening on the trigger. The Long Mountain March gave him a peek into that pit. He had no desire to repeat the experience. Of course, Fidel might tempt him but for the most part Chico considered himself inactive; a former war-junkie.

                              *   *   *

While the Hoa Hao monks were at evening prayers, Chico Reyes sat in a small alcove in a house on the south side of Hue near the old French *Cercle Sportif.* Dinner with Han's family had been a mercifully brief affair involving simple food and cautious conversation. The manager of a newly-privatized furniture factory married to an English-speaking school teacher could not afford intrigues...particularly since he was heavily involved with his guest in a currency manipulation scheme. They were all out of the house now, strolling along the banks of the Perfume River, giving their honored guest privacy to make his overseas call.

He squinted at the faded face of the old rotary phone, checked the numbers on the note and began to dial. It took three tries before he heard the beeps, hums and hisses of successful entry to an overseas cable trunk. A phone in Havana growled twice.

"Ola, Sergento! Como esta?"

"Bien, Commandante...muchas gracias. La linea esta claro, verdad?" Chico listened carefully for the response.

"Si, Sergento. La linea esta sempre clarissimo en la noche." Safe to speak freely.

"How are you, old friend?"

"Worried...as usual. There has been some turbulence here. Old walls may come tumbling down. Our bearded friend talks of retiring. Progressives are champing at the bit. It's all such a pain in the ass..."

"You have always survived the purges, Commandante."

"Things are more precarious now, Chico. Real trouble, I think. The business in Yemen did not go well. Found myself running...from friendly fire."

"You should retire, Commandante."

"There are those here who agree with you, Chico...most forcibly. In fact, I think I may be on the trading block."

"Which team, Commandante?"

"The Yankees...who else?"

"Perhaps that's a good deal. The Yankees have very good lawyers who might be able to negotiate a favorable settlement for you."

"And if a trade is made, Chico...how long do you think it would take them to find out about the Long Mountain situation? You remember the methods...no one can resist... given the proper application of stress and chemicals."

"Even so, they would need proof..." Chico felt his hand tremble and pressed the receiver tightly to his ear. "...and there were so few of us...no one who was there would ever..."

"Our friends over there kept a file, Chico...the Laos File. It is kept under tight security somewhere in their Central Museum in Hanoi. I have only learned about it recently. American dogs are on the scent. I have had to make some moves...eliminate some potential sources of information. It has been costly and not always successful. Our Asian friends in America botched the last job. We have a problem, amigo...a serious problem. There is a man with the Yankee team there now...he knows most of the story and he is searching for the rest of it. Now that we know a record of events exists, there is always a chance he will find it."

"Our friends here will never let that happen. They have too much at stake with the Yankees."

"Don't bet your life on it, Chico. Scapegoats would be at a premium. Certain heads would have to roll; perhaps an international tribunal. You remember our promise? We may die...but never in prison."

Chico's fingers were numb. He rolled his shoulders forward against the pain in his chest. It felt like he'd swallowed an ice cube that lodged at the base of his throat. After all these years, the madness was upon them again.

"What must be done, Commandante?" Through the handset he heard his voice take on the old timbre; the resigned growl of the loyal NCO.

"Preserve the status quo, Chico. There is no problem unless proof is found, you understand? And that must not happen. The Yankee on the visiting team must be taken out of the game. Once he is gone, the trail grows cold. But it must be quick, comprende? We don't want him sharing information or theories..."

"I am flexible, mi Commandante."

"Bueno. A package will arrive for you from Danang... tomorrow or the next day. There are pictures, a dossier... credentials...everything useful I could find...including some of your favorite cigars. You will have to suit up and be ready to play. Can you do that, Chico?"

"There is still some of my old equipment left..."

"Retrieve it. If we don't win this one, we will play no more."

Former Sergeant Chico Reyes hung up the receiver, left the house on the south side of Hue and began to walk west toward the Hoa Hao temple. The cicadas chirruping in the banyan trees along the river bank sounded oddly warlike on this peaceful evening; automatic weapons firing short, sharp bursts. His shambling pace steadied into a march. He lifted his head to stare at the shower of stars in the night sky over Southeast Asia. Before daybreak he would have to find a lantern, a shovel and the box of weapons carefully buried twenty years ago.

11. Haiphong

Shake Davis let Commander Jeff Ault off at the entrance to one of the huge harbor's finger piers. With Lieutenant Pham waiting patiently at the wheel of the balky, rough-running jeep, he watched Jeff lead his escort in a charge up the gangway to the forward brow of a former Soviet Navy Stenka-class fast corvette. No question, his roommate and traveling companion was a seagoing sonofabitch who loved the feel of deckplate underfoot.

Jeff would get his fill of that if the crusty old PAVN Navy officer at Haiphong Naval headquarters was true to his word. This morning, while Shake and Pham sat quietly sipping tea, the Commander led Jeff out onto his balcony, handed over a pair of binoculars and began pointing out highlights in a harbor that was once a prime American bombing target. There was the new corvette, a PAVN flagship Krupny-class destroyer, A Petya II-class frigate, several Polnocny-class tank landing ships and a flotilla of the swift little Chinese-pattern motor torpedo boats that patrolled the country's coastline. The visiting American sailor was welcome aboard any or all of them...after which the resident PAVN Commodore would be delighted to discuss a number of items he felt were required to bring his little fleet up to Chinese intimidation speed.

Jeff was delighted; full of questions and observations. While the two ship-nuts became instant buddies, Shake found himself grudgingly admiring the PAVN Commodore. The guy came off like a cross between John Paul Jones and Popeye the Sailorman. To hear him tell it, he was the logistics guru who planned all the waterborne resupply and infiltration from north to south for three of the heaviest war years which led him to command of harbor defenses at Haiphong. And he was a patriot, proud of his gnat-size Navy's record against the haze-grey American juggernauts.

Shake half expected the Commodore to break into a sailor's hornpipe at any moment, but the guy was no bullshit artist; no maritime gloat-worm. In a fight he would likely take his lumps and keep coming; boring in broad on an enemy's beam until he found a way to slip in the kill-shot...then he'd come about to police up survivors.

Jeff was enthralled, but Jeff had spent his war outside the shrapnel fan; steaming on the Yankee Station gun-line where the face of the enemy was mostly MIG blips on a radar screen or muzzle-flash from truculent shore batteries. Shake had seen the other side of the coin. The congenial sense of admiration and empathy he felt for the Commodore was unsettling.

"He's a pisser, ain't he?" Commander Ault bounded down the headquarters steps, heading for the jeep.

"Yeah, he's a...a real pro." And I ought to hate the bastard but I don't.

After Commander Ault disappeared into the bowels of the frigate, Shake and Lieutenant Pham wheeled toward a remote section of the harbor complex which served as headquarters for the PAVN's solitary Naval Infantry battalion. Their schedule was open-ended and tied mainly to the time Commander Ault decided to stay in Haiphong. Shake thought two days...maybe three...but now he was hoping for more time to look beyond the machines, over the gunsights, into the minds of these soldiers. There were revelations here; lessons to be learned.

"Is the Commodore a Party member, Pham?"

"I don't know..." The question seemed to surprise his escort officer. "I don't think so. Not many people are these days. If he was...a man of his years and war experience...I think the GPD would have gobbled him up long ago."

"Are you?"

"A Party member?" Pham laughed and shifted gears to grind around a slow-moving truck. "You must understand...the Party is a thing which advises...shapes policy...and not much more. We are Vietnamese before we are anything else."

"So you are not a Party member?"

Pham shrugged and fished in his pocket for a cigarette. "I am a Vietnamese soldier. When my country's best interests are served by the Party, I suppose I am a member. When they are not...I am still a Vietnamese soldier."

Nice dodge. Sincere enough...and familiar to any professional in uniform. It's not what your country can do for you. It's what you can do for your country. I may not like the Commander-in-Chief worth a shit, but I'll carry out his orders. And when he makes the moves I like, by God, I'll even register and vote for him.

The PAVN Naval Infantry compound was a relatively small area, a cluster of huts surrounding two large warehouse-type buildings. The grounds were immaculate and well-tended, a refreshing change from the garbage-strewn docks of the harbor complex. They motored past a working party scrubbing at a sandstone wall as Pham suddenly began to chuckle. He braked the jeep to a squealing stop and pointed at the laborers.

"Perhaps that will give you some idea about party popularity these days..."

Shake uncoiled from his seat and stared. Three soldiers wearing Navy tabs on their fatigue uniforms were swabbing at some graffiti under the guidance of a sergeant. Four bold capital letters...XHCN...and something written below it. He started to move closer and read the rest, but Pham shook his head.

"The sergeant would be most embarrassed, Shake..."

"About what?"

"This writing. X-H-C-N...our abbreviation for socialism...xa hoi chu nghia. But someone has written a different translation. The smaller writing says xao het cho noi. It is a very popular joke."

"Help me out here, Pham..."

"Xao het cho noi...means `so deceitful you can't tell the difference.'"

"And they get away with that...on a military base?"

"Of course not..." Pham put the jeep in gear and rolled on toward the warehouses. "That is why it is being scrubbed away. But still...it is a very popular joke."

And a damn good indicator that the average Vietnamese trooper...like most other military people around the world...came equipped with a sensitive bullshit detector. How many times has some rear-rank bush-rat depicted the Marine Corps' eagle, globe and anchor as a vulture perched on an eight-ball pierced by a fish-hook? Or some clown performing make-work at the end of his tolerance tether changes Semper Fidelis to Simply Forgetus. There's a warm-and-fuzzy for you...Mac Marine and Luke the Gook are brothers under the skin.

After a brief meeting with Pham's commanding officer, Shake was given the run of the compound. Unfortunately, there wasn't much to see and not many regular line troopers available for him to interview. Most of the battalion was deployed aboard ships in the South China Sea, steaming to help divert yet another Sino-Vietnamese crisis over Hainan Island. Those regular Naval Infantry troops he did spend some time with asked more questions than they answered. His high-speed Seiko diver's watch was a major focal point as were his speed-lace combat boots, a turquoise ring and his wear-faded camouflage utility uniform.

The troopers talked about the amount of range time they got with their weapons, the shortages of ammo and equipment, the disjointed PAVN promotion system and the differences between field officers and party hacks, but mostly they wanted to know about western pay scales, food and consumer goods. A discussion of infantry mortars somehow wandered into the relative merits of American motorcycles. The troopers he talked to were polite, forthcoming and of one voice concerning American efforts in Vietnam.

Yeah, sure...better weapons would be nice; more gear would be handy...but when are we gonna be able to get our hands on the neat stuff everyone else has already got? Quite familiar with vague responses and impossible promises, they merely nodded when Shake said he didn't know.

He showed professional interest in everything, chatting and joking to the extent of his Vietnamese, keeping it light until he felt fairly certain he was hearing opinions rather than rote responses. There was no anger or animosity reflected in conversations with the enemy. In fact, it was obvious by the time they entered the command messhall for a lunch of pork and rice that the young soldiers considered him much more a visiting fireman than a potential arsonist. While it was omnipresent in signs, slogans and posters, politics seemed to be tacitly ignored in the ranks. Even when a question or passing remark made reference to the war between America and the SRV there seemed to be no squeamishness or discomfort. You did this; we did that...and out there in the bush who really gives a shit why? Once you're committed to doing something, technique is always more interesting than motivation.

Toward the end of the day, Shake reviewed what he'd heard, trying to come up with a bottom line he could draw in his report on the PAVN Naval Infantry. At least one thing was clear. These young soldiers were something other than hidebound communist zealots. In fact, he strongly suspected the keen edge of political fervor had been dulled in PAVN ranks and much of the militant rhetoric had leaked out of the Vietnamese war-bag since the end of active hostilities. Like their counterparts on the other side of the Pacific, these kids would fight resolutely and competently when and where they were told. At the tactical level that telling would be done by senior NCOs and junior officers. The key to PAVN combat effectiveness rested there. As a former vertebrae in the Marine Corps's enlisted backbone, Shake was anxious to get a handle on the attitudes evinced by the old sweats wearing stripes.

He crawled over a few rattle-trap BTR-60PB armored personnel carriers, noting they were basically Soviet monkey-models, gutted of anything approaching technical sophistication. A platoon of five PT-76B light tanks, typical armored fire-support for PAVN Naval Infantry, were in sad mechanical shape despite the ministrations of a greasy gang of mechanics who laughed and joked as they struggled to bring their worn-out charges back to fighting trim.

It was all low-tech; antiquated even by third world Soviet-client standards, but nobody in the battalion area seemed at all concerned. Little David faced a great Chinese Goliath with a pocket full of low-end river rocks but nobody was sweating the situation. Rolling south in a pissed-off, ground-gaining mode, Chinese field commanders would be significantly under-whelmed.

Pham called to him while he was inside one of the PT-76's checking the headspace and condition of a DShK-38 heavy machinegun. Standing on the ground next to the tank was a slight man - short even by Vietnamese standards - wiping his greasy hands on an old piece of mattress ticking.

"This is Senior Sergeant Na..." Pham pointed at the little man and smiled. The PAVN NCO squinted up at the American visitor but gave no acknowledgement of his introduction. He kept wiping his hands, turning his head one way then another like a little dog sizing up a new human in the house.

"Sergeant Na has been a tank soldier for a long time. He was in action against the Americans at a place called Lang Vei..."

Little piece of military history standing here looking like a shade-tree mechanic from some grease-pit along Route 66. This guy was in one of the PT-76 tanks that hit the Special Forces/Civilian Irregular Defense Group camp west of Khe Sanh. Would have been during Tet...early '68. Major flap over that one; the first time we found out the NVA had armor south of the DMZ.

Sergeant Na wadded the rag, stuffed it in a back pocket and cleared his throat. "Were you there...at Lang Vei?"

"No. I was east of there at Khe Sanh. We heard of your attack...with the tanks...but we were busy with other concerns at the time."

"I lost my tank there..." Na nodded and glanced at the line of PT-76's in the maintenance yard. "One man...an American I am sure...fired a rocket. Just one round from..." Na seemed to search for a word and motioned, pulling something apart and mounting it on his shoulder.

"A LAW...Light Anti-Tank Weapon." Shake translated the concept and Sergeant Na nodded gravely.

"Yes. A small weapon but it destroyed my tank. He was very brave...this American. I hope he lived. I would like to meet him."

"And I think he might like to meet you, Sergeant Na. Maybe that will be possible one day."

"If you see him, tell him one man survived from the tank he killed. I am here...when he is ready to talk."

He was about to suggest that was unlikely, but Sergeant Na had said his piece and wandered off toward the warehouse. Lieutenant Pham said they should go. He lived in Haiphong and had not been home to visit his wife and son for two weeks. A major dinner was laid on and Shake was invited as an honored guest to stay the night in Pham's house.

As they rumbled out of the Haiphong Military Complex heading for the teeming suburbs, he was certain of one thing that should be plain in his after-action report. Socialist ardor was significantly low on the list of PAVN motivations these days. When the combat pucker-factor ran up around plus four, there would be no rabid communist fanatics in Vietnamese bunkers just as there would be no hard-boiled atheists in American foxholes.

12. Hanoi

Chico Reyes dismounted from the creaking, over-crowded bus near Hoan Kiem Lake and paid the driver's assistant to help him lever the heavy equipment bag off the roof of the vehicle. His trip north to Hanoi was on a strictly cash-and-carry basis. He stood in the dark beside the heavy canvas satchel, a stocky, bald but otherwise unremarkable traveler in urban standard shirt and trousers. If he was questioned at all, the credentials certifying him as a Nicaraguan air-conditioning consultant on an SRV contract would cover nicely. Beyond that, the wad of American currency provided by Fidel in the mission package would insure unrestricted passage wherever he needed to go.

He was at the starting line armed with pictures, a description and local point of contact. The key now lay in finding his target and picking a spot to...

"You are the passenger from Hue?" A Vietnamese with scraggly chin whiskers and a hoarse whisper of a voice emerged from the lakeside shadows and approached. If the man sported three identical ballpoint pens in his left shirt pocket, Chico had met his Hanoi contact, a senior official in the Nghe Tinh Group.

"Yes, can you recommend a place to stay?" The Vietnamese had the requisite pens. He offered his hand and motioned for a cyclo.

"I am Duc, Group 875. The others are waiting..." He pointed at the canvas satchel. "Is this yours?"

Chico shook the man's hand and nodded. "I'll handle it, comrade. Just my personal things...and some tools." He picked up the bag containing a folding-stock AKS-47, a disassembled Dragunov sniper's rifle with light-intensifying scope, four F-1 hand grenades, along with modified and suppressed Tokarev TT-33 and Makarov pistols. Dumping it on the seat of the cyclo, he climbed aboard and made room for Duc.

                    *   *   *

Fortunately, the weapons and small amounts of specialty ammunition buried in a metal air-drop container long ago had survived internment. Beyond transportation, intelligence and billeting, his logistics problems were solved. Fidel assured him the ideological strings were still taut and the Nghe Tinh militants would provide whatever he needed to make the mission work.

Taking a circuitous route through the Thirty-Six Streets area, Duc directed the cyclo driver to a small two-storey building with barred windows. A sign above the entry advertised millinery products and materials. Duc paid the driver, opened the door, and headed up a creaky staircase to a windowless room on the top floor. About a dozen Nghe Tinh loyalists rose from the shadows and stared at their visitor.

Chico declined the beer he very much needed, accepted a cup of lukewarm tea and stared around the room. It was hard to distinguish much in the murk, but everyone seemed his age or older...hard-liners, idealists dedicated to socialist hegemony or frustrated veterans snubbed up short of post-war promises. In the mission notes Fidel described them as urban-underground militia, rabid anti-Americans: dedicated Ho Chi Minh visionaries who believed the current Vietnamese leadership was engaged in a treasonous sell-out of all they fought for over the war years. Duc seemed to be the spokesman.

"An appeal for our help has been made through the socialist brotherhood. What do you require of us?"

"Mostly information, comrades..." Chico dug in the satchel and extracted photographs from an envelope. "I need to find this man and track him." He handed Duc the pictures of Chief Warrant Officer Shake Davis from Fidel's intelligence dossier. There were four grainy but clear close-ups obtained by agents on NATO maneuvers. After a glance, the Nghe Tinh Group leader passed them along to the members.

"This man is here in Hanoi?"

"Yes, I believe he is. He is an American soldier as you can see from the photographs...a member of the group that arrived here last week."

"I presume your mission is to kill him?"

"That is correct, comrade." Playing a disinformation game with these old veterans would be less than useless. Either the fire still burned in their bellies or it did not. Best to play it straight and find out right now.

"Why is this man a target, comrade? There are certainly more significant Americans here..."

"It has to do with something that happened during the War of Liberation. This man was involved in certain criminal activities..." Chico sipped tea and considered the cover story he'd been instructed to provide. "You have heard of the Americans' Phoenix Project...the terrorists who tortured and killed so many in the south. This man was one of the most active assassins."

"This will require some discussion and planning, comrade. Meanwhile, you should rest from your trip." Duc nodded at one of the men near the door. "Comrade Tien will take you to his home and give you something to eat. We will meet again tomorrow night." Realizing he would have to play this game by their rules, Chico nodded, picked up his satchel and followed his escort down the stairs. The low, angry rumble at mention of the Phoenix Project indicated the proper buttons had been pushed. It was now merely a matter of patience and opportunity.

Duc polled the membership for discussion but there were no significant objections. The Nghe Tinh Group had been aching for an opportunity to derail the burgeoning, treacherous relations between Vietnamese leadership and the opportunistic Americans. Here was a chance to send the old enemy running for cover and transmit a bold message: The revolutionary fires still burn in Vietnam.

Some general reconnaissance and surveillance plans were established before the meeting adjourned. Duc stood near the door, shaking hands and chatting until the last member approached and handed back the photographs of Shake Davis.

"You can be especially valuable in this project, comrade. We can use any information you may be able to dig out of the GPD."

"Of course, comrade. I will have a report for you tomorrow night." Than Duc Minh plodded slowly down the stairs and out into the muggy night air, unsure about what he'd heard and seen. His arthritic knees were trembling and his lungs felt as though they'd collapsed inside his chest. In the mist rising from the Red River he saw old ghosts swooping and soaring.

The Cubans are back...one of them anyway...the shorter of the two that survived the Long Mountain March. He is not a pile of hyena shit somewhere in Angola. He is here in Hanoi on a mission to kill an American...a man whose face looks vaguely familiar.

It was all too much to contemplate. Certainly the man in the photos was the same American who came to the Central Military Museum asking questions about a name in the Laos File. And the file contained very specific references to the Cubans and their role in what happened.

Somehow the American knew about the Laos File. And somehow the Cuban knew what the American knew. And old sparks could quickly become raging fires. Minh shook his finger at the ghosts lurking in the mists.

Go back to your graves. Rest easy, comrades. I am still on guard.

13. Haiphong

He was monitoring a morning PT period in the Naval Infantry compound when Commander Jeff Ault arrived sporting a PAVN rank badge pinned to the pocket of his khaki uniform. While the escort officers went for tea, they watched a gaggle of mechanics, technicians, and clerks go through a series of fluid tai chi stretching exercises.

"They give you a ship to go with the badge, Jeff?"

"No...but they let me conn that corvette into the pier this morning. Got fairly frantic at the end. I had Thien translating commands he'd never heard before."

"How they lookin' sailor-wise?"

"Sailors are OK...pretty good deck and gunnery skills. Snipes don't know shit from Shinola but they seem to keep the boilers lit and the ships steam somehow. Mostly they need A School stuff, technical instruction. Good team of Chiefs in propulsion rates would set 'em straight pretty quick. The officers are interesting. Shore-huggers, you know? Don't much care for blue water. They been trained to work within spitting distance of the beach."

"Politics?"

"Never came up. They got Uncle Ho's portrait hung up in the mess, but I'd say what drives their ships and sailors is Navy crude and rice. There was a political officer aboard...GPD guy...but they seemed to tolerate him more than listen to anything he had to say. Only time I spoke to him he wanted to know how soon I thought American container ships might arrive."

"Uh-huh. Assuming something can be done to square away their economy, these guys are poised to become conspicuous consumers. Given free trade and a little surplus cash, they'd all probably head for home."

"Could be...anyway it's something we should mention in reports. If the military gets the shitty end of the economic stick, they might not have a military..."

"Unless there's a war."

"Yeah, they don't respond well to threats. Anyway, it's too early to draw conclusions. There's lots more to see."

"You going back out?"

"Roger...we both are but not right away. Message from Chan this morning. General Thurman's been playing travel agent. We have a mission."

"What's the deal?"

"Cook's tour. You, me and the escorts head for Hanoi this afternoon, quick brief and then back here to pick up a ship which takes us south. We split up down there. I do the Navy stuff starting at Cam Ranh Bay and you do the grunt stuff...drive up the coast and stop when you see soldiers."

"Christ, I don't know if my back will survive another road trip in a Russian jeep."

"Relax, you get a break on the trip back to Hanoi. Thien laid on a helicopter. He says it's a low-mileage, previously-owned Huey...only flown on weekends by a teenage warrant officer out of Pleiku."

14. *Hanoi*

In the villa provided for him by the Presidential Envoy, Rockwell Thurman poured short measures of scotch for himself and the leader of his Military Contact Team. Twilight of another full day of bureaucratic convolutions, political machinations and unmarked minefields. He'd have to be disciplined or the whiskey level would quickly drop to match his morale.

"Goddammit, Gordo...we've got to kick-start this thing. One more planning session that leads to nothing but another planning session and I'm gonna kill somebody..."

Major General Gordon Fowler sipped scotch and watched his boss pace the breezy room. Rock Thurman was used to seeing wheels turn when he flipped a switch. He had all the duty experts in place and marking time but so far government inertia had kept the green light glowing solid amber.

"What's the problem, Rock...aside from your own impatience?"

"I wish it was just me wanting too much too fast, Gordo, but there's more to it...much more...and I'm gonna need your help."

"Anything I can do..."

Thurman snagged the scotch bottle and scooted a chair next to Fowler's. "We got one too many American generals in Hanoi."

"Al Varney? I just met with him yesterday. He's as frustrated as you are."

"Listen, Gordo, I don't want to start some kind of military shooting match here but you gotta know, Al Varney is the reason we can't get off first base. I just found out about it."

"I don't get it. Al's a damn fine officer...under a lot of pressure from home, you know? And the Joint Task Force for Full Accounting is operating on a completely separate agenda. How is he getting in the way?"

"Let me give you an example. I've got Mawk Arnold down at Vinh...labor, materials, everything in place to start the road-building project...but the government keeps stalling. The PAVN engineers don't show up. I can't get a straight answer, so I check up on the QT and find out it's the PAVN dragging their feet..."

"What's that got to do with Al? PAVN problems are my bailiwick."

"Let me finish. Turns out General Varney is exercising leverage he doesn't have. He got to his GPD counterpart and quietly passed the word. If they want that road...and he knows they do...they better cooperate a lot better in the MIA search project."

"What?"

"Yep. I shit you not. He's turned the whole thing political. If the Vietnamese want what we're offering they better play ball on the MIA issue."

"General Varney doesn't have the authority to make demands like that."

"Tell that to the PAVN. Probably sounds like a typical American subterfuge to the boys in the GPD. I don't wonder they'd believe it."

"Well...Christ, Rock! You're operating under a Presidential mandate. Why don't you just have Al ordered home?"

"I made a few quiet noises about that yesterday night on the secure circuit. Shit hit the fan. Folks at home might see it as shutting down the search efforts, giving up on the MIAs. That's sure as hell what Varney would call it if he suddenly found himself relieved."

"Let me talk to him..."

"Uh-uh. Bad idea. We'd just wind up making some kind of deal with the JTF and I don't want that. The MIA search is one thing; our strategic aims are another. Where the two missions cross, we cooperate...but we can't have one tied to the other or we'll never get anywhere. What I want you to do is talk to the PAVN leadership. I want you to assure them as a military man that what we're trying to do over here is separate and distinct from the MIA search."

"You want me to sabotage General Varney..."

"Bullshit, Gordo. I want you to tell the truth...to the right people."

"Who would you suggest?"

"Seems to me you go to the most respected name on the list. That's why I've set up an appointment for you with General Giap."

"Might be the wrong guy, Rock. He's mainly a show pony these days. Remember they levered him out as Minister of Defense in 1980 after he advocated another long war of attrition against Pol Pot."

"Yeah, and they dropped him from the Politburo in '81. But General Giap still has tons of influence with the Army leadership and my sources tell me he's mellowed considerably; wants to see his country on the road to prosperity before he dies."

"The final victory..."

"What's that?"

"I was thinking of Clausewitz. There is only one decisive victory: the last."

"Might not be a bad approach. Give it a shot."

"I'll do it, Rock...but I gotta tell you, I won't like it much. They never really won, you know...against us on the battlefield."

"I believe someone said that to Giap before, Gordo. And as he said then, that might be true but it is also irrelevent."

*   *   *

Despite a sudden Red River rain squall that blew up enroute and nearly drove the shuddering Huey down into a nest of high-tension wires, they raised Noi Bai Airport, dodged a Royal Thai Airlines commuter on final approach and thumped down on the arrival apron.

Commander Ault and the escorts ran quickly out of the rotor wash, but Shake stood next to the shivering bird for a few seconds to wave at the pilots and the grinning crew chief who handed him his overnight bag. Delay had everything to do with gratitude and nothing whatsoever to do with the aircrew. The pilots flew like ham-handed mule skinners and the crew chief doused him with rank hydraulic fluid while attempting to repair a leak by wrapping adhesive tape around a spurting line.

Still the creaky old Bell workhorse, abandoned by previous owners on the flightline at Phu Bai, took all the punishment her current tormentors could dish out and still beat the air over Vietnam into submission. He fondly patted a patch of bare metal showing through a shoddy paint-job, got control of his wobbly knees and joined the others milling around Major Chan Dwyer and two vehicles for the trip into the city.

They spent a quiet two hours pounding on laptops at Contact Team Headquarters, stored the files and made hard copies for Chan. The itinerary laid out for them by General Fowler was pretty much as Jeff Ault indicated, open-ended and broad-ranging. Return to Haiphong tomorrow morning, pick up a ship headed south, disembark with escorts at Cam Ranh Bay and see everything available to be seen on the way back to Hanoi. The lack of specifics in the orders threw Lieutenant Pham into a panic which drove him up Dien Bien Phu to the Citadel where he could use tactical radios to alert field commanders that they might find an American in their midst anytime over the next two or three weeks.

Chan handed over stacks of currency and messages. There was just one for Shake, a cryptic note from Tracey saying how glad she was that he was doing his bit and supporting the President. She was enjoying school and had a nice evening with First Sergeant Rea and his family.

"Everything OK at home?" Jeff Ault signed for his money, stuffed it in a briefcase and headed for the door.

"Yeah, fine. You go on ahead. I'll catch up with you later for a beer." He scooted a chair up next to Chan's desk and slouched into it.

"How's it going with you?"

"Pretty fair. I managed a day off while you guys were up at Haiphong. Got to see the Ho Chi Minh Mausoleum and the Central Military Museum."

"There's a fascinating place. Marine I met from the JTF took me over there last weekend. Amazing..."

"No news on that other thing...the deal you told me about at El Toro?"

"No joy...unless you count the fact that nobody's tried to kill me lately. I take that back...the dip-shits in that helicopter today were definitely trying to kill me."

"But you sniffed around? Asked questions over at the museum?"

"Yeah. I talked to one of the curators...Major Hiep I think his name was."

"That's his name all right..."

"You met him?"

"Uh huh...in fact, I've got a date with him tonight."

"You got a what?"

"A date with Major Hiep of the General Political Directorate and the Central Military Museum. We're going to the opera."

"They've got an opera?"

"They've got one and I'm gonna go see it."

"Well, how about that shit..."

"Don't fall apart, Shake. It's platonic. His CO is coming along...female-type colonel. She's GPD also. Hiep makes any moves on me and he'll get a very nasty evaluation."

"Guess that blows away the dinner invitation I was gonna offer."

"Yeah, but all is not lost. I'm gonna see what I can find out about the Laos File."

"I tried that. Nada. Hiep acted like he'd never heard of it. Seemed to be telling the truth..."

"Well, I'm gonna probe a little anyway. Can't hurt, can it?"

"Guess not. I'm trying to set up a meet with the museum's chief archivist. Kind of an end-run around the GPD officers. This JTF guy I was telling you about seems to think he might be a better source."

"Well, keep me posted. I'll do the same." Chan checked her watch and thumbed a button to punch up Eastern Standard Time. "Almost the witching hour. I've gotta make my Stateside calls."

"I'll head for the hotel and leave you in peace...provided you'll give me a rain-check for the dinner."

"Soon as you get back from your field trip. Promise."

As Shake Davis disappeared through the exit, Major Chan Dwyer pushed the probe of an HF scrambler through the phone cord and began to punch numbers. A machine in the DIA communications suite at Bolling Air Force Base would tape her up-date, filter the distortion and print a hard-copy for the man who called himself Bayer.

*   *   *

Shake Davis crossed the street and negotiated with a cyclo driver who was in final stages of having one of his tires repaired. It would only be a minute or two before the old one-legged guy who did the patch work would finish putting the wheel back on and they could head for the hotel. He was morosely contemplating a night of warm beer and sea stories with Jeff Ault when he noticed the cripple squinting at him; a cold, furtive look that alternated between his face and the hub nut he was twisting with a rusty crescent wrench.

Probably war-wounded, he thought climbing into the repaired cyclo. Probably a former NVA grunt who thinks I'm the very same evil American bastard that blew his leg off. He was about to say something but the cyclo driver rang his bell and pushed off into traffic.

*   *   *

Old Tran the tire repairman found Duc and the Cuban drinking tea. He sat and handed the photo to the Cuban. "I have found your man. He came out of the new office the Americans have on Dien Bien Phu Street. He told a cyclo driver to take him to the Dan Chu Hotel."

"Excellent work, comrade!" Duc shook Tran's hand and then turned to their guest. "What else can we do for you?"

"I will need some help keeping track of his movements and contacts..." Chico Reyes pocketed the photos of his target and squinted into the gloom at the rear of the room. There was something vaguely familiar about one of the men in the shadows back there. But there was no light in the stuffy room except for the puny glow of a single naked bulb hanging from a frayed wire over his head.

"Yes, we anticipated that." Duc motioned toward the figure in the shadows. "Comrade Minh works in the archives of the Central Military Museum. He informs us the GPD publishes an itinerary that outlines the Yankees' daily activities. What have you discovered, Minh?"

The familiar figure rose from his seat on a pile of jute sacks but made no move to step into the light. "The man you are after stays at the Dan Chu when he is in Hanoi. According to the itinerary I saw, he and another American officer will drive to Haiphong tomorrow morning..."

Even the voice was familiar. Chico knew this man, he was sure of it. Minh? My God, could it be...

"I'm having trouble hearing, comrade. Can you come closer?"

"Come forward with your report, Minh." Anxious to please the visitor, Duc moved to the rear of the room and shoved Minh toward the splash of pale light. Unable to resist and anxious to avoid a scene, Minh shuffled forward into the light and stared into the Cuban's black eyes. It was such a long time ago, perhaps he would not remember.

"Your man is at the Dan Chu Hotel. Tomorrow he is scheduled to drive to Haiphong with another officer. They will board a ship and sail to Cam Ranh Bay. The itinerary from the GPD says they are due to arrive there in three days time. There was no further information..."

The Cuban's eyes drifted to the scar but there was no flicker of recognition. He merely nodded and turned to Duc. "I think I should travel south also. The job will be more easily done away from Hanoi. What would you suggest, comrade?"

"Roads are in bad repair and not very reliable, comrade. I would suggest you travel to Ho Chi Minh City by train. We will provide you with a Nghe Tinh Group contact in the south."

"Good. I will leave by train tomorrow." Chico Reyes stood and moved toward the door realizing he had just stumbled on an opportunity to amplify Fidel's orders and tear out the very root of this entire problem. Minh could lead him to the Laos File...and then he could eliminate another surviving witness. "You have my thanks, comrades. When this war criminal dies it will be in the name of the Nghe Tinh Group."

After the visitor left, the group members sang a few of the old patriotic songs, toasted dead comrades with warm beer and then began to drift toward their homes. Minh waited until everyone left the room and then cornered Duc, the stoic political officer, veteran of many battles, including the one in Hue. His nerves were frazzled, a fit of the old combat shakes, and he needed to talk to someone, lighten the load, lift his spirits.

"I think our visitor is lying to us, comrade."

"Why do you say that, Minh? The instructions to help him came directly from our man in the politburo."

"I must tell you something, Duc. And you must swear to keep the secret."

"How can I swear, comrade? I have no idea what you wish to tell me."

"It is a thing that has remained secret for more than twenty years...since the War of Liberation. It is a thing very few people know and if it is revealed, it would dishonor those who fought and died."

Minh looked up from pouring the last of a beer into two glasses. "On our side or theirs?"

"On our side, comrade. Some terrible things were done."

"It was a long time ago, Minh..."

"Not so long ago that the Americans have forgotten. Do they not still comb the country looking for the ones who are missing?"

"Yes, they are like ghouls...snapping turtles who will not let go."

"Then they must never discover what is in the Laos File. I know this Cuban and I believe the reason he is here is because of that file."

*　　*　　*

Minh felt better when he left the building, a little drunk and a lot relieved, two hours later. He sucked greedily at the muggy night air and turned toward the river banks. High tide fog was roiling off the water but he spotted no ghosts. He began to hum. It was a good sign and he had plans.

Duc had agreed to guard the secret and listened quietly as Minh told him about events in 1972 at Ban Karai along the great trail. Minh agonized over breaking the sacred trust - even with someone as sympathetic and understanding as Duc - but he needed a confidant. Recent events were more than a little disturbing. First the Cuban emerges from some nightmare, and then Major Hiep says the Americans want to meet with him. It was no simple series of coincidences and his reliable old combat instincts were tingling.

*   *   *

"So, comrade...you survived." The voice came from a dark shape in the fog, but Minh knew immediately who it was. The Cuban had recognized him after all. He stopped and waited passively until the tall figure emerged into the clear.

"As did you...and now you have returned."

"But I never left, you see?" The Cuban's teeth flashed in the dark but Minh quickly dropped his gaze to keep an eye on the man's hands. "I have been living here since the war ended, living peacefully with the monks in Hue."

"What do you want with me?" Minh flicked a glance down the dark street and spotted the headlights of a truck. It was heavily-loaded and moving slowly. He would need to time his move but the drifting fog would help.

"A little help from an old comrade. I need to find the American...and I need to find a certain file which I hear is kept in the museum where you work. I think you should get that file and give it to me, Minh. I will destroy it. After that, everything is conjecture...hearsay."

The truck was grinding slowly nearer. It would pass in the next minute. "I know nothing about such a file. If it exists, it would be kept under the tightest security and I would not have access..." Minh kept his eyes on Chico's hands.

"Then we should go search for it together..." The Cuban's left hand disappeared into a trouser pocket; the right drifted toward the small of his back.

Minh saw the move and darted into the street, barely clearing the truck's hissing radiator. Lack of practice and the suppressor tube screwed onto the muzzle of the Tokarev cost the Cuban a couple of extra seconds on his draw. Minh heard two slugs slap through the metal skin of the truck. If more were fired the suppressor and a blaring horn kept him from hearing.

He disappeared into the fog, running as hard as his creaky knees would allow. Nostrils flared, heart hammering inside his chest, eyes wide and dilated, he felt the old familiar bite of adrenaline. He would be hunted now, as he had been for so many years in the jungle. It was terrifying to be back on the razor's edge but Minh was an older, wiser man in the skin of the predatory animal he had been during the war. He ran through the dark, heading for home, hoping for enough time to pack and leave before the Cuban found out where he lived.

*   *   *

Shake and Commander Ault were on a second beer, drowning a skimpy dinner and half-listening to a swishy waiter whine his way through a maudlin song on the karaoke machine that was the Dan Chu Hotel bar's only non-alcoholic recreational asset. The hotel's power supply ebbed and surged which made the music alternately sharp and flat. The grinning waiter didn't seem to care as he chased the key up and down the scale.

"God help us..." Jeff Ault shook his head and watched the only other roundeyes in the place - a pair of whiskey-soaked Australian contractors - bolt out of the bar. "You're a trained killer, Shake. Shoot that bastard."

"I'm outta practice. Could I just win his heart and mind instead?"

"Negative. He's got to die...or we've got to drink a whole hell of a lot more beer." Fortunately for the waiter, a beer resupply arrived in the hands of Lieutenant Colonel Mike Stokey who slipped into the bar behind the departing Australians.

"You guys are gonna need these..." Stokey placed beer bottles on the table and centered a silver flask engraved with the Jack Daniels logo. "Boilermakers are the only known antidote for karaoke night at the Dan Chu."

"Thank God for reinforcements." Shake introduced a fellow Marine to his roommate. "Between the songbird up there and Jeff's ship talk I was getting desperate."

"Good trip up to Haiphong?" Stokey unscrewed the top of his flask and poured a measure into their glasses.

"Not bad. Doors seem to be open wide." Jeff Ault tasted his boilermaker and grinned. "Anyway, we're headed back up there tomorrow morning. Gotta catch a ride south and continue the inspection tour."

"Ah, shit, shoulda checked..." Stokey handed Shake a note with a name and time scrawled across it. "I had you set up for a meeting with the archivist, Sergeant Minh...over at the museum. Ten tomorrow morning."

"We'll be halfway to Haiphong. Can you reschedule for after we get back?"

"Guess so. Major Hiep said the guy wasn't going anywhere. Interesting character. I asked about his wartime service. Does the 800th Battalion, 6th NVA Regiment ring any bells?"

"Hue...northside." Shake shook his head and reached for the flask. "Tough bastards...very tough."

"That's what I heard. Can't say I'm sorry I missed that one..." Stokey trailed off and turned his head to watch a tanned visitor walk up to the bar and order beer.

"What's up, Colonel?" Jeff Ault turned to look at the bald-headed roundeye who leaned on the bar and spoke Vietnamese with the bartender. "You know that guy?"

"New face in town. After you're here a while, you come to recognize most of the roundeyes but I've never seen this guy."

"Probably just got in."

"Nah. He's been around for a while. Check out his feet. Tougher than nails...sandals...this guy's been living native."

"Looks Hispanic...Cuban or Nicaraguan?"

"Not likely...unless he's a hold-out from the old days when Fidel and the Nico's had regular contingents over here."

Jeff Ault helped himself to another slug of whiskey. "Well, I'm betting he's a Cuban."

The boilermaker turned bitter in Shake's mouth and he stared at the man, trying to convince himself Ault was way off base. "What makes you say that?"

"Trust me on this. I spent three years at Gitmo. You learn to spot the type."

Lieutenant Colonel Stokey shrugged and turned back to his drink. The singing waiter was about to conduct another assault on their senses. "Guy's probably got a Vietnamese wife and kids somewhere down south...up here on business or something."

Shake was getting nervous. The tan man looked like he was recently out of the bush; carried himself erect, shoulders back, weight centered...like a soldier.

"Or he could be shopping..." Commander Jeff Ault tore the filters off two Marlboros and made himself a set of earplugs. "I read a piece in the Tribune says Castro is buying rice from the Vietnamese."

The bald man glanced in their direction, shook his head at the caterwauling waiter and grinned. He claimed to be Nicaraguan in Hanoi on business when Mike Stokey sidled up next to him and ordered a round. He was still hunched over his drink when Shake and Jeff Ault called it a night. Assuming the creaky elevator to be out of service as it generally was, they climbed the stairs discussing the trip. "Got most of my packing done before you came back to the hotel..." Ault stabbed his key into the lock and swung the door open. "I just loaded up on skivvies and socks. Ship's laundry ought to be able to handle my khakis."

"Assuming they've got laundries on their ships..." Shake strolled to the flimsy dresser where he'd laid out clean camouflage uniforms before joining Jeff in the bar. Adding the jeans and shirt he was wearing and stuffing it all in a seabag would just about complete his preparations for the road trip. He peeled the shirt over his head and noticed Ault's B-4 bag sitting on the end of his bed. Jeff's bed on the other side of the rickety nightstand was empty and unrumpled. He couldn't remember seeing the bag there before he left the room earlier in the evening.

"How come you stacked your bag on my rack?"

Ault poked his head out of the small bathroom and stared at his bag. "I didn't put it there. Last time I saw it was on the end of my bed." Carrying his shaving kit, he walked out of the bathroom and headed for the bag. "Probably the maid. I'll move it..."

"Don't touch it, Jeff!" Ault froze in his tracks and stared at Shake. The Marine slowly slid to his knees and peered at the half-packed canvas bag. "There's something wrong here. I can feel it..."

Without touching the bed or the bag, Shake cautiously maneuvered around to stare at the grey, government-issue suitcase. It seemed to be OK; just misplaced. Jeff slung it on the wrong rack in a hurry to get down to the bar, or the maid moved it when she made up the beds. No, the beds had both been made when he got back to the room.

"You sure you didn't put it here?"

"Swear I didn't, Shake. Unless I'm suffering a serious brain-fart, I specifically remember packing most of my gear and then putting the bag on my bed...handy so I could stow any last minute stuff."

"Well, I'm not buyin' the maid proposition. She'd already been in here when I got back to the room and I didn't see your gear on my rack before I left for the bar. Grab me a coat hangar..."

He took the wire hangar and slid it carefully under the B-4 bag. Halfway through the slow traverse it hit something. Shake put his ear next to the hangar and sawed it back and forth. Metal on metal. Something's under there and it's made of metal.

"Jeff, I don't like the feel of this. I've seen too many fucking boobytraps. Put your hands on the bag and press...not too hard...just an even pressure. I'm gonna see if I can snake my hand under there by pressing down on the mattress. You gotta keep pressure on from the top."

Shake depressed the mattress and flattened his hand into a thin blade. "If you hear a metallic sound...a snap or pop...hit the deck immediately." Millimeter by millimeter he wormed his hand under while Jeff kept a steady downward pressure on the bag. Five minutes passed in what seemed like an hour before he felt it. Metal...neutral temperature...round base...dollars to dog-shit...it's a grenade.

"Listen, Jeff, don't get your bowels in an uproar..." He carefully inched his hand farther under, moving his fingertips minute distances to feel for the arming lever. It was where he expected, wedged against the bottom of the B-4 bag. "We got a grenade under here. There's no pin and the spoon is resting against the bag."

"Shit, man! Leave the bastard where it is. Let's call somebody to disarm it."

"Not that easy, shipmate. We'd be here all night waiting on some kind of PAVN EOD and then they'd probably blow it in place which would scatter your skivvies all over the area..."

"Fuck the skivvies. Leave that thing alone."

Shake felt his hand cramping painfully. Decision time or the muscles might convulse and trip the boobytrap. "I've done this kind of thing a few times before. Just gotta have patience and a little manual dexterity." He felt for the end of the arming lever with his thumb. If he could hook his thumbnail on the lever and get a fingertip or two around the body of the grenade, he might be able to trap it long enough to get a better grip. A lot depended on how strong the spring pressure was on the arming lever. Hard to tell from feel what kind of grenade it is...

He felt the ridge of the arming lever dig painfully into the tender meat under his thumbnail. Poising his left hand in position to smash down over his right, he stared up at Ault and raised his eyebrows. "When I give the word, you carefully lift the bag. When you've got all the weight off the bed, get the bag the hell out of the way so I can get two hands on this thing in a hurry. Got it? All right...now!"

Jeff Ault did as he was instructed and found himself staggering back from the bed on shaky legs. He barely noticed Shake's left hand strike like a cobra before he tripped over a pair of boots and fell flat on his back with the heavy bag over his face and chest.

"The line is clear...shooters put your weapons on safe and stand up."

Ault scrambled to his knees and stared at Shake Davis who was squeezing a mustard green grenade in his hand. Strange looking device...definitely a hand grenade...serrated body like the old World War II pineapples, but different...with a long silver tube protruding from the top. Shake held it tightly in his left hand while he flexed the cramps out of his right.

"Standard pressure-release boobytrap." Shake walked across the room, snagged a sewing needle from his mending kit on the dresser and shoved it into the fuse to serve as a temporary safety pin. "This is a Soviet F-1, old model frag. They use the RGD-5 these days..."

"Who gives a shit about the nomenclature?" Jeff moved to examine the disarmed grenade. "Question is who put it here...and why?"

"Why is pretty simple..." Shake bent the makeshift safety pin double with a pair of needle nose pliers until he was confident it wouldn't fall out of the grenade and undo his good work. "The idea was to fill our asses with shrapnel, which...given the bursting radius of this little beauty...would likely have resulted in one or both of us making that long, lonesome return flight in a bodybag."

"Who would want to do that?"

"Beats the shit out of me..." But it doesn't really. So the bald-headed bastard who says he's a Nicaraguan is a Cuban, right? No matter where you go, there you are. I ask about the Laos File and I'm number one with a bullet on the hit list. What the fuck is in a 25 year-old file that makes it worth killing to hide? Get this road trip out of the way and I'm sure as hell gonna find out...

"Listen, Shake...we better find Chan and let her know about this."

"You handle it. I'm gonna go back down below and see if I can find that prick we saw hanging out at the bar. He planted this frag and I'm gonna find out why."

*   *   *

While his target frantically searched the hotel for him, Chico Reyes stood in the shadows across the street from the Dan Chu watching for signs of alarm or panic. Nothing but sleepy staff milling about their chores. Nearly an hour since the Americans left the bar and he'd watched them climb the stairs headed for their room before he left the hotel. So...the boobytrap failed. Irritating but no great problem. Five American dollars to bribe a room clerk, two minutes flat to pick the flimsy doorlock and who knew? He might have saved himself a long trip south. Survival demanded he wait now.

He'd just have to open the range, presume the quarry knew he was being hunted, and snipe the nosey bastard somewhere along the road between Cam Ranh Bay and Hanoi. Graciously facilitating his mission, the Nghe Tinh Group had ticketed him on a noon train that would put him in the area near the time of the target's scheduled arrival. That left him a few free morning hours for a side-trip to the Central Military Museum where he might find the Laos File, Than Duc Minh or both if he was lucky.

*   *   *

Frazzled from a sleepless night roaming the streets and dodging shadows, Minh reported for work at the usual time, fairly certain the large number of soldiers and police in the vicinity of the Citadel would keep the Cuban from making an overt move. The gate guard was alerted to let him know immediately if there were any foreign visitors. He unlocked the office and stowed his old rattan suitcase under the desk.

Mrs. Ngoc commented on the luggage as he crossed the courtyard but he told her it was to carry the fruit and pastry he planned to purchase at lunchtime...a little party for one of the children who shared his quarters. She shrugged and squawked about some dusting that needed to be done in the exhibition hall.

Fine; it would give him something to do before the tea break at nine when he could put the first phase of his plan into effect. He switched on the overhead lights, checked to see that none of the neon tubes needed changing and then ran a dusting cloth over a captured American sensor device. Such a joke, this effort to sow the great trail with electronic eyes and ears, comic relief for the Group 559 soldiers who found the sensors.

They looked like slim shell casings, pointed on one end to bury themselves in the dirt after being dropped from aircraft. The end which stuck up above ground was festooned with plastic fronds supposed to make it resemble a jungle shrub. Eyes accustomed to all types of jungle flora quickly spotted the difference between plant and plastic.

The Americans called them ADSIDs...Air Deliverable Seismic Intrusion Devices...and he'd seen hundreds of them along the trail, planted there to detect movement and provide marauding bombers with targets. Minh and other Group 559 members located the ADSIDs, dug them up and hung them in trees, deep in vacant stretches of jungle where the wind blew them around and banged them into tree trunks. A neat and reliable way to insure the Americans monitoring the sensors dropped their bombs well away from active supply routes.

It was just one of the ways the soldiers of his army proved themselves to be smart and innovative, tenacious in the face of superior firepower and technology. It reminded him of the noble, silent sacrifice of...what was the number these days? Eight hundred thousand killed in action? A million? No one knew for sure...nor were they likely to ever know. The teeming, scrabbling, selfish...yes, ungrateful people of Vietnam didn't know and they didn't care as long as the rice bowls were full; as long as there was money that had value, a way to buy what their brave martyrs would never have. Minh folded his dust cloth neatly and headed for the stairs leading to the archives. His duty, even if it was his last, was to comrades living and dead.

Promptly at nine when the first wave of visitors completed their tour and the museum staff generally disappeared inside offices for tea and respite, Minh rose from his desk, felt for his keys and walked down the long row of files, stopping at the padlocked cabinet - Row C, fifth from the end - keyed the lock and removed the Laos File from its accustomed place.

He relocked the cabinet, walked back to his desk and turned off the hotplate, slid the volatile red logbook into his humble suitcase and headed for the door. A bus for Hue left from the city central depot in just under an hour.

*   *   *

Chico Reyes dawdled at his morning meeting with Duc, drinking strong coffee and stifling yawns. After a restless night wandering unfamiliar streets searching for the little scar-faced bastard, he'd given up shortly before dawn. In the end it was easier to catch Minh at the Central Military Museum and - if the opportunity presented itself - take care of business. Assuming success, Fidel would be delighted and generous.

He checked his watch and glanced again at the name Duc had scribbled on a small piece of notebook paper. A man named Thuy was scheduled to meet him at Phan Rang south of Cam Ranh Bay with a fast car.

"This man is reliable?"

"One of the best. He has been a stalwart of the Nghe Tinh Group in the south."

"Combat experience?"

"Comrade Thuy was a platoon leader in U Minh 2nd Infantry Battalion operating out of An Xuyen. His unit was the scourge of the Mekong. You will find him quite suitable for your purposes."

Shaking Duc's hand, Chico thanked his Hanoi host, paid for the coffee and pocketed the contact information. It was time for the mission to begin and timing was critical to survival. He would make one quick pass at the museum. If it was too crowded or if Minh was not there, he would call if off and re-focus on the American.

He hailed a cyclo, gave directions and reviewed his schedule as the driver pedaled into light morning traffic. Thirty minutes to search the museum...then a cyclo ride to the nearby train station. With a little luck and a conductor who rolled his train on time, he'd be well clear.

Arriving ten minutes before his self-imposed deadline, he left his heavy equipment satchel and a wad of dong with the ancient guard at the museum's wrought-iron gates. Noticing the old man's nicotine-stained fingertips he pressed a packet of Japanese cigarettes on him and asked where he might find Than Duc Minh.

The old gatekeeper stared at the visitor - cutting his eyes from the tan face and round dark eyes to the heavy satchel on the ground - and counted his blessings. It was a slow day at the museum but his luck was on the fast track. Just an hour before he'd collected another package of cigarettes from Minh in exchange for an alibi. This man was clearly the reason the senior sergeant had needed one.

"I last saw Minh about a half-hour ago..." True enough as he'd passed right through these gates carrying a suitcase. "You'll probably find him in his office...the archives...just through the main exhibition hall and up the stairs at the rear." Payment received and earned. Minh was nowhere on the museum grounds, but the bald-headed visitor would have to find that out for himself.

The door at the top of the stairs that led past the rank latrine area was padlocked. Chico checked his watch. No time to set an ambush. He searched the exhibition hall, spending a few valuable minutes running his eyes over the Great Trail mural, remembering a day in 1972 that ultimately drove him on this mission, but Minh was not there. He checked the Dien Bien Phu diorama building, the courtyard, the warren of cubbyhole offices where officers and military scholars drowsed over their studies. Nothing.

Assuming Minh was at work where he was supposed to be and the gatekeeper's sighting was accurate, there was only one possibility remaining. He checked his watch again and headed for the main administration building. Doors to several of the offices off the main hallway were closed. Minh could be in any one of them, napping, drinking tea, on an errand. He was running out of time.

"Museum staff only in this area. Can I help you, sir?"
He turned to see a wispy woman in PAVN uniform, brushing at a clump of unruly hair and carrying a stack of papers. As she approached he noticed she wore the rank tabs of a Lieutenant Colonel and she was staring at him intently, squinting, questioning as if she recognized him. Impossible. He hadn't been in Hanoi for twenty years...but she was old enough to have met him during the war. Chico stared back, looking for clues but there was nothing about her that sparked memories from those days.

The woman officer stopped in front of him and he saw her pencil-thin eyebrows arch. She made a slight wheezing sound and began to fuss with the stack of papers crooked in her elbow. Probably put off by my appearance, he told himself. They can't get many foreign visitors in a place like this.

"I'm sorry if I've strayed, colonel. I was looking for the archivist. Some research I want to do..."

"No access to archives without written permission. We have rules and they must be followed. Who are you, sir?"

Chico reached for the doctored ID papers and handed them to her. "Armando Guitterez, Colonel. Heating and air conditioning engineer...from Managua. My papers..."

She examined them closely; again giving him that quizzical look. "Well, you can't get access to the archives with these. You'll have to see the administrative section of the General Political Directorate and make application."

"Perhaps if I could just talk to your archivist, colonel. I'm on a fairly tight time schedule."

"Senior Sergeant Minh knows the rules as well as I do, Mr. Guitterez. He can give you no information without prior approval from the General Political Directorate. You must make application for access."

Chico nodded, retrieved his papers and checked his watch. Too late for any more hunting. Minh would simply have to live for a while longer...at least until he'd taken care of the American. He'd be lucky to make the train if it left on time. "I will make application and come back. Thank you, colonel."

Mrs. Ngoc slumped against a damp wall and watched the tall visitor amble down the hallway and out the door. It was him, no doubt. Older, thinner; bald now...or simply a shaved head to change his appearance...but it was him. She remembered his dark, intense eyes; his fluent Vietnamese tinged with just a hint of his Spanish roots. Of course, he would not recognize her. She was young and pretty in those days when she saw him nearly every night. She was flushed with passion and desire when he came to pluck his officer out of her bed in the Cu Loc neighborhood where they had established a secret nest.

Why was he here after so many years; using an assumed identity with patently false papers? And why did he seek access to the archives? Unless...the Laos File? Mrs. Ngoc leaned against the damp walls of the museum hallway and felt an unaccustomed flush rising along her neck to her cheeks. There was an emergency number her former lover had given her; a way to reach him anytime, anywhere, but she'd never tried it.

Would it still work? Was he still alive? In favor or purged? Would he welcome hearing from her after all the years? Nonsense, she chided herself. She swept into her private office and poured tea to calm jangling nerves. It was a full five minutes before Mrs. Ngoc began digging in the files to find the long-hidden and nearly forgotten contact number.

*   *   *

They sat silently in creaky wicker chairs on a breezy veranda overlooking a grove of rambling banyan trees. Watching an orange slice of sun sink beneath the horizon, General Gordon Fowler felt himself relaxing for the first time since he and Major Chan Dwyer had been ushered into the small, secluded cottage that served as General Vo Nguyen Giap's retreat. A senior PAVN aide who introduced himself as a doctor politely informed them the General was ailing and asked them to be brief.

Fowler, in dress uniform for the occasion, complied, limiting the requisite pleasantries and conversing directly with Giap in French. Although fluent in the language, Chan let the discussion flow around her, returning Giap's pleasant smiles and listening carefully for nuance in what was being said by the senior officers. She admired the opening gambit and watched the ancient Vietnamese warrior's reserve melt as Fowler plowed common ground, calling himself a simple soldier uncomfortably saddled with political burdens.

Yes, Giap had nodded his understanding and smiled, these things become larger parts of our duties as we rise in rank. On the other hand, he continued lifting a bushy grey eyebrow, our knowledge of battlefield tactics sometimes makes the job easier. Fowler agreed and got to the meat of his message. In simple, disturbingly candid terms, he outlined the IRDG situation, flowing seamlessly from strategic to practical concerns. Chan had never seen her boss more cogent or persuasive.

Despite festering wounds on both sides, Fowler said, it is pointless to argue that the war between America and Vietnam has not ended. It is equally pointless to argue about who won and who lost. In war, everyone loses.

Giap nodded, shrugged and studied the smoldering cigarette between his nicotine stained fingers. We must look to the future and forge new alliances against common enemies, Fowler continued. In the end, a soldier's ultimate mission is to insure the security of his nation and the future of its children.

General Fowler saw the glint in Giap's eye and plunged toward the bottom line. The IRDG, acting on orders from the President of the United States is here to do that...and our efforts have no direct connection to the search for missing persons...on either side. In fact, they are separate and distinct issues which must not be allowed to interfere with each other. We will make no progress, forge no mutual defense against future Chinese aggression if the search for missing Americans is allowed to tie the normalization process into knots. These efforts must be parallel and not interdependent.

Giap pondered that and leaned forward across a low coffee table, staring deeply and directly into Fowler's eyes. He seemed wispy and frail; clearly in failing health, but the old campaigner could still read a political map. "This seems to represent a significant change in your country's position on missing Americans..."

Chan Dwyer let her eyes shift to General Fowler. This was the nut of the issue at hand. In effect, Giap was asking if America was ready to admit the vast majority of their Missing In Action soldiers would likely never be found. Was a new generation of Americans, ascending to power over their Cold War predecessors, ready to write the Vietnam experience off as a bad job poorly handled? Would the world's proudest superpower admit a loss at arms and accept the consequences? She knew it was squeezing painfully on Fowler, putting his ingrained sense of duty and honor at odds.

Fowler uncrossed his legs, rested his elbows on his knees and took a deep breath. He seemed to be searching beyond the verbal horizon, looking for a trail free from mines and boobytraps.

"It represents a passage of time," he said with hints of Texas roots sliding through his French. "It represents an acceptance of certain realities, a willingness to come to terms with the past and avoid disasters in the future."

"Just so," said Giap, smiling and nodding. "Just so. And a Vietnam strong enough to scare off the Chinese dragon offers America stronger footing in Asia. You can understand a certain reluctance on the part of my people to become puppets. We have been forced to dance at the end of too many strings."

"Just so," General Fowler agreed. "But there are no colonial strings attached to the IRDG rebuilding efforts. We wish to help you because it is the right thing to do after so many years of hatred and bitterness. Our tradition, our American ethic demands it. Modern history will attest to that. If a democratic society emerges in Vietnam, we are pleased certainly... and we believe a truly free society will emerge in this country once the people of Vietnam see the benefits and prosperity it brings. We have watched you move away from old alliances toward genuine independence. Americans understand, admire and respect such things...even among former enemies.

"I wish to assure you, General, that our efforts to help Vietnam rebuild will continue as long as they are welcomed and that there is no cause and effect relationship between those nation-building efforts and our continuing search for information about our missing soldiers. I have come here to ask you to help us make that point clear to your current military leadership."

Vo Nguyen Giap struggled to his feet and winced briefly, swaying and searching for balance. A solicitous aide appeared at his elbow but Giap dismissed him with instructions to prepare drinks for the visitors. Chan noticed the falter in his step, the tremble in his hands and the livid spots on his pale skin that signaled serious infirmity. Vietnam would be staging another full-blown state funeral in the near future.

"I would like to see my country serene, strong and free," Giap whispered, "just once before I die. Above and beyond the politics...it is what I was fighting for all those years."

At sunset they were sipping cognac, watching murky dusk descend over the countryside. Giap was a frail specter slouched in a wingback chair, the familiar face a mask of contemplation lit by the glow of his cigarette. His voice when he finally spoke was barely audible above the croaking chorus of tree frogs in the banyans surrounding his retirement retreat.

"And there is no hook in this bait, General? You would not have us become addicted to prosperity and withdraw your support when the Vietnamese do not meet your...cultural expectations?"

"General Giap, I don't think Americans have a lot of cultural expectations..." He smiled and reached over to pat Chan Dwyer's shoulder. "As you can see, we are a nation composed of many different cultures. Americans these days are focused on peace and prosperity. What we are trying to do here is really just an extension of that. As strange as it may seem in a lot of ways, helping you is simply helping ourselves in the long run."

Following a long silence, Giap crushed his cigarette and folded his hands. "Perhaps what you say is true. Perhaps the time has come for trust..."

"I think so, General."

"And perhaps such resolve should be tested..." Giap shifted his glance to Chan Dwyer and smiled. "Do you have a religion?"

"I have certain religious beliefs, General. My father was a Catholic, my mother is a Buddhist."

"Perfect!" Giap laughed and lit a cigarette. "You would have made a perfect Vietnamese, Major. Our struggle has roots from the same two trees. It was what drove me to become an atheist, a communist. But we are a spiritual people and I have spent some years now studying the ways of Buddha. There is much wisdom to be found there...especially for old soldiers." He turned slowly to look at Fowler and began to recite.

"A wise ruler is always thinking of his people and does not forget them even for a moment. He thinks of their hardships and plans for their prosperity. Wherever he goes, fighting ceases and ill-will vanishes. Because his rule is based on truth, he is invincible. There is no dissension among his people and, therefore, they dwell in quietness and safety..."

"Wise words, General..."

"And perhaps it is now time to heed them. Perhaps now it is finally time for truth. If not now...then never. I do not have long left in this world...and I would like to leave it with a sense of honor...toward my people and toward our enemies...or former enemies if what you have told me is true."

"General Giap...I don't know what to say."

"You have said all that you need to say. Now it is my time to speak. I will pass your message to the army high command. And I will give you a gift which you may not want. It is time for me to shift a burden I have carried for too many years. We must meet at the Central Military Museum. I will reveal some things to you...and we will see if your country is truly ready to forgive and forget."

                              *   *   *

A stiff north wind shoved at the stern of the Stenka class corvette as it plowed through South China Sea whitecaps. The ship pitched steadily, making 25 knots with the wind, holding a sliver of land on the starboard beam and outrunning the monsoon rains that were now drenching her homeport at Haiphong. Shake Davis stood forward in the corvette's sleek bows, sheltered from the wind by an antiaircraft mount, and watched as the land mass to his right rose slowly on the horizon. There was no perceivable cant in the deckplate underfoot, but they were clearly angling toward shore. He was beginning to see detail in the distant smudge; fecund smells of shoreline vegetation and coastal fishing villages floated faintly over the corvette's decks.

"Lung full of that will take you back twenty years, won't it?" Commander Jeff Ault, wearing a foul-weather jacket stenciled

USS INCHON, eased into the lee side of the AA gun mount and expertly cupped his Zippo against the wind to light a cigarette. "Keep me belowdecks blindfolded for six weeks and I'd still know when we hit the South China Sea. Nothin' in the world smells exactly like it."

Shake shook his head at the ear-to-ear grin. A kid in a candy store. At sea Ault was in his element and all was somehow right with the world. An attempt on their life the night before, duly reported to Chan Dwyer and then promptly forgotten. "Funny, I always associated the area with the smell of camphorwood, cordite and burning shitters."

"Which proves beyond a shadow of doubt that you fucking grunts have no soul. You'll feel better once you're on the road and the monsoons start soaking your ass."

"Well, it's that time of year, ain't it?"

"It is. Monsoons marching south and you're marching north. Should meet up with the rains somewhere around Chu Lai, I figure."

"You will, of course, be warm and dry at the officer's mess ashore or in some cozy wardroom..."

"Of course...which prompts me to remind you of what General Fowler and Major Dwyer had to say before we left. Be ultra-fucking-careful out there."

"I'll watch it..."

"And check six at all times."

"I will."

"And tell me why it is that someone's trying to kill your sorry ass..."

"Long story, Jeff. Has to do with POWs or MIAs. I might be into something that's way over my head. There are some serious people who don't want me to find out what it is."

"That all there is...or is that all you're willing to tell me?"

"It's complicated, Jeff...and I haven't even got it completely figured out yet. I'll tell you everything I know after chow tonight if you want."

"Check. See you in the cabin right after fish heads and rice. Meanwhile, check that out..." Ault pointed toward the looming shoreline off the starboard quarter, much closer now and dotted with small fishing sampans. "The captain's mission includes shoreline surveillance so he's gonna run close tonight and tomorrow. Know what that is?"

Shake stared at the shoreline, cut in two by a wide river that flowed from inland; perpendicular to the ship's course.

Large hill masses to the south of the river looked vaguely familiar. He had a visceral feeling about the place but it was hard to identify from the seaward angle.

"Seventeenth parallel, son. That's the DMZ; high ground to the south and west is Con Thien and Gio Lin. Water's the Ben Hai River. You ought to recognize your old stomping grounds. See you after chow..."

Shake moved to the starboard lifelines, feeling the steady spit of rain on the wind and staring at the lumpy, scarred hills rising like blisters above the flat savannah of elephant grass that flanked the Ben Hai River. They called it The Trace, a roiling pit full of vipers, a sweltering swatch of head-high razor-edged grass, always chockablock with infiltrating NVA. He remembered his time in the barrel up on Con Thien, the place of angels, where a warning order for a patrol into The Trace always sounded like an apology. Sorry guys, but we gotta go out into the Trace again; we gotta get a bunch of you killed on a little stroll by the banks of the Ben Hai.

15. The Trace - 1970

"Sorry 'bout the quick turn-around, people, but we got a little problem out in The Trace. Helo inbound twenty mikes. Saddle up and go light. Weapons, ammo, water, split kit and fighting gear. Sgt. Davis, they're ready to brief you up at the COC."

Con Thien supposed to be a respite; short stop-over to rest Recon Team Slingshot after five nut-shrinking, no-slack, no-sleep days on the far side of that fucking Ben Hai blue line. Four days of pouring sweat and scoping gooners at play in their own backyard. And hell yes, to state the fucking obvious, there is a shit-pot full of them over there masked by Signal Mountain and they are indeed headed south by night in big goddamn droves. What else can we do for you, Colonel? Five fucked up, brain dead Recon Marines on final approach to a hard landing from a Dexedrine high standing by for orders...and ain't there somebody else somewhere on this fucking hill capable of doing whatever it is?

It is an aviation problem...or rather a problem with a Marine who formerly aviated...in an A-6 Intruder. Seems this particular bird from one of the Marine all-weather attack squadrons at Danang selected an egress route off target that included air space guarded by a very efficient, highly-pissed gook triple-A battery. Said battery ripped the living shit out of the Intruder, fucking up the flight controls and the pilot who just managed to make the Ben Hai before he died...leaving his bombardier-navigator with nothing to do but scream for help and punch the fuck out.

Wingman pushing bingo fuel reported the BN down in the tall grass of The Trace. He saw a good chute and heard the guy check in on his survival radio. All kinds of high-speed rescue rangers headed for the area but the ground-bound BN had a pressing problem while he waited for transportation. He was in the middle of a mess of gooks who also saw a good chute as well as a golden opportunity to snatch a POW and move him north in record time. What he needed was a brace of bodyguards who could buy him some time until the Jolly Green appeared overhead. What he needed was fellow Marine ground-pounders out there with him...a gang of King Hell bushbeasts who could tuck him under their reeking armpits until the cavalry arrived.

Questions? Well, hell, Sgt. Davis...once he's cozy aboard the rescue chopper you and your guys do what you normally do. You just melt into the tall grass and disappear. Head south toward Con Thien; we'll leave a light on for you and pump a bunch of arty out there if you think you need it.

Skids of the slick barely brushing the elephant grass when Kid Crewchief grins at the lunatics sitting in the doors and gives the go sign. Last known position for your guy on the ground, gents. Kindly exit quickly as that shit clanging into the fuselage is most definitely enemy ground fire.

Gook gunner held the departing helo in his sights until it staggered out of range then began a ball ammo search and traverse through the elephant grass looking for us. Long gone and moving southwest by that time. Let the bastard waste ammo on weeds. If the downed flyer was running, he'd head south toward the high ground in friendly hands. Push him on the guard frequency and set up a meet.

"Lazy Two...Slingshot on the ground with you. Say your position, over..." Nada. C'mon Marine Corps Nasal Radiator. Check in on the net. Gotta find you before they do.

"Lazy Two...Slingshot is a friendly patrol. Talk to me so we can set up a meet, over."

"Slingshot...Lazy Two..." The voice was weak, shocky, disoriented. "I'm busted up. Where are you guys?"

"Out here in the weeds with you, Lazy Two. We're gonna police you up and take you home. Can you move?"

"Both ankles hurt...something on the ejection...hard to move unless I crawl..."

"OK, Lazy Two...we'll come to you. What can you see from your position?"

"Weeds...tall grass...I'm in a hole...bomb crater, I think..." Christ...there's at least a thousand fucking bomb craters in The Trace. Bastard could be anywhere and time is tight. Gooks gotta be looking hard as we are. Heads up; identify common ground.

"Lazy Two...we need directions. Look around...see if you can get your head above the grass for a minute. Can you see a stand of low trees?"

"Rog...yeah. Low trees to my right front." Stand of scrub to our left front. West by south of us about 300 meters. But where are the gooks?

"Uh, Slingshot...I've got some flares in the survival gear...pencil flares...I can give you a marker..."

"Negative, Lazy Two! Negative on the flares until we get closer. We got bad guys out here..."

"I got...I hear movement to my rear. Is that you guys?" No way...and no use lying to the man.

"Negative, Lazy Two. We'll be coming from the other direction. Move toward the stand of trees. Low and slow. We're gonna see if we can slow up the competition."

Switch freqs and dial up the Fire Direction Center at the Rockpile. Eight-inch tubes back there can put it in a pickle barrel...assuming good firing dope to the gun crews...and that's up to me. Lucky...they've sent so much HE and shrapnel out into The Trace that the map's riddled with pre-plotted targets.

"Iron Hand...Slingshot...emergency fire mission for your eight-inchers follows. From Bravo Tango zero-three, add 150...left 100...adjust fire...how copy, over?"

"Slingshot...Iron Hand...say the nature of your target, over."

"Iron Hand, just fire the mission! This is an emergency. We have a friendly flyboy on the deck and he's being chased by bad guys..." Cease and desist the fucking back-chat. Rounds inbound and we move out in a hurry. Fuck the mines and fuck the unexploded ordnance laying everywhere and fuck the slow, silent tactical movement...it's nothing but a three hundred meter footrace.

First eight-inch HE rounds crunch into the Trace. Battery two...and right where we want it. "Lazy Two, Slingshot...that's our arty. Where's it landing in relation to your pos, over?"

"Slingshot...it's behind me...maybe a little to my right..."

"Good deal, Lazy Two...that's where we want it. Are you in the trees yet?"

"Slingshot, that's negative. Can't move very fast. Maybe another hundred meters...I don't know. Where are you?"

"Lazy Two...we're headed for those trees just like you are...runnin' like hell. Just keep moving toward the green..."

"Better put a rush on it, Slingshot. I...I've got company over here. Bad guys heading in my direction. I can see 'em now..."

Move, move, move! No time to calculate adjustments for the guns. Just tell 'em drop five-zero and fire for effect. Another hundred meters to the green...storming through the fucking Trace like a herd of panicky water-boos. Bleeding like stuck hogs from the grass cuts. Ankles and knees screaming from impact with unseen crap underfoot. Like running through a goddamn swamp and...there's his chute! Fifty meters! Pump some rounds to the right of the trees. Gooks gotta be coming from there...

"Lazy Two...Slingshot...with you fifty meters...hang on, we'll be right there..."

And nothing...except five short, sharp pops. Aircrew issue .38 revolver...and no return fire. They want him alive...and it's just too fucking late.

"Lazy Two...Slingshot...was that you firing? We're almost there..." And the mocking voice from the survival radio.

"Xin Loi. He go Hanoi. You come visit him there..."
And a wall of winking muzzle blast out of the trees. Pinned down hard in the high grass. Locked down tight, panting and gagging in the muck and dust while some English-speaking gook travel agent books another American for an extended stay at the Hanoi Hilton. And what's next, Ricky Recon? How you gonna act now that you blew the mission?

"They've got him. Check the arty. Can't take a chance on killing our guy. Push the air frequency and gimme the handset..."

"Jolly one-five...Slingshot on the ground. How copy, over?" Air Force Jolly Green Giant HH-53 rescue helicopter somewhere on station. Engine roar and blade clatter from the southeast.

"Slingshot...Jolly one-five with you on guard. Any sign of our boy?"

"Jolly...be advised the bad guys have got him. We were a day late and a dollar short."

"Slingshot...we still might have a chance here. Can you locate the bad guys and keep an eye on them for us?"

"Jolly...Slingshot, roger. Clear the air space to the echo and we'll bring some artillery onto their rear guard. I believe they'll move our boy north for the blue line. Soon as we can move, we'll be on their heels..."

Eleven perforated former gooks in the former treeline following the arty strike. Small consolation but the zip in charge must see it as fair trade for an American POW. Sneaky Pete mode now...snoop and poop...follow the track. Gooks leaving plenty to follow. Anxious to get their prize across the Ben Hai.

"Jolly one-five...Slingshot. We are in a little patch of green just sierra of the blue line. Our boy is in sight. They're carrying him on some kind of stretcher. He said his ankles were injured..."

"Slingshot...continue to observe. We are in contact with highers to see if there's a plan, over."

"Jolly one-five...we need some directions in a hurry. They're rigging a raft to float him across..."

"Slingshot...stand by..."

"There ain't time to stand by! He's in the water. I'm gonna put some artillery over there on the north bank..."

"Slingshot...negative...I say again, negative on the arty. Our highers don't want to take a chance on hurting the good guy..."

"He's already hurt. That's a Marine out there, goddammit...and he's gonna be hurt a lot worse if we don't do something in a hurry!"

"Slingshot...stand by..."

And he's fifty...maybe seventy-five meters away. Dirty, sweaty, bloody, fighting two broken ankles and a hopeless future...when he swivels his head on the makeshift raft. Gooks pushing him into the sluggish current and his eyes locked on the southern banks of the Ben Hai...a last look at freedom. Longing...pain...desperation...and he sees me. I fucking well know he sees me. Small shake of his bloody head. No use. You people let me down...and I'm gone.

Nothing we could do...short of suicide...or killing him during a firefight we couldn't win. And no way to forget the look in his eyes as he was trundled across the water into hell. No way to forget that...not ever.

16. Hue - 1996

After checking in with his sister, assuring her his stay in the small, cramped quarters she shared with husband and three children would be short, Senior Sergeant Tran Duc Minh walked across the newly-restored Nguyen Hoang Bridge toward the teeming market area on Hue's north side. His intention was to buy plastic sheeting to wrap the Laos File logbook and then find a safe place to hide it in or around the Imperial Palace...one place he felt sure no amount of reconstruction or building boom would ever disturb.

Yet as he paused amid the trestle spans of the bridge his old comrades detonated and dropped on the first day of their Tet attack on Hue to keep enemy reinforcements from rapidly crossing the Perfume River, he wondered if it wouldn't be better to simply heave the damned thing over the side; let the only record of that nightmare wash out to sea. Why not just do it and be done? Send word to the Cuban that his worries about the Long Mountain March were over; call off the dog.

No, not the Cuban bastard. Not him. He'd stay on the trail until the last witness was dead. The Laos File was the death knell. At least one of the bastards was still alive - cruel karma after all these years - but he wouldn't be for long if the contents of the file were revealed. Of course, Minh realized as he watched the muddy Perfume River slide beneath his sandals, that threat was what put the pig Chico on his trail. But why now? What had changed in the past few days?

Why now after decades of abject silence, after all the turbulent post-war years when he could have obliterated both evidence and witnesses with relative impunity? Unless...unless the Cuban bastard never knew the file existed. If that was true, only one possible scenario made sense: the Americans.

Somehow the Americans got wind of the story and began their own investigation into events at the Ban Karai Pass. That would account for the inquiries about the Laos File at the museum. And then Chico or his informants - discovered the Yankees were conjuring dangerous ghosts. Something like that would flush him from under the rocks. Something like that would have the Americans screaming for vengeance and put Chico squarely in front of a firing squad...or worse.

Minh walked off the Nguyen Hoang bridge headed for familiar territory on Hue's north side. Somewhere up ahead among the warrens and crannies of the Citadel was a safe spot for the Laos File. By now, the Cuban and a few powerful players in his own government would know he'd stolen it. That made Senior Sergeant Tran Duc Minh a fugitive and the record he carried in a simple straw hand basket his only life insurance.

17. Hanoi

Fortune smiles, thought Major Hiep, as he led the group of very distinguished visitors through the museum courtyard toward the archive section. Mrs. Ngoc off searching for that idiot Minh, and who should show up at the museum but General Vo Nguyen Giap, the country's most venerated hero, and an American General, the senior soldier of the American contact team. He'd requisitioned a cleaning crew from the administrative support section just this morning when he found Sergeant Minh absent from his post and the place was spotless. If General Giap was conducting a tour for the American visitors, he could point with pride at pristine symbols of victory.

They stepped into the main exhibition hall and Major Hiep paused to flick on the lights, smiling proudly at the American woman officer who'd spent such an enjoyable time with at the opera. He'd invited her to visit anytime, but he hardly expected her to show up the very next day in the company of such senior officers.

A chilling thought crossed his mind as he watched the Americans and General Giap pause by the Great Trail display. The American woman had been discreet but persistent in conversation; asking him probing questions about American prisoners. He'd mentioned the complete records contained in the museum files. Could that be the reason the visitors asked for immediate access to the archives? And on the very day the chief archivist goes missing...

General Giap crossed the main hall and leaned on his bamboo cane as he led the American visitors slowly up the stone stairs. Major Hiep excused himself as he pushed by the American woman officer and fumbled with his ring of master keys.

"The archivist is absent today, General Giap. My apologies. I will have the door open in a moment..."

"Sergeant Minh? He is absent from his post?" The old warrior's voice was sharp and snappish. "Where is he?"

"We are trying to find out, General. He is an old man, perhaps he..."

Major Hiep wisely shut up when he saw the angry squint of General Giap's dark eyes. The general bobbed his chin at the padlock and Hiep snapped it open. It was dark inside so Major Hiep rushed to throw open the shutters admitting pale rays of afternoon sunlight. The archive area remained in gloomy shadow. Hiep scurried toward a bank of lamps.

"Do not trouble yourself, Major. We will only be here for a short time." General Giap consulted a scrap of paper from his pocket and then began to pace slowly along the rows of filing cabinets, counting as he walked. He stopped at Row C, counted five cabinets from the end and then pulled at a key suspended from his uniform buttonhole by a length of braided leather. He unlocked the cabinet and spent a few moments pawing through the top drawer.

"Major..." Hiep rushed to join the general in the banks of filing cabinets, leaving the two Americans staring into the shadows after him. "...where is the file normally kept in this cabinet?"

Hiep kept his voice low and confidential. "Does the General mean the file concerning Americans in Laos?"

"Of course I mean that file, Major. It is always kept here...under my orders. But it is not here now. Where is it? Has it been moved?"

"No, General! That file is never moved. No one sees it except..."

"Sgt. Minh..." The old general smiled and shoved weakly at the heavy file drawer. "...and he is missing from his post?"

"Yes, General. The last time anyone saw Sgt. Minh was yesterday morning...here at the museum."

"And you have checked his quarters?"

"Yes, General. Mrs. Ngoc sent a guard yesterday afternoon and she is out looking for him now. He has not been seen."

Vo Nguyen Giap nodded and gestured with his cane at the two Americans. "Turn on the lights, have someone prepare tea and then station yourself outside the door, Major. Let no one approach or enter until I tell you different."

As Major Hiep rushed to carry out his orders, General Giap limped from the shadows and motioned for the American visitors to take chairs. He let himself down slowly into Sgt. Minh's chair behind the single rickety desk in the anteroom and steepled his fingers. General Gordon Fowler and Major Chan Dwyer exchanged a questioning glance and then concentrated on Giap as the old general began to speak. His voice was solemn, reedy and resigned.

"I will tell you a story now...about Laos and about a large number of your countrymen. You will find what I have to say shocking...perhaps beyond belief. Yet, for now, you must take my word that these things happened. The proof I was going to offer has...disappeared."

18. Stateside

The man called Bayer punched the stop button on the mini-cassette recorder and scanned the two pages of notes he'd taken while listening to the decrypted voice message from Chan Dwyer in Vietnam. On the other side of the desk, Bayer's boss sat with his eyes closed and his chin bobbing over steepled fingertips.

"Most of it's just like we figured...assuming you can credit the source."

"Good Lord, Robert!" Beal waved a hand dismissing the thought. "Who would know better what happened to those men in Laos?"

"So why does Vo Nguyen Giap, former Commander-in-Chief of the PAVN...the guy who will be at the center of the shit-storm if the story goes public...suddenly decide to let us in on it?"

Beal leaned forward in his wheelchair and snatched at the recorder. He cued the tape, listened, rewound a bit more and then punched the play button. "Listen again, Robert...listen carefully." Chan Dwyer's phrases were distinct over the electronic sibilance imparted by the scrambling equipment.

"...he didn't seem to be apologizing. It seemed to me more like a welcome, uh...unburdening, I guess is the word that fits. It was all fairly straight-forward. The POWs were meant to arrive alive and well in Hanoi. Those were his specific orders to the Group 559 people. He was very clear and emphatic about that. He blames what happened primarily on the Cubans... specifically the two mentioned in our Ops-BG material...Fidel and Chico. Colonel Armondo Ochoa-Desidro is the guy all right...he's Fidel...and totally out of control, according to Giap..."

Beal stopped the tape and shoved the recorder back across his desk. "Giap's in no danger...at least not from this incident. He gives up the story, verifies it with some remorse, calls it a mistake and points his aging finger at the Cubans. Wouldn't surprise me if he's ultimately viewed as a compassionate statesman who finally cleared the air and brought the whole goddamn thing full circle."

"They can't dodge the shrapnel on this one, Rod! No way! This gets out, people will be screaming bloody murder, Congress will slam the cash box shut on this normalization thing and we'll see an international war crimes tribunal that will make Nuremburg look like traffic court."

Beal shook his head and wheeled his chair toward a coffee urn in the corner of the office. "Ten years ago...even five years ago...with a different President in the White House...maybe. But not now, Robert. Not when the economy is slumping, trade balance is badly skewed on the export side and industry is pressuring Congress for lucrative overseas markets.

"Clinton's spin-specialists will eliminate the negative; accentuate the positive. An answer - after all these frustrating years of silence - brought to us through the altruistic senti-ments and good conscience of an old soldier about to fade away. More importantly...the principal villains are not Viet-namese...but Cuban."

"That's gonna be a long credibility stretch for most Americans, Rod..."

"Nonsense! Most Americans are so self-absorbed they can't see dog shit on their doorstep. Vietnam's a non-issue...has been for a decade now. Listen, I took a look at my grand-daughter's high school history book last week. You know how much they covered Vietnam? Three fucking paragraphs, Robert. Ten years, a whole generation of young Americans wiped out and it gets three paragraphs in a history book!"

"Yeah...everybody remembers who won the Super Bowl; nobody remembers who lost. We got short memories when it comes to something unpleasant. So what now, boss? If the file has gone missing - presumably with this caretaker guy from the Central Military Museum - we're back where we started."

"Hardly, Robert. In fact, we are in fairly good shape here." Beal sipped lukewarm coffee and wheeled his chair back toward the desk. "All we need do now is simply stir the stick."

The man called Bayer clicked his pen into action and poised it over a yellow legal pad, waiting for instructions. He'd worked with Beal long enough to recognize when a plan of action was formulating in the man's brain.

"Pass word through our man in Cuban State Security. We are ready to make a deal for Ochoa-Desidro."

"He'll know about it 15 minutes after we make the overture..."

"Precisely. And he'll run...probably by sea and then by air through Bangkok. Alert our guy in Hanoi to get on the case...drop everything else. Go after the file...get on the trail of this Minh guy. Be there when Fidel shows and put him under wraps. I want him here and I want him alive."

"He won't be worth much unless you've got the Laos File, boss."

"We'll have the Laos File in short order, Robert. Trust me on this. We'll have the file and I'll have my Cuban right where I want him. All our man has to do is follow the hounds. Now that Giap's let the cat out of the bag, the Vietnamese will be falling all over themselves to find that file."

"It's not like 'em, boss. You gotta figure they'd rather stonewall this thing. The Viets have never much given a big rat's ass how they stand in world opinion."

"They do now, Robert, now that the IRDG is in place and about to resuscitate their country. They'll do anything to open the trade gates. Now comes this opportunity to clear the air and dodge a bullet at the same stroke. Consider. This is certainly the first the current Vietnamese government will have heard of the fate of our men captured in Laos. With the file in hand, they can stage a dog and pony show: show the world that what they've been saying all along - in other words, their official position on Americans missing in Laos - has been the truth...as they knew it. The Cubans were behind what happened...apparently the file reflects that conclusively...so the Vietnamese leadership won't be held accountable in the court of world opinion."

"And people are gonna buy that? When they find out the file containing the whole story was right there in Hanoi all the time?"

"Of course, they'll buy it! It was a conspiracy on the part of a few people high in Hanoi's wartime leadership. They're all dead or discredited now. It's perfect. It's another Oliver Stone movie."

The man called Bayer snapped his ballpoint out of battery and started for the door to the classified message center. "One last thing, boss. What about Davis?"

"Redirect the assets we've got on him, Robert. Davis is out of the loop now...a nonplayer."

19. Cam Ranh Bay

Shake Davis frowned at the shivering hulk of the GAZ jeep and winced as the driver elicited an agonized metallic squeal by stepping on the brake pedal. The grinning soldier-chauffeur ordered up by Lt. Pham while the corvette was docking at the huge deep-water port facility left the engine running - more or less - and began to heave baggage into the backseat. Pham moved forward to assert his authority as navigator and overall honcho of the upcoming road-trip while Shake moved up the greasy concrete quay to find Jeff Ault watching a gaggle of deckhands double up the corvette's forward mooring lines.

"Guess I'm gone in the next few minutes..."

Ault eyed the Soviet jeep and grinned. "All set, are you? I see the local motor pool spared no expense."

"I'm gonna be in traction next time you see me, for Christ's sake. Anyway, I'll be checking in with Chan at each stop...assuming we can find phones along the route."

"Well, I've got the itinerary Pham provided. I'll call it in and they can double-check on your progress from that end. Headed north from here, right?"

"Yeah, first stop is Tuy Hoa...couple of infantry battalions spread around up there. Shame we can't zip down south first and get a look at what used to be Saigon."

"Not to fret, pal. I'll take that mission for action."

"You fucking sailors get all the good deals."

"Which is exactly as it should be. Only those with stature and experience can provide meaningful intelligence on bars and whorehouses...which, I'm told, are still flourishing in the workers' paradise now known as Ho Chi Minh City."

Shake grinned and saluted. "If there's nothing else, Commander, I'll move out smartly."

Ault returned the grin and reached into a canvas gym bag at his feet. He handed over a bulky package wrapped in a worn towel from some BOQ he'd visited. "Little giftie for the road..."

Shake unfolded the towel and caught the dull metallic sheen of a pistol slide. Colt...Government Model, 1911A1, and in good shape at first glance. "Where the hell did you get this?"

"War souvenir according to the Chief Bosun who was anxious to barter it for my extra Seiko and an old pair of boondockers. There's a second magazine and 10 rounds. I didn't get a chance to test fire it, but it looks good."

"I won't need it, Jeff..."

"You fucking well might, if what you told me aboard ship is gospel. That grenade deal left me shaky about having you mill around unarmed. I think you got some people running scared around here, Shake, and evidence indicates they're not averse to blowing your ass away."

Shake rewrapped the pistol and stuck out his hand. "Thanks, Jeff. Like all good grunts suitably armed, I am now ten feet tall and bulletproof."

"Just keep your ass covered, kiddo. Check in when you can and don't go poking around in too many shit-piles."

Back at the loaded jeep, Lt. Pham introduced Private First Class Son Xuan who was selected for the trip because his father, a former Saigon cabbie, had taught him rudimentary mechanics and some useful phrases in English which he was anxious to try out on Shake Davis.

"OK, numbah one GI. We go Tuy Hoa. You souvenir me one cigarette."

Shake tossed a package of Marlboros into the front seat and climbed in the back. As they swung out of the Cam Ranh port facility onto Vietnamese Highway 1 headed north along the coast, he noticed Xuan's AK-47 and a bag of extra magazines on the floorboard. As he'd done at the beginning of hundreds of convoy runs elsewhere on this infamous road, he checked the chamber for a ready round, clicked the weapon onto safe and placed it near his knee where he could reach it in a hurry.

*   *   *

Fifty kilometers to the south of Cam Ranh Bay, near the dilapidated rail station at Phan Rang, former Master Sergeant Carlos Alejandro Reyes dumped his bulky kit-bag in the back of a sleek black Citroen sedan and slid into the front seat next to Thuy, his Nghe Tinh Group contact. The man had cold, hooded eyes and the flat, emotionless stare of a combat veteran. Comrade Duc had chosen wisely.

"A very pretty vehicle, comrade. You don't see many of them these days."

"A legacy from different times. I work as a mechanic in the government transportation facility at Cholon. It is not hard to find parts."

"You have been briefed on the situation?"

"Yes. Comrade Duc sent a message from Hanoi."

"Good. And the Americans?"

"Arrived at Cam Ranh Bay yesterday. One of them went south, the other headed north in a jeep. I am told you are interested in the latter."

"Correct. Do you have any idea where he is headed?"

"He will not be hard to find." The Nghe Tinh man pressed the starter button and the old Citroen rumbled to life. The engine sounded smooth and powerful which pleased Chico since speed was now a primary element in the chase.

"Head north," he said wallowing into the cracked leather seat for comfort. "First we find him, then we move ahead and search for a suitable place..."

"Ambush," said the Nghe Tinh man as he released the clutch and steered the Citroen onto the Route 1 access road. "I am familiar with the concept."

20. Hanoi

"You are familiar with the subject of this missing material?"

"In general terms...yes, of course, General. It has been some time since I read it."

General Nguyen Phu Dinh, Chief of Staff of the Peoples Army of Vietnam, glanced up at the nervous, disheveled female officer standing before his desk. He was by nature a chivalrous man, usually genteel around women in or out of uniform but the exhausting round of meetings he'd just completed left him short tempered. Lieutenant Colonel Ngoc, Head Curator of the Central Military Museum, could damn well stand there at attention until he was finished with her and do without tea or amenities.

"It is your responsibility, is it not, to safeguard any and all material entrusted to your care...particularly material that is considered most secret?" He watched the beads of perspiration forming at Ngoc's receding hairline and felt pangs of pity. The woman was caught in a box she could not open.

"Under direct orders from General Vo Nguyen Giap, the material was the responsibility of Senior Sergeant Tranh Duc Minh. I must assume he has stolen it."

"Just so, Ngoc...and what would cause Senior Sergeant Minh to do that...now...after all these years?"

"I believe it has something to do with the Americans, General." And the Cubans, she thought, particularly the Cubans...but General Dinh could do without that information. "My staff reports that two of them visited recently, asking questions about a missing American...one of those names contained in the Laos File. Sergeant Minh was aware of the inquiries. As you know, he was with Group 559 at the end of the war..."

"What are his intentions, Ngoc? Will he destroy the file?" General Dinh dearly wished the fugitive sergeant would do precisely that and put an end to some of his recently-discovered problems.

"I do not think so, General. Minh's status is dependent on his relationship with General Giap. I do not think he would destroy the material without consulting General Giap."

"Well, that has not happened. I spoke with the General this morning. He has heard nothing from Minh...which brings us back to you, Ngoc. Do you have any idea where Minh might have gone?"

"He has family in Hue, General...a sister I believe."

"Very well..." Dinh scribbled a note on the pad at his elbow. "Is there anything else I should know?"

Mrs. Ngoc sensed a chance to further incriminate the scar-faced weasel that put her under the deadly guns of the PAVN high command. "I believe Senior Sergeant Minh is a member of the Nghe Tinh Group, General. He may have appealed to them for assistance."

The PAVN Chief of Staff pinched his broad nose and tried to will away the throbbing behind his eyes. The more he fished, the muddier the waters got. "You are dismissed. Say nothing to anyone of this matter. Hold yourself available to report here on short notice."

Alone for virtually the first time since rising on a confusing day, he dug in a desk drawer for the strong East German aspirin tablets he favored and swallowed two of them with water. He'd had no time to eat and the aspirin would likely add heartburn to his headache but there were more pressing problems at hand.

He was under binding orders from Premier Do Muoi to drop everything, find this bastard Sergeant Minh and rescue the Laos File...if that was still possible. The Premier had explained in nagging, unnecessary detail how diplomatically critical it was. Vital to the future of the nation. Bigger and more important than any mission since the end of the war. General Giap - consider him nattering old fool or supreme patriot - still had the influence to set big wheels in motion. There was no turning back; no denying the truth or calling out the propaganda pundits to obfuscate the issue.

Fortunately, the current leadership - both civilian and military - could truthfully claim ignorance when the story was told...and that would not be long now that General Fowler had the ugly gist of it direct from an unimpeachable source. The Americans would at last have answers about their men missing in Laos and, incriminating as those answers were, the vast majority of the guilt could be dumped squarely on non-Vietnamese members of the socialist fraternity.

All the requisite hold-harmless documentation was contained in the Laos File. He would have to move quickly and decisively...especially if the Nghe Tinh Group might be involved. If a bunch of bitter old soldiers got their hands on the file, it would be lost forever. They would not understand the new and vital necessity for full disclosure. Members of the Nghe Tinh Group had their own view of the way the war was fought and they would never allow that honorable, heroic perception to be confused by contrary facts.

General Nguyen Phu Dinh knew differently, of course. He'd been a company commander for the last three long years of the war with the Americans. He was well aware of many brutal, heartless acts and cruelties that exceeded the general ravages of combat...but this business with the American prisoners was incredible even to an old, experienced soldier. He'd been genuinely shocked at the morning briefing. From a professional military viewpoint and from a personal perspective, what happened was outrageous. No wonder it was such a closely guarded secret. No wonder Giap had used his still considerable influence to keep the information under wraps.

Well, he thought as he swiveled to reach the secure phone on the small bookcase behind his desk, it is time for damage control. He pressed a four-digit key code and Nguyen Van Linh, communist party chief of the Republic, answered an identical phone in his office near the center of the city.

"We have a lead. He may have gone to Hue where he has family."

"Good. I have been in contact with Havana. The Cubans are not happy...but that cannot be helped at this late date."

"And our two gallant wartime allies?"

"One missing since 1975. Never returned to Cuba and presumed dead. The other very much alive and - listen to this, Dinh - about to be turned over to the Americans!"

"So? All that's needed now is the file and the fall-out will be greatly diminished. Our General Varney and his ghouls can go home with evidence in hand."

"Finding the file is your business, Dinh. You heard Do Muoi this morning as well as I did: Quick action, full disclosure. We are to appear as shocked as the Americans will be."

"That will not be hard. I have received some information that the Nghe Tinh Group may be involved. This man Minh is apparently a member."

"Very well. The dissidents are my concern. I will look into it. Keep me informed."

General Dinh disconnected and reached for another phone that provided a direct line to the PAVN military command center. The Duty Officer responded before the second ring.

"Find Captain Mai Van Hung of the Z-18 Company. Have him here in my office in one hour or less."

*   *   *

Unfamiliar with remote message machines, Colonel Thanh Thi Ngoc shouted into the phone trying to elicit a voice beyond the electronic tone she heard when her call was answered at the Cuban Embassy. In frustration, she disconnected and sought help from the supervisor at the Central Telephone Exchange.

"A very important call..." she insisted when the shift supervisor complained of over-taxed circuits and other priorities for the few available lines, "...most urgent business of the General Political Directorate."

"Then why not use the military exchange? They certainly have better equipment and..."

"If this call could be placed through military circuits, I certainly would not be here, comrade. There is a reason why I must use your lines. Will you help me...or shall I call my headquarters and let them explain priorities?"

The shift supervisor was in no mood to tangle with the military...certainly not the power-players in the GPD who were unaccustomed to having their methods questioned. Better jobs than his had been lost as a result of lesser confrontations.

"I will clear a line. Where were you calling?"

"The Cuban Embassy."

"Cuba?"

Mrs. Ngoc nailed the bureaucrat with a reproachful glance and flipped pages in her pocket notebook. "The Cuban Embassy in Hanoi. This is the number."

The shift supervisor donned a headset and manipulated switches on his console. He punched in the number pointing to a phone on a nearby desk. "We have a clear line. You can take the call there."

Mrs. Ngoc picked up the receiver, listened to the static for a moment and then heard the phone on the other end ringing. After three rings she heard the frustrating electronic tone and shouted at the supervisor.

"There! That's the same thing that happened when I tried it before. There is something wrong with the line."

"It is a machine on the other end." The telephone supervisor shook his head at her ignorance but carefully kept his face hidden. "The party you are calling has installed a recording machine. You may speak now and leave a message."

When she did not respond, the supervisor turned to stare at the GPD officer. She covered the mouthpiece with one hand and pointed at the door with the other. He got the message and walked toward a small break room in the back of the exchange.

Mrs. Ngoc felt foolish talking to a tape recorder. Trying to make her voice sound young and seductive, she phrased her message in short sentences full of references she was sure Fidel would recognize. "I have had a visit...from our friend...the one who used to call for you in Cu Loc? I am curator of the Central Military Museum these days and our friend was seeking access to the archives. Perhaps he was interested in certain material concerning the Truong Son Corps in 1972? I thought you would want to know...that material has disappeared. It has been stolen. The authorities here are mounting a search for it. That is all I can say now. I hope you are well. I hope you will call..."

She gave her number at the museum, hung up and left the central telephone exchange. Negotiating sluggish traffic on Dien Bien Phu Avenue headed back to the Central Military Museum, she was ruthless at horn and wheel. She cursed pedestrians, motorists and cyclo drivers loudly and mercilessly. Between confrontations she cursed herself for acting like a moonstruck schoolgirl, and praised herself for taking the initiative in a situation that hopefully would improve her status and security. In fact, if she was able to do this one thing right; if she was able to leverage her value in this quest, her old lover might turn out to be the ticket she needed to leave a frustrating life behind and reap some reward – finally – for all her years of service and sacrifice.

A glance at her reflection in the rearview mirror nearly brought tears. A beautiful, passionate man like Fidel would have aged handsomely. He'd have loved a hundred women since their nightly ravishings at Cu Loc. Even if he remembered the heat of that flame, he'd have no time for a parched old cow in Vietnam. She'd have to do everything in her power to change his mind.

21. Cuba

Crouched in a thick copse of palm and pine on the beach near Cienfuegos on his country's south coast, Colonel Armondo Ochoa-Desidro heard the motorized patrol roar along the road to his rear. Half an hour before that, he'd watched an Mi-8 helicopter cruise slowly overhead, playing a light over the plunging surf line; searching the white sand for a fugitive who might be anywhere in the island's forty-two thousand square miles. In the next five minutes or so one of the heavily-armed, shallow-draft patrol boats would pass, hoping to stopper the ocean bolt-holes most fugitives used to escape from Cuba.

Ochoa-Desidro was worried but not about his ability to escape the Cuban State Security forces searching frantically for him all over the island. He was too old, too experienced, too wealthy and well-connected for the bumblers out here in the boondocks to have a shot at him. Even the relatively sharp KGB-trained operatives in Havana were not hard to dodge and duck given the early warning provided by his well-paid informants in Castro's corrupt Interior Ministry.

What worried Colonel Ochoa-Desidro as he waited for a signal from the gloom beyond the surfline was his future...beyond Cuba, beyond Vietnam, the unexpected detour he was now having to make. Just five short years ago, had the bottom fallen out - as every clandestine operator in the business knew it might at any time - he could have disappeared seamlessly into Eastern Europe. After years of looting and generous salaries from wealthy despots and dictators around the world, he was well-heeled in precious metals and more solid, negotiable currencies than he could recall. Shadow warriors like Ochoa-Desidro did not survive long without carefully prepared and protected "spook stashes" for those times when international tides turned unexpectedly.

Now - at the worst possible time for him naturally - the gutless former zealots of Europe and Asia decide the price of the prize is too high. Nowhere safe in the former Soviet Union. His oldest cronies in the communist underworld would sell him out for a case of vodka these days. Old allies meant nothing anymore. It was the old enemies that never forgot...like that American bastard from the Bay of Pigs. His confidant in the Foreign Ministry said his ass was definitely on the auction block and Rodney Beal of the American DIA was high bidder.

His original plan had been to head for the Orient. He'd thought to join his old *compadre* in Vietnam, rent protection until the heat died down, and retire to greener pastures in Bangkok or Rangoon where his oriental language skills would keep him on top of things. But the stop in Asia would be brief now; a way station while he handled some unexpected business. He could become like the former Nazis, hunted and haunted everywhere, unless he managed to deal decisively with the Laos affair.

Colonel Ochoa-Desidro heard the burble of patrol boat engines and flattened himself next to the dark rubber bulk of his equipment bag. The bright beam of a xenon searchlight speared the tree line, swept over his head twice and then moved on, probing the beach to the west of his position. He propped himself up on his elbows and stared out beyond the whitecaps marking the offshore reef. No signal yet from the smugglers in the flat-black speedboat hired for the run to Santo Domingo but they'd wait until the patrol was well down the coastline. They were both expert at this kind of thing and paid well beyond what they might expect for turning him over to the authorities.

Keeping his eyes on the dark horizon, he went over the itinerary, cobbled together rapidly after he retrieved the startling message from Vietnam on the dead-drop phone planted in the storage area of a sugar cane processing plant on the fringes of Havana. That equipment - upgraded periodically until it was no longer necessary for him to do anything but dial a number and transmit tones to retrieve messages - had been a lifeline for many years. Mostly he got good news: valuable intelligence, job offers, contacts, training opportunities for people who needed his unique talents and were willing to pay handsomely for them. Occasionally, a bombshell dropped like the one from the old *puta* in Hanoi, transferred from his special voice mail at the Embassy. He'd long forgotten that he even gave her the number when he left Vietnam after the debacle at Ban Karai Pass.

Fortunately she had not forgotten and was smart enough to call when the flames of an ancient fiasco suddenly threatened to burn her old bedmate. Ochoa-Desidro barely remembered Ngoc beyond a few basic details. She was married to a PAVN officer; a minor functionary in the GPD herself. He recalled a ravenous she-devil, a sexual enthusiast, an acrobat who tested his stamina and slaked his frustrations during the time he was dealing with the American prisoners at Cu Loc. A woman who survives in the GPD, a woman who runs the Central Military Museum in Hanoi, does not take risks unless there is still a smoldering fire in her belly.

He would certainly return Ngoc's call; probably from Vientiane after he successfully negotiated his planned passage through Santo Domingo, Lima and Kuala Lumpur to find Chico and ensure destruction of that damning file. Ngoc would be very glad to see him again...and very handy in getting the job done. It boiled down to a footrace: The Vietnamese authorities versus Fidel, Chico and Ngoc, together again. No contest, he assured himself as his eyes detected a blip of light on the dark slash between sky and sea.

Three green...three red. His ride was idling offshore. Colonel Armondo Ochoa-Desidro flashed the designated response and clipped the mini-light to his jacket. He slung his waterproof kit bag onto his back and bit into the hard rubber mouthpiece of the excellent American Dreager LAR V rebreather strapped to his chest. Glancing cautiously up and down the beach, he opened the compressed air propulsion valve on the ultra-quiet, bomb-shaped Scuba Scooter, pulled the dive mask over his face and dashed for the water.

If all went as planned in the next 10 days or less he'd be well under cover and comfortable in the Congo or Zimbabwe. South America was preferable, but the Americans had too many tentacles there these days.

22. Hanoi

"Air transportation has been arranged. You will take whatever assets you think necessary, proceed to Hue and find this man. Quickly and quietly." General Nguyen Phu Dinh shoved a photograph of Than Duc Minh across his desk. It was a grainy black and white from Minh's Central Military Museum employment file.

"At least there will be no need to copy and distribute the picture," commented Captain Mai Van Hung as he studied the ravaged features of his quarry. "Anyone who sees this man will remember him."

"Use whatever methods you deem appropriate, Hung. Just remember, the material he has stolen is more important than he is. It is the file we are after..."

"And we are fairly certain he has not destroyed it, General?" The Commanding Officer of the elite Z-18 Special Operations Company was fairly certain of what he would do if he were this little rodent Minh. He'd consign such material to flame and ashes long before it could cause harm to the nation he was sworn to protect. As he often reminded his dedicated, deadly soldiers when the Z-18 was called on to deal with "internal problems" at one place or another in the country, the enemy is anyone who will not obey or abide by the will of their leaders.

"Our opinion is that Senior Sergeant Minh would not destroy the file for a variety of reasons. He is under orders from General Giap personally to protect and preserve the material. An old soldier such as Minh is likely to consider such orders sacred. From a more practical point of view, the material in the Laos File proves that Minh and other members of Group 559 - and by extension the Peoples Army - were not completely to blame for what happened to the Americans in Laos."

"How much time do we have, General?"

"You have as much time as you need. If you become convinced he is not in Hue, search elsewhere...but proceed carefully. Do not frighten this man into doing something rash."

"Very well, general..." Captain Hung stood and saluted. "My men will be in Hue tomorrow. Is there anything else?"

"Just be aware that this Minh is a member of the Nghe Tinh Group. Those hardheads may attempt to interfere or get their hands on the file to destroy it. See to it that does not happen."

23. I Corps

Tran Duc Minh was savoring the pungent aroma of an excellent crab soup when his brother-in-law rushed into the tiny restaurant on the south bank of the Perfume River near the sports stadium. Minh motioned to a chair across the table but his brother-in-law was in no mood to eat a relaxed lunch.

"Soldiers," he whispered looking around the restaurant for uniformed patrons. "They came to the house an hour ago. Very tough men. All business...and all looking for you."

"Why?" Minh felt his appetite, so keen just a few minutes ago, fade to a dull ache below his belt.

"They didn't say...but you are in trouble, Minh. These men are going to find you."

"You told them I was here...in Hue?"

"Your sister did. She was afraid for the children. I am sorry for that."

"She had no reason to lie. She knows nothing about why I came to the city."

"Nor do I, Minh. And please do not tell me. If I know nothing, I will say nothing. They left two soldiers at the house, so you will not be able to go back for your things." Minh's brother-in-law dropped a plastic shopping bag near the table. "I was able to bring some clothes. You should change out of your uniform and go now. They are searching everywhere."

Minh stared longingly at the crab soup, thanked his relative and picked up the shopping bag. "They will leave you in peace shortly. When they do not find me here, they will move on." Minh glanced at the crowds outside the restaurant. With a face like his, even a sea of people provided no anonymity. "Don't worry, brother. You will see me no more in Hue. Enjoy the soup. It's very good."

He ducked into shadows twice along the southern fringes of Doc Lao Park near the Perfume River's edge as truckloads of soldiers roared by on Tran Cao Van Street. They were the ones searching for him; specialists brought in for the job. It was easy to tell them from the bored teenagers stationed nearby at Hue's garrison command. These men were older, harder; wrapped in better uniforms and equipment. Very likely from the Z-10 or Z-18 Special Operations companies in Hanoi, Minh suspected, noting the scaled-down version of the familiar AK-47 most of them carried. Only special troops got the relatively new AKSU-74 which fired a smaller 5.45mm round.

These hard young men would turn Hue upside down in an attempt to find him but Minh had more time in the soldier game...both as hunter and prey. He saw the high walls of Tu Do sports stadium; wondering what instinct guided him in this direction when he spotted two small boys splashing each other by hurling a soccer ball into a puddle of dirty water near a storm drain. Of course, he smiled at a memory from Tet Nguyen Dan, the Year of the Monkey, and dashed across the broad avenue, heading for an area he remembered on the east side of the stadium.

For three days before the assault on Hue began on January 30, 1968 Minh and his comrades from the Reconnaissance Platoon of the 800th Infantry Battalion lived in and ran scouting operations out of the labyrinth of inter-connected storm drains beneath Hue's city streets. Built by the French in the mid-nineteenth century to direct and divert the flow of the Perfume River's complex of feeder streams and canals, the sewer system allowed them to move virtually everywhere undetected, popping up when and where they wanted simply by lifting one of the concrete slabs that provided access to a broad, pervasive underground highway.

Than Duc Minh milled around the block of sidewalk on the stadium side of Tran Cao Van street where he recalled there was an access to the tunnel system. He found the place in the dark shadow of a teak tree and probed with his fingers. Yes, it would lift easily. The sky above him was filled with dark, scudding clouds and the air was heavy with moisture. It would rain soon but the brunt of the monsoon deluge was a day or two away from starting.

If he could escape flash floods; steer clear of heavy run-offs for a while, he'd be safe. When the street cleared of nearby traffic, he stooped quickly, shifted the concrete slab to one side and disappeared.

*   *   *

On the road rolling north out of Tuy Hoa, crossing what used to be the MACV operational boundary between II Corps and I Corps, Shake Davis was busy stuffing plastic sheeting around the windshield on the passenger side of the GAZ jeep where the rubber sealing strip had rotted. Heavy rain squalls hit just south of Qui Nhon and by the time they reached the outskirts of the city water was blowing through every crack and crevice of the vehicle.

While Shake and driver Xuan stopped to affect some jerry-rig waterproofing, Lieutenant Pham caught a ride into the city to check with the commander of the unit they were scheduled to visit. He was back in less than an hour, soaked to the skin and not at all happy to report there would be nothing of interest for them to see at Qui Nhon. Combat units of the 48th Regiment, 320th Infantry Division were doing flood control and road repair work at Binh Dinh northwest of the city. Unfortunately, the phone lines were down and it would be evening before they could even report the situation to Hanoi.

After a quick meal, Pham checked with a southbound bus driver and discovered the weather was slightly less miserable to the north. They could either kill the day, call in and spend the night at Qui Nhon, or push on and hope for better luck with the elite 126th Naval Group at Quang Ngai.

Shake was reluctant to climb back into the soggy jeep and subject his lumbar vertebrae to the pounding of stiff suspension rolling over the inevitable gauntlet of monsoon potholes. In four days on the road he'd learned that Private First Class Son Xuan considered turning the wheel to avoid various road hazards akin to abject cowardice. It would be a rough trip but making it would put him in the southern reaches of old I Corps, the 1st Military Region; familiar territory and the site of most of his combat experience in Vietnam.

"We can't get much wetter than we already are. Let's push on and I'll call Hanoi from Quang Ngai to give them an update on our progress."

Two hours later, satisfied that Xuan had no suicidal intent and lulled into a stupor by the slow, nearly useless sweep of the wiper on his side of the windshield, Shake was nodding off. From the backseat Lt. Pham spotted a familiar landmark and announced they were about 20 kilometers out of Quang Ngai.

"There was much fighting here in 1969," he said. "My father was involved..."

Yeah...much fighting. Shake Davis squirmed some of the wrinkles out of his soggy skivvies and let his chin drop to his chest. There was much fighting at Quang Ngai...and it was a stone dickhead.

24. Quang Ngai - 1969

Roughrider convoy rolling south out of Chu Lai. Elements of the 4th ARVN Armored Cavalry Regiment roaring in to rescue a gaggle of their headquarters hacks in a desperate punch-out with NVA sappers trying to file a claim on the provincial capitol at Quang Ngai. Five sand-bagged six-by's led by two jeeps sizzling through the monsoon rain giving the stoic troopers crammed into the truck beds their first bath in weeks.

Miserable little shits now but they'll be wishing for nothing more than a wet, cold ride in the other direction by the time we hit the city. Initial reports garbled and panicky. Shades of Surprise '68, it's another Tet Offensive! Call it Mini-Tet or Round Two of the Great Uprising That Never Was. Landlines cut after the first call for help. Major attack. Sappers methodically hitting strategic targets with high explosive. NVA infantry moving on the regimental headquarters. No air support due to this fucking zero-zero weather.

More information gleaned from ARVN defenders when they finally check in on the tac radio nets. Scattered friendly units cut off and surrounded throughout the city. No sign of hit and run. NVA apparently making a major play for control of the area. Send help and send it now or the gallant clerk-typists and fat cats of the Quang Ngai garrison command will be greatly inconvenienced.

At Danang to the north little hands flutter over big maps. Well hell, we got us a glob of mechanized infantry right here north of Quang Ngai city. They've only been in the field on scrounge rations for two weeks in a running gunfight with them little pissants in the 2nd VC Infantry Regiment. Search the whorehouses. Round up the American advisors. Make sure they take along the jarhead that just checked into the unit out of the hospital. Be good experience in joint ops. Maybe the Army guys can teach him how we do things in this A-O.

So the Army guys all pack into the lead jeeps with heaters and canvas tops. The jarhead - assigned to the unit because some stateside computer running Tricky Dick's retrograde Vietnamization Program declared him an excess asset - winds up bead-blasted by rain sheeting off an M2 heavy-barrel .50 caliber machinegun in the ring mount of the third truck. It's like standing in a wind tunnel while some sadistic asshole soaks you with a fire hose.

Skating through a hard curve at the 10K marker. First refugee gaggles headed away from the city under siege. Strobing flashes on the horizon. What looks like lightning from the low cloud cover is really a major mortar attack. NVA 82mm tube crews pounding the piss out of Quang Ngai. At least we ain't the only ignorant bastards who believe you can save a place by destroying it.

Water-logged ARVN prives in the trucks have got the picture now. Lock and load. Some fumbling with cold-numbed fingers. Silly grins mask the fear they're feeling. Poor bastards can't even smoke a cigarette to distract them from what lies ahead: Yet another battle in the long war that's been a total immersion experience since the day they were born. Spend any amount of time with these guys and you learn quickly they don't waste precious minutes fantasizing about peace or hoping for an end to it all. Combat becomes a permanent lifestyle. It's over when you get your dumb ass killed...and not before. There it is. Live with it while you can.

Closer now...beginning to pinpoint specific sources in the roar and rattle ahead. ARVN checkpoint guarding the main artery approach to Quang Ngai blown high and wide. Five...six...dead behind a 106mm recoilless rifle. Gooks must have been in a hurry to pass that prize. Or maybe they're still...

"Rockets! Swing right...goddammit! Don't stop!"
Gasping...dizzy...slammed hard into the breech of the fifty. Fucking driver saw the flash from the tree line. He knows better than to hit the brakes. Grinding crunch from up front...smoke, fire and small arms. Bastards hit one of the trucks or a jeep with an RPG.

"Reverse! Turn it around...get the fuck outta here!"
Driver grinding the guts out of the gearbox. Trying to duck incoming and twist through the pile-up. Both rear trucks slewed sideways across the road. Hydroplaned like beer mugs on a wet bar when the drivers stomped the brakes.

ARVN troopers mashed and bashed all over the area, scrambling around like maggots in a stump. Gotta bring some to get some, people.

"Open fire on the tree line! Stay in the trucks. Open up!"
Haul the heavy fifty around, flip the trigger safety bar free and mash with both thumbs. Lean back and let the big Browning roll. Watch the tracers. Walk the heavy slugs along the base of the tree line. Got to get on top of this situation in a hurry. One jeep burning up front and the other tits-up in the

ditch to the left of the road. No sign of survivors...which might make me the lone roundeye in this particular shit sandwich.

Wave of wet heat from the rear. Feel it before you see it. Crispy Critters in the last truck by now. No surprise when you're playing with the pros. Classic convoy ambush. Gook RPG gunner cooking by the book. Hit the lead vehicle then scramble along the road and clobber Tail End Charlie before the rats can reverse out of your trap.

ARVN troopers bailing over the side away from the incoming. Maybe thirty still functional including my driver who just volunteered into the grunts. No time to look for the *dai huy*, but if the ARVN CO is still alive, he'll round up the strays. Key is to give 'em a little time.

Gooks along the spine of the linear ambush well aware of that and dead-set against it. At least two RPD machineguns sweeping the stalled convoy, probing for meat, blasting through tires, gas tanks and side panels. And that fucking RPG gunner just put a rocket into another truck! Heat and flames driving the ARVN into the off-side ditch. Won't be long before the gooks cross the road and start rolling up flanks.

Bail out is the smart move. Only a genuine dumb shit hangs up here in the turret ring drawing lead like a fucking magnet. So...let's just see how many rounds this big sonofabitch will fire before the barrel burns out. Let's just see if I can find that efficient little bastard with the B-40 rockets and put him out of business. And...please Jesus...let a little fifty caliber suppressing fire prompt the ARVN troopers to counter-attack across the road before my ass gets blown out of this truck.

"Go! Now, goddammit! Go! Across the road! Charge into 'em."

Smoke rolling off the barrel and breech of the Browning. Hard to see where the rounds are hitting. Won't matter in a minute or two. Either I bleed to death through the bullet hole in my thigh or the flames from that burning saddle tank will cauterize my ass out of the fight for good.

Below me a muddy wave of pissed off manpower. *Dai huy* shoving troopers into the fight and screaming into a handset for fire support. ARVN blowing through the treeline...on the move and pushing hard. Time to un-ass this blowtorch of a truck and seek shelter elsewhere. Fight's over...until it starts again... somewhere down the road...anywhere in this fucking Vietnam.

Just another day in the life of Marvin the ARVN. Another day; another dong. There it is.

25. Quang Ngai - 1996

At the 10K marker south of Quang Ngai city, driver Xuan downshifted, accidentally bumping the gear lever into Shake Davis' left thigh. The painful impact, on a slight concavity where puckered scar tissue covered an old war wound, jolted him awake. He waved a hand at Xuan's apology and rubbed at his eyes. Rain had tapered off to a light, steady mist prompting Lt. Pham to curl up under a poncho on the backseat bench. The GAZ slowed, balking in the lower gear as it powered into a tight right turn.

*   *   *

Chico Reyes felt the water pooling at his hips wash forward to settle under his belly. He sighed and cursed silently as cold seeped into his guts. This stuff is for younger men...or for men like Thuy who can focus on age-old hates and make the discomfort disappear.

Below his perch fifty meters above and to the right of the road, he caught the pale outline of Thuy's face pressed tightly against the stock of an AK-47. In a ditch on the other side of the road, the Nghe Tinh zealot had found a perfect position to key the ambush by sweeping his fire across the target at pavement level.

Reyes checked his watch and reviewed the situation. He could find no problem with preparations. They'd caught up with the target at army headquarters in Tuy Hoa. Thuy's reconnaissance had been complete and professional. During a loose, day-long surveillance while Chico stayed out of sight in the city, he noted the vehicle type and identity number, the American's escorts and their arms, and discovered from one of the local soldiers that the visitors would be leaving the next day for Qui Nhon.

Initial plans for an ambush along a lonely stretch of road between Tuy Hoa and Qui Nhon were spoiled by sheets of blowing, blinding monsoon rain. They pressed north at all speed the Citroen would handle in the storm, searching for a better opportunity somewhere behind the southbound weather front. At noon, cruising in steady drizzle, Thuy steered the Citroen through a blind curve and punched it into a farmer's access road where it would be hidden from the highway.

"Here," he announced switching off the engine. "We can hit them just after they come around the bend. They will see nothing until it's too late."

They spent the next twenty minutes checking fields of fire and watching traffic patterns. The rain was keeping people off the road except for a few over-loaded buses. Quang Ngai was only ten kilometers to the north allowing them ample opportunity to disappear as soon as the job was done. Nothing more to it. Just do it.

Chico Reyes heard the revving engine on the other side of the curve and the whine of a protesting transmission as the driver downshifted. This is it, he thought catching Thuy's affirmation signal. Target in sight. Ninety rounds of ball ammo in spare magazines on his chest pouch and thirty rounds of armor-piercing in the weapon. He focused on the tip of the front-sight post, nested it tightly in the notch of the rear leaf and watched the slatted grill of a GAZ jeep bend around the curve.

*   *   *

Shake Davis caught the billowing muzzle flash from their left front and reached for the steering wheel already bucking violently under Xuan's startled grip. They were just managing to hold it on the road against the wobble of two blown tires when fire from another direction slammed through the hood and killed the engine. Rounds were thumping loudly into the jeep as Shake struggled with Lt. Pham for possession of the AK-47 on the floorboards.

Pham leveraged the weapon free and kicked at the rear door, rolling out onto the wet pavement. Shake started to haul Xuan out from behind the wheel when a thumping burst shattered the windshield. He felt the sting of glass shards and saw blood on his hands as Xuan slumped across the seats. The driver's face and neck were distorted by at least three hits. There was no time to count...or fool with first-aid for a dead man.

Several rounds snapped close by his ears as he dove for the ditch on the right of the road. Trying to orient himself to the threat, he scrambled in the soggy muck and poked his head over the berm. Fire from his left front, on the other side of the road, ricocheted off the macadam and tore up the embankment at his back. He cringed below road level and duck-walked along the ditch until he was driven back by a muddy shower of rounds from his right rear.

Nice work, assholes. Classic ambush. And I am in no fucking position to counter or reciprocate. Believe I've been in this position before...somewhere right around here as a matter

of fact. Chased by a steady stream of incoming, Shake
scrambled along the ditch to the stretch directly behind the
riddled jeep and found Pham cradling the AK-47 tightly against
his chest.

Shake reached for the weapon but Pham retained full and
powerful possession. His dark eyes were wide and glaring
through a mask of mud. He was breathing in short gasps,
swallowing hard against the bile rising in his throat.

"Ambush, Pham!" Stating the obvious seemed to catch his
attention. Pham shifted his gaze to Shake and nodded grimly.
"We're gonna have to fight our way out of it!" Before they could
formulate a plan, Shake heard someone moving through the
thick bush that covered the ridge above them. "They're moving
on us. Give me the weapon!"

Plunging fire tore into the ditch splashing water and mud
over them. Pham's left leg spasmed as a round blew through
the calf. He rolled away trying to escape the fire sweeping down
from above but Shake snatched him by the belt and hauled him
up and out of the ditch. Crashing into a bamboo thicket, they
scrambled into defilade from the shooter above and out of the
direct line of fire from the man across the road whose view was
blocked by the riddled jeep.

Peering through the wet bamboo, listening to the slow,
deliberate movement of the shooter on the ridge, Shake
realized whatever they did, it would have to be quick. Dying in
place was not an option in his playbook. He forced himself to
think, squeezing tightly on Pham's bicep to keep the man
focused on their predicament rather than the pain in his leg.
Glancing over his shoulder, Shake saw the ragged hole in
Pham's blood-soaked trousers and hoped the bullet had missed
the bone.

"How's the leg?" Pham squirmed a little, testing mobility
as best he could in the prone position. "Not too bad. I think I
can walk...but where?"

Nowhere, pal. We aren't gonna walk away from this one.
Move forward and the guy across the road takes us out. Move
back and we run into the asshole on the ridge. Move right or left
and they've both got a shot. What we need is supporting
arms...or a fucking air strike...bring a little napalm to bear on
the situation...

Shake stared at the wrecked hulk of the jeep wishing he'd
been smart enough to snatch Ault's souvenir pistol before he
bailed out of it. But he was here and the .45 was over there,

across that slick pool of...fuel! Leaking all over the road from the punctured gas tank!

"Listen to me!" He stuck his nose close to Pham's ear and whispered urgently. "I'm going to set fire to the fuel out on the road. When it goes you get yourself across the road, into the ditch and take out the guy over there."

"What about this one?" Pham nodded toward the bush at their rear.

"He's moving...and he hasn't seen us yet or we'd be dead by now." Shake dug in his trouser pocket, found his Zippo and checked it. Flame jumped on the first stroke of the flint wheel and he silently blessed a bunch of skilled and conscientious people in Bradford, Pennsylvania. "When I give the word, you fire a burst up into the bush...try to pin him down for a minute before I go. There's just the one magazine, so be sure to save ammo for the one over there."

It was a crap-shoot with heavily-loaded dice, but Shake couldn't imagine what else to do. He nodded and watched Pham roll onto his back, aim the AK up at the bush, and return the nod. "Now!"

He heard the familiar cracking of the AK on full-auto and blew out of the bamboo, vaulting the ditch and sprinting for the middle of the road. His boots lost traction in the oily pool near the jeep. An unexpected and completely uncontrolled hook-slide saved him from the shooter in the ditch on the other side of the road who spotted the move and fired high. He was adjusting; sending rounds rattling through the driver's side of the GAZ, searching for his target when Shake Davis rolled over in the pool of high-octane fuel and fired his Zippo.

*   *   *

Pham gasped at the pain that shot up through his leg into his belly as he jumped into the ditch on the far side of the wet road. He caught a glimpse of movement to his right and saw a long, twinkling arc of cartridge cases as the low shooter pumped ammo at Shake. Hoping fervently none of the rounds found flesh, he was hit by a searing blast of super-heated air that drove him to the bottom of the ditch.

He recovered just in time to see the shooter scrambling down the ditch in his direction, snapping an empty magazine out of his rifle and reaching inside his shirt for a fresh load. In a flash, Pham noted the man was an older Vietnamese...civilian clothes but clearly a veteran from the way he manipulated the weapon...and then his training kicked in. He shouldered his weapon just as the shooter racked the AK bolt to chamber a round. As he squeezed the trigger, Pham's front sight was outlined clearly against the muzzle flash of the shooter's return fire.

*   *   *

He could feel the flames chewing at his wet uniform as Shake snaked an arm into the jeep and snatched the bundle containing the pistol and ammo. He gasped against the burning pain in his exposed neck and ears, but the air scorched his lungs and sent him scrambling madly away from the roaring ball of fire he'd just ignited.

His clothes were burning by the time he sucked in the first breath of cool air outside the inferno. He launched himself headlong into the muddy ditch and began to roll, splashing muck and water over the stinging flesh of his head and neck. He heard a fusillade of fire from the opposite side of the road but there was no time to see how Pham was doing. He was dead or alive. Either way the shooter on this side would have to be handled before they were home free.

Quickly unwrapping the precious pistol that gave him a slim but survivable chance, he jacked a round into the chamber and began to slither uphill into the bush.

*   *   *

Chico Reyes dropped to a knee when the heat from the blazing vehicle washed over him. It didn't take him long to figure out the unexpected turn of events. Fuel caught fire, he decided, and began to shove through the thick tangle of vines that grabbed at his legs. No time for stealth now, he realized. The fire will attract unwanted attention and the American is still alive.

These things never go exactly as planned, he reminded himself as he worked his way downhill toward the road. There are never any guarantees. His first shots should have killed the American. Then he missed the bastard on a clean shot down into the ditch. Chico cursed himself for that failed opportunity. Nothing but nerves; a jangling rush of unaccustomed adrenaline that snapped his eyes shut and caused him to jerk the trigger.

I'm too old for this shit, Chico admitted as he angrily pulled his foot free of a tree root. Too old, too soft; too long from the battlefield. The sniper rifle would have been a better idea. He should have found a hide and sniped the bastard at Tuy Hoa or Qui Nhon instead of turning a simple mission into a full-fledged fucking tactical exercise. Now he would have to find the American and kill him at close range. He was not averse to it; simply out of practice.

*   *   *

Shake heard the thrashing in the bush somewhere to his right front. He'd been hung up on enough wait-a-minute vines in enough jungles to realize what was happening. The shooter was losing patience. He was pissed off about the failed ambush and anxious to get the deed done before somebody spotted the smoke from the burning jeep and came to investigate.

There's the edge, he told himself as he dropped to his belly on the soggy jungle floor. A man who's fighting the jungle is out of control...and a man who's out of control can be killed. The shot would have to be clear and precise. That required close range given the untested pistol which was all he had. If he missed or if the weapon failed to fire, there would be no second chance.

Shake forced himself to study the jungle from a snake's perspective. As he listened to the shooter above him charge on, he began to see patterns in the nest of thick vines, stems and roots that criss-crossed his immediate vicinity. He focused on a thumb-sized green liana vine that snaked off to his right front across a low tree limb to disappear into what he hoped was the shooter's downhill path.

He jerked sharply on the vine and listened as the shooter reacted. The noise of his movement ceased almost immediately. Shake could almost see him...dropping to a knee...looking around carefully...eyes on a direct line with the muzzle of his weapon. He jerked on the vine again and heard the rasp of material on vegetation as the shooter changed direction. He slowly shoved the pistol forward with his right hand, keeping his left lightly draped over the vine which now served as an early-warning tripwire.

*   *   *

Lieutenant Pham got his breathing under control and snapped a quick look around a bend in the roadside ditch. No sign of the man with whom he'd exchanged fire moments ago. He was virtually sure he'd hit the man but there was nothing lying in the bottom of the ditch but an empty AK magazine and a pile of expended cartridge casings.

He's gone...scared off, Lt. Pham told himself as he checked the magazine and chamber of his weapon. Both were empty. He thought of his wife and son in Haiphong and wondered how they would survive if he was killed in this muddy ditch. He wondered who had ambushed them and why anyone would do such a thing to him. Of course...it was not him they were after. He was just an unfortunate who fell into the killing zone. They were after the American.

Pham raised his head just a fraction to peer over the rim of the ditch into the jungle on the other side of the road. He thought of his father who warned him against being a soldier. Just because you have no war, the old jungle fighter told his son, it does not mean you have peace.

*   *   *

He felt the vine tremble and took the slack out of the pistol's trigger. It slid smoothly back with no grit in the creep until the rear of the trigger stirrup contacted the smooth face of the disconnector. The merest pressure of his fingertip would now trip the sear and fire the round in the chamber...but that had to come at exactly the right time when the muzzle was pointed at exactly the right place.

He closed his eyes and forced his breathing to become slow and shallow. His fingertips played lightly on the vine through which he could sense the shooter's movement, feeling the trembles, tugs, and jerks like a fly fisherman plays a small trout. He heard a footfall, a squishing, as the shooter settled his weight and paused. Turning his head slightly to the right he saw a sandal touched by the soggy cuff of dark trousers.

When the heel of the sandal rose, indicating the shooter was on the move again, Shake stood silently, saw the target less than four feet away staring in the wrong direction and brought the front-sight blade to bear on the man's ear. He squeezed the trigger twice but the second shot went high.

The first heavy .45 slug slammed through Chico Reyes' ear canal into his brain and dropped him to the jungle floor like a wet sandbag.

*   *   *

Limping painfully uphill through the jungle toward the place where he heard the boom of a weapon that was definitely not a Kalashnikov assault rifle, Pham hoped he'd find Shake Davis. If there was another ambusher armed with an unfamiliar weapon, he was a dead man.

At a flat spot some twenty meters above the ditch he saw a pair of sandal-shod feet sticking through the bush. They were still and bent at odd enough angles to convince him the owner of those feet was probably dead. He carefully separated the surrounding vines and got confirmation.

The right side of the man's head was dented and distorted. The left side was missing completely. Barely enough remained for Pham to be certain the man was not Vietnamese. He was wondering about that when Shake Davis nearly froze his heartbeat, stepping out of the bush and glaring at him over the slide of a pistol.

"Did you get the other one?" Shake slipped the pistol into his waistband and bent to examine the corpse.

"I'm not sure. I emptied the magazine at him. He fired back. I ducked. When I looked, there was nothing."

"Who is this bastard...and what did we do to piss him off so badly?" Shake was examining a clutch of papers from the dead man's trouser pocket.

"What do his papers say?" Pham noticed the official Vietnamese government stamps on several of the documents.

"They say he is a man named Guitterez...some sort of technician from Nicaragua...but that's nonsense."

"How do you know?" Pham stared at the documents Davis handed him. They all looked legal and genuine.

"Think about it, Pham." Davis shrugged, winced and stood over the body. His uniform hung in charred tatters; his face and hands were seared a bright pink. "Why would a Nicaraguan technician visiting here want to ambush us? And this bastard is no Nicaraguan anyway. He's Cuban."

"How can you know that, Shake? There is barely enough left to see he was a man."

"He's a Cuban. Trust me on that. Was the other guy a Vietnamese?"

"Yes, I'm sure of it. I saw him clearly."

"Then we've got a real pressing problem, Pham. Let's get out of here and see if we can make it to a phone."

"Quang Ngai is about ten kilometers from here." Pham limped along following Shake through the jungle. They were about a kilometer north of the ambush site when they heard engine noises and stepped out onto the highway.

Pham stood fearlessly in the middle of the road waving his pith helmet and the empty AK-47 until a wheezing mini-bus, loaded inside and out like a gypsy wagon, skidded to a halt. The driver and his capacity load of frightened passengers were shouting and pointing back down the road, trying to do their civic duty and report what they presumed was a terrible accident involving a government vehicle.

Pham shouted for silence, helped Shake squeeze into the bus and ordered the driver not to stop until they reached Quang Ngai.

*   *   *

Thuy lay in a hollow behind a fallen palm log for a full hour before he slipped across the road and discovered the ambush had failed miserably. He was hurt but alive, which was more than he could say for the man he found with the bullet in his brain on the other side of the road. The American was no easy mark. Underestimating that had cost the Nghe Tinh Group's foreign friend his life.

The Citroen was undisturbed where he left it and Thuy felt strong enough to drive it to Tuy Hoa. The flow from his left arm and hip had slowed to a seep and the pressure bandages he fashioned and tied tightly over the wounds seemed sufficient to keep him from bleeding to death. He started the engine and wheeled the car onto the highway heading south.

Fortunately, he'd been quick-witted and experienced enough to leap sideways, away from the unexpected meeting engagement with the soldier in the ditch. He survived...but so did the American...which meant the mission was not complete. Now he had to find a working phone and report the situation to Comrade Duc in Hanoi. If there were no further orders, he'd look for a doctor.

*   *   *

With Lieutenant Pham firmly bedded down in the PAVN hospital at Quang Ngai and assurances from the army doctor that he would live a limpless life if fortune continued to smile, Shake Davis made his meeting with the Provincial Military Commander and a bloodless civilian from the Vietnamese State Police.

Both departments rushed details to the ambush site immediately after Shake and Pham arrived and laid out the bare bones of their story. Two hours later they had cleared the road and returned with the corpses. The second shooter had not been found, but they were still looking.

"You have no idea who the dead man was..." The police official was examining the documents Shake handed him. "...or why he would want to harm you?"

"I really don't." Shake was determined to keep what he suspected confidential, at least until they let him make a call to

Chan Dwyer in Hanoi. "You can see his papers indicate he's a Nicaraguan..."

The PAVN officer seemed stunned, unhappy with this turn of events in his otherwise quiet command. "I was unaware we still had Nicaraguans in the country. I thought they left when the Russians did."

"It is a big country and full of foreigners if you know where to look." The policeman handed the documents to an assistant and thumbed through a notebook until he found the detail he wanted to explore. "You said that you shot this man with a pistol?"

"That's correct."

"And where is that pistol now?"

"I lost it...somewhere in the jungle...while Lt. Pham and I were trying to get away from the ambush." Actually, it's right outside under a potted plant where I stuck it when we arrived... anticipating this very question...but you don't need to know that. "I'm sure your men can find it out there."

"Where did you get this weapon, Mr. Davis? You are aware that it is against our law for any foreigner to possess weapons while in the country."

"Yes, I'm aware of the law, sir. The pistol was given to me...a gift...a sort of war souvenir."

"A Vietnamese gave you this pistol?"

"That's correct, sir."

"Would it do me any good to ask you who that was?"

"No, sir. It would not. The weapon saved my life. I'm obviously indebted to the person who gave it to me, so I don't want to get him...or her...in trouble."

The PAVN commander picked that point to exert his authority. "The pistol is not important! In the end, it's fortunate that he had it. If it's significant, we will search for it. Since Lt. Pham was on an official assignment when he was wounded and an army vehicle was involved, the army will investigate this unfortunate incident as a matter of jurisdiction."

The policeman was either unwilling to challenge the army or anxious to unload the problem. He shrugged and snapped his notebook closed. "I remind you, Mister Davis, it is a serious violation of our laws for you to have a weapon while you are in Vietnam."

"Thank you, sir. I will bear that in mind."

"In the meantime," The PAVN officer checked his watch and pointed at the phone on his desk. "I have been in contact with the command center regarding your tour of our units. They feel it would be better if you returned to Hanoi...at least until we can assure your complete safety from this kind of incident."

"I understand." Shake nodded and smiled. There was nothing he wanted more right now than to be surrounded by police and soldiers in the national capital. Wrapped in the relative safety of that cocoon, he could press on and solve what was threatening to become a sordid murder mystery.

"I'd like to use a phone to call my headquarters, if I may...and I would like to commend Lieutenant Pham for his bravery in this incident. His superiors should know that he saved my life."

"It was the other way around according to Lieutenant Pham." The officer stood and motioned for a PAVN NCO. "But I will pass your comments along to Hanoi in the official report."

Shake followed the NCO down a dark hallway toward a private office. The place was apparently used for document storage. It smelled of wet paper and mildew. There was no desk but there was a phone on top of a stack of cardboard boxes. Shake nodded his thanks, shut the door after the escort and peeled melted plastic off his soggy notebook to find the Contact Team number in Hanoi. He gave it to a switchboard operator, hung up the receiver and dropped wearily onto a pile of paper to wait for the connection. Ebbing adrenaline levels left him feeling weak and numb.

There was no question in his mind about one thing. That stiff lying outside wrapped in a muddy poncho was the same man he saw in the Dan Chu bar...ergo, he was the same sonofabitch that planted the grenade booby-trap. And there were a few other issues becoming slightly less cloudy. The Laos File had to be real...had to be the impetus for all this...and its disposition was a very high priority on someone's agenda. That someone was almost certainly a Cuban...or a bunch of Cubans...so Gus was on the right track. The information in the Laos File was something certain Cubans would kill to keep secret. And that led to all kinds of wild-ass speculation about their involvement with POWs in Laos...

The phone chattered rudely and he snatched it out of its cradle. Chan Dwyer's voice was like a soothing opiate on his jangled nerves.

"Hi, Chan. Contrary to popular belief, the wayward Marine is alive and well."

"Where the hell are you?"

"Quang Ngai...at the PAVN headquarters. We had a little problem on the road."

"We heard. General Fowler's all over this thing. Are you OK?"

"I'm all right. Pham's a little worse for wear but I'm fine.

"What happened?"

"I thought you guys got the story..."

"Your version..."

"Well, on the surface of it, we got ambushed on the road between Qui Nhon and Quang Ngai. Two shooters. Pham got dinged. I got one of the guys. The other either took off or Pham nailed him and he crawled off into the bush. They're still looking. Anyway, we commandeered a bus and hauled ass for here. End of report...except for one other item. You remember me telling you about the incident in Miami?"

"Right. The thing in Little Havana."

"That's it. Well, the guy I nailed? He was the same nationality as the guy in Miami. On top of that, me, Ault and Colonel Stokey spotted this guy in the Dan Chu bar just prior to the boobytrop deal. Does that tell you anything?"

"It tells me you need to get back here ASAP. There's been a major break in the Laos File situation..."

"Jesus, Chan! Not on the phone..."

"Doesn't matter anymore, Shake. General Fowler and I had a meeting with General Giap that you should have attended. The cat's out of the bag, buddy. There is a Laos File. And it does, indeed, confirm much of what your friend suspected. It was in the archives at the museum all the time..."

"Was?"

"It's not there now. Best guess is that the guy in charge of the archives took it. He was under direct orders from General Giap to protect the material. General Fowler suspects when you guys started poking around, he panicked and split with it."

"Well, that'll be the end of that."

"We don't think so...and neither do our hosts. Seems the file is much more incriminating to the Cubans than it is to the Vietnamese. Naturally, our hosts would like to document that fact."

"Explains a thing or two about recent events, doesn't it? What did the Cubans do? What actually happened?"

"That's something you better hear from the horse's mouth, Shake. General Fowler and General Varney have been conferring with each other, the White House, Pentagon, State...damn near everybody. It's a fairly incredible story."

"I'll bet it is. Wish to hell Gus was still alive to hear it."

"Obviously, we're all anxious to get the details...all the names...who hit John, you know. It's gonna be serious business when the lid blows off."

"How can you do that...if this guy stole the file?"

"Well, right now a man by the name of Sergeant Minh is at the top of the Vietnamese most wanted list. The PAVN dispatched troops to Hue to look for him. It's a major effort...and he's pretty hard to miss. Veteran...with a big, ugly scar on the right side of his face. They'll have him and the file before long."

"He's in Hue?"

"Everybody seems to think so. Apparently he's got family down there. They're serious about this, Shake. They'll find him. Believe me, it's in their own best interest."

"So, you guys want me to get back to Hanoi?"

"Roger. General Fowler's orders. He's making arrangements for a plane or chopper as soon as the weather down there clears. Meanwhile, sit tight where the PAVN can protect you."

"Let the PAVN protect me...life is so full of little ironies."

"Listen, Chief Warrant Officer Davis, you do as you're told. There may be more than one Cuban in the woodpile...so to speak."

"Yes ma'am. Well, you know where to find me."

"See you soon, Shake."

He hung up and sat for a few moments with his head between his knees, trying to digest what he'd heard. In a little while, America would have her answers about MIAs in Laos. It would not be good news...but it would be news. It would be an end to the agony. And all because his lunatic old Sergeant Major had a hunch. But for Gus Quick, the truth might never have been revealed.

And what was that truth? He still didn't know. Would anyone ever really know? Would the Laos File become another Warren Report? Shake felt the hollow form in the pit of his stomach.

The source after all this time is none other than General Vo Nguyen Giap? Please. There's got to be a glitch somewhere. What if the whole thing is a scam designed to shift blame for whatever happened from the Viets to the Cubans?

Shake struggled to his feet thinking about his promise to Gustav Quick...and about 213 Americans who were almost home...almost. He let himself out of the office and walked down the corridor toward the PAVN command suite. The senior NCO seated outside the commander's office door seemed anxious to help.

"Will you ask the Colonel if I might have a ride into Quang Ngai? I need to buy some clothes."

While he waited for his ride outside the PAVN Provincial Headquarters, Shake retrieved the pistol and shoved it under the tatters of his charred shirt. When it came down to a choice between legal and alive, there was no choice. And when you're running short of allies, you can always count on Colonel Sam Colt.

*   *   *

When his two PAVN bodyguards had their jeep parked near Quang Ngai's bustling central market area, Shake pulled out his cash reserve and blatantly thumbed through the large wad of local currency. The underpaid NCOs just as blatantly ogled the overt display of more cash than they would see in a year of soldiering for the state.

"None of this is mine, you understand." Shake grinned and shook his head, one old trooper to a couple of others. "My government gave me this and told me to spend it on whatever I needed. It's much like an official order, isn't it?"

Oh, hell yes. The NCOs couldn't agree more. You get money and orders to spend it...well, there's just one thing a soldier can do.

"It will probably take me some time to find clothes to fit. I'm a little bigger than most around here." The NCOs watched Shake peel off a sizeable sum and agreed that shopping would take a while.

"Why don't you help me carry out my orders? You take some of this and buy lunch...maybe a beer or some cigarettes... whatever you like. I'll find some clothes to fit and meet you back here."

The NCOs climbed out of the vehicle, looked around to be sure there were no obvious threats in the immediate area, then pocketed the windfall and melted into the throng. Shake ambled along until he found a stall featuring a fair selection of fashions from Taiwan.

He grabbed a pair of extra large Wrangler knock-offs, the only knit shirt he could find that looked like it would stretch over his frame and a windbreaker that might keep him reasonably warm and dry. The shopkeeper was so happy to move the out-sized merchandise with no argument over the asking price that he was glad to give the big American spender the benefit of his extensive knowledge regarding cross-country bus schedules.

Thirty minutes after he arrived, Shake Davis was in his new clothes and on his way out of Quang Ngai. The chatty bus driver told him the weather was poor along the route, but he expected to make Hue with no problem.

26. Hanoi

Comrade Duc, nationwide Nghe Tinh Group coordinator, placed the phone receiver back on its cradle and then put the entire unit back in the drawer of his old desk in the fabric shop. His secret line - normally so quiet he was in the habit of periodically checking for a dial tone - buzzed twice in the same day. Neither call brought him good news.

First the hasty report from Thuy letting him know the Cuban was dead...and the American still alive. Then this strange communication from the very man who installed the private line and used it only in dire emergencies. Duc rose from his desk and stood near the cranky old hotplate at the rear of the shop. He made tea and let his mind wander over what he knew and what he had just discovered.

He could not see the whole picture, but certain blurred images were coming into focus. This business of the Cuban going after the American for something to do with the Phoenix Program was subterfuge of course. Minh saw through that. The Cuban was after the American because the American either knew or was about to find out what was in the Laos File. Fine so far. It was in the interest of the Nghe Tinh Group to cooperate in keeping such information confidential.

In fact, when he learned of the Cuban's failure, Duc had been prepared to have Nghe Tinh operatives in the south deal with the American and finish the job. Then the call from one of the country's highest-ranking public servants...and one of the Nghe Tinh Group's most valuable clandestine advocates.

"There is a man, a member...Than Duc Minh. He is a traitor...to the country and to the cause." As usual when he used the secret line to reach Duc, the Chairman of the Vietnamese Communist Party neither identified himself nor wasted time on preamble. "I believe he is in Hue; possibly staying with a sister. He has stolen a document which must be destroyed."

And the line went dead. No specific instructions; no further explanation. Duc sipped his tea and admired the intricacy of a spider web angling across a corner of his shop. How complicated some traps can be, he thought, as a few more images shimmered into focus.

Clearly the document in question was the Laos File and that file must no longer be the deep, dark secret Minh presumed it to be. Hence the Cuban chasing the American...but what about Minh? Given what he said the file contained, any threat of imminent exposure should have prompted him to destroy the document. So why didn't he simply do that? Why steal the file and run?

Because Minh was more to blame for what happened to the Americans than he admitted that night after the meeting when he spilled his guts? No...all the more reason for him to destroy the Laos File and any evidence it contained. Because Minh and his Group 559 companions were not to blame and the Cubans were? Possibly...it explained the sudden reappearance of the Cubans after all this time.

If Minh has the Laos File, what is he planning on doing with it? Comrade Linh called him a traitor. What would a traitor do with something like the Laos File? The answer startled Duc so badly he spilled tea on a bolt of valuable Chinese silk.

He would turn it over to the Americans, of course. And that must not be allowed to happen.

*   *   *

Lieutenant Colonel Mike Stokey snapped the lid shut on the suitcase-sized satellite communications unit and glanced at the one-time message pad on which he'd scribbled a long set of four-digit code groups. The message, up-linked in Washington according to the Address Indicator Group and blasted down from the bird on a secure frequency to Hanoi, was unusually long. Normal comm from his DIA control was terse and inevitably the same simple instructions: Continue current mission under current cover. Report all JTF-FA findings and activities via Blowback.

Blowback was the DIA Southeast Asia Control Element in Bangkok which operated independent of normal U.S. intelligence activities centered on the American Embassy. Military Intelligence types rarely trusted or shared information with their civilian counterparts at CIA Langley so for the past year while he worked a day-job as one of General Varney's MIA field investigators in Vietnam, Stokey sent regular, detailed reports and analyses to Bangkok where they were edited or expanded and fired off back-channel to the Pentagon. Stokey's presence on the JTF gave DIA an exclusive asset in Hanoi.

Still, it was relatively rare for the guys in the Five-sided Wind Tunnel on the Potomac to communicate directly with their man in the field. The last time was two weeks prior when a sat-comm message advised him that Major Chan Dwyer, the nominal admin officer of the IRDG's Military Contact Team, was in reality an MI officer and also a DIA undercover asset.

Dwyer had likely gotten a similar advisory concerning him, but tradecraft and separate missions dictated they each keep their own counsel barring emergencies.

Now for some reason he was anxious to discover, Washington had sent him what looked like a short novel. Although the high-speed, burst-transmission equipment handled the message in less than two minutes, it would likely take Stokey an hour or more to decipher it. Each cluster of four random numbers corresponded to a word or phrase in the day code for the date indicated in the message date-time group. He found the code reference where he kept it taped to the underside of a dresser shelf and began to work.

Two hours later he was in the JTF transportation office arranging for a flight to Hue. He told the Vietnamese booking agent it would be a quick trip, pointing to the small canvas bag containing his shaving kit, cash, credentials and some spare clothes. That and a ride on the first thing smoking south was all he needed. Unless you counted the M-9 Beretta nine-millimeter pistol riding in a holster at the small of his back.

*   *   *

"He what?" Major General Gordon Fowler was in shirt sleeves and sweating through another of the Dan Chu Hotel's periodic air conditioning failures.

"Disappeared, sir." Major Chan Dwyer had done all the checking she could to determine Shake Davis' whereabouts before trekking from her office to give the boss the bad news. "The PAVN command at Quang Ngai is in a bit of a flap over it. Seems he went into town to buy some clothes, sent his escorts off on a shopping spree and then never showed up to meet them."

"Do they think he's still in Quang Ngai?"

"They're combing the city, General...but I suspect he's gone. Probably to Hue."

"The Laos File?"

"That would be my guess, sir. As I explained to you, he's got a personal stake in this thing."

"Well, he's gonna have a problem keeping his ass attached when I get hold of him. This is a damn delicate situation and we don't need cowboys operating on their own agenda. Did you explain that to him on the phone?"

"I briefed him on the situation, sir. And I gave him a direct order to remain in Quang Ngai until we sent transportation to fly him to Hanoi."

"Sonofabitch! I got General Varney and Mr. Thurman in here trying to figure out what we're gonna do when the Viets find that file. This kind of shit I don't need right now."

"General, I know Gunner Davis fairly well. I could probably find him in a hurry...at least before he gets himself in trouble down there."

"Yeah..." General Fowler mopped at his face and considered the diminutive officer he'd come to like and trust for her calm professional manner and solid performance. This was no time for chauvinism or gallantry. "I need someone down in Hue to monitor the situation and keep me briefed. I'll call the Air Force guys out at Noi Bai and lay on a flight. Better take that Captain with you as liaison and translator. What's her name?"

"Ding Dong's as close as I can come to it."

"OK, you guys get down there today. Call me when you're set up...and let me know immediately when they find this guy Minh."

"Yessir. Anything else?"

"No...wait, you better get a message to Commander Ault. Tell him to drop what he's doing and meet you in Hue."

"Think I'll need reinforcements, sir?"

"Can't hurt to have him there. Both he and Davis have anchors on their asses. Maybe the Navy can help you talk some sense into the Marines. When you find Davis, have Commander Ault hog-tie him and see that he gets back here."

"Yessir. I'll call you from Hue tonight."

                              *   *   *

"If you are going to a party, Colonel Ngoc, you may be delayed." General Nguyen Phu Dinh intended to rake her over the coals; vent a little of the frustration he felt over the lack of progress in Hue, but the woman's pitiful efforts at making herself look seductive left him unfocused.

"I was on my way to the airport, General. An old friend arriving for a visit..." Despite the general's glare, she knew her appearance had an effect on him. A woman could sense these things in a man. Her decision not to change into her uniform when the call came to report to the PAVN Chief of Staff had been correct. If this did not take long, there would be time to get her hair done before Fidel's flight arrived.

"Has there been any communication from Sgt. Minh?" General Dinh lowered himself into his chair thinking that the traditional *ao dai* was a beautiful frame for a woman's form...provided the woman had the necessary form...which Mrs. Ngoc did not.

"No, General. My staff has been instructed to report anything they hear from Minh to me immediately. He has not checked in but we are watching his apartment. He has not been found in Hue?"

"He has not...but he will be...assuming he is there."

"Of course. A man who looks like Minh cannot hide. It is simply a matter of time."

General Dinh thought of impressing Ngoc with the urgency of the situation but quickly dismissed the notion. The fewer people who knew how close the nation was to a major international incident, the better. He nodded and checked the notes from his investigators combing Hanoi for any sign of Minh.

"On the day Sgt. Minh disappeared you had a visitor at the museum; a foreigner with papers indicating he was a Nicaraguan contract engineer. Do you recall seeing him?"

Mrs. Ngoc glanced down at her fingernails to hide her surprise. She would like to have them manicured. Everything had to be as perfect as age would allow. "Yes, General. I recall the man. He said he wanted to do research but he had no clearance from the GPD. I sent him on his way."

"Did he mention the Laos File?"

"No, General...but he did want to see the archives."

"Very well. That will be all. You may go and meet your friend."

Mrs. Ngoc rose and smoothed the front skirt of her *ao dai*. She could not probe too deeply, but Fidel would be interested in why the army was inquiring about his old partner. "This Nicaraguan may come back to the museum, general. Is he wanted? Should I detain him?"

"That would be neither necessary nor possible, Mrs. Ngoc. He was killed yesterday while attempting to ambush one of our American visitors. Fortunately, the American survived...which saves us from at least one diplomatic disaster."

Mrs. Ngoc fought hard to keep her expression neutral but the PAVN Chief of Staff was staring at his desktop, leafing through a report. She swept through the door of his office in a whirl of white silk trousers under blue brocade skirts. There was no need to be at Noi Bai early. An old friend on the airport security detail promised her visitor would be cleared with minimum delay. She still had an hour left to primp.

*   *   *

She looked like a simpering old nanny goat. The years had not been kind to Ngoc but none of that mattered now. Ngoc was a tool: adjust as required and use to get the job done. He reluctantly draped an arm around her spreading waist, letting his hand lightly caress her hip as they waited for his baggage to arrive at the terminal.

Ngoc had influence and wielded it well. His Peruvian passport and the pricey visa he'd purchased after calling her from Bangkok were barely out of his hand before the arrivals clerk banged his entry stamp on them, collected his fees and with a nod to Ngoc waved Colonel Armando Ochoa-Desidro through the checkpoint.

He was nearly staggered by the cloying wall of humid air that assaulted him outside the terminal. He'd forgotten the slimy feel of Vietnam on his skin. Of all the third world toilets and equatorial shit-holes this had been the worst. He wondered as he had so many years before if it wasn't something in the stifling, dank air that drove men to acts of brutality. Or perhaps it was the maddening disharmony in the howls and hums of the spoken language. He forced himself to smile at Ngoc as they squeezed into her sagging Lada sedan.

She hammered him with memories and overt flirtations while he struggled to recall enough of the vocabulary to seem interested. He lost patience with it when they got stuck in an airport exit traffic snarl.

"Please, Ngoc! We will have plenty of time to catch up...but there's more pressing matters just now. I must contact Chico..."

She had planned on breaking the news gently, hoping it would not spoil her chance to rekindle the old passions. She laid her hand lightly on his upper thigh.

"There is bad news..."

"What? Has he been arrested?"

"He has been killed...yesterday near Quang Ngai in the south. Something to do with an attack on one of the Americans visiting here..."

Ochoa-Desidro digested the news, fighting to keep his expression suitably stoic; hiding the shock he felt trying to erode his self-control. "He was a good friend...a good soldier."

"I had no idea he was even in the country. Perhaps I could have helped him...if I had known...what he wanted."

"Cigars..."

"What?" Ngoc applied sufficient pressure on her horn and nearby bumpers to wedge the Lada into a moving traffic lane.

"Chico always wanted cigars..." They were coursing along a main artery now bringing him back into the heart of darkness that Hanoi had always represented to Colonel Ochoa-Desidro.

"Well...he was not looking for cigars at the Central Military Museum...was he?"

"No, of course not..." It was so like Chico to panic and blunder beyond his orders. It was stupid to try and destroy the file itself. In Hanoi? At the Central Military Museum? Good God!

"He was after the Laos file..."

"More precisely, he was after an American who knew about the file." If Chico had simply taken care of the American snoop he would not be here trying to defuse a potential disaster. "I have spent the past six months and a considerable amount of money trying to deal with that situation."

"The American is still alive." Mrs. Ngoc wheeled into the courtyard of the stained stucco building where she lived with another civil servant's family. By virtue of her rank and position in the GPD, the entire ground floor was her private quarters. "If you wish I can find out where he is."

"The American is a secondary concern now." Colonel Ochoa-Desidro unfolded from the car and hefted his battered suitcase from the trunk. "You said the Laos File has been stolen?"

"Yes, but it will be found shortly." Mrs. Ngoc led the way through a small foyer. The house smelled seductively of the incense she had burning in her bedroom. "The army has men looking for him now..."

"For the man who stole the file?"

"Yes, of course...for Sergeant Minh, the man who stole the Laos File from the archives. Let me take your bag into the bedroom. You would probably like a bath..."

"In a little while, Ngoc..." Now that he was in a position to confront the threat, Ochoa-Desidro had to quickly formulate a plan of action and that would be driven by priorities. First find that goddamned file and destroy it. Then deal with the American. "Where are they searching for this Minh? Here in Hanoi?"

"We believe he has gone to Hue. He has family there. The army has been combing the city for him. They will find him soon. As I told General Dinh...a man with a face like Minh's cannot hide."

"What's wrong with his face?"

"Ugly! Crushed and scarred on one side. He always looks as if he's sneering at you..."

The colonel let himself down slowly onto one of Mrs. Ngoc's Chinese lacquered chairs and rubbed at the painful throb in his temples. He was certain now why Chico had been nosing around the Central Military Museum. "This Minh...is he a veteran? Did he make the Long Mountain March?"

"Well, yes...he served with Group 559 after he was wounded. He compiled the Laos File under direct orders from General Giap. Do you know him?"

"I remember a scar-faced man..." It never rains but it pours. Minh? He didn't recall the name but the face? Unforgettable. The same little prick who tried to take charge when the bombs fell. The same horrible gargoyle who tried to back them down when the shooting started...

He opened his eyes to see Ngoc place a brass tray on a table at his elbow. It held delicate tea cups, sweet rice cakes and a half-liter bottle of Johnnie Walker scotch whiskey. He reached for the liquor, unscrewed the cap and swallowed a healthy jolt.

"I need a gun, Ngoc..." She was on her knees before him, gently rubbing his thighs.

"There is my pistol..."

"Makarov?"

"Yes, standard issue..."

"Fine...but I will also need something heavier."

"Why, my love?"

He took another swallow of whiskey. The burn in the pit of his stomach felt good. Like an old war wound, it reminded Colonel Ochoa-Desidro that he was still alive and in the fight.

"We are going to Hue."

"After Minh?" Mrs. Ngoc felt a burning in her thighs. She was sure the hot flush on her face was melting through the make-up. She was alive again; vital, vibrant and aching for the feel of his body crushing into hers.

"Yes. You understand this is vital to me, Ngoc. I must find Minh and the file. If you have any feelings for me...in the name of the love we once shared, you will help me do this."

Ngoc stood and took his hand. She stared into the dark eyes that still drove her mad. "I will arrange everything," she said softly, tugging him toward the bedroom. "Trust me."

Colonel Ochoa-Desidro took another fortifying drink of whiskey and followed.

27. Hue

As the wheezing vehicle neared the An Cuu Bridge on the southern outskirts of Hue, Shake Davis struggled forward and conferred with his pal Sam the bus driver. Throughout the five hour trip over rain-slick roads, the laughing extrovert played both Dutch uncle to his nervous passengers and consummate wet weather wheelman.

Shake spent enough time with the driver at stops along the route to discover a number of interesting things. Over the war years Sam worked his way up from itinerant laundry man for the Marines on Hill 327 to shuttle bus driver on the air base at Danang. Of course, that was just to make ends meet. After dark, Sam worked in a Viet Cong munitions factory out by Marble Mountain. He claimed to have made some of the best hand grenades ever tossed at the guys who employed him on his day jobs.

Sam had a cousin...or an uncle or an in-law of some sort - it was difficult to decipher exactly...who hosted the best restaurant in Hue. He tried to invite his American passenger for a discount meal, but Shake wanted to get off at the An Cuu Bridge. He wanted to enter the city the same way he had so many years before...walking in the rain.

28. Hue - 1968

Stand down my dyin' ass. Tet Truce...ceasefire...the big three-day skate. Alpha One-One in the rear with the gear...warm and dry and Phu Bai. Kiss my motherfuckin' ass and ceasefire this, you rat-bastards.

Ain't supposed to be here until tomorrow...and then just to guard the goddamn squids and their landing area on the Perfume River. Ain't supposed to be walking into Hue behind a fucking fifty-ton mortar-magnet of a tank. Ain't supposed to be wet, miserable and nursing a plus-four pucker factor.

Above and beyond all that...something about this deal ain't right. If there's a whole shit-pot full of gooks trying to overrun the doggies holed up in the MACV Compound somewhere up ahead there, how come they leave the An Cuu Bridge over the Phu Cam Canal alone? Spend some time watching Luke the Gook at work in the field and you know he's no dumb-ass.

Luke knows he's got a couple battalions of Marine Corps man-killers milling around Phu Bai just eight miles south of here. Luke knows if he starts any shit in Hue, those Marines are gonna come screaming up the road, across that Bridge, and try to stick a bayonet up his ass. Luke's outfits always pack enough H-E to blow bridges. And Luke soldiers by the book...which says you ambush along an enemy's primary axis of advance.

So how come we get across without having to pay the toll? Two platoons of grunts, a couple of army Dusters with ass-kicking quad-fifties aboard and five Marine M-48 tanks make it across the bridge to huddle up at a traffic circle like a contingent of combat tourists?

Skipper and a couple of other officers he policed up along the road over there at the Esso gas station trying to figure that one out. No pump-jockey present to ask directions but we ain't gonna get lost. MACV Compound's about a click straight up Highway 1 to the north. Take the road to the left across those sugar cane fields and you get a nice look at the Hue cathedral...just before you run into the provincial prison. It's a no-brainer, Skipper. Hey-diddle-diddle; right up the middle.

Gunny Canley out of the huddle and headed this way. Big bastard's wearin' that boy-have-I-got-a-deal-for-you look. Gonzalez and his guys get the sweep across the open cane field to check out movement over there. Thank you, Jesus. And we go with the track-rats in one tank...Alpha four-three...Dink

Buster...right up this long, lonesome road. And be sure to call if we find work.

Alpha four-three grinding north with grunts on the flanks and fanned out to the rear. Big diesel blowing hot exhaust...takes an edge off the chill from pissing cold rain. Close enough to snatch the T-I phone from its mount on the tank's right rear, it feels like cuddling up to a pot-belly stove in a snow-storm. Drawback is danger-close proximity to a big-ass target that even a blind gook can hit. There ain't a grunt breathing - ours or theirs - that can resist shooting at a tank. Fucking things draw fire like a trophy buck on the first day of deer season and deflect it with extreme prejudice at grunts dumb enough to get too close.

Spread the platoon out right and left...below the level of the road and slightly to the rear of the lead tank. Commander of four-three buttoned up inside advises the other four vehicles are moving up behind us. Dusters back by the circle chopping the hell out of something. Still no incoming but that can't last. Tanks on the move with no cover...grunts in the open...tall buildings ahead perfect for plunging fire. If there's NVA around they will definitely piss on this parade.

Major flash from the left front. Gook B-40 rocket gunner on a rooftop slammed one into four-three. Shrapnel cut the corpsman in half. Skipper's radio operator down hard. Told 'em to stay behind me, goddammit!

Small arms smacking off the tank. Here we go...up to our assholes in it now. Four-three...you guys OK in there? Target's a B-40...brick building at about ten-thirty or eleven. Either on the roof or in one of the second floor windows. Saw the flash when he fired. Yeah...clear out here. Just nail the fucker.

Squad corpsman from third platoon headed out after the casualties. Won't make it through the incoming. Stay down, doc! Goddammit, let the tank work! He's down...either took one or concussion from the 90mm knocked him off his feet. Alpha four-three biting back hard. Ninety milimeter blasting chunks out of buildings up the street. TC on the fifty caliber up in the cupola getting his licks. Can't hear the sixteens over the racket but grunts are definitely in the shoot and move mode on the flanks. Squad leaders hauling 'em down the dinky little streets on both sides of the main road.

Time to check off the party line. Tankers have got more business than they need anyway. Four-three...gotta go. You got friendlies on your right and left moving up the street.

Recommend you try to stay ahead of 'em. Good luck, people...and thanks for your help.

Second squad in a sharp firefight on the left. Gooks bunkered in at the windows of a stucco building. Grunts in defilade behind a low stone garden wall. Two down and bleeding on the sidewalk. The rest popping up like prairie dogs; splashing rounds on full auto...looking for a break. Just might be able to give 'em one if there's a way to work in close.

Times like this a blooper is the answer. Second squad's M-79 man sprawled in the street. Guy who tries to retrieve the weapon won't make it back through the shit-storm. Straighten the pins on two frags and stuff them in top pockets where they'll be handy. Gotta get in under one of those windows.

Don't over-think it. Don't calculate the odds. Just go...go...go! Hard crack in the head. Helmet gone. Down in the dirt...dizzy as hell...halfway home. Incoming shit smacking all around...how can the bastards miss? Do the cockroach. How low can you get? How fast can you crawl?

Under the window tucked into the shrubbery like some kind of fucking aphid. Zip machinegun pounding out rounds two feet above; firing over a stack of chewed-up furniture. Muzzle gas stings like hell this close. Gunnner can't expose himself to nail me without getting his ass handed to him. Grunt's wet dream. Frag in the window...pitch hard...the other one. Now! Stick the muzzle in right behind the blast...haul back on the trigger...redecorate the fucking place with ball ammo.

Get some, Two Bravo! Good squad leader, Tom Donlon. Saw the break and hit the hole. Grunts repossessing the place. Second squad in...gooks out. Don't let 'em mill around, Donlon. Get a corpsman on the wounded guys and head out toward the main road. Just catch up with the tanks and keep moving. Yeah, there it is. You got their fuckin' ceasefire hangin'.

Dead gooks in three rooms. Four...maybe six...doesn't matter. There's a whole hell of a lot more between here and the MACV Compound. Fresh meat by the looks of 'em...full uniforms...haircuts...no festering jungle sores. And they ain't playin' games. This ain't gonna be like shooting at shadows in the bush. This is gonna be assholes and elbows...house to house...close-quarters...and we ain't even started.

The NVA have come to Hue...and they're here to stay. We are in a world of shit.

29. Hue - 1996

The house had been re-stuccoed and whitewashed but he could still spot the divots on the face of the garden wall where the gook gunner tried to take Corporal Donlon's Two Bravo out of the fight for Hue City. And that hedge...where he hunkered down to frag the house...seemed bigger; better concealment back then.

The tree-lined streets of Hue were peaceful and bustling. The people he passed on the way into city center seemed prosperous and serene. Still he could not shake the dread he felt entering Hue for the second time in his life.

Walking back toward the main road, in the same direction he'd followed the tank so long ago, Shake Davis remembered the extraordinary number of times he nearly died in Hue. He'd been lucky...way beyond lucky...to walk out of that fight... bloody and battered, but still upright and still mobile.

Right here, right in this place, he'd spent the absolute, no-contest, most gut-wrenching, horror-filled three weeks of his life. Nothing before or since had even come close to the sheer emotional impact of his time in Hue. This was the epicenter of his nightmares, the genesis of his recurring war-sweats.

Walking north toward the Perfume River and the Citadel on the other side of it, he hoped there would be time to see the city, revisit other battle sites, engage in a little regression therapy. But first he had to locate a man named Minh and read the Laos File. That much he owed to Sergeant Major Gus Quick and a lot of other guys...including himself.

                  *   *   *

The wild flight from Hue in the four-engined Antonov AN-12 had bored through a major weather front sweeping south from Hanoi. Captain Dinh Duong had been sick much of the way which prompted Major Chan Dwyer to make soothing reassurances she didn't really believe. She was more than a little relieved when the aircrew finally planted the aircraft on the runway at Phu Bai in a light but steady monsoon mist.

While she retrieved the luggage from the back of the airplane, Captain Duong staggered off to find a phone and army transportation that would take them up the road to the garrison command at Hue. In her briefcase Chan Dwyer had notes gleaned from Shake Davis' personnel records listing the units he'd fought with during the battle for Hue in 1968 and a copy of Eric Hammel's *Fire in the Streets*, an excellent overview of the action. Beyond a vague notion she might find the Marine revisiting old haunts in his quest to find the Laos File, she had no specific plan of action.

Two hours after touchdown at Phu Bai, a PAVN driver deposited them at the Thua Thien Provincial Military Command Center on the south side of Hue. The PAVN garrison commander ordered to host their visit had offices in the cruciform complex on Le Loi Street which runs parallel to the Perfume River. Across the rain-dimpled water Chan got her first look at the massive walls of the Citadel and tried to imagine what it must have been like for the Marines in 1968, attacking against fanatical defenders with nothing but balls and bayonets. Her already high opinion of Shake's combat prowess ratcheted up another notch. If a man like Shake intended to hide, he'd be hard to find.

The PAVN garrison commander offered them tea and introduced a Captain Mai Van Hung as the officer in charge of the search for Minh and the missing documents. Hung was stiff but polite until the senior PAVN officer left them alone in a spare office down the hall. He smoked and stared while Duong explained their mission to monitor the progress of his search and look for an American officer who was also supposedly somewhere in the city. When she finished speaking, Hung stubbed out his cigarette, put his hands on his hips and launched into what any experienced soldier would instantly recognize as an ass-chewing.

He barked into Captain Duong's face for three long minutes, occasionally stabbing a finger at Chan, then hitched at his pistol belt and slammed out of the office. Chan gave Duong a minute to recover and then tried for an English translation.

"I take it Captain Hung is a little less than glad to see us..." Duong shrugged and stroked one of her pigtails. It was a habit Chan had learned to read as a sign of frustration in the otherwise stoic PAVN officer.

"Captain Hung believes we are spies sent here to spur his efforts in finding Minh. His soldiers have been everywhere in Hue with no success. His troops are now expanding the search south toward Phu Bai and he orders us to stay out of his way. He said he does not need or want any help from two women."

"Is that all he said?" Chan grinned at Duong and waited patiently until the Vietnamese returned her smile.

"There was more. Captain Hung does not have a very high opinion of female soldiers. You have a phrase...a boar pig?"

"Male chauvinist pig is the phrase, I think. Don't let it bother you, Duong. The military...yours and mine...is full of them. Most male soldiers simply can't stand the thought that a woman might do as well as they do in a dangerous profession. It's a painful blow to the male ego."

"This is not a common thing in Vietnam. We have traditions in which women have shown great courage in battle."

"Yeah, I know. But when you get right down to it..." Chan smiled and pointed at her crotch. "...traditions don't mean much up against what you might call the glandular imperative."

Duong pondered the area indicated and frowned. "Maybe we should try Chinese..."

"Wouldn't help. The thing is...well, there's a point in being fair-minded and impartial beyond which most military men can't go. Regardless of what they say, when it comes down to hardship or danger, they want to be the ones putting their lives on the line. They want to preserve that chance at glory and it seems...somehow terribly diminished...if a woman shares in it."

"It doesn't make much sense...to a woman."

"No. But it is a fact of life that's unlikely to change for a while yet. What did Captain Hung have to say about finding Mister Davis?"

"He said he is too busy to search for lost Americans. If any of his men should spot a wandering American, they will report it. Otherwise, we are on our own."

"Probably just as well. Can we work out of here?"

"Yes, the colonel has offered this space and a telephone. There is a barracks nearby where we can sleep."

"Okay. I've got to make a call to Hanoi and then we need to come up with a search plan. I've got a few ideas on that. Why don't we get established...and then we can ask around the bus terminal and check the train station."

*   *   *

Lieutenant Colonel Mike Stokey shrugged into his raincoat, dodged around the huddle of civil servants and soldiers waiting for their bags to be off-loaded from the Mi-14 helicopter, and headed for the terminal access road. Trudging through ankle-deep mud, dodging spray from passing vehicles, he made his way to Vietnamese Highway 1 and looked to the right.

Up that road eight kilometers was Hue where his orders indicated he'd damn well better find a man named Minh and a very important wartime document. That simple little chore done, he was to hang out; keep tabs on man and material, until the real rat showed up to strike at the bait. He'd been assured in the message from the DIA case officer it would happen... sometime soon...as long as Minh and the document remained missing.

Background information on the general situation and on the supposedly inbound Cuban had been detailed. The action portion of the message was typically open-ended and vague. They told him what to do; not how to do it. Still the emphasis was clear: Nail the Cuban...then let the PAVN deal with the Laos File as a collateral issue. Working from that point, Stokey developed his own set of assumptions. Chiefly that the Cuban was unlikely to emerge if Minh was in hands of PAVN authorities.

The key, he decided on the bumpy trip from Hanoi to Phu Bai, was to find Minh - who presumably had the document referred to as the Laos File - before the PAVN forces already searching Hue found him. Then he'd have to invent a way to assist the guy - either directly or by inhibiting the PAVN search - in staying loose until the Cuban showed up to make a play.

The message had been very specific on one point: Do whatever's necessary to spring the trap. In his canvas satchel was an unusually large slug of contingency cash - hard American currency - he was authorized to spend in the effort. Given his experience with the Vietnamese in this area - uncommon greed and common fear of anything to do with the army - the money made him feel a little better about the daunting task ahead of him.

Spotting a taxi with a dozing driver at the wheel, Mike Stokey rapped politely on the window and began to haggle over the price of a ride through the rain to Hue. Deal made, he climbed into the back seat wondering where Shake Davis was at the moment. Probably up to his ass in mud watching some broke-dick PAVN platoon stagger through assault on a fortified position. Too bad the guy wouldn't be in on the big break. It was sure as hell old Gus Quick's theory and Shake's persistence that was about to pay off in a big way...in a lot of big ways...for a lot of deserving people.

*   *   *

Comarade Duc's two companions from the direct action cell of the Hanoi Nghe Tinh Group were exhausted and complaining as they stood in the neatly-tended yard of a house on Tinh Tam Street on the eastern edge of the Citadel. They were both beyond fifty and hard-pressed by a nine-hour, high-speed trip from Hanoi to Hue through driving monsoon rain. The ordeal sapped much of their enthusiasm for the mission but Duc had pressed them and a Nissan van full of leaky black-market gasoline containers to the limits with no smoking and little time to eat or rest.

They had no more than cut the engine at a car park on Hue's south side, when Duc had them unloading heavy bags and charging across the Nguyen Hoang Bridge on foot to make a scheduled meeting inside the Citadel walls on the north side of the city.

"You endured much worse than this during the war," Duc reminded them as they stood in the steady rain waiting for someone to answer a knock on the ornate door at Number 15 Tinh Tam. "Remember our comrades who died for victory...and stop complaining."

A stocky individual with a milky, blind left eye opened the door, glared at the drenched visitors and motioned for them to enter. Duc quickly shook hands with the host and sent his companions to the rear of the house where a simple meal was waiting. In the sitting room at the front of the house, he greeted four Nghe Tinh comrades from his old command, the Political Action Cadre of the Tri-Thien-Hue Military Region.

Each of them bowed respectfully to the man who brilliantly master-minded the great purge of traitors and collaborationists in their city. Back among them was the single-minded, efficient, avenging scourge of Hue, the man who swept toadies and traitors from the streets during Tong Kong Kich-Tong Khoi Nghia - the General Offensive-General Uprising - of 1968.

Duc settled into a chair with no inquiry concerning his old comrades' health or welfare. It was like him to waste no time on social graces.

"What news?"

"He is here...or he was here in the past two days." Vung, the one-eyed senior Nghe Tinh comrade in Hue, uncorked a bottle of vintage rice wine and poured a cup for Duc. "We have been out and about since you called. He stayed a night with his sister and then disappeared. The army has been looking but never in the right places. What do you expect from simpletons who have never seen the elephant or heard the owl?"

Duc tasted the wine. It reminded him of the vintage they'd shared after dealing with the traitors in Hue so many years ago. More than a thousand Saigon puppets danced lively in those days...until patriots permanently cut the strings. All of them deserved to die and rot in the mass graves Duc and his cadre ordered dug in and around Hue. He had no regrets then or now.

"And so? Is he still in Hue?"

"We believe he is, Comrade Duc." Vung poured a second serving of the vintage wine. "We believe Minh has gone underground...a familiar place where no one who is not a veteran of the fighting in Hue would think to look."

"The sewers..." Duc felt a flood of strength and vitality flowing into flaccid muscles and creaky joints. "Have you searched?"

"No. We decided it would be better to wait for your instructions. But he has been seen, mostly at night when he emerges to buy food."

"Excellent! Here in the Citadel...or south of the river?"

"Both sides apparently. But I would guess he is on this side of the river. The monsoon rains will have made the sewers on the south side difficult to navigate. As you know, the water drains from north to south."

"We will begin this evening, comrades." Duc studied the fading French map Vung placed before him. It was essentially a grid outlining all the city venues within the six square kilometers encompassed by the Citadel. It was also the very same one they'd used in 1968 to plan the entry and occupation of the city. "How many men are available?"

"We are four...plus yourself and the two from Hanoi. It should be enough."

"And weapons?" Duc was sketching search grids on the map. He felt younger than he had since the time in 1968 when he was at the peak of his form. He was back in business; back on the field of his greatest triumph.

"Whatever you brought from Hanoi..." Vung motioned for his comrades to join him around the map. "...and we have grenades...Kalishnikovs as required...some American rifles... limited ammunition. There are pistols...some explosives. How much can we need to eliminate one traitor?"

"Remember the way it was in the War of Liberation, comrades..." Duc waved away the offer of more wine. "Nothing is as simple as it seems. Before it's done, we may need more

than we have. Minh is only a secondary target. We must find
him and follow him to the Laos File. That is the mission..."

*   *   *

From the narrow ledge where he slept in the sewer system
confluence under Mai Thuc Loan Street, Minh wrapped a thin
blanket around his shoulders and watched the water level rise.
In the yellow glow of his candle he could see chunky detritus
bobbing in the dark current running swiftly beneath him. It was
raining steadily now and by tomorrow the growing torrent from
storm drains would force him out onto the streets.

Hopefully, he thought as he shifted to let his legs dangle in
the frigid water, the soldiers will be searching elsewhere by
then. Gurgling intestines reminded Minh it was time to emerge
for the single meal he allowed himself each day. He had no
watch and there was no way of telling in the dark tunnels under
Hue whether it was day or night above, but his stomach was a
reliable time-keeper.

His gut said it was time to refuel, so Minh felt confident it
would be dark when he popped up from underground on the
gloomy section of street less than 500 meters from the eastern
edge of the Imperial Palace. If the rain had not driven her away,
he'd find the street vendor there and buy a meal of rice, *nori*
and bean sprouts. If he was lucky there might be a fish
available. The vendor was very good at preparing the small,
bony perch her young sons pulled from the Perfume River each
day. More importantly, he'd discovered on the first night he
stopped at her cart that the woman was a mute, victim of some
surgical butchery visible along the length of her throat. She
asked no questions and was unlikely to be pressed for answers
by anyone searching for him.

Crouching under the section of pavement he used for
access and egress, Minh listened for noises or voices to indicate
traffic above him. As usual this late, this close to the seat of the
ancient emperors which still inspired a certain distant
reverence and awe among residents of the city, Mai Thuc Loan
Street was quiet. He flexed and pushed on the heavy concrete
slab, sliding it to one side just enough to allow him to vault up
and swing his legs over the edge.

Minh stood quickly, replaced the sidewalk section and
looked carefully up and down the street. It was dark and silent
except for the sigh of a soft wind blowing through the steady
monsoon rain. He pulled the cheap, plastic poncho from his
belt and draped it over his head. Turning left, keeping his face

hooded, he followed the pungent scent of *nguoc mam* and coconut oil down the sidewalk.

The mute vendor bowed politely and held her kerosene lantern close to the fare on her cart as Minh decided on his purchases. He splurged on two of the fishes, pointing at several other items as the woman manipulated her long chopsticks and placed his selections on a strip of pressed palm leaf. She smiled as he handed over the money required and wrapped his dinner in newspaper to keep it warm and relatively dry.

Minh thanked her and glanced carefully around the nearly deserted streets. There was no lighting except for what spilled from unshaded windows and the moon was only an insignificant glow in the cloudy night sky. He tucked his meal under the poncho feeling the warmth against his stomach, and decided to risk a quick trip to check on the Laos File.

Walking west along the 15-foot-high northern wall of the Imperial Palace he kept a sharp watch for soldiers but the Z-18 troopers he'd seen everywhere on the north side of Hue for the past two evenings had apparently shifted their search pattern. Along the half-mile walk he saw only three vehicles poking along through the downpour. He seemed to be alone on the street except for a couple of old men sharing a cigarette under the bonnet of a cyclo near the northwest corner of the palace. They took no notice as he slipped by on the other side of the street and turned left onto An Hoa Street headed for Nha Do Gate, one of nine such formal archways that provide access through the Citadel's thick walls.

Ahead in the gloom he picked out the torpedo shapes of three giant bronze cannon parked in a battlement guarding the gate. Their muzzles were aimed to cover the river from which the French siege engineers thought trouble might come in 1820 when the great fortress was completed. The ornately-decorated guns, known as double-cannon, were gifts from the French architects who copied the Citadel after the pattern of the Imperial City in Peking. The 12-ton weapons, layered with a thick patina of verdigris, fascinated Minh from the first time he saw them during a perimeter patrol when his unit held the Citadel against the attacking American Marines. There were times during that slaughter when he wondered if there was a way to fire those cannon; somehow stuff them with powder and blow the enemy away in a shower of heavy shot.

But the bronze cannon flanking the Nha Do Gate had never moved and Minh was fairly certain they never would. No one was interested in such ancient artifacts these days and visitors to the Citadel rarely even noticed the huge guns except as back-drop for family photos. That was the reason he chose to hide the Laos File in the barrel of the cannon on the right facing the Perfume River. It was usually in full shadow - either of the battlement wall or the other two guns - as the sun passed over the area. The right-hand cannon was the ignored orphan of the trio as indicated by the layer of muck and soggy leaves Minh scraped out of the muzzle and carefully replaced to hide the Laos File until he could decide what else to do with it.

Days of agonizing over that question had not brought him to a satisfactory conclusion. All he really knew was that the file must be kept from the Cuban who would destroy it...and from the Americans who would use it to dishonor brave soldiers who simply did their duty. Beyond that, Minh refused to speculate. Whatever punishment the army decided to impose for stealing the Laos File was a matter to be considered only after the current danger passed.

Drawing near the stone portico of Nha Do Gate, Minh heard the hiss of rubber tires in the rain and the grind of a bad bearing to his rear. He snugged himself up against a tree and peered into the dark. A cyclo was approaching along An Hoa Street. As he watched from the shadows, the vehicle passed slowly and he clearly saw the same two men who had been smoking on the street corner. One of them was peddling the cyclo and keeping his eyes diverted to the right. The man in back peered steadily to the left. They did not appear to notice him against the dark, irregular bulk of the tree.

Halfway down the street, short of the gate and the cannon, the cyclo stopped. Both men dismounted, conferred for a minute and then changed places with the man in back now doing the peddling and most exposed to the rain. Guard relief, thought Minh as he wrapped the poncho tightly around his body to keep it from flapping in the wind. Soldiers do that; not poor cyclo drivers and passengers with enough money to afford the ride.

As the cyclo turned and ground slowly back up the street toward him, Minh decided to forego his visit to the hiding place. The Laos File was safe or these people - whoever they were - would not be out searching for him in the monsoon rain.

His meal was cold and congealed by the time Minh made his way back into the sewer system. He ate it mindlessly, crunching on the fried fish and watching the cold, dark water rise toward his sleeping platform. He ate every crumb and chucked the wrapping into the stream so it would not draw more hungry rats than normally visited during nights in the dark tunnels. In the morning he would have to risk exposure to search for a hiding place above ground. Minh hoped for nothing more than a restful sleep, but the nightmare denied him even that.

30. Hue -1968

Wind...rain...a little rice...one machinegun...two rifles. Not much else...except for enemy soldiers. Just a single three-man cell outposted at the Dong Ba Tower. Captain Phuong says there are more coming...veteran men...pulled from the fighting around Khe Sanh. They will come, he says. They will come charging to the rescue through the Huu Gate on the opposite side of the walls.

Probably a lie. At least it makes the two children feel better. So young...those two...like green bamboo. They bend but do not break. Let them whisper and wish. What does it matter?

Don't worry, Minh. We will be reinforced. We can hold, Minh...just until the new men arrive. Some similar nonsense each time an American pops up to fire. Soon now...they will come...right over the rubble...right there where the machinegun is sighted. And then we will see what we will see.

Hoping for reinforcements. Silly as hoping for a glorious death. Important thing is not to die at all...unless there is absolutely no other option.

"Listen carefully..." Distract the children from fussing with a short supply of grenades. Damn things are wet and won't work anyway. "...our task is not to stand and fight the Americans. Trinh Sat soldiers are the eyes and ears, remember? When they come we will fire the ammunition we have...slow them up...and then escape out the back of the tower. If anything happens to me, you go toward the river...find Captain Phuong and report."

Mortars. Two...three...small ones. The little stovepipes that advance with the American infantry. Hitting high and low on the Dong Ba Tower. Easy...wait. The infantry will come soon. Just one can of ammunition. Fire that and go. Let the brave reinforcements take over and keep the Americans off this section of the wall.

At least Captain Phuong did not lie to the Trinh Sat veterans...old bamboo is strong enough to stand the truth. If the Americans manage to get up on the walls, we will all probably have to die here. Orders. No retreat. We stand like the great mountains to the west. While the National Liberation Front flag flies over the Citadel, there is no escape from Hue except death. Code of the Liberation Army: Obey the orders received. Sacrifice myself for the people's revolution. Maintain the honor of the revolutionary soldier.

Now! There! Right there! Fire! Shift the shoulders, move the muzzle. Fire in small bursts. How many of them? Death of a child. One less weapon in the Dong Ba Tower. A bullet in the nose and no face remains. Bad death...but there is no good death. At least the other child will understand that much.

Too much fire. Too many weapons aimed at this machinegun. Burning...my neck? No. Just a spent cartridge from the other child's Kalashnikov. Don't bother with the grenades! Reload...reload. Be ready...just the rest of this and we go. There! One waving his hands...get the leader...and four running behind him! Shift and squeeze the trigger. Let it pound...let it burn...blow them off the walls.

Go...now! Shove the child down the staircase at the back of the tower. Machinegun red hot and smoking...almost too hot to carry...but it will be needed elsewhere. Out of the Dong Ba Tower and...Americans! Two near the wall...black rifles rising to fire. Empty machinegun...and the child stands like a statue! Shoot! Too young...too late.

Jam the red-hot barrel into an exposed white neck. Lunge for the second murdering dog...a black one...who wants to live. The child's rifle speaks through me. That one will fight no more. But the hive has been broken. Wasps and hornets buzzing everywhere. His comrades are coming. Rifles crack and bullets whine off the old stones of Dong Ba Tower.

Run now! Run or die! Run and report. The Americans are on the walls. Only the karma of a good soldier to protect my back from the stinging insects of death. Only that and nothing more...and please let it be enough. Down off the walls. Turn toward the palace...the flag...find cover...find the unit and report. The Americans are on the walls! The children are dead! Born in the north. Died in the south.

Death wind blows in Hue. Americans are on the walls...and they will not be stopped.

31. Hue -- 1996

As the eastern horizon slowly faded from black to pale grey, he saw a small swarm of fireflies sweeping toward the southern shore of the Perfume River. Pulling himself up from a reeking pile of nets, he extended a hand beyond the canvas shelter at the stern of the wormy old sampan on which he spent the night. Still raining but that was nothing more than minor discomfort to the men approaching with lanterns to launch their boats before dawn. Fish don't mind monsoon rain and after an hour or two of hauling nets neither would the fishermen.

A thin, white-whiskered old man limped up to the boat and hung his lantern from a bow stanchion. He waved two assistants to work and handed Davis a plastic box of hot food. It was part of the deal they struck at dusk the previous night. Shake got accommodations including water-bed and continental breakfast. The old fisherman got a gob of cash and the promise of a bonus if he told no one about the guest sleeping on his sampan.

Shake handed over the hush-money, accepted the morning meal from his host and stepped ashore. The old man grinned and cackled. The American and his cash were welcome back anytime. Nodding thanks, Shake shrugged into his windbreaker and walked west toward the foot of the Nguyen Hoang Bridge. It was still too early for much pedestrian traffic and he wanted a roof over his head while he ate whatever was in the box.

He ducked under a bridge overhang wishing he'd thought to buy a hat in Quang Ngai. He could probably pick one up at the market or in one of the shops here on the south side of Hue, but that involved a little more exposure than he cared to risk.

South of the river, the city was crawling with troops. The special ops types he spotted patrolling search quadrants yesterday would be after Sgt. Minh and the Laos File but they'd police him up too. More than likely General Fowler knew by now he had a loose cannon on deck. Chan would point toward Hue...and he was probably the poster boy on a military and police A-P-B.

He spent the shank portion of his first day in Hue dodging patrols. The few people he was able to interview - or bribe - said they hadn't seen a scar-faced man. He struck out at the bus depot and Hue's train station was being watched by a contingent of PAVN soldiers. He flashed a little more money around but by dusk he'd only collected an entourage of greedy kids who would gladly take him right to the scar-faced man...for a nominal finder's fee.

Only one semi-valid lead surfaced. He was wandering along Le Loi Street, dodging soldiers, cops and ghosts, nearing the walled court of the Cercle Sportif and remembering a vicious fight for the riverfront club built as a high-tone French and Vietnamese social center in Hue. A pair of meandering state policemen drove him behind the walls. He stood cringing very near the same place he'd cringed in 1968 when Hotel Company, Two-Five was beating the bulldog shit out of the place in an all-out effort to permanently cancel the NVA's club membership.

The cops continued up Le Loi and he was about to venture back onto the boulevard when a guy hawking rice and vegetables from a stand in the area got him interested in a quick meal. It was idle chat that paid.

What are you doing here? Looking for a man. Vietnamese? Yeah, guy with a scar on his face. Saw him...night before last. Really? Bought some rice from me and then went across the bridge. Haven't seen him since.

It wasn't much and there was a lot of area inside the Citadel across the bridge, but it was all he had. Problem is, Shake Davis realized as he munched a rice cake and stared across the Perfume River at the dark mass of the Citadel, that's the one place I really don't want to go. Something dreadful about the place, swollen with evil portent like a dark alley in a bad part of town. There be dragons...and demons and God knows what the fuck else.

Mainly, Shake realized as he watched the raindrops pelt the river surface in the dim glow of dawn, over there is fear, a soldier's most malignant enemy. Over there along those walls is where that cold, clammy claw finally gripped his teenage heart and squeezed so hard his fucking eyeballs nearly popped out of his skull.

It was probably right about there. He held his hand at arm's length, sighting along his fingers as the walls of the Citadel shed shadow and emerged from the gloom on the other side of the Perfume River. Probably about two fingers to the right of the area where that huge-ass NVA flag flew. Right about there playtime ended. All the good things were gone after what happened up there. All the sweetness turned sour. Images of honor, courage and destiny turned into abstract shit stains on those walls. And no matter your age or station, if you survived, you came down off those walls an addled, quaking, incontinent zombie forever marching in the ranks of the walking dead.

On the other hand, Shake Davis told himself as he walked up onto the Nguyen Hoang Bridge and headed for the Citadel, if you're going to wrestle with a demon, you've got to step into the ring.

*   *   *

Minh slithered into his poncho, pulled the hood over his head and faced east. A greenish glow was visible on the horizon but rain-swollen clouds would keep the sun from brightening the day much beyond monsoon gloom. And the steady spit from those clouds would keep most people under shelter.

He was more than a little reluctant to go back up on the walls of the Citadel. Something deep in his heart ached as he stood by the interior base of the walls near the Nha Do Gate and pondered the proposition. Just up the muddy ramp and a right turn...about fifty meters...and he would be right back in the belly of the beast that haunted his sleep.

Why do it? He wondered as he mounted the slippery ramp and began to climb. Aren't the memories of that night, of the green-eyed monster who bit my face, vivid enough? At the top of the ramp Minh turned right and glimpsed the soggy flag of his country barely stirring in a soft, wet wind over the Citadel. It was a depressing sight, totally unlike the vibrant 54-square-meter NLF banner that snapped defiantly from the tall flagpole during Tet Nguyen Dan.

This flag seemed limp, listless and exhausted by the burden of national pride it was supposed to carry. Much like the people of Vietnam these days, Minh thought. Wrung out, numb and staggering under the burden of the great victory. This is not the way it should be. The people should not lose for having won.

Still, the flag is a symbol of the reason he wound up in Hue...then and now...and there can be no retreat. The demons are still here. Minh sniffed the humid air and felt the dull ache in his heart become a piercing pain. He rested on a rock and put his head between his knees.

The smell of battle was clear and strong: something rotting under the mud, gunpowder, cordite, coppery stench of fresh blood, cloying stink of vegetation and old earth plowed by high explosive...permeating the ground beneath his feet. These things are a combat soldier's karma, he reminded himself as he rose and began to walk. A soldier cannot run from them. A soldier must fight through these things and face his demons.

He remembered a series of reinforced underground bunkers built by the Japanese during an earlier war. Those bunkers had been a safe haven after Captain Phuong was killed and no one remained to enforce suicidal orders. It was from those bunkers that Minh and the remnants of his platoon emerged to make a break through the Americans on the walls. If he could find them, if they had not caved in or been destroyed, the old Japanese bunkers might once again save his life.

Minh felt stronger as he began to pick his way over the humps and muddy moguls of the old battleground. I should have come here to face the demons long ago. Perhaps now I can kill them.

*   *   *

Major Chan Dwyer, U.S. Army and Captain Dinh Duong, Peoples Army of Vietnam, stood in the rain outside the Hue bus terminal near Doc Lao Park, surrounded by a frenetic cordon of kids. Ignoring Duong's warning when they emerged from an early morning search for signs of Shake Davis, Chan dug in her kit-bag and offered two pieces of hard candy to a skinny, shivering urchin and his little sister who looked like she was suffering from rickets. Ten seconds later they were under siege.

Duong shook her head and shouted at the sea of upraised hands and agonized faces. "Be quiet! Go home! You should not be here begging a visitor for candy."

"Sorry, Ding Dong..." Chan fished in her bag for another two or three candies and tossed them into the mob. "It's hard not to..." The remainder of her comment was lost in the din of twenty kids fighting for the treats. Duong waded into the fray, barking and shoving, until the kids began to disperse.

The little girl with the swollen stomach lost sight of her brother and began to scream. Chan picked her up to keep her from getting trampled but the child bawled in terror, struggling and staring wide-eyed into Chan's unfamiliar face.

"Give her to me..." Duong took the girl in her arms and began to speak softly in Vietnamese. When things calmed, the brother returned and stood watching the two women from behind a nearby tree. Duong motioned for him to approach and he reluctantly emerged from hiding.

"Take your sister and get out of the rain. You should not be here bothering the passengers." The boy accepted custody of his snuffling sister and shoved a small chunk of candy in her mouth. All was immediately right with her world.

Duong softened and squatted to chuck the little girl under the chin. "Where do you live?" The boy waved a hand in vague direction somewhere behind the bus terminal. "Why don't you go home and get out of the rain?"

"I thought there would be money..." He glanced at Chan Dwyer and nodded. "Yesterday there was money offered."

"Who offered you money yesterday?"

"Another foreigner. He wanted to find someone...but he would not believe I knew where he was."

Duong stood and switched to English. "If you have some money...not much...I believe we may have some information concerning Mister Davis." Chan dug bills out of her uniform pocket and let Duong select what was required. Squatting again, Duong showed the boy the cash.

"This is for you if you tell me the truth. What did the foreigner look like?"

"He was a man...very tall...with short hair like a soldier." The boy's eyes remained riveted on the money. "He said he was looking for a man...a Vietnamese man...with a scar on his face."

"Did you know where the scar-faced man was?"

The boy stared at the ground and sucked hard on the candy in his cheek.

"The truth..."

"No. I just wanted the money...for my family."

"And when was this?"

"Yesterday...just before dark. The foreigner was asking everyone in the bus terminal."

"Was he wearing a uniform?" Duong gestured at Chan in camouflage field jacket and battle dress. "Like that one?"

"No. He was wearing American jeans...and a red jacket. But he had soldier boots like those."

"Where did he go?"

The boy waved toward Le Loi Street in the direction of the Nguyen Hoang Bridge. "Somewhere down there. It was getting dark..."

"Did you follow him?"

"He told us to go away. He spoke the language very well...but he would not give me money."

Duong handed over the cash and watched as the boy snatched his sister's hand, heading for home to announce a windfall. She turned to Chan and smiled.

"Mister Davis was here yesterday evening...asking about Minh."

"The boy saw him?"

"Yes. His description was accurate. Apparently Mister Davis was wearing blue jeans and a red jacket."

"That would be it. The people at Quang Ngai said his uniform was ruined and he went into town to buy clothes. Did the boy know where he went?"

"This way..." Duong led off down Le Loi street. "The boy seemed to think he was headed for the bridge."

"And the bridge leads across the river to the Citadel. That's where we should be looking."

"The Citadel is a big place, Major Chan, nearly six kilometers. He could be anywhere."

"He fought on the walls. He once told me it was a turning point in his life. If he went to the Citadel looking for Minh, he won't miss the chance to walk that ground again. Believe me, Mister Davis is like that."

"Yes, I have seen our old soldiers do the same thing." Duong pulled her army poncho over her head and tucked at stray strands of wet hair. "It is difficult to understand unless you have been a soldier and fought in a war."

*   *   *

On the other side of the bridge, Lieutenant Colonel Mike Stokey, U.S. Marine Corps, turned his back to the wind and walked northeast toward a shrapnel-scarred structure identified as Dong Ba Tower on the tourist map he picked up at the Cercle Sportif. Hell of a fight up there, he thought, as the gate beneath the tower came into view through the morning mist. And Minh's outfit was defending according to the research. Good place to start looking now that he had a defined search area.

Dame Fortune smiles on old recon guys. No reason to think she'll start frowning now. His first stroke of luck was yesterday evening when he bought a bowl of noodles and sat wolfing them under an umbrella at the Cercle Sportif. Man who sold him the meal was chatty and amused at the spurt of foreigners eating from his cart. Wanted to know if there was some special tour or wartime reunion in progress.

"Why do you ask?"

"It's just unusual. We don't see many foreigners around here anymore...especially Americans."

"There have been other Americans here?"

"Well, just one...yesterday. He had rice and vegetables... spoke the language as well as you do."

"That's interesting..." And it's got to be Shake Davis. And he could only be here for one reason. "What did this man look like?"

"Would you like some *pho ga*...or fish? The fish is very good today."

Stokey took the hint and held out his bowl. He reached in his pocket for money and peeled off the tab plus a generous tip. "Tell me about this other American."

"Big man...wore civilian clothes...but I know a soldier when I see one. He didn't seem to care for the police much."

Stokey chewed on a hunk of sticky rice and pondered the revelation. It's Shake...and if he's dodging he's probably here on his own hook...very likely against express orders to the contrary. Could well be he knows something I don't.

"Did this man say why he was in Hue?" Stokey let the vendor see the color of more cash.

"Said he was looking for a scar-faced man...a Vietnamese. I told him I saw the man. He asked where; I said here...and then he headed across the bridge to the north side. The American paid for his meal and left. Last time I saw him, he was walking down by the river bank."

Stokey finished his food and forked over more cash for one of the mimeographed Citadel maps the vendor offered for sale. Even narrowed down to the north side of the city, a detailed search would take days or weeks. He didn't have that much time if he intended to find Minh before the army did...or before Shake Davis got lucky and compromised the mission.

At least the PAVN hadn't scored yet. That much was clear from the nearly-constant patrol activity. What he needed was an edge, a focus for his efforts. He hailed a cyclo and told the driver to take him to the House of Tradition. His work with the JTF had made him intimately familiar with the mini-museums dotted around the country near every major battle site. They usually contained fairly-detailed wartime records.

He spent an hour wading through patriotic screeds and nationalistic bullshit before he finally ran across an NVA order of battle for the Tet 1968 campaign in Hue. The 6th Infantry Regiment had been in the thick of the north side fighting. Minh fought with the 800th Battalion of the 6th Regiment. Bingo.

Tracing the battalion's ebb and flow as the American Marines pounded at them in an effort to breach the Citadel walls, Stokey studied and annotated his tourist map. When the House of Tradition closed, he left with detailed notes and a strong hunch about where he might find Than Duc Minh.

*   *   *

It was overgrown, weedy and hard to recognize, but Shake was sure this was the place. Over there was the flagpole. There the southern edge of the Imperial Palace. Dong Ba Gate on the right. Thuong Tu Gate on the left. Right around here...we were dug in vacated NVA fighting holes when the bastards jumped us.

He moved toward a mound of trash-littered earth that felt familiar. They were probably hiding behind it. Waiting, arming the grenades...and on us so fast...like they just exploded up out of the dirt. There was a strange tingling numbness in his legs as he walked up on the mound and surveyed the land atop the eastern edge of the wall. It felt as if he'd been wearing shorts and shuffling through a virulent patch of poison ivy.

He walked down off the mound toward a depression that might have been his hole that night. Something besides triangulation was telling him he was in the right place. Something wafted up through the weeds like an electric current; growing stronger as he neared the fold in the muddy earth. He was nearly there when he stumbled, the toe of his boot caught on something solid rooted down among the weeds.

Shake Davis squatted and brushed at the foliage. His fingers probed the mud and felt rusty metal. A helmet...an American helmet...or what was left of one. He dug it out of the muck. Not much left...liner and webbing long gone. Camouflage cover rotted away...rusty rents in the steel...but then it had been half-buried here for a long time. American fighting men wearing helmets like this had been absent from these walls for 30 years.

It could be, he speculated lowering himself into the wet weeds and letting his legs dangle into the muddy depression, that it might have been his fighting hole. Why not? Who could say that this rusty relic was not the very helmet he'd used to drive off the gook who tried to kill him...right here?

Lightning blazed over the mouth of the Perfume River and in its flickering light, Shake Davis saw images from that night. He saw the muzzle flashes. He saw the sparking trail of the incoming grenades. And over there, just behind that hump...

Shake Davis saw a figure in a green rain-slick poncho walking up over the top of the mound. It was hard to note detail in the gloom and the shadow of the poncho hood but the man was a Vietnamese. And he was searching...for something or someplace. The man stood on top of the mound, his poncho whipping in a sudden gust of wind, and slowly surveyed the stretch of wall from left to right.

Lightning cracked suddenly nearby and thunder rumbled over the walls. Both men flinched and ducked instinctively. Shake understood in that moment that the man was a soldier...or had been one...who fought in Hue. The move to duck incoming was instinctive...and indistinguishable from his own. He stood slowly, emerging from the high weeds with the rusty helmet in his hands.

The soldier atop the mound spotted him then. He gasped, staggered and clutched at his chest. The mound was empty in the next lightning flicker. The man in the poncho was there one moment and in the next he was gone. Shake ran to the mound and shouted in Vietnamese for the man to stop...come back...he meant no harm.

The soldier was below him on the ground, gasping with his head drooping between his knobby knees. Shake could see the white pucker of scar tissue on the man's corded calves beneath rolled up trouser legs. Shrapnel and jungle sores...and fear...of old ghosts like me.

"You were here," he said softly walking off the mound and kneeling by the gasping man. "So was I."

The man straightened slightly, fighting for composure. He appeared to be in some pain. Shake pulled a green military bandana from his pocket and offered it to the old soldier, wishing he had a canteen to share. The man accepted the bandana and mopped at his brow. When he finally threw back his shoulders, the poncho hood slipped off his head.

Their faces froze inches apart. Adrenaline surged stretching eyelids until they glared at each other like cornered rats. Thunder boomed and their necks snapped as if they'd both been shot in the forehead at close range. They recoiled, scrambling for distance. Both men fought to discount the ugly truth hammering at them.

"You!" Minh tried to stand, edging himself up against the mound but the pain in his chest made his legs numb and rubbery. "How can this be...how can you still be alive...how can you be here?"

He glared into the green eyes of his demon and tried to will strength into his limbs. Fate called on him to finish the fight...or die. Minh recognized fear in the green eyes that haunted his nights and he drew some strength from that.

"Sergeant Minh..." Shake Davis got his knees under himself and coiled to spring. He kept his gaze riveted on the man's disfigured face, slowly reaching for the pistol in his waistband. He gripped the weapon but did not expose it as Minh reached out for the rusty helmet and shook it at him.

"Was this the weapon?" Is this what you used that night?" He leaned toward Shake and canted his head to reveal the full extent of the damage. "Have you come here to savor what you did?"

Shake flopped back down into a puddle of muddy water and gave in to the shock. Gradually, confronted by this mangled veteran, he accepted the surreal truth. They were not strangers. He'd met Minh, the scar-faced man who stole the Laos File, before...right here on these walls...right over there in a muddy hole.

And those scars...I put them there. I nearly killed this man...and now we are here again...and I hope he doesn't attack...because I can't kill him...not now.

Shake felt tears welling and gasped to choke back the sob heaving up from his chest. It was too much after so long. All the burdens of all the brutality in all the battles of a lifetime at war came crashing down on him. In the face of his old enemy he felt weak, hopeless and defeated. If this sick old man wanted to kill him now, he could try again and so be it. There'd be justice in that. Death would likely be more pleasant than what he'd inflicted on Minh for a lifetime...in the struggle to live just one more day.

"It sounds so stupid...after all this time...to just say I'm sorry...but I am."

"Sorry? You are sorry?"

"Yes. Sorry it was you...sorry it was me. Sorry for all the pain. Sorry it had to happen at all."

Minh stared into the monster's green eyes and for the first time saw something besides hate, lunacy and blood-lust. He saw himself: the same anguish, pity and pain reflected in his own eyes when he allowed himself to look deeply into a mirror. It is not so obvious, he realized, but this man is also terribly scarred.

"I don't know your name..."

"Davis...Sheldon Davis."

*   *   *

"He is there...but not alone." The Nghe Tinh operative who shadowed Minh from the moment he emerged from the sewers at dawn stood before Comrade Duc at the base of the ramp hiding a folding-stock AK-47 under his poncho. "There is a man with him...an American I think...blue pants, red jacket."

"What are they doing?" Duc realized he would have to commit now, work fast and be ruthless if the Americans had gotten to Minh. Very likely he or one of the heavily-armed Nghe Tinh men huddled against the rain across the street would have to kill an American. The thought disturbed him in one way and pleased him in another.

"Nothing. It appears they are just sitting in the mud... talking."

Duc nodded and worked the slide of his Tokarev pistol to chamber a ready round. "I will make contact and get Minh to turn over the file. Spread the men out in firing positions along the wall. Be alert. If there is one American, there are likely more."

Walking rapidly up the ramp leading to the top of the wall, Duc checked over his shoulder. The Nghe Tinh comrades were responding like veteran soldiers. He was well covered. It only remained to get his hands on the Laos File and see it destroyed. His comrades would deal easily and efficiently with Minh and the American once that was accomplished.

*   *   *

"Is it true that you have the Laos File?"

"What do you know of this..." Minh gasped but he was not looking at Shake Davis. He rose on rubbery legs and stood staring beyond the American at a figure approaching in the steady drizzle. Shake stood and turned to see an elderly Vietnamese sauntering toward them with his hands behind his back. He was smiling, like an old gentleman enjoying a stroll in the rain.

"Greetings, Comrade Minh..." The visitor kept his eyes locked on Davis but there was nothing in his voice or manner to communicate a threat. "We must talk privately, Minh. I have come a long way to see you."

"What are you doing here, Duc?" Minh seemed surprised but not fearful. He obviously knew the man so Shake simply waited to see what developed.

"I have come after the material from the museum, Minh. It is imperative that you turn it over to me."

"I cannot do that, Duc. You know the nature of the material..."

"Precisely...which is why it must be destroyed. Now turn it over to me and your comrades from the Nghe Tinh will help you hide. We can get you out of the country."

"I am under orders from General Giap to safeguard that material."

"Oh? And is that why you are meeting with this American?"

Shake began getting the picture at mention of the Nghe Tinh Group. He moved to put his body between Minh and Duc. "This man goes nowhere...and neither does the Laos File." Shake reached for his pistol just as Duc's hands flashed from behind his back. The muzzle of the Tokarev was pointed directly at his chest.

"Drop the weapon!" Duc motioned toward a mud puddle at his feet. "Drop it here. I have killed Americans before and I will not hesitate to kill you now."

Shake slowly completed the draw, flashing his attention between Duc's face and the pistol in his hand. A firefight would be futile. At this range Minh would certainly catch a round and the Laos File would either be lost or destroyed. He carefully leaned forward to drop the cocked and locked .45 into the mud puddle at Duc's feet.

He spotted the rusty helmet just six inches from his hand and made his move so quickly that Duc never saw the uppercut coming. In the first vicious stroke he smashed the steel pot into the wrist of Duc's gun hand. The Tokarev barked once but the bullet sailed high and right. On the backstroke he brought the helmet down hard into the right side of Duc's head. Shake saw blood over the ear as Duc staggered and tripped, sprawling on his back in the mud.

Minh shrugged by to get at Duc but Shake shoved him back and fished wildly in the puddle for his pistol. He was bringing it to bear on Duc's prostrate form when a wicked burst of incoming fire showered them with muddy water.

Should have known the asshole wouldn't show up alone. Shake went prone behind a small hummock of old tree roots wishing he'd had time to put at least one round into Duc before things turned to shit. From the sound of it there was more than one shooter in the action.

As incoming rounds pounded at him, chewing away at barely adequate cover, Shake heard a rustling to his rear. He squirmed to see Minh's poncho on the ground. Minh was not in it. Snapping the safety off the Colt he pumped two rounds in the general direction of the incoming and vaulted behind the dirt mound.

Minh wasn't there either. Better cover gave Shake a chance to turn his attention from immediate survival and look around the area at his back. Minh had to be somewhere. He didn't go down in the first burst...and an old soldier was not about to stand around providing a handy target.

He spotted movement in the tall grass at about the same time one of the shooters did. Minh was low on his belly and slithering like a lizard away from the fight. Rounds mowed a chunk of weeds directly in Minh's intended path and Shake saw the grass begin to bend in a different direction.

"Stay down, Minh! Find cover and stay put!" He winged a few more rounds over the top of the mound then covered to check the magazine. Four rounds remaining. At his back the tall grass was still except where AK ammo chopped at it.

*   *   *

Mike Stokey scrambled up the muddy ramp and onto the walls just in time to spot Shake Davis bashing away at someone with what looked like an old helmet. Shake had found Minh but there was trouble of a serious nature with a third party. He heard a pistol shot and snatched at the Beretta as he lurched for cover behind a pile of masonry rubble.

Suddenly the world between him and the three struggling men exploded. He squinted against the glare of muzzle flash and spotted at least four shooters hammering away at Davis and Minh. Older guys...civilian clothes...had to be Nghe Tinh fanatics...intent on killing Shake and the man he'd been sent to find.

Stokey steadied the Beretta and wedged his wrist between two large masonry chunks. Bringing the front sight blade to bear on the nearest shooter, he saw the man roll over to change magazines and put two rounds into his chest.

*   *   *

While he was trying to think of something semi-intelligent to do about his very precarious situation, Shake sensed a drop in the volume of incoming fire. He listened carefully and thought he heard the sharp pop of a pistol, a new voice in the din.

He crawled to the edge of the mound and sneaked a look through the weeds. One of the shooters stood suddenly, spun to the rear as if headed out of the fight, then crumpled and dropped. Shake was sure he heard the bark of a pistol. Might be Duc, he thought, but Duc had disappeared. Probably crawled off somewhere...and he sure as hell wouldn't be shooting his own guys.

Someone was evening up the odds out there. Shake Davis slithered around on his belly and began to low-crawl in the direction Minh had taken. He was grateful for the gift of life but his benefactor would have to wait for the hearty handshake.

*   *   *

On the street below the eastern wall, Comrade Duc paused to tie a clumsy bandage over the painful gash in his scalp. His heart was hammering in his chest reminding him with each thump that he was alive...in service again...at war with the bastards who threatened the nation.

It was no great trick to crawl away under the line of fire when he saw Minh making his escape. Let the Nghe Tinh comrades deal with the American. He knew what Minh was running after and he intended to be present when the traitor retrieved it.

Duc scrunched himself down behind a hedgerow near the Nha Do Gate. There was an access ramp just beyond the gate near those three old cannon. If Minh dodged the fire and continued to his rear, he'd come off the walls and escape down that ramp.

Duc was listening to the snarl of small arms on the wall above him when his quarry came stumbling and sliding down the ramp in a whirl of bony arms and legs. Minh regained his feet, glanced around quickly, and charged off in the direction of the cannons. Duc shifted the Tokarev to his uninjured left hand and followed.

*   *   *

"My God! Those are gunshots." Unexpected as they were on a quiet, misty morning in Hue, Major Chan Dwyer had spent enough time on ranges to recognize the rapid racket of AK-47s and the hollow boom of a GI .45. She and Captain Duong stood under the arch of the Thuong Tu Gate closest to the north end of the bridge over the Perfume River. The firefight echoed and ripped on the rim of the Citadel walls somewhere to their right.

"What can be happening?" Captain Dinh Duong turned to see a few straggling pedestrians on the Nguyen Hoang Bridge scramble to make way for a Z-18 Company patrol running hard toward the sound of shooting.

"Get those soldiers and head them in this direction." Chan pointed at the patrol and gave Duong a shove. "I'll see if I can find out anything."

She jogged inside the Citadel and looked to the right just as a man with a bloody bandage on his head ran by in the opposite direction. He shouted something and pointed a pistol at her. Chan Dwyer was flat on her belly in a rain puddle when two rounds passed close over her and went whining off the mossy stone of the archway.

"So that's what it's like," she thought. "That's what it's like to be under fire."

*   *   *

Than Duc Minh was trying to ignore the painful pounding behind his ribs as he hung from the muzzle of the right-hand cannon with one arm and scooped debris with the other. There was no time to build a careful pile of stones as he'd done when he hid the Laos File. Now that he needed to retrieve it from the maw of the great gun, he had to leap up and hang from the barrel like a jungle monkey.

Just up the street on the walls to the east he heard the firefight diminish. An odd sensation occurred as his scrabbling fingers felt plastic wrap and the bulk of the Laos File. He was hoping the American would escape. The Nghe Tinh comrades doing the shooting would be from a direct action cell. They were fervent haters who would kill Sheldon Davis with neither compunction nor compassion. What conceivable karma...what horrid mistakes in life...could bring such a man to death in Hue when he'd so barely escaped it once before?

Minh jerked the Laos File free of the great cannon and dropped to the ground. The awful pain moved around to his back and made it hard to breathe. He wanted to rest for just a moment, but there was no time. The Nghe Tinh would sweep along the walls and be on him soon. He had to head northwest, toward the Huu Gate and the old Japanese bunkers. He had to buy time and protect the file.

"Minh! Stand still...do not move." Duc stepped around the carriage of the cannon and pointed the Tokarev at the plastic bundle Minh clasped to his chest. "Give me the file."

He moved forward, pressing Minh against the damp stone of the battlement and snatched at the file. Minh held tight staring at the muzzle of the pistol just inches from his eyes. Duc stepped back and leveled the weapon.

"I will not wrestle with you, traitor..."

Minh tried to keep his head erect and stare death in the face as he'd done so often on the battlefield. He watched Duc's finger flex at the knuckle putting pressure on the trigger and then bowed his head, telling his Lord in the last moments that he had done what he could to do his duty.

The boom of the pistol shot was heart-stopping, huge and amplified; clanging off the cannon and confined by the stones of the battlement roof. There was pain in Minh's ears but the rest of his body seemed normal. He felt something crash into him driving the breath from his lungs as he slid down the mossy wall.

"Get up, Minh! We've got to go..."

Minh looked up into the green eyes of the demon. His old enemy from so many nightmares was shouting for him to rise. From the dead? How could he do that?

Minh looked down and saw Duc sprawled across his knees in a spreading pool of dark blood. There was a single oozing hole at the base of the neck. Duc's eyes were wide and staring as the last time he'd seen them but beneath the lifeless eyes there was no lower jaw. Just the eyes, a nose and bloody mush.

"Is that the file? Is that the Laos File?" Shake got an arm around Minh and lifted him upright.

"You saved my life..." Minh blinked and shuddered, trying to deal simultaneously with seething emotion and cold reality. So many things remained unexplained in life; so many twists and turns unrelated to justice or reason, but this was beyond yin and yang. This was beyond simple checks and balances.

"Our war's over, Minh...once and for all. If you want to run, go...but leave that file. I need to know what's in it. I owe that to a lot of people...living and dead."

Minh glanced down at the file and back up at Shake Davis. For the first time in thirty years he saw a man and not a monster. He nodded once and moved to pry Duc's Tokarev from a death-grip.

"I command the detachment now." He stuck the pistol in his waistband and peered out into the gloom. An army patrol was flooding into the Citadel but they were turning in the wrong direction. "Is this acceptable?"

"You know the area better than I do." Shake checked the magazine of his pistol. Only one round remaining and no telling what Minh might do with the ammo in the Tokarev. "I need to know what's in that file. If you'll show it to me, I'll go where you lead."

Minh motioned for Shake to follow and scrambled up a littered stone staircase to the surface of the northwestern wall. As they headed for the Huu Gate, dodging and weaving like soldiers in the assault, a fresh firefight broke out to the rear.

"What the hell is happening back there?" Shake saw muzzle flashes but they were too distant to make out detail.

"My countrymen are killing each other." Minh crouched behind a section of wall and peered over the side. He could barely make out the arched window and rusty bars but this was the area. Somewhere near here was an entry to the old Japanese munitions bunkers beneath the walls. He motioned for Shake to remain in place and began to crawl forward feeling among the high weeds with his hands.

It was near the root of a small nippa palm Minh didn't remember, but the spongy wood and rusty hinges appeared as he scraped at the mud. Under this lid should be a stone staircase leading to a water-tight storage room. It was small and confining with only one tiny barred window for ventilation but fourteen men had hidden in it at one time. It would do to shelter two more fugitives.

Shake helped him dig and in a few minutes they managed to lift the rotting cover and reveal the entrance to the bunker. Minh led the way into the dank, choking hole. At the third step he paused to light the stub of a candle he pulled from his pocket.

* * *

Mrs. Ngoc slipped the Sanyo VC3000 transceiver into a leather pouch at her hip and walked toward the space along the highway outside the Dong Ba Gate where she'd parked the Lada. It would likely remain there forever, she thought sadly. The ten-hour push from Hanoi to Hue had stressed the engine and transmission beyond endurance. The poor thing was barely puttering when they crossed the bridge last night.

No matter. Mrs. Ngoc was well past considering consequences. There would be other cars...bigger and better... in other places...with plenty of money and plenty of time. She was committed to a future beyond grey walls, grinding boredom and political rhetoric. Her Cuban would lift her beyond all that...or give her the gift of death.

With a little luck they would be gone the instant this business was finished. He promised they would as he was pulsing between her thighs. And men do not lie at times like that. Just this business to handle and they'd be gone...south to

Cam Ranh Bay where passage to another world was merely a matter of money and connections.

Colonel Armando Ochoa-Desidro emerged from the bushes beside the Lada and motioned for Ngoc to hurry. She joined him with a hug but he pushed her away and snatched at the radio.

"Does it work?"

"Of course. There is only one issue radio and only one frequency. The same here as in Hanoi...merely a matter of finding the correct channel."

"What was the shooting about? What did you hear?"

"There was a battle on the walls..." She turned to point. "...back there between the two eastern gates. A patrol from the Z-18 Company engaged some men with rifles. I heard the commander say they were Nghe Tinh..."

"Any word of Minh or the American?"

"No. They have called in the police. The search continues."

"You have fresh batteries?"

"Yes. This one and two more."

"Good. We will find a place to stay inside the Citadel and monitor the military frequency. When they find Minh, we make our move."

"And then we go?"

"Yes, Ngoc...how many times must I tell you?" Colonel Ochoa-Desidro stepped back into the bushes beside the highway and knelt to retrieve the case containing a special weapon that cost him two hours delay and five hundred American dollars on the trip south.

A hard-to-find former ordnance soldier in Vinh, a friend of Ngoc's dead husband, got instantly rich by selling the centerpiece of his secret wartime collection, a Swedish Carl Gustav .45 caliber submachinegun with an integral silencer once used by American Special Forces. Overwhelmed by the windfall, he threw in thirty rounds of subsonic nine-millimeter ammunition at no additional cost.

Colonel Ochoa-Desidro folded the stock of the weapon along the receiver and tucked it beneath his raincoat. He nodded at Ngoc and walked toward the Dong Ba Gate into the Citadel.

"Bring the extra batteries and keep an ear on the military channel. They'll find the bastards eventually. When they do, I want to know about it."

Mrs. Ngoc, in full uniform of a GPD Colonel for the advantage that might provide, stepped off with her Cuban. Striding along at his side, she felt more alive than she had in thirty years.

*   *   *

"Major Dwyer?"

Chan turned from watching Z-18 Special Operations Company troops collecting bodies and weapons on the walls above her. A man was standing near the arched bridge over the moat leading to the Imperial Palace. He was in shadow and making no move to join her on the street.

"I'm Major Dwyer. Who are you?"

"Mike Stokey, Chan...JTF. The name should be familiar."

It was. The classified advisory sited him as an asset working a parallel operation, independent from her tasking in Hanoi. Chan glanced up the street where Captain Dinh Duong was busy chattering on a radio cadged from one of the Z-18 NCOs. She would be occupied with sending an after-action report across the river for a while.

"I need to kind of stay low profile, Chan. Can you step over here?"

She joined him in the shadow and shook hands. "Didn't expect to see you here, sir. Are you working or just slumming?"

"Working...but that's just between you, me and the boys in the back. I need a favor."

"Official favor?"

"Yep. I've got to police up a guy down here. Major international player. He's supposed to make a try for the file."

"What's your mark got to do with the file?"

"Can't say. Need-to-know. But we're doing the rest of the world a good turn, believe me."

"Is this guy a Cuban?"

"He is...and that probably means you know the rest of the story."

"Background said there were two primary players. Shake blew one of them away down at Quang Ngai. This has got to be the other guy."

"Check...and he's going stateside to face some very unpleasant music."

"The Vietnamese are just gonna let you walk away with him?"

"Gladly. They want no part of him. There'll be a C-141 idling on the runway by the time I get his butt back to Hanoi."

"What can I do for you, sir?"

Stokey nodded toward the clutch of soldiers up the street. "That little firefight a while ago was unfortunate." Z-18 reinforcements were flooding into the Citadel now that everyone involved in the search knew which side of the river to cover. "Did my best to bust Shake and Minh lose from it...but I wasn't planning on having the army all over the area."

"They were in that fight with the Nghe Tinh?"

"Yeah, both of 'em...serious situation until I added my two cents worth. If anybody asks how come a couple of those guys were dinged in the back by pistol rounds, you don't know a thing."

"No problem. So Shake and Minh got out of it OK?"

"Yeah. I've got 'em covered. That's where you come into the picture. I need to keep the PAVN looking elsewhere until my mark makes his play...ensure the guy doesn't get blown away by some trooper before I get to him."

"After what just happened we'll play hell convincing them to look anywhere but here in the Citadel."

"It's a big place, Chan. And I don't think I'll need that much time. Sources put my guy in Hanoi day before yesterday. He's gotta be here in Hue by now." Stokey turned and swept a hand over the area to their rear. "The key is to keep the PAVN search parties away from the northwestern sector."

"I'll do what I can, sir."

"That's all you can do. Thanks." Stokey turned to walk over the moat bridge into the grounds of the Imperial Palace.

"Colonel Stokey..."

"Yeah?"

"I, uh...is Shake gonna be OK?"

"Hey, he's a Marine, right?" Stokey smiled and waved as he melted into the shadows. "We're harder to kill than whorehouse crabs."

Chan walked up the street to where Duong was watching a clutch of National Policemen load Nghe Tinh casualties into a jeep. She pulled her counterpart aside and pointed at the Sanyo VC3000 portable radio.

"Can you get Captain Hung on that?"

"Yes, of course. He is in the Command Post on the other side of the river. Reception is very good."

"OK, tell him Minh has been seen in the southeastern sector of the Citadel."

"How do you know this? Captain Hung will want to know the source of the report."

"Tell him it's a woman's intuition..."

*   *   *

Mrs. Ngoc holstered the radio and traced a rough square on the Citadel map with her fingernail. "Somewhere here...between the Dong Ba and Thuong Tu Gates."

"Good...excellent." Colonel Ochoa-Desidro studied the map looking for a strategic location which would put him in place to intervene once the army located Minh and the Laos File. A disturbing thought nagged.

"Will he have the file with him? Or has he hidden it somewhere?"

"Minh is no genius, my love...nor is he completely stupid..." Mrs. Ngoc held the radio to her ear for a moment before deciding the transmission was unimportant. "He knows the noose is tightening. He will likely be trying to get out of Hue...and I should think he would take the file with him to keep it from being found by search parties."

"Yes..." And if he does not have the file when I get my hands on him, there are ways of finding out where he hid it. Take him, take the file; and then kill him. Or take him, find the file; then kill him. One simply takes longer than the other. In these cases, all you can do is hope for a little luck.

"We will move to the northern corner of the Palace, Ngoc. That puts us in the approximate center of the search area."

*   *   *

They sat huddled around the guttering candle, staring silently at each other in the dim yellow glow. Air in the old bunker was foul and thick. Both men tasted it in small, reluctant sips, much more intent on what was roaring through their minds than what was entering their lungs.

"You almost won you know." Minh brushed fingertips over his scars. "I almost died."

"Yes...it looks like the damage was severe. You were lucky you didn't bleed to death."

"I always wondered...were you badly hurt? How much damage did I do?"

"You came very close yourself, Minh." Shake pulled open his knit shirt and leaned into the light to expose the white ridge of scar tissue on his chest. "The doctors told me your knife missed the main artery by less than an inch."

"An inch?" Minh held his fingers apart trying to judge the unfamiliar measurement. Shake took his hand and squeezed the fingers closer together.

"By such small amounts...we win or lose."

"Nobody won in that fight, Minh. We both lost."

"The dreams..."

"Yes. I have them too...and you are always there."

"Where is all the hate?"

"Gone. It always goes...when you realize your enemy is just another man...just another soldier trying to do his duty."

"That's how you think of me?"

"It is now. Before this you were the black-eyed monster of my nightmares."

"And you were the green-eyed monster..."

They smiled and studied the glow of the candle.

"You stayed in your Marine Corps..."

"Yes. I had nothing in common with civilians. Didn't like them much. I was comfortable as a Marine...among others who understand me."

"I understand you..."

"I believe you do, Minh."

"Did you marry? Have children?"

"I was married but that is finished now. This is my daughter...my only child." Shake reached for his wallet and pulled out Stacey's high school graduation picture in cap and gown.

"A scholar. She is very beautiful."

"Yes...she is everything to me."

"And if I had killed you that night up on those walls, she would never have been born." Minh handed the photo back and nodded. "I wish I had known this. It makes me feel better."

"Did you marry?"

"No. There was a girl in Hanoi but..." Minh pointed at his face and looked away for a moment. "When this happened I sent her a letter. I told her not to wait; that I expected to die in the south."

"I'm glad I didn't know that. It makes me feel worse."

"Do not. If you feel worse, then our meeting has no purpose. I cannot believe that."

"No. We have come together again...in this place after all these years...for a purpose." Shake tapped his finger on the Laos File. "Tell me what's in here."

"I cannot. There is information in this file that would cause my country harm. If Americans knew what happened in Laos, brave men would be dishonored."

"Minh, I received a call from Hanoi two days ago. General Giap has told my General Fowler the story of what happened in Laos..."

"No! This cannot be true!"

"It is true, Minh. My word of honor. The soldiers searching for you have been ordered to find the file and return it to General Giap who will turn it over to us."

Minh closed his eyes and tried to suck sufficient oxygen out of the fetid air in the bunker. There was a tingling in his hands; a dull ache in his shoulders and biceps.

"Minh...are you all right?"

"No. I am miserable..."

"Why, Minh? It's over..."

"I was in Laos...with Group 559..."

32. From the Laos File - 1972

There were twenty in my group. All in bad shape; some worse than others. Two hobbling on broken legs which did not knit well. Three others with large sores on their swollen feet. They were all thin with visible ribs and swollen joints. A sparse diet of rice and a few vegetables does not wear well on American meat-eaters. It was all the Pathet Lao fed them and only slightly less than we had to eat at trams or stations along the great trail.

We had 200 kilometers to cover in order reach the assembly area at Ban Karai Pass where the Americans would be turned over to officers from the General Political Directorate. For the trip I allotted thirteen to fifteen days at around fifteen kilometers per day.

It would not be easy on the prisoners but we were ordered to pace it so that none of them died. Prisoners were to be safeguarded. Those were strict orders with the Group 559 leaders held accountable. From stations along the trail to the north and south other small groups of prisoners transferred from Laotian control were also being sent north. We heard there were as many as two hundred, maybe more.

All Yankee prisoners were being assembled in Hanoi against the great day when the nation was united, the puppets defeated and the interlopers driven from the land. It would be soon...very soon, we were told by the political cadre. Le Duc Tho was already in Paris negotiating the American surrender. The prisoners were an important bargaining chip in these negotiations.

As senior man of the detachment at Base Area 609, I signed for the Americans. This made them strictly my responsibility. An interpreter was present to translate my briefing into English. I told them what was expected. Simple really. Do as you are told. No talking among prisoners. Obey all orders from the guards. Any attempt to escape or cause dissension will be dealt with most harshly. It was obvious these men were beaten regularly by the Pathet Lao. There was no requirement to explain the terms.

As we moved them to the assembly area an officer from our GPD and another man - the translator said he was a Russian - turned over a large envelope to the Pathet Lao. It was money. How much, I don't know but it must have been a large amount. We were told the prisoners were very valuable...those were the exact words...and very great pressure was put on the Laotians to give up custody of the Americans.

They did not look very valuable....dressed in tatters; shoeless and shivering. It did not take a doctor to see the majority of them had malaria or pneumonia. I was worried that some might die of sickness along the route and asked for extra medicines. For once there was no argument. We were ordered to make sandals for them from old truck tires stored at the depot. All in my group were air pirates with tender feet and no experience on the ground in hostile jungle. Food, utensils and equipment for the trip were made into bundles and given to the prisoners to carry.

We began the Long Mountain March sometime in early December. I do not recall the exact date. It was called the Long Mountain March because the great trail ran roughly parallel to the Truong Son or Long Mountain range that separates Laos from Vietnam. We moved only at night to avoid American aircraft which ranged up and down the great trail almost every day. We could see the damage they inflicted everywhere. Burned trucks, valuable equipment bent and blasted into rubble by the bombs and rockets. We passed the graves of many men who died on the trail before they had a chance to fight.

Walking at night was most difficult, especially when we passed through areas riddled with the great craters caused by bombs from the American B-52 aircraft. We called them "whispering death" because they flew so high that there was never a warning sound before the jungle exploded to swallow you up.

When we passed the Group 559 *binh* trams or units manning the antiaircraft gun or SAM missile batteries, we slowed. They always lined the trail to jeer at the Yankee air pirates. Seeing enemy airmen on the ground and in bad shape was good for their morale. But most times we were alone on the first part of the march. Only five guards but there was little chance of prisoners escaping. Where would they go?

Our route northward was clearly designated. We were not allowed to deviate unless it was an emergency. Other prisoner escort groups moved along different trails parallel to our route. The idea was to keep each group separated as much as possible in case of air attack.

During daylight hours we made rough camps under the jungle canopy. There are special stations for overnight stops where tall trees are lashed together forming a solid roof. It is safe to make small fires in these places and we often had tea after the prisoners were inspected and ordered to sleep. We could hear American planes searching overhead, but we did not worry. As long as we could hear them we were safe.

All five of the Group 559 men in my group carried green bamboo sticks which we used much like farm children use them to herd water buffalo. Prisoners sometimes wandered or stumbled due to fatigue or injury. We prodded them along with the bamboo sticks. We had to discipline prisoners only twice before we reached Tchepone which was the halfway point in the journey. I whipped Prisoner Number 154 across the back of his legs for moving up and down the ranks whispering to other prisoners. This was expressly forbidden and might have been an attempt to organize an escape.

Comrade Hanh, who lost his mother and two sisters to an American bombing raid on his home at Vinh, beat Prisoner Number 211 severely for refusing to bury his waste. This incident exceeded the punishment required. Although I understood Hanh's anger, I was forced to criticize him before the other guards. Comrade Hanh was warned to maintain the proper spirit and composure or he would be reported to the cadre at Tchepone.

We reached the halfway point with all prisoners intact. We were fourteen days on the trail at this point and ordered to rest for three days while other groups of prisoners were assembled. The rest was very welcome and charge of our prisoners was given over to the GPD cadre at Tchepone so we would have time for relaxation.

On the third day at Tchepone, the Group 559 comrades were assembled to receive fresh food and other supplies for the remainder of the trip to the Ban Karai Pass. The trouble began at this point. We were informed that a total of 213 American prisoners were now assembled and all would be moved north as a loose group. We were to remain dispersed for safety but maintain contact between groups. There was no explanation for this change of tactics other than a need for greater speed and control so that the prisoners all arrived at Ban Karai at the same time. Since this violated the proven principles of safe movement along the trail, I assumed the change was politically grounded.

At dusk of the day we were to begin the second half of the march, we were introduced to two volunteers from the Cuban

Socialist Republic. Their names were difficult to pronounce so we were told to address one as Major and the other as Senior Sergeant. The adjutant of the Group 559 detachment told me they were privately known as Fidel and Chico. He also informed me that the Cubans were specialists in prisoner interrogation.

The senior Cuban chose to travel with my group and immediately challenged my authority over both escorts and prisoners. By dawn of the first day on the trail to Ban Karai we had our first shouting match. One of our prisoners - Number 166 - walked with a crutch and slowed our progress to the best speed he could make. The Cuban known as Fidel accused the prisoner of malingering and broke the crutch. When other prisoners tried to help the crippled man, Fidel beat two of them with a split bamboo cane. One of the men was bleeding before I could put a stop to it.

On another occasion the following night, the Cuban officer expressed his hatred for Americans by burning a prisoner with a cigarette. I could discern no reason for this treatment and ordered him to stop. He drew his pistol and threatened to shoot me. There was a Group 559 officer at the head of the column, but I was afraid to leave my command and seek his help.

The Cuban spoke our language very well and during the day when we rested the prisoners he would talk to us about his hatred of Americans. Apparently this had something to do with an attempted invasion of his country. He likened that incident to the American invasion of our country and many of the Group 559 comrades expressed sympathy. Many of us had fought the Americans in the south and were familiar with their brutality in combat. All of us had suffered under the shock of their bombs along the great trail.

By the evening of our fourth day on the trail the prisoners were very close to Ban Karai Pass and I was very close to losing control of my group. The Cuban seemed to breathe hate. He was a vicious man with little of the true revolutionary spirit.

We were camped at T-14 just south of Ban Karai when the American B-52s struck at dawn. There was complete panic as the jungle on both sides of the trail erupted in great geysers of dirt and deadly shrapnel. Such terror and helplessness breeds insanity. I have seen it before and I saw it that morning.

There must have been a great number of the American B-52s bombing in formation. The effect was excruciating. It was like watching the earth split under your feet as you are pounded down into the fires of hell. Those around me, both prisoners and guards, were bleeding from mouth, nose and ears due to the concussion of the bombs. The situation was utter chaos.

The long string of bombs drove groups together as if they were sheep seeking safety in a herd. Large groups of prisoners and guards ran into a common area to escape bombs falling in front and in back of them. It was like watching great swarms of beetles crawling and clawing in mindless frenzy. As the bombs continued to fall, men began to die...escorts and prisoners disappearing in shattering explosions with nothing but bones and pink foam at the bottom of smoking bomb craters.

In the midst of the chaos many prisoners tried to escape through the jungle. The Cuban officer grabbed a rifle and shot three men. He then turned it on a group of prisoners huddled near the edge of the trail. This was my group and before I could stop him, the Cuban killed all of them. The other Cuban then joined him and fired into another group of milling Americans.

As bombs continued to fall, several Group 559 men also began to execute American prisoners. I could not identify them, but I saw at least three of our men joining in the slaughter. An officer from the front of the formation tried to stop it but no one could hear him in the roar of the bombs. I saw the Cuban shoot in the officer's direction. I did not see the officer again until the raid was over. He was dismembered but there were bullet holes in what remained of him.

Blood lust was raging and I do not think anyone or anything could have stopped what was happening. The situation worsened when several American prisoners retrieved discarded weapons and began shooting at the escorts. We had our own little war on the trail under the brutal rain of the bombs. I criticize myself harshly for failing to do more to stop it. In fact, I hid behind fallen logs in the jungle some distance from the trail.

There were hundreds of bombs and I do not know how many were killed by them nor how many were killed by gunfire from the Cubans and our own Group 559 escorts. I know only what I heard and saw as I wandered back toward the trail.

Gunfire continued for some time after the bombers passed on their way back to bases in Thailand. I could hear firing constantly as I picked my way through the shattered trees and cratered earth. What the targets were I was not sure and I dreaded to think that they were executing more prisoners.

However, I am forced to conclude that is exactly what happened. It is my opinion that no one involved in the incident wanted to take chances on surviving witnesses. When I made my way back to the trail, I found only the two Cubans and six other men from Group 559 still alive. The entire trail for nearly a half-kilometer resembled a slaughterhouse. In all my years as a soldier I have never seen such devastation. We were all in shock; amazed at what occurred. Except the Cubans. They both seemed to think the slaughter was justified. The senior Cuban spent much time and effort justifying his actions. He cautioned each of us to remember the Americans had tried to escape under cover of the bombing. He pointed to several dead Americans with rifles in their hands and said we acted in self defense.

In the final accounting there were forty-three Group 559 comrades killed by bombs or bullets. All 213 American prisoners were killed in the same manner. While I did not personally inspect each body, I can attest to more than 100 who died from gunshot wounds.

Burying the bodies in bomb craters took three days. We carefully marked the spot on a map and compiled a complete list of prisoner numbers and names. We then proceeded to Ban Karai to report the incident to the regular army command there. I was immediately placed under arrest along with the surviving Group 559 escorts. I never saw any of them again and I do not know what happened to the Cubans.

33. The Citadel - 1996

"My God, Minh...all of them?"

"Yes. We searched the jungle and made sure of the count. All of them...all 213 Americans."

Shake sat in the dark, breathing in little pants, trying to work up some outrage over what he'd learned. He closed his eyes and focused on the vivid images from the Laos File but all he felt was a deep, aching sadness. It was all so senseless, and - like many of the instances in combat he personally experienced - as much the brutal result of terror, anger and frustration as anything else. Above all, to any true combat veteran, to anyone who had watched brains bend and human beings morph from righteous warrior to mindless brute, it was understandable. Never justified perhaps...but understandable.

"Only this..." Minh's voice was a hollow whisper in the dark. "In all the battles over all the years...only this I truly wish had not happened."

"I think I understand what occurred out there on the trail, Minh. We called those air strikes Operation Linebacker. The idea was to make a show of strength and power...put the Paris peace negotiations back on track."

"The bombs were not to blame...at least not in this case."

"That depends on how you look at it. I saw men snap under pressure of constant shelling at Con Thien and Khe Sanh. There's only so much anyone can take. Have you ever heard of Shakespeare?"

Minh was silent for a long moment, struggling with something in the dark. When his hand appeared in the orb of candlelight, Shake accepted a yellowed slip of paper and unfolded it. It was a page torn from a copy of Julius Caesar. Minh had underlined a passage and written a rough Vietnamese translation in the margin.

"`Cry `Havoc!' and let slip the dogs of war.' Yes. It's what I was thinking. It's what happened on the Long Mountain March, isn't it?"

"Yes..."

"It wasn't the first time. It won't be the last. Do you remember My Lai, Minh?"

"I remember what we heard. Quang Ngai Province. Civilians were executed by American soldiers."

"That's right. About 150 men, women and children gunned down when the dogs of war got loose. It must have been much the same thing, Minh. Inexcusable, unforgivable but under-standable...if you have heard the owl and seen the elephant."

"Yes. Inexcusable, unforgivable...I know these words. What will happen now?"

"To you? Probably nothing, Minh. There will be anger and resentment...just as there was after My Lai. There are those who will never understand anything about what happens in war and we will certainly hear from them. But the truth about the Long Mountain March is right here. The evidence is clear. You were not to blame."

"It is why General Giap made me compile and keep the record. It is why he would never let me destroy it."

"I guess he expected this day would come. Let's get it over with, Minh. There are a bunch of families in my country who need to know about this. It will be painful but the knowledge will bring its own kind of peace."

"It's not so simple. We may have escaped the Nghe Tinh but there is still the Cuban..."

"No...we don't have to worry about the Cuban, Minh. I killed him...near Quang Ngai two days ago."

                              *   *   *

The rain over Hue had dwindled to a mist when Shake and Minh emerged from underground. They stood on the surface of the northwestern wall and blinked; letting their pupils absorb the light. A fuzzy orb of sun hung somewhere behind the low clouds overhead. Heat convection was causing billows of knee-high fog to roll down the streets of the Citadel. The place looked dank, dreary and medieval as if they were standing atop the ramparts of some ancient Scottish keep.

Shake eyed the plastic-wrapped package in Minh's hands. "You'd better tuck that somewhere out of sight...at least until we find a patrol."

"You do it." Minh shoved the Laos File at Shake and shook his head. "I have carried it with me for too many years."

Shake tucked the file under his shirt at the small of his back and wedged it tightly into the waistband of his trousers. "There's just one other thing we probably ought to deal with..." He hoisted the .45 pistol from a pocket and walked to the outer edge of the wall. "I have been reminded by the police that I shouldn't have this."

He pitched the Colt toward the moat and watched it splash into the muddy water. Minh stared at him for a long moment and then tossed the Tokarev after it. That done he nodded solemnly and led the way down off the walls.

Treading tentatively, feet and lower legs lost in the fog, they made their way down Mai Thuc Loan Street walking along the rear wall of the Imperial Palace. Shake was explaining details of the ambush at Quang Ngai to Minh's obvious pleasure when they spotted the flashing lights of a radio jeep. Two PAVN soldiers stood smoking near the vehicle which sported a tall radio antenna.

"Here we go..." He smiled reassuringly at Minh. "That looks like a command car of some sort. We should find an officer or they can call one. You do the talking."

"Do not hand them the file!"

"Don't worry about that, Minh. We turn ourselves over to the army but we don't give up the file until you personally have a chance to hand it back to General Giap. You have my word on that."

The senior soldier near the command car was jabbering into his radio by the time they came within shouting distance. His partner sprinted toward them on the other side of the street to cut off any attempted escape.

"We are the ones you are looking for," said Minh as they continued to approach the jeep. Shake glanced over his shoulder to see the escort trooper had now crossed the street and was following them with his weapon leveled.

"I am Senior Sergeant Minh, assigned to the Central Military Museum in Hanoi. If you have not already done so, call your officer."

The senior soldier smiled and raised his radio but before he could press the transmit button his head snapped hard against his shoulder and he staggered sideways. Shake heard the rattle of a bolt and the spit of a silenced weapon. The escort soldier behind them crumpled and disappeared into the fog.

Shake and Minh dove for the pavement in the veteran soldier's ingrained reaction to incoming fire, hoping for a moment to scramble for weapons. He was fumbling in the low fog layer, trying to locate one of the fallen troops when a wet boot slammed across his neck. He felt the heat from a suppressor tube near his cheek and inhaled the strong stench of trapped muzzle gas.

"On your feet...quickly! Do exactly as I tell you or you die right here."

Shake felt the pressure come off his neck and stood to see Minh on the other side of the jeep with his hands laced behind his head. The woman holding him at pistol point was dressed in the uniform of a senior PAVN officer.

"Now, Ngoc! Send the transmission."

Shake was prodded painfully in the back and forced in the direction of the Imperial Palace. They were headed across the arched moat into the palace grounds as he heard the woman bark into a radio.

"Emergency! Two men shot. Fugitives moving northwest on foot. They are heading toward the Tay Loc landing field!"

Shake still hadn't gotten a good look at the man with the silenced sub-gun at his back, but the PAVN officer herding Minh was playing some kind of game. Tay Loc landing field was a short airstrip inside the Citadel walls but well to the northwest of them. She was misleading the soldiers. Deliberately, of course...which meant she was not on the side of the good guys in this situation.

They were herded up the broad stone stairs leading to the spacious antechamber where the ancient Vietnamese emperors held court. He glimpsed the ornate thrones on a dais along one wall before they were shoved into an alcove. A solid shield of intricately-carved wooden screens kept them from casual observation as they were forced up against a marble wall.

Shake turned to face their captors and saw the man holding the Swedish K was a Latino. Can't figure the woman...but discounting involvement by South American terrorists...I'll bet this bastard is a Cuban named Fidel.

"Face front, Minh! And give me the file...quickly!"

Minh turned slowly when the woman officer barked but he seemed to be in shock; staring fixedly at the Latino. He was having trouble standing upright and his breathing was labored.

"You...you can't be here. You are dead..."

"This is no time for reunions, scum! The file...where is it?"

"We will let you live, Minh..." The woman officer waved her pistol in Minh's face. "But you must give us the file."

"You get nothing from me, Mrs. Ngoc. As a patriot and a soldier, I have nothing but contempt for traitors..."

For a moment it looked to Shake as if the old woman was going to repay that compliment with a bullet but the Latino waved her off and moved in on Minh. "I should have killed you a long time ago, you scar-faced sonofabitch." He whipped the sub-gun down and fired a round into Minh's left kneecap. Minh groaned loudly and collapsed into a panting lump.

Shake saw blood pooling beneath him on the marble floor of the throne room. "We don't have the file, pal. It's hidden and you'll never find it if you keep that shit up."

Fidel swung his muzzle onto Shake but before he could bore in after information a pistol shot echoed loudly off the walls. A chunk of carved wood flew off the screens at his back and sent Fidel to his knees searching for a target.

There was no one visible in the gloomy interior of the throne room but Shake recognized the voice. "Put the weapon down on the ground...slowly. You too, Colonel Ngoc! Put the weapons down and back away from them."

Nothing happened for too long and Lieutenant Colonel Mike Stokey stepped out of the shadows to show them the Beretta. "You've been traded, Colonel Ochoa-Desidro. No place for you to go now but right along with me. Put the weapon down and we'll make it easy."

Stokey moved closer and improved his angle. "If you want to make a nineteen hour flight to the States with a bullet in your ass, that's fine by me. Either way, you're going..."

Colonel Armando Ochoa-Desidro and Mrs. Ngoc moved to obey Stokey's command, placing their weapons on the floor. Mrs. Ngoc began to weep and the keening frayed his nerves. "Shut up, you old hag!"

Shattered dreams simply notched up the volume of her wails. Stokey had to shout to be heard as he moved in on the captives. "Shake, how about you police up a weapon and give me a hand here?"

Shake bent to retrieve the Swedish K which momentarily put his body between Mike Stokey's muzzle and Fidel. The move was swift and effective. Fidel snapped his boot into Shake's neck, grabbed Mrs. Ngoc and fired her at Stokey like a live cannonball. Stokey found himself wrestling with a wildcat, trying to push her away and get his weapon back on target.

In the scuffle, Fidel snatched the sub-gun and hauled back on the trigger sending ten subsonic rounds through Mrs. Ngoc into Mike Stokey.

Shake recovered in time to grab Ngoc's Makarov pistol and roll behind one of the throne room's giant pillars. He winged two quick rounds from behind the upright, missing with both but the unexpected return fire drove Fidel scrambling for cover.

Shake rose to a crouch and studied the situation. Stokey was ten feet away lying motionless under the sprawled form of Mrs. Ngoc. A growing pool of dark blood beneath the jumble indicated both were likely dead. He'd be joining them in that state if he moved from cover to check. Minh was alive and trying to crawl out of the beaten zone. What he needed was some noise to attract attention.

Shake fired a round from the pistol and Fidel responded but the suppressed spit of Swedish K wasn't going to draw a curious crowd. Shake checked the Makarov magazine. Four rounds...and no reloads in sight. There were at least two spare magazines jammed into Fidel's belt which put Shake at a distinct disadvantage in terms of basic firepower.

He heard footsteps pounding on marble and glanced to see Fidel sprinting for cover behind another pillar. He's working the angles...trying to get me to unload on him...then force me into a corner. But he won't kill me outright...not as long as he believes I know where that goddamn file is.

He heard slithering noises and looked to see Minh crawling toward him. There was a smeared blood trail to mark the distance he'd covered. In another second or two at that pace, Shake could reach out and snatch him into cover.

"C'mon, Minh...just a little more." Fidel sent another burst into the pillar and Shake responded with half his remaining ammunition. Immediately after the second shot he ducked out, grabbed Minh by the collar and pulled him close. They were out of the line of fire but that wouldn't last. Outgunned, with Fidel closing on them and no way of telling if anyone was responding to the gunfire, flight seemed a much better option than fight.

Shake Davis stood, hauled Minh upright and squatted to loft him into a fireman's carry. Minh groaned and Shake shifted to ease the position across his shoulders. "Hold on tight, Minh. We are about to haul ass." He fired the Makarov to slide-lock then dropped it and ran for the wide doors of the throne room. Incoming rounds whined off the marble as he blew through the entryway, down the staircase and turned right headed for the moat bridge.

*   *   *

Captain Dinh Duong waved her radio in the air to attract Major Chan Dwyer's attention. They were strolling discreetly behind a wall of PAVN soldiers sweeping near Tay Loc for signs of Minh or Shake when the call came.

"A report from the police! Gunshots at the Imperial Palace. Two people injured...an American and a Vietnamese."

The PAVN patrol was piling into a truck with Captain Hung shouting for speed. His driver whipped the command jeep around in the narrow street and mashed the accelerator. He was barreling by the two women with the truck in noisy pursuit when Chan saw brake lights. Captain Hung appeared around the front of the jeep and shouted something.

"He wants us to come along," Duong translated. "There is something wrong."

They sprinted for the jeep as another transmission came in over the radio. Duong listened as she ran. "Yes, one American and one Vietnamese shot at the palace...but the Vietnamese is a woman."

*   *   *

"What's the latest, Lieutenant?" Commander Jeff Ault checked the sonar fathometer on the conning display of the 40-foot motor torpedo boat and saw the bottom shoaling rapidly as they approached the mouth of the Perfume River.

"Very confused..." The skipper of the jumpy little Chinese-pattern gunboat had been monitoring the local frequency since a port turn to avoid a storm front put them on a direct course for the city. "I'm now hearing that two people have been shot...one American and one Vietnamese."

"Goddammit..." He might be too late. That American down in Hue might be Shake. It was sure as hell likely. The message from Chan told him to get to Hue ASAP because Shake had slipped his leash. But he'd been aboard a frigate steaming well to the south. It took a full day to arrange transfer at sea to the torpedo boat and a plea to the Commodore in Hanoi for clearance to make for Hue at best speed. Another day of pitching and puking in that goddamn storm...and he might be too late.

On the other hand, Commander Jeff Ault told himself as he eyed the drenched Vietnamese sailors manning the deadly DShK-38 .51 caliber machineguns fore and aft, Shake Davis is one tough sonofabitch. I'll believe somebody managed to kill him when I see it...not before.

"Lieutenant, I have a feeling your firepower might come in handy up ahead there. And I'd suggest maybe you'd want to put your crew at battle stations."

"Serious trouble you think?" The torpedo boat CO shouted into his intercom and there was an immediate flurry of activity around the conning station.

"I don't know," Jeff Ault watched the course indicator swing as the Vietnamese helmsman put his rudder over and steered for the river, "but a good captain sails into harm's way looking through his gunsights."

Ault stared into the fogbank that obscured the entrance to the river. It was guarded by shifting sandbars and flanked by treacherous mud flats. A prudent sailor approached the inland waterway with caution even in fair weather.

"All ahead full!" Ault grinned at the Vietnamese officer in the green glow of the instrument panel and bent to stare at the depth gauge. Fuck prudence...

*   *   *

Chan Dwyer helped Captain Duong and a PAVN medic sort out the carnage in the throne room of the Imperial Palace. Commands echoed and boomed off the marble walls as Captain Hung searched the immediate area and ordered patrols to fan out across the Citadel.

"This one is dead." Duong pointed at Mrs. Ngoc's lifeless form as the medic turned to Lieutenant Colonel Mike Stokey. Most of the low-velocity killing rounds had lodged in Ngoc saving the American's life. Stokey had bloody splotches on his hip and ribcage but he was clearly a survivor. He coughed bloody foam from a punctured lung and tried to sit up as Chan ran to his side.

"My guy..." he panted. "Colonel Ochoa-Desidro. Cuban bastard we been after for a long time. Primary target. You're gonna have to take him."

"Where's Shake?" Chan watched the medic at work. He seemed to know what he was doing to stop the bleeding.

"Couldn't see much after I got hit. If he isn't here, then he got away. The Cuban will be after him. Orders are get the Cuban alive. He goes back to the States..."

Two PAVN soldiers arrived with a collapsible stretcher and the medic supervised getting Stokey loaded on it. Chan walked alongside them toward the throne room exit. "Any idea where Shake and Minh might be headed?"

"He's a Marine, right?" Stokey grinned through the pain and ran a hand across his bloody mouth. "He'll head for the beach."

Chan whipped out her Citadel map and quickly oriented it. The nearest exit leading to the Perfume River was the Dong Ba Gate about three city blocks to the north.

"Ding Dong!" She shouted over the din of orders and radio transmissions. "Ask Captain Hung for a patrol...in a hurry!"

*   *   *

Shake had no particular plan in mind except to stay ahead of Fidel and out of his line of fire. Adrenaline surged through his body in huge quaking jolts. Minh felt like nothing more than a moderately heavy rucksack hanging from his shoulders as Shake sprinted down the fog-shrouded streets.

He felt trapped and channelized by the walls, buildings and byways of the Citadel. Infantryman's instinct told him to run for open ground, search for space to maneuver. Above the swirling fog layer about a block ahead he saw a tall tower and a dark archway: Dong Ba tower guarding a gate. He remembered the fight in 1968. They massed just below the tower on the other side of the walls to make an assault with nothing but water and a narrow strip of muddy ground at their backs.

He heard pounding footsteps to the rear as he dodged and zig-zagged across Mai Thuc Loan Street heading for the gate and escape from the confinement of the Citadel walls. The Cuban was somewhere behind in the fog. Shake fervently hoped the Laos File still firmly tucked at his back was enough to keep Fidel from simply blowing them both away the first time he got a clear shot.

Rounds stitched the stone of the Dong Ba Gate as Shake blew through it with Minh bouncing and groaning on his shoulders. Intentional miss...warning shots, Shake realized. The bastard was still after the file and that was the only thing keeping bullets out of their backs.

Minh was groaning, trying to talk but there was no time to listen. Through the stone tunnel and across the exterior moat bridge, Shake began to think they might be able to lose Fidel in the swirling fog. He sucked up a new strength as he spotted a copse of low, wind-warped trees near the point where the river mouth widened to spill into the South China Sea.

Hitching Minh a few inches higher on his shoulders, he charged across the mud-flat for nearest cover. It was like trying to run through glue. He barely managed a lurching stagger in the muck. Monster footprints in the mud would lead Fidel wherever he went. He fell twice, losing precious time and distance, before he made the tree line.

He was certainly no expert but Shake felt confident he was seeing a man suffer a serious heart attack as he gently eased Minh down into the mud and forced himself to think around the pounding in his brain. There was no help for Minh...no other place to run...no boats conveniently beached nearby... and he could see Fidel just fifty meters away in the fog; following the muzzle of his weapon across the mud-flat.

He needed a weapon in a hurry...but there was nothing...and then it struck him. The Cuban bastard was focused on the Laos File. He'd go for the file, first and foremost. Shake reached beneath his sweat-soaked shirt and retrieved the package. If he worked it right, the Laos File might be all the weapon he needed.

Quickly checking Fidel's progress through the mud, Shake pulled the red logbook from its plastic wrapping and slithered to a forked tree near the edge of the water. He stuck the book among the branches in plain sight above the low fog and crabbed back behind the trunk of the tree. It would have to be a quick move...quick, efficient and devastating.

"Laos File is in the tree...straight ahead. You can have the sonofabitch!"

Coiled to spring when the time was right, Shake heard the wet squish of Fidel's boots as he pounded through the mud to reach the file. He heard the rattle of branches as the Cuban snatched his prize. Off to his left he heard the throb of marine engines. A high-intensity searchlight stabbed at the trees behind him. Fidel would be turning toward the threat. He coiled and sprang from hiding.

Colonel Ochoa-Desidro spun at the sound of a rush and swung the Laos File logbook in a vicious back-handed arc. The blow caught Shake Davis flat against the left ear sending a jolt of pain through a burst drum into his brain. He rolled into the mud, scrambling to recover and looked up into the suppressor tube of the Swedish K submachinegun. Expecting a vicious little spit to be the last sound he heard on earth, the massive crack racketing through the trees nearly stopped his heart.

He rolled right as the searchlight stabbed directly into Fidel's startled face. A heavy machinegun thudded loudly from somewhere in the fog out on the Perfume River and huge gouts of wet mud marked a line near the Cuban's feet.

"Freeze in place, asshole!" Commander Jeff Ault's familiar voice buzzed through an amplifier. Shake followed the searchlight beam to its source and spotted the bulk of a gunboat idling just offshore. "Put your weapon on the ground and raise your hands."

Colonel Armando Ochoa-Desidro turned his head slightly and caught sight of a PAVN patrol thrashing through the mud to cut off any escape in the opposite direction. If nothing else, long years of hard soldiering around the world taught him to recognize a hopeless situation. He placed his weapon on the ground and raised his hands, mentally reviewing the catalogue of information he might be able to trade with the Americans for certain concessions.

Shake Davis stepped from the tree line and shouted at the gunboat. "Jeff! It's Shake! I'm gonna back this bastard off and get his weapon."

"Hey, Jarhead! He's all yours...compliments of the Navy...ours and theirs."

Fidel was standing immobile, squinting into the bright light as Shake approached determined not to make a second mistake. "Back up, pal. Three steps...very slow."

The Cuban wrenched his feet from the mud and complied as Shake picked up the Swedish K and covered him. The first soldier to reach them was a Vietnamese Special Operations officer who slapped manacles on the Cuban in a very efficient manner. He was being led back toward the Citadel when Shake moved to intercept the escort party. He stopped Fidel with a hand on his chest.

"I don't know what's gonna happen to you now, you sonofabitch, but you ain't no soldier. Soldiers don't do the kind of shit you do. I'm a soldier...and that's the only reason I don't kill you right now...right where you stand. God knows you deserve it."

There was more he wanted to say but Chan Dwyer pulled him away from the confrontation and into a hug. He squeezed her shoulders and watched Fidel stagger away through the mud flanked by two PAVN guards. It felt like some vindication for Gus Quick...for Ken Quick and the other American POWs slaughtered in Laos...but not much.

"Mister Davis! Please come quick!" Captain Dinh Duong was standing at the tree line motioning for him. She shouted for a medic and he realized what was happening. He'd forgotten about Minh.

He lay pale and gasping, arching his back against the terrible pain in his chest. Shake dropped to his knees and took up the shout for a medic. Minh reached up and put a hand on his neck. Shake was pulled down close to the brutal scars he'd inflicted so long ago.

"Over now...all is forgiven..." Minh gasped and whined against the pain that was killing him. "We can go home now...we can sleep..." The frail hand dropped off his neck and Shake Davis caught it in his own. Minh was through talking forever. He barely managed a final, feeble squeeze to let his old enemy know the war was over at long last.

34. Washington, D.C. - 1997

They stood at the back of the throng on the mall between the Lincoln Memorial and the Washington Monument. The VIPs disappeared shortly after the ceremony, their brief respite from the grinding business of government or national defense over until the next call to show the flag. Clustered around the new stele of black marble added to the Vietnam Veterans Memorial were mostly kin of the 213 Americans whose names were etched on the slab. The tears were relatively few; the grief mostly subdued and internal. Over the decades it took for these names to finally appear among the others listed as killed in the Vietnam War, the families had mostly cried out the pain of their loss. There were grown children, grandchildren and great-grandchildren here who knew the men listed only as vague notions or grinning snapshots in fading family albums.

"Christ, when we waste 'em, we waste 'em big time, don't we?" Lieutenant Colonel Mike Stokey swept his eyes across the long, dark line of the monument and tugged at his overcoat collar. There was a wet hint of rain in the air.

"At least they know the end of the story..." Shake Davis noted grim smiles; hints of peace and pride on faces reflected in the polished surface of the black marble. "It ain't they lived happily ever after...but it's an ending. People I talked to said it was important. They can get on with their lives."

Rain began to fall gently, slowly driving most of the visitors away from the wall. Umbrellas, raincoats and civilian attire gradually gave way to boonie hats, faded field jackets and camouflage as the eternal parade of vets and Nam-junkies resumed their vigil among the memories. Shake saw Chan Dwyer and his daughter, home from college for his retirement ceremony at Quantico, threading through the crowd.

"We got it, Dad...just before the rain started." Tracey parted her raincoat to reveal a lead-pencil rubbing of Ken Quick's name. "Look OK?"

"It's fine, honey." Shake slipped an arm around his daughter and kissed her cheek. The vibrant life he felt in her reminded him of Minh, buried now with special permission of the Vietnamese Government on the walls of the Citadel beneath the Dong Ba tower. General Giap pulled the necessary strings and made sure Shake stayed for the funeral. That had been a special moment, providing its own sort of closure.

Now it was time see what else was out there...beyond the memories, the terrors and the trepidations of an old soldier out of step, out of uniform and low on ideas for the future. He re-buttoned Tracey's coat and draped an arm across Chan Dwyer's shoulders. They'd been seeing a good bit of each other since orders brought them home to testify before the special Congressional committee investigating the Laos File and events on the Long Mountain March. It was less than ardent: comfortable, casual, interesting. Maybe there was something else in it. Maybe later.

"Think it'll rain on your parade tomorrow?" Chan had taken over as master of the planned post-retirement reception at Quantico, bugging him relentlessly until he came up with a reasonable guest list.

"Probably. Maybe it'll keep the crowd down to a bare minimum. I don't know how many more memories I can take."

"Bet your ass it'll rain on Shake's parade," Mike Stokey beeped his car to life and opened the doors. "This is a Marine Corps function...right Chan? If it ain't rainin', we ain't trainin'."

They stopped at a Georgetown fern-bar and huddled over a round of micro-brews Tracey insisted on tasting. She'd heard most of the story in bits and pieces over the past week from one or the other of the people involved but there were still a few nagging questions.

"Tell me about this woman Ngoc. I'm still confused about her."

"Wages of Fidel's wartime dalliances," Mike Stokey shrugged and explained the connection. "She was his lover when he was working on American POWs at Cu Loc prison camp. Just one of those quirky coincidences that happen, you know? She finds out he's still around...in jeopardy over the Laos File...and tries to re-kindle the old flame."

"But he killed her, right?"

"Actually, he was trying to kill me...but it's safe to say it was an unrequited love affair."

Shake Davis grinned at his pals and whispered. "You two spooks cleared to tell me what's happening now?"

"You know most of it, Shake." Chan patted his hand and smiled. "Congressional hearings; lots of noise, and not much substance. Apparently, Minh was the last survivor of the march...except for the two Cubans. The Vietnamese are eating a little humble pie in their own self-righteous fashion. Communist infra-structure is rapidly disassembling. The IRDG is still over there plugging away at it. Nation-building efforts continue. Won't be long before the big foreign trade scramble starts."

"What's happening with Fidel?"

"Let me put it like this..." Mike Stokey tossed his credit card on top of the bar bill. "Our boy is in hands of appropriate authorities and singing like a big-ass bird. We are learning many interesting things which may put Fidel's namesake in the shitter once and for all."

"Don't suppose they'll hang the bastard and let me pull the lever?"

"Not likely, Shake...but I'm told there's a big, horny S and M freak who needs a cellmate up at Rahway."

35. Ozark Mountains - 1997

"That's the story, Gus...everything I know, everything that happened on my watch."

He rolled the rubbing from the wall and stuffed it into a water-tight canister from a mortar round. The entrenching tool that served as Sergeant Major Gustav Quick's gravestone was rusty but still functional enough to dig one last hole. Shake Davis set to work burying the son beside his father in the thick Ozark loam.

When the job was done he replanted the marker and stood watching sunbeams sparkle on the lake below the mountain. "We got the last victory, Sergeant Major. We brought 'em home."

A soft breeze blew up from the lake through the pines carrying the scent of spring. He walked down off the mountain feeling fortunate and joyful; a surviving soldier finally at peace.

Dale Dye is a Marine officer who rose through the ranks to retire as a Captain after twenty-one years of service in war and peace. He is a distinguished graduate of Missouri Military Academy who enlisted the United States Marine Corps shortly after graduation. Sent to war in Southeast Asia, he served in Vietnam in 1965 and 1967 through 1970 surviving 31 major combat operations. Appointed a Warrant Officer in 1976, he later converted his commission and was a Captain when he deployed to Beirut, Lebanon with the Multinational Force in 1982-83. He served in a variety of assignments around the world and along the way attained a degree in English Literature from the University of Maryland. Following retirement from active duty in 1984, he spent time in Central America, reporting and training troops for guerrilla warfare in El Salvador, Honduras and Costa Rica. Upset with Hollywood's treatment of the American military, he went to Hollywood and established Warriors Inc., the pre-eminent military training and advisory service to the entertainment industry. He has worked on more than fifty movies and TV shows including several Academy Award and Emmy winning productions. He is a novelist, actor, director and show business innovator, who wanders between Los Angeles and Lockhart, Texas.

Made in the USA